T0207639

A LOST GENERATION

RONALD S. ZIMNEY

iUniverse, Inc.
Bloomington

A Lost Generation

iUniverse books may be ordered through booksellers or by contacting:

iUniverse
1663 Liberty Drive
Bloomington, IN 47403
www.iuniverse.com
1-800-Authors (1-800-288-4677)

Because of the dynamic nature of the Internet, any web addresses or links contained in this book may have changed since publication and may no longer be valid. The views expressed in this work are solely those of the author and do not necessarily reflect the views of the publisher, and the publisher hereby disclaims any responsibility for them.

Any people depicted in stock imagery provided by Thinkstock are models, and such images are being used for illustrative purposes only.

Certain stock imagery © Thinkstock.

ISBN: 978-1-4620-7110-4 (sc)
ISBN: 978-1-4620-7112-8 (e)
ISBN: 978-1-4620-7111-1 (dj)

Library of Congress Control Number: 2011962284

Printed in the United States of America

iUniverse rev. date: 12/8/2011

Chapter 1. The Meeting. Autumn, 1981.

Oh my God, it's him! Lilly's pulse quickened. Although she had known of his presence in the community for years, events that morning had provided her with an opportunity to meet him. Lilly's heart skipped a beat when she realized Roger had spotted the open seat at her table for two. It was probably the only remaining empty seat in the packed dining area of the fast food restaurant.

He had made a beeline for her table, weaving between the small square tables with their painted blue and white checked square tops. She could still hear the words of Police Chief Harley Johnson, "Hell no, I'm not going to arrest him. He lives in the country. I'm deferring this to Oscar. He's dealt with Roger Hartec before." Oscar Thompson was the county sheriff.

"May I share this table with you, ma'am?" Roger politely inquired of Lilly. He stood tall above her, holding his tray, awaiting permission.

"Why yes you may," Lilly stammered, embarrassed by her response. *What will I talk to him about?* She was a little apprehensive about his reputation for violent behavior. She had seen an example of that this morning. However, his actions also revealed the respect he has for women and children.

In the community of Ashland Falls, Minnesota, hearsay and rumors were never in short supply. Lilly's late husband had been fond of saying that rumors, in this community, were spun so hard and fast that they soon became legend and then gospel. The second year after her husband's death, when she started dating, the rumor mill had her married off four times.

Lilly was jolted back to the present when she nervously looked up at Roger to see him, with his head bowed silently saying grace. There are many churches in the city of every denomination, but she had never seen anybody say grace in a public eating facility. Roger stood out as obviously not of Scandinavian descent. Dark black eyebrows accented his dark brown hair. He commanded a strong presence and Lilly found his rough-hewn features attractive. *Eastern European,* she thought.

Lilly had been meaning to order fireplace wood from Roger. Although he was recommended as the best dealer to do business with, rumors about his violent actions had prevented her from making the call. She thought talking about an order would be a good way to start a conversation.

"Do you still have fireplace wood for sale?" Lilly inquired.

"Yes I do ma'am," Roger replied. "I delivered a load this morning. I'm a little overdressed for firewood delivery. I read about the Americana Display at the museum last night and decided to take it in, before I made my delivery and purchased supplies." His demeanor displayed no concern about the earlier incident.

"You did stand out," Lilly interjected, with a smile that she was feeling a little guilty about.

Roger emitted a subdued guffaw, followed by a low snicker. "I suppose I was a little hard to miss. I think I'll be arrested before I get out of town. However, lunch with you will make it worthwhile," he said, with a smile.

"Oh, I don't think you will be arrested," Lilly responded. "Lawrence got a good chewing out from Oscar and Harley. Harley said, 'Your displays are provocative, inflammatory and a waste of taxpayer's money.' Oscar said, 'As soon as you have to install plate glass in front of one of your displays, you need to recognize that as a clue that there is something wrong with your thought processes. Just call in the nearest pedestrian from the street to help you with your thinking.'"

Lilly and Roger chuckled in unison at Oscar's observation. "I thought the best part was when Harley said, 'this incident would have happened yesterday afternoon when Officer Slocum saw your display, but he couldn't pick up the park bench.' I guess with all the Vietnam War veterans in this area, what Lawrence did wasn't too bright."

"Slocum is a runt all right, good man though," Roger said, as he took the last bite of his sandwich.

Slapping the table in front of Roger, Lilly said, "Do you know it took four men to remove the park bench from the display? But enough of this, can you deliver a load of wood next Saturday morning? I would like a cord, but I don't think I can get a full cord in my garage. Do you deliver half cords?"

"I don't normally deliver half cords," Roger replied. "Not much profit left with the price of gas. When it jumped from thirty-five cents to two dollars a gallon several years ago, it became the biggest expense for just about every business."

Roger withdrew a pen and note pad from his left shirt pocket. "However, if you provide coffee, not only can I deliver a half cord, I'll help you stack it in your garage. Just don't tell anybody though, could be construed as an implied warranty."

Leaning forward and looking at Lilly, his green eyes dancing, Roger said, "Your address and phone number ma'am. I need to be able to call you if my truck breaks down. It's mighty old."

Lilly felt a warm flush rising up her neck to her cheeks as she gave Roger her telephone number. She hadn't given her telephone number to a man in years. A year after she had been widowed, she had tried dating. Each date had been a disaster. It seemed a dinner date was supposed to be followed by a quickie in her bedroom, and she would have none of it. She had cut off all relationships and resigned herself to widowhood.

Lilly knew Roger never stacked firewood for his customers. He delivered with an old dump truck. He always informed the customer to mark the spot and he would dump.

"Okay, next Saturday morning it is," Roger said, as he finished writing her order in his notebook. He slipped the notebook and pen in his shirt pocket and grabbed Lilly's coat off the back of her chair as she stood up. He helped her into the coat. This courtesy was completely unexpected. Lilly found the attention a little embarrassing, although pleasing. She felt as if she were being courted.

"May I escort you to your vehicle, ma'am?" Roger asked, as he offered Lilly his arm. "Mighty slushy and slippery out there."

"Lilly," she said, "and yes you may." Her apprehension of the past, regarding the rumors of his reputation for violent behavior, was fading. Now she found him interesting and exciting. *I better be careful. This guy could be a heartbreaker. I suspect he is much younger than I am.* Together they had exited into the parking lot, carefully stepping into the tracks of tires encased by three-inch walls of slush. They made their way over to Lilly's car.

As Roger held the door open for her, a police cruiser pulled up in front of them in the street. It had to stop for a line of traffic backed up at a red light. It was Officer Randy Slocum. When Randy spotted the two of them, he momentarily turned on his siren to get their attention. Then he gave a two-thumbs up signal to Roger. The light changed and he moved down the street.

The traffic was heavy that beautiful, sunny day. The slush on the streets and parking lots slowed the pace of everything in the city. It was early afternoon, and the sunny warmth was infectious. The populous was very cheerful and courteous in spite of the slow pace.

Lilly worked her way around the parking lot to the street. The traffic was steady, and she thought she would be a long time getting into the street. She noticed Roger's truck in the flow of traffic off to her right. *He must have parked in the street. That's what I should have done.* Finally a driver on her left stopped short in the bumper-to-bumper traffic and left a space for her to cross his lane of traffic. Lilly could proceed now because the traffic light at the end of the block had stopped the traffic in the westbound lane.

Lilly waved a thank you to the driver on her left. Then she proceeded into a left turn onto the street. It was only a few blocks to her house on Oak Street. It was a small comfortable, retirement cottage built in the early fifties. She shared the cottage with her black and white tomcat, Sylvester, since she had been widowed ten years earlier.

Lilly's husband and two teenage sons had been killed in an auto accident. Now at almost age fifty, Lilly couldn't see the possibility of starting a new family. Her volunteer work, teaching Sunday school and helping with the Cub Scout troop, helped fulfill her motherly instincts.

It was her work with the Cub Scouts that had started that day's adventure. The Scoutmaster had eight Cub Scouts who had wanted to see the new display set up at the County Museum.

The display had gotten considerable press coverage, in the local paper, as this annual event usually did. However, the Director's thinking was considered controversial, bordering on un-American. Opening days were usually poorly attended in spite of the free refreshments offered. Lilly had informed the mothers of her eight charges that she would provide caramel rolls, milk and orange juice for their breakfast before the opening. Lilly knew that most people preferred to sleep in on Saturday mornings. She thought that providing breakfast would encourage the parents to have the children ready for the eight a.m. opening.

The scoutmaster's wife, Sally, had agreed to deliver the children to the museum in her station wagon at seven forty five A.M. Then she would trade vehicles with Lilly. The Scoutmaster had been called out of town, so Sally agreed to help Lilly as much as she could around her appointments.

Lilly had spread the fare she had brought to the museum on a table in the conference room. There was a forty-cup coffee maker on the counter near a kitchen sink. Alongside the coffee maker were packets of sugar, powdered creamer and a tray of cookies.

About seven forty, Lilly's charges had arrived. These were members that had a keen interest in history. They were excited about the day and were busy guessing what they were about to see in the displays.

At seven fifty five a lone figure had strolled into the room and drew a cup of coffee. Lilly observed him disdainfully appraising the cookies. They were pathetic looking pastries with the appearance of under baking, yet hard as a rock. "You may share our caramel rolls if you wish," Lilly cheerfully said. "We also have plenty of milk and orange juice. Help yourself."

"Thanks," the man said with a smile. He picked up a napkin and placed a caramel roll on it.

"You're sure lucky, mister. We would've eaten all those rolls if we could've," a cub scout said. "Mrs. Larsen sure is a good cook."

"By gosh, I believe you know what you're talking about young fellow," the man said, after washing the first mouthful down with a drink of black coffee.

"Come children, the display is opening," Lilly said, as she placed her left hand on the shoulder of one boy. Out of the corner of her eye, Lilly could see the man staring at the boy. *Or was he staring at her ring-less fingers?*

Lawrence, the Director, was unlocking the door to the exhibition room. He would provide commentary for the new display. As they started down the hall of displays, Lilly noticed the man did not follow. He seemed to be more interested in the caramel rolls.

It soon became obvious that Americana was a display of American culture as seen through the eyes of the disruptive anti-war activists. Large pictures of college campus demonstrations were displayed with text messages of what these disruptions were supposed to have accomplished. Excerpts from college campus speeches were emblazoned across the walls of individual booths. Examples of the practice of civil disobedience, as proposed by Henry David Thoreau, were displayed in many booths. However, the part about sacrificing liberty for one's beliefs wasn't included.

As they had turned the corner of the first hall, they came upon a booth that was protected by a sheet of plate glass. Inside was a white china toilet bowl. Alongside the bowl was a small wooden table. An American flag was draped across the table with one end in the toilet bowl. Above the display on the back wall was a sign proclaiming: "The Flushing of America."

The children were horrified. As cub scouts they had been taught respect for the flag. Although many can't read all the words used in the texts, the symbolism wasn't lost on any of them. Timmy Johnson started to cry. He pointed at the display and sobbed, "No, no." Lilly gently moved him along to the next display booth and Lawrence's further explanations of the displays.

After viewing a few more displays, Lilly became distracted with two boys who had lost interest and were wandering off. After she had gotten the two of them back with the group, she was horrified to see Timmy back in front of the glassed in display sobbing. At that moment, the man they had shared the rolls with came around the corner and observed the small boy crying. Looking up at the man Timmy pointed at the flag and sobbed, "No, no."

The man gently picked up the small boy and walked over to Lilly and the group. He set the boy down next to Lilly and said, "Stay here with this lady and your buddies." Looking at Lilly, he said, "Lady, please keep these children right here." Then he went back to the end of the long hall where a heavy cast iron park bench had been placed for a rest stop. He picked up the park bench and flung it through the plate glass window. The glass was thoroughly shattered. The man stepped inside the booth and gathered up the flag. He returned to the group and presented the flag to the cub scouts. "Here, this belongs to you fellows. I reckon you boys know how to display it properly."

Looking at Lawrence he said, "Many a mother has received this flag in exchange for a son who gave all. We should remember and respect that."

Lilly observed the look of fear on Lawrence's face. He was ready to take flight when the man executed a smart about face and walked away.

Chapter 2. First Date.
Winter, 1981-82

The late November day had broken foggy with a cool crispness in the air, an indicator of a slow coming warm up. The earlier snow had melted. Now a brilliant sun was burning off the fog to reveal a landscape dressed in heavy hoarfrost.

"All of nature is dressed in wedding lace," Lilly said to Sylvester as he jumped up to the kitchen windowsill and slipped behind the curtain to observe the scene.

Lilly was bursting with exuberance this cold morning. Roger had called the night before to confirm a ten a.m. delivery. It had been a week since she had met him and placed the firewood order.

This morning had Lilly feeling like a teenage girl. She was nervous about her hair and already had changed her earrings three times. *All this preparation for a date stacking firewood in her garage.* Lilly laughed at herself. *Some date! Oh, she was such a fool. This was just a business transaction. Roger couldn't possibly be interested in her.* Still, her friends described her as, "That beautiful blonde with a nice figure." *Perhaps Roger had been attracted to her. Oh! He probably was a flirt who left a trail of broken hearts. Why couldn't she get him out of her mind? He had to be much younger than she was. He had to know that. Well, she might just as well do her best to please.* Her kitchen was filled with the aroma of fresh baked caramel rolls and fresh brewed coffee.

Having heard a noise in the street, Lilly had rushed to a back window and pushed aside the lace curtain. She was able to better observe Roger's old truck turn off the avenue onto Oak Street. She quickly got into a coat and stocking cap and grabbed a pair of gloves as she passed through the door. Lilly hurried to the end of her driveway as Roger pulled the truck in front of her in the street. He had his side window rolled down.

"I parked my car in the street so you could back down the driveway to the front of the garage," Lilly said. "We can stack the wood inside along both walls and I'll still be able to get my car in."

"Gottcha," Roger said, as he ground the transmission into reverse.

Lilly could see he had anticipated the back in and had stopped in the middle of the street. She studied the magnetic sign on the door of his truck as he backed down her driveway. It was a square rubber sign of black letters on a brilliant white background. The sign read, "Firewood for Sale." Under that, in smaller letters, was Roger's telephone number. The sign was a bold contrast on the red truck door. Roger stopped and Lilly could hear him setting the hand brake.

Roger opened the door and hopped out of the cab. He walked to the back of the truck. Then, studying the distance between the garage and the truck, he said, "Perfect. Just the right distance to dump without knocking the garage down."

"When you're done dumping, we can have some rolls and coffee before we take on the task of stacking," Lilly suggested.

"Great," Roger replied. "I've been thinking about those caramel rolls all week."

He pulled himself up into the cab. Pushing in the clutch, he ground the shifter into a gear. When the transmission stopped grinding, Roger pushed a hand lever in. Then he bumped the shift lever into neutral and let the clutch out. The hoist lifted the box up, and the wood slid out. Roger pulled the hand lever out, and the box fell down on the truck frame with a loud thump. Turning the ignition switch off, Roger depressed the clutch and ground the shifter into a gear.

"Got to leave it in a gear." Roger explained. " Once before the parking brake band had cooled down and expanded. My truck rolled into the street."

"That sure was a lot of grinding noise. Is your truck in need of repairs?" Lilly inquired, as she observed him through the open cab door.

"Nah," Roger replied. "This model has the last of the crash box transmissions. Everything built after this has what is called synchromesh. Then it's possible to shift without all the grinding and noise. All the young fellows who work for me get real excited about the prospects of driving Old Red, until they learn what a crash box is all about. Then they go for the newer trucks."

They were silent as they walked to Lilly's back door. After they had entered Lilly's neat cottage, Roger bent over to unlace his heavy boots. He stacked his vest, gloves and cap on top of his boots. Then he reached up to help Lilly take off her wraps. Lilly had been so intent on watching Roger that she hadn't gotten around to taking off her coat.

"Come on in and sit," Lilly said, as she led him into her kitchen. It was a small kitchen and dining nook combination. It had an eastern exposure window over the kitchen sink.

Roger sat down at a small, square table already set with utensils. Lilly poured coffee into mugs and set a plate of warm rolls with a tray of butter on the table. Then she sat down across from Roger. They both prepared their rolls in silence.

Lilly was feeling a little awkward and wondered if the wood stacking would be done in silence too. She desperately searched her mind for a topic of conversation. Finally she said, "Mrs. Gustafson, your bookkeeper, is a member of my church. She's a charming lady. She always does a lot of volunteer work."

"Oh, oh," Roger said. "I'm going to have to start bribing her, if you start asking her for information."

Lilly could feel a flush rising up her neck to her cheeks. *Oh my goodness, this is a date. He said he didn't deliver half cords.* She quickly pointed to the fireplace in the front room. "It will be nice to have a fire in there again. I didn't use it the last two winters because

I didn't have any wood. I'd used all the wood that came with the place when I purchased it."

"Well, I'd be right proud to stoke it up for you anytime," Roger said with a forced nervous chuckle.

Lilly detected a little flushing in his handsome, well tanned, smiling face. She decided it was time to learn more about this strange man. What she had heard about him in the past didn't seem to fit. He actually appeared to have a shy streak. She wished she had inquired about him with Lori Gustafson.

Lilly had become good friends with Lori Gustafson and Jenny Thompson. Neither of these ladies ever tried setting her up with men. She had removed herself from others who were prone to do so. She made a mental note to make some inquiries of Lori.

"Have you ever been married, Roger?" Lilly asked.

"Ah, actually twice," Roger said, his face growing dark. "Both ladies divorced me."

"Oh, I'm sorry to hear that," Lilly said. "I do hope the separations were amiable."

"Oh yes, quite so," Roger said, as his demeanor brightened.

Lilly was feeling brave now. She felt she had command of the situation. *Why should she depend on second hand information? She probably could get all the information she needed right from the horse's mouth. The worst that could happen was for Roger to tell her to buzz off. It didn't appear it would go that way. Roger seemed to be struggling, as she was. Besides, she was too old to be wasting time.*

"They were much younger than I was," Roger continued. "Seven or eight years. I think my medals enthralled them. I used to keep that stuff displayed on a wall. When they realized I was a mere mortal, the shine wore off." They both chuckled at Roger's observation.

"Did you love them, Roger?" Lilly asked.

Looking into Lilly's eyes, Roger replied in a very serious manner, "Yes I did. However, it takes two people in love to produce harmony and happiness. I was smart enough to know that. Just-barely. But still smart enough." Roger smiled, clearly amused by his self-depreciation.

This is all very interesting, Lilly thought. *He definitely wants a relationship, but, with me? Both of his ex-wives were much younger. But, he said they divorced him,* she argued with herself. *Is it my being older that interests him? Some-how I must approach him about our age differences.*

"Well lady, I think we better get to stacking wood," Roger said, interrupting the silence.

"Yes we must," Lilly agreed. She welcomed the prospect of being outside in the cool crisp air, with all the frozen wedding lace clinging to everything. There would also be a bonus this day, a nearness to Roger.

They had carried the wood into the garage and stacked it against both walls in silence. Occasionally they stopped to observe hoarfrost dropping off the trees in giant chunks as the sun warmed the limbs. By early afternoon, all remnants of the wedding lace would be gone. As Roger and Lilly called each other's attention to giant clusters about to fall, Lilly found herself wishing Roger would take her into his arms.

"Goodness how time flies," Lilly said. "It will be lunch time before we're done. I'll be pleased to make a sandwich for you, Roger. What's your favorite sandwich?"

"Bacon, lettuce and tomato on toast," Roger answered, as he smiled at Lilly. He appeared enthused with the suggestion of lunch.

"I believe I have the ingredients for that. Mayonnaise?" Lilly inquired.

"Heavy on the mayo," Roger said, as Lilly took a push broom off the wall and started sweeping up bark. "Here, let me do that while you start the sandwiches," Roger stated. "If you give me the keys to your car, I'll run it back in for you. Where do I put the bark?"

"In the metal trash can in the corner," Lilly said. "I'll use it for kindling."

"Okay lady, I'll be in before you have those sandwiches ready," Roger said, with enthusiasm.

"Great, see you soon," Lilly said. She really didn't want to be away from Roger that long. But, she was happy with the prospect of more time with him.

Roger came into the cottage as Lilly was finishing frying bacon.

The toast was up in the toaster cooling for the mayonnaise. Roger took off his boots and stacked vest, cap and gloves on top as before. *Creature of habit,* Lilly thought.

"Off to your left is a bathroom to wash up," Lilly said.

After he had completed his clean up, Roger entered the kitchen and inquired, "May I help you? I can set the table if you direct me to the utensils."

Why, oh why did those two ninnies throw this one back? Lilly mused. "Sure, the cabinet next to the corner on your left. The silverware is in the drawers below. The one Sylvester is sitting in front of. Put on glasses as well as coffee mugs, if you like milk with your sandwich."

After the table was set and sandwiches completed, Roger and Lilly sat down across from each other. "You may say a blessing prayer," Lilly said.

Roger said a before and after prayer familiar to Lilly. "I like to do the thank you up front," Roger explained. "Sometimes it's hard to remember to thank our Lord once the belly is full."

"That is thoughtful of you, Roger," Lilly agreed.

All through the meal Roger appeared rushed. He would glance at his watch and ponder, while they ate their sandwiches. Finally he admitted that he was a little pressed for time. "I've committed to several pickups for tomorrow. I have to finish splitting what I've got left," Roger said. "I'm normally sold out this time of year. I like to be done with the wood business before the permanent snow cover for the season arrives. If I get the splitting done this afternoon, I'll be out of business for this season tomorrow."

"You have time for a piece of double chocolate cake and a cup of coffee, don't you?" Lilly inquired.

"Only if you promise to let me take you out for dinner next Friday evening." Roger said, with a smile, as a flush rose up his neck and faded into his well-tanned cheeks.

Lilly chuckled pleasantly at his discomfort. "Well, I certainly can't eat all this cake by myself. I guess I'll have to accept your offer. Is there anything I can do to help you get your wood ready?" She asked.

"Oh no. It's very dangerous work," Roger said. "I'll get it done before dark. But I'm going to have to keep my nose to the grindstone. After he'd finished a large piece of cake and his second cup of coffee, he rose from the table.

Lilly followed him to the door. After he had put on his boots, vest, cap and gloves, Lilly grasped the front of his vest on both sides and pulled on it. "Now you be careful," she admonished. "If it's such dangerous work, maybe you shouldn't be out there alone."

"Been doing it for years. I'll be okay. See you Friday evening. Six okay?" Roger asked.

"Sounds terrific to me," Lilly said, as Roger stepped through the door and closed the storm door behind him.

Lilly was thrilled about how the first date had gone. Even more so with the promise of a second date, that could only be construed as just that. At the same time she began to feel some apprehension about how little she knew about Roger. Outside of the stories she had heard about his violent episodes on the gossip chain, she knew only what she had learned today.

Lilly decided to call Lori Gustafson. Lori had worked for Roger ever since he had moved into the area. He had purchased the failing lumberyard where Lori worked. Lilly dialed Lori's number and was relieved when Lori picked up on the second ring. Lilly hadn't gotten a chance to chicken out.

"Gustafson's, Lori speaking."

"Hello Lori. This is Lilly Larsen. I'm calling to chat and seek some advice."

"Shoot honey, I'll do what I can," Lori said.

"Roger Hartec just delivered a half cord of fireplace wood this morning," Lilly said.

"A half cord? Roger doesn't do half cords. You must have winked at him. Beauty certainly opens gates. How do you wink at a man over the telephone?" Lori inquired.

"I didn't place the order over the phone," Lilly said. "We ended up sharing a table at Tops last Saturday at noon. I placed the order then."

"That must have been soon after that ruckus at the museum," Lori stated. "By the way, I understand you had eight cub scouts in that little cottage of yours for half the morning. How did you keep them entertained?"

That part was easy," Lilly replied. "The scouts were pretty excited after meeting Roger Hartec. They spent the rest of the morning telling tales of his exploits, like he's a combination of Paul Bunyan and the Lone Ranger." Both ladies chuckled at Lilly's description.

"He's become sort of a legend in the rural areas north and east of Ashland Falls." Lori said. "The country folks there respect him. They're not prone to rumors like the town folks. Honey, are you the reason he caused that ruckus at the museum? So he could corner you at Tops?"

"How could he know I would be at Tops?" Lilly asked, with a hint of exasperation in her voice.

"Settle down honey. Just teasing you," Lori said. "What advice were you seeking?"

"Well, well, " Lilly stammered, becoming aware of a hot flush rising on her neck and cheeks. "Roger asked me to go to dinner with him next Friday evening. I said yes. Then I realized I knew very little about him, out side of what I've heard on the rumor mill. None of what I've heard there has been good."

"Oh posh!" Lori exclaimed. "Roger's a pussycat. In fact Janice and I refer to him as the pussycat. He's so opposite of his reputation. What you heard from the cub scouts is probably more accurate then anything else you've heard. Sure he has problems. What combat veteran doesn't? Roger would never hurt anybody who didn't deserve a hurt or two. You should see the way he protects the Shore kids. Their dad's a drunk. Roger is the best thing that happened to them. After Danny Shore went into the Army, his sister, Janice, stepped into his job. Those kids would've had a hard time in school without the money they make working for Roger. They had lived in near destitution until Roger started paying Danny. Roger always sees to it that they have the transportation they need. He carries them on his employment records as his son and daughter. Danny was under age when Roger hired him. Janice is still under age; she's only fourteen."

"How does he get away with that?" Lilly interrupted.

"Roger said that with all the broken homes he doubted any investigating authorities would question the different surnames and home addresses," Lori explained. "He's been doing it for seven years and has gotten away with it so far. I've had to show the records three times and only once was I questioned about it. Roger had told me that if I were questioned to tell the truth and he would handle it. However, I thought, what the heck, this is such an easy question to answer. I told the man that the kids' mother never married Roger. She just wanted the child support checks. The man got a sad look about him and said, 'Yes, that's a problem with to many divorce laws. The father can end up making support checks and taking care of the kids. It's not right.'"

"There's also our age difference," Lilly said. "I'm sure I'm older than he is."

"How old are you, honey?" Lori inquired.

"I'll be fifty in December," Lilly said.

"Whew," Lori whistled. "I'd never have put you a day over forty. The Lord sure has been good to you, honey. Looks, good figure, good cook and now a very eligible bachelor hot on your trail. You're one lucky doll. I've noticed something a little different about Roger since the museum incident. He's usually depressed after a violent episode. This time he wasn't. He's in love! I just know it."

"Oh my God!" Lilly exclaimed. "Please don't spread that around."

"Your secrets safe with me, honey," Lori said. "I can also tell you he's thirty-seven. He's the same age my Chester would have been. They were both born in May---just a few days apart. I don't think your age is going to make any difference to Roger. When's your birthday? I'll subtly give him the information. That way you won't have to broach the subject."

"December sixth," Lilly replied. "Thank you Lori for helping me with this. I appreciate the information. I know I can trust you."

"Wait a minute Lilly," Lori said. "Were you in fear of harm when you saw that incident a week ago?"

"Not for myself or the children," Lilly said. "He was so gentle and caring with little Timmy Johnson. We thought Lawrence was in for a thumping though. Roger really chewed him out. He said,

'Many a mother received this same flag in exchange for a son who gave all.' Several of us were in tears. I think Lawrence would have been too, if he hadn't been so scared."

"Good. I lost my son, Chester, in that damn war," Lori said. "Naturally, I think Lawrence got his due. It's people like him who caused that war to be conducted in the fashion that it was. Our warriors got a raw deal. Chester was one of the wounded that was tipped off their stretchers when they returned home. In spite of not being able to stand up, he fought back. Chester pulled a rioter down to his level and gave him a good thumping. The rioter Chester thumped came from a family of means. So that rioter's family was pushing to have Chester prosecuted for assault and battery. They probably would have succeeded if Chester hadn't died from a jungle virus shortly after the riot. Chester tried to ease my burden, when he knew he was dying," Lori sobbed. "He insisted that men like him, who didn't have to reenter society, were the lucky ones. Chester said, 'Mom, over fifty thousand of my generation will be sacrificed in a war we aren't allowed to win. Secretary of Defense, McNamara admitted as much when he resigned last February. I believe we're a lost generation.'"

Lori was crying. Lilly could hear her blowing her nose. Lilly reached for a tissue from the box on the telephone table to wipe the tears from her eyes and face. "I'm so sorry I brought back such horrible memories," Lilly said, as she sniffed back her own tears.

"Oh, sometimes it feels good to talk about it and have a good cry," Lori said. "This was one of those times." Lilly was surprised how quickly Lori regained her composure.

"I have to admit I can be prejudiced when it comes to Roger," Lori continued. "Sam and I are his surrogate parents. We've had him over here a lot and he always takes us out on Mother and Father's days. I know he's killed a lot of people. Our country trained him to be a killer. He was doing his duty. His was a problem of being born at the wrong time. We can't blame these men for that. We must give them a chance."

"Thank you Lori. I needed this chat," Lilly said, still wiping tears from her eyes. "Good bye and thank you ever so much, again."

"Goodbye Lilly. May God bless you.

Chapter 3. The Courtship.
Winter, 1982

Lilly had been seeing Roger regularly since their first dinner date. He had taken her to dinner with Sam and Lori, as their guests, to celebrate her fiftieth birthday. Before they had left her place, for the supper club, he had presented her with a fiftieth birthday card and a very expensive necklace with matching earrings. Roger had helped Lilly change into the gift set so she could show it off that evening. Lilly had planted a very passionate kiss on Roger to show her appreciation and growing affection.

Roger had escorted Lilly to his annual Christmas party. She had met all his employees. Lilly and Roger had been Christmas day guests of Lori and Sam Gustafson.

At the beginning of February, Roger had purchased advance tickets for the play Brigadoon. That production was being presented by the community college the last week of February. Their tickets were for the Saturday evening performance. They had made plans for dinner before the play. Now a week before the planned weekend, the weather bureau was predicting a severe blizzard would sweep into the area late on Saturday.

Lilly had volunteered to be on the dishwashing and cleanup crew for her church's annual soup supper Thursday night. She would be working with Lori Gustafson and Jenny Thompson. The three ladies had volunteered so that they would be working together. Lilly found this threesome always made for a pleasant work environment.

Jenny had started that evening's gabfest. "When will we hear the wedding bells?" she inquired of Lilly.

"I, I, don't really know," Lilly stammered, as she felt heat rush into her cheeks.

"Is something wrong honey?" Lori inquired.

"Roger has tickets for the play at the college Saturday night. I'm hoping for something to happen then," Lilly confided. "However, the weather bureau is predicting a complete white out for Saturday night."

"Oh yes, Oscar was talking about receiving the warnings. It's going to be an Alberta Clipper," Jenny said. "However, true love knows no bounds. You don't expect a storm to stop Roger, do you?"

Before Lilly could respond, Lori said, "Janice is always teasing Roger. She keeps asking him, 'When are you going to whip the words on Lilly?' Lord, how he blushes. She was really impressed with you after the Christmas party."

Lilly laughed. "Yes, she gave me a big hug in the powder room. She said, 'Please take good care of our pussycat.'"

"Maybe Roger needs a push," Lori suggested. "He's been burned twice you know. He's always looking in the paper and asking about places to take you on dates. It was Janice who told him he doesn't need to take you somewhere on each date. She said, 'If Lilly doesn't want to spend a lot of time alone with you, she could be a gad-a-bout. Bad news, Roger.'" The three women laughed at Janice's brashness.

"Well, we've spent several evenings in together. I've encouraged it and I do enjoy cooking for Roger. He's so complimentary and not at all fussy. We've even done some light necking. But, he's never made a pass at me," Lilly said. "I know he's a good Christian. But, he doesn't like to go to church. He knows the Bible well. When I chided him about not keeping holy the Lord's Day he said, 'every day is the Lord's Day. Sleeping through a sermon on Sunday doesn't meet our commitment for the other six days.' I couldn't argue with that. But there just seems to be something missing in his life that I can't explain."

"Like maybe a childhood honey," Lori said. "Well, take it from me, there isn't one. Sam and Roger are from similar backgrounds. Sam ran away from one foster home after another until he was old enough to enlist in the service. One night when they were playing cribbage, Roger told Sam that his parents gave him away when he was nine years old. Roger thinks they sold him."

"Oh my God!" Lilly gasped. "One time I asked him how many brothers and sisters he had. He said, 'about fifteen or twenty. I don't know for sure. Lost all track of them years ago.' I was so shocked; I didn't pursue it any further."

"There you have it honey," Lori said. "Sometime you should check to see if Roger knows how to pout. My Sam couldn't pout to save his life. Instead the effort causes him to laugh. There never was an opportunity for these men to exercise that childhood expression. Now that they're adults, their facial muscles won't respond. It seems pouting is something you have to learn as a child. When you get to know Roger better, you will come to recognize this void in his life that he isn't even aware of. He's damaged merchandise, honey. But, that doesn't mean he won't make a good husband."

"He has a high regard for the female gender," Jenny intoned. "Somewhere in his life there had to have been a good woman."

"Maybe he finds me to nosy and bossy," Lilly said. "I'm sure a lot of men do. Or, maybe he is incapable of having sex. Maybe that's why he hasn't made a pass at me."

"No, I don't think so," Lori said. "I know his previous wives made the move on him, or so he says. Maybe you're going to have to try that."

"Oh shush! I couldn't do something like that," Lilly exclaimed, as she felt her face turn hot.

"Well you better gal, if you know what's good for you," Lori exclaimed. "Some fellows need a shove. I just know he's in love with you. He doesn't know how to proceed and he needs your help. If he doesn't make a pass at you-make a pass at him. What have you got to lose?"

"Oh yes," enthused Jenny Thompson. "We French women

are trained by our mothers and aunts to manage a successful relationship. Let's look at what we know. You say he's kind, gentle and attentive, yet shy. We also know he's been burned twice. I think you must take the lead now, if you know he's what you want."

"That's right honey," Lori said. "It's time for you to seduce him."

"In France, the women had a saying," Jenny said. "A successful wife is a lady in public, a chef in the kitchen and a whore in the bedroom." All three ladies broke into laughter.

"People think I spoil my Oscar," Jenny continued. "I've been criticized for mixing his drinks and plumping his back cushion for him. They also tell me he uses very coarse language. I know he does. I've overheard him using coarse language when he's talking with other men. However, he's very attentive to my needs. He never uses coarse language in my presence. He knows I absolutely detest taking out the garbage. You know, not once since I met the man in France, have I ever taken out the garbage again. Oscar chided my younger brother about manners. So Pierre took over the task until Oscar and I were married in Paris. I'll gladly mix his drinks and plump his pillow, just so I don't have to take out the garbage. I guess that's what love is."

"Whew!" Lilly exclaimed, as she put the finishing touches on drying the counter top. "I think I've met the first two requirements for being a successful wife. That third requirement is kind of scary. I wish he would make a pass at me."

"Well honey," Lori said, as the three women were getting into their outdoor clothes, "He's in love with you and he's probably running scared of losing you, if he makes the wrong move. He'll probably court you forever if you don't get it through his thick head that you are ready for much more. Good night gals."

"Good night Lori," came two replies in unison.

Saturday morning broke bright and clear with no hint of a storm. Roger was at Lilly's at 6:30 p.m. for their dinner engagement.

"You look stunning tonight," Roger said, as he helped Lilly into her coat. While inhaling over her head as he wrapped the coat around her, he said, " Smell real nice too."

Lilly chuckled. "It's amazing the things we chicks do to please our roosters. I hope they appreciate it."

"Oh I do missy beautiful, surely I do," Roger replied.

As they had come out of the restaurant-there is a decided feeling of a winter storm in the air. A bone chilling blustery wind had replaced the cold stillness. All that was lacking for a blizzard was falling snow. They drove to the theatre in Roger's four-wheel drive pickup.

"I left the yard early and dug a service truck out of cold storage because of the impending storm," Roger explained.

"I'm glad you did, Roger. You're truly a thoughtful person," Lilly said. She was also thankful because the pickup was so high that Roger had to manhandle her into it. It gave her an opportunity to give him hugs and plant thank you kisses on his lips. Roger appeared to be enjoying her attentions.

Inside the theatre, Lilly snuggled into Roger's right side. When he placed his right arm around her neck, she kept it there by playing with his fingers. She noticed other people paying particular attention to the two of them, but she didn't care. She wanted this man.

At intermission it was announced on the P.A. system that a blizzard was in full force. The announcer advised anybody living beyond the city limits to go home now! The theatre would honor all tickets at a later date.

"Oh, you must not try to get home tonight Roger," Lilly exclaimed. "I'll put you up in the guest room. It would be way to dangerous for you to travel out in the country."

"Thank you Lilly. Now we can see the rest of the play. The best part is ahead," Roger said.

"You've seen this play before?" Lilly blurted out, before catching herself. A pang of jealousy swept over her at the thought of some other woman on Roger's arm. Remembering her nosiness, she made up her mind not to pursue the subject any further.

"Oh yes," Roger explained, "the original movie has been on television many times. I thought you would like it because of the wonderful music and the mythical and romantic story line."

After they had returned to their seats, Lilly nestled onto Roger's arm. She said a quick thank you prayer for the storm keeping Roger in town tonight. The last half of the play put them both in a romantic mood. Roger was pecking her on her cheek at regular intervals. She responded by squeezing his hand and turning her head up to receive a kiss on her lips.

After the play was over they went to the foyer. "I think you should wait here while I go out to start the pickup," Roger said. "It's so cold blooded it needs to run for a least ten minutes before it has enough power to pull itself out of its tracks. I'll be right back."

While Roger was gone, Lilly chitchatted with people she knew. The conversations were mostly about the weather with a few references about her and Roger.

Roger came back in. Looking at his watch he said, "Seven more minutes and we should be ready to go."

By the exit door, waiting for their husbands to come and pick them up, gathered several ladies. Some men, like Roger, were waiting longer for cold vehicles. There was a lot of kidding and exaggerations about who owned the coldest vehicle. It was a merry crowd as it thinned and the exaggeration became more enhanced.

The ten minutes were long gone as several ladies took advantage of meeting Lilly's escort and congratulating him. Lilly was enjoying the attention. However, she could detect Roger's growing uneasiness.

"Roger, the ten minutes are long past," Lilly interjected. "I think we should be going." They stepped out of the building into the blowing, swirling, snow. The few women left followed them. Their husbands were all waiting curbside in running vehicles.

Lilly and Roger moved swiftly to their vehicle midway down the lot. As Roger boosted her into the pickup cab, she exclaimed, "Hurry Roger! Get yourself into the cab. I'll get this door." Roger bent into the wind and rushed around the front of the cab and climbed in. The cab was over warm and Roger reached to shut down some of the heat, while getting the windshield wipers going to remove the melted snow and ice.

"This was truly a wonderful evening," Lilly said. "I'm so glad you agreed to stay in town tonight. I couldn't bear the thought of you being stranded in this truck, somewhere on a county road."

"Yes, I think it would be wise for me to stay in town," Roger responded. "I believe you're right."

"Course I am," Lilly said, as she chuckled and chucked his chin with a mittened hand.

The conditions of the streets were horrible. State plows had kept the state highways open. The main through fares were plowed. The secondary streets were unplowed and littered with stuck and abandoned vehicles.

"Here we are," Roger announced as he pulled up to Lilly's house as close as he could. They were along side of the garage and somewhat sheltered from the blizzard's gale forces.

After entering the house and dumping their wraps, Lilly said, "Follow me and I'll show you where you can sleep." They walked down a hall and Lilly opened a door to a small room with a full-sized bed. The bed took up most of the room. "You may sleep here, or just follow me," Lilly continued. She led Roger to the end of the hall and opened a door to a large spacious bedroom with a full bathroom and queen-sized bed. "You may share my bed with me if you wish."

Roger's reaction to Lilly's offer was one of stunned silence. Finally, he found his voice, "Gosh Lilly, I could never share a bed with you without getting ah, ah, ah, getting frisky," he stammered.

Lilly looked up at Roger. Smiling, she put a hand on each side of his face. "Trust me, love, a women doesn't offer to share her bed with a man unless she wants him to get frisky. Actually, she would be insulted if he didn't get frisky." She could see the relief in Roger's face. A bright smile lit up his features.

"I'll go to my sewing room and retrieve a pair of my late husband's pajamas for you," Lilly said, "I spotted a pair I haven't made into a quilt yet. I'll be right back dear." Lilly retrieved the pajamas and rushed back through her bedroom door. She was half expecting Roger to be gone. Instead, what she saw caused her to stop short with an audible gasp. Roger was standing next to her bed buck naked with a full erection.

Roger was startled by her gasp. "I, I'm sorry," he stammered.

"No, no, don't be sorry darling," Lilly said, as she flung the pajamas in his direction. "Don't bother putting those on yet, Roger. Hurry! Open the bed and help me out of my clothes."

Lilly awoke with her and Roger's bodies entangled. She carefully extracted herself from the entanglement and propped herself into a position where she could look into his sleeping face. Through his opened pajama top, she gently blew across the brown hair on his chest and lightly kissed his lips. His heavy peaceful breathing was a comfort to her. They had made love twice and then showered together. After returning to bed, Roger had made love or as he put it, "Pestered her again." She hadn't thought that was possible. She wished this night could last forever.

Roger had told her several times that he loved her. She had complimented him and expressed her love for him as well. Now, she wondered if he would propose to her.

With her finger, Lilly traced the round pattern of scar tissue where a bullet had passed through Roger's upper body. It was the large pattern of the exit wound that corresponded with a smaller entry pattern on his back. There were two small entry patterns on his left leg just above the ankle. There was a corresponding pattern of one much larger exit hole on the backside of his leg. This exit pattern was clearly made by shattered bone. Lilly wondered about this. She made a mental note to ask him about it at an opportune time.

Lilly could hear the storm abating outside and decided to wake Roger up. She planted a big wet kiss on his lips, jolting him awake.

"Wow!" Roger exclaimed, "I'm in love! I would like to wake up like this every morning."

"Is that a marriage proposal?" Lilly inquired.

"Oh I'm sorry dear," Roger said, "I should have proposed to you long ago. I was afraid you would say no. I've had enough experience with rejection. Then this all came on so sudden. Still, I've known for some time I wanted to be your husband and provider."

Taking Lilly's hand, Roger looked into her eyes. " I truly love you Lilly. Will you marry me?"

"Yes darling, yes," Lilly said with glee, as she smothered him in kisses. They were jolted back to the present world when Lilly's clock radio came on. Commentary about the storm was the news. A rundown of cancellation notices began.

"Oh Roger," Lilly exclaimed, "Services at my church have been postponed until this afternoon. We can walk there if the streets haven't been cleared. Will you please come with me? I must show off my fiancé. There won't be many people there because of the storm."

"I sure will darling. My time is yours. But what are we going to do about this?" He pulled his pajama bottoms down to reveal an erection.

"My goodness Roger, I never thought that was possible," Lilly said. Although her muscles were sore from last night's activities; she wasn't about to pass this up. Slipping out of her nightclothes, she pulled Roger down on top of her and said,"You must pester me again."

After they had showered, Lilly inquired of Roger, "Do you need some clean underwear? I still have some of my late husband's around."

"That would be nice," Roger said. "You sure did a great job of messing mine up in the theatre last night."

"Thank you Roger," Lilly said, as she dug in a drawer for the underwear. "I guess I didn't realize I was having that kind of effect on you. I appreciate your frankness."

After dressing they had gone into the kitchen and both got involved in making breakfast. The sun was shining brightly and the wind was almost gone. There was a lot of rumbling and banging in the street as plows progressed with the clearing. Soon the squawks of back-up signals were heard as dump trucks progressed into snow removal.

"We should be able to get your driveway cleared out before the church service," Roger said.

"How about your place," Lilly inquired. "Will it be difficult to clear?"

"Oh we need not worry about that for a few days," Roger said. "Then we'll both go out there and look the joint over. You'll need to decide which place we will live in after we're married."

This was a jolt for Lilly. She hadn't given that aspect any thought.

She had assumed she would finish out her days in this cottage, since she had become a widow ten years ago.

"Do you have a nice place?" Lilly inquired.

"I think so," Roger said. "I hope you like it. It's southeast of the city where the hills meet the prairie. I purchased the land when I came here nine years ago. I built the house a few years after that. It's not completely finished yet. It will be easy to make changes if you wish."

Chapter 4. The Engagement. Winter, 1982

It had been three weeks since Roger had proposed to Lilly. They had spent every night together at Lilly's place. Then on the following weekend they had moved all her belongings out to his place. Their engagement had been announced and the impending wedding date set. However, Lilly still didn't have a ring.

Lilly fondly remembered going out to Roger's place for the first time that Monday after the storm. Roger had come to her place at noon with the plow truck. They had eaten lunch together. "I'll plow the driveway while you get a feel for the place," Roger had said. "Do you think we should take Sylvester along to get his opinion of the of place too?"

"Sure, why not? Lilly had said. "Lets get bundled up and I'll track him down."

Lilly had felt a great deal of apprehension as they turned into the long driveway. It was a two-story house set on a walkout basement. One full wall of the basement was exposed. From the direction they approached, it looked like a three story house. Attached to the basement was a two-stall garage with independent doors. A fully enclosed deck was above the garage.

"The deck above the garage can be converted into a screened deck during the warm months," Roger had explained. Roger had stopped the truck in front of the garage door and hopped out to open the door. "Got openers; just don't have them installed yet." He had opened the garage door and then came back to the truck to help Lilly get out. They had walked inside of the garage to a steel entry door about midway down the left wall. Inserting a key into the lock, Roger turned it and pushed it open. Then bending down, he had surprised Lilly by scooping her up in his arms and carrying her inside. Sylvester had scampered in behind them. "I read somewhere that this is how this is suppose to be done," he had said. Then he set her back on her feet and kissed her.

"Thank you," Lilly had stammered. She had hoped this didn't mean it was settled and they would be living out here.

They had walked around the corner of a short wall. There was another door that Roger opened to reveal an elevator. "Step in please," Roger had said as he scooped up Sylvester. When the three were in the elevator's car, Roger said, "Now push the button with the one on it.

Lilly had pushed the button and felt a slight jolt, as the elevator started lifting. Shortly it stopped and the door opened. Sylvester had shot into the room while Lilly stepped through the doorway. She had realized she was in the kitchen. It was a bachelor's kitchen, completely devoid of decorating, strictly functional. Sylvester was already up on the kitchen sink looking out a window. Lilly had followed him to the window. She caught her breath when she had seen the view.

The window overlooked an orchard of fruit trees and Mountain Ash. A colorful array of birds had been working on the berries of the ash trees. To the right of the orchard was a natural meadow. That meadow blended into rolling cropland all the way to the horizon. To the left was the driveway they had come in on. The driveway was recessed below the higher ground of the orchard and both sloped east all the way to the mailbox. Sylvester had definitely been pleased.

Lilly had backed into Roger. Leaning her head back against his chest, she sighed, "It's beautiful Roger. I think you have Sylvester sold."

"Darling, you haven't seen everything yet," Roger had said to her. "Let's take the elevator to the top floor." He had taken Lilly's arm and escorted her back into the elevator. When Sylvester had seen them leaving, he had hustled down from the sink and shot into the elevator. Looking up at Roger and Lilly, he scolded them with a, "Meow."

They both had chuckled at Sylvester's antics. Then Roger had pushed the button with the two on it and up they went. The elevator door opened into a wide hall. At the end of the hall could be seen a large, brightly lit room.

Escorting Lilly down the hall, Roger had explained, "This is just a big empty space. I have a desk and bookcase that can be moved wherever."

They had entered a large naturally lighted room, almost totally devoid of furnishings. There weren't any blinds or curtains.

Lilly had gasped at the three direction panoramic view. "Roger! This is beautiful." The countryside all around the house was rolling hills. To the west and south was a vista of rolling corn and grain fields, now blanketed in snow. The view to the east was the same as the view from the kitchen window. It was more expansive because of the additional elevation.

From a picture window in the master bedroom was the northern view toward the city. The hills rose to higher heights before the terrain started to drop away to form the lower elevations of the city. "The elevation of Main Street is actually lower than our basement floor," Roger had informed Lilly.

Lilly had turned to face Roger. Laughing and giggling, she had rapidly pounded softly on his chest with both of her clenched fists. "Oh Roger, how soon can we move me out here? I think I've died and gone to heaven. Thank you, thank you," she had said, as she kissed him.

As they looked for Sylvester, Roger had said, "We should be able to get enough of your belongings out here on Saturday so that you can be out here from then on."

Why didn't you finish this room?" Lilly had inquired.

Roger had put his arms around Lilly and said, "Darling, I just ran out of ability here. I thought the rest would need a woman's touch. As far as I know, you're the only woman who has ever been up here. I hope you will make this as pleasing as your cottage."

"Oh I will darling, I will," Lilly had assured him.

Just then, Sylvester had shot out from behind the bookcase, bent on another adventure. Roger had scooped him up as he passed by.

Lilly's thoughts returned to the present. She was enjoying the view from the family room. She had spent most of her days up here decorating, since moving in. It had been three weeks of working alone and no ring on her finger. Pangs of loneliness were creeping in. She had confided in Lori her concern. Lilly had insisted that Roger should pick out the rings himself. Now after this long delay, she's been thinking that might have been a mistake.

The ringing of the telephone interrupted Lilly's daydreaming. Glancing at her watch, as she walked to Roger's desk to answer the phone, she realized it was closing time at the lumberyard. *Roger would be home soon.* "Hello," Lilly said into the receiver.

"Lilly, Lori here. The mystery of the ring has been solved. He's bringing it home to you right now. My lord, what a rock!"

"He's shown it to you?" Lilly questioned, disappointment clear in her tone.

"Yes Lilly. That's why I called. I made an excuse to stay late. I thought this could be a problem, and I wanted to talk to you," Lori said.

"Well I'm certainly angry with him for doing that," Lilly said. "I should've been the first one to see the ring."

"That's how I thought you would feel. Remember when I told you he was damaged merchandise? This is what I was talking about. Roger and Sam are from similar backgrounds. Each had no childhood to speak of. As soon as they were old enough to be cannon fodder-they were sent off to war. Now honey, you must understand they've had few opportunities to learn societies' niceties. Roger doesn't know any better. Don't be angry with him; he's fragile. He implicitly trusts you. He would never intentionally do anything to hurt you. When you are hurt, you must reach inside yourself for understanding. My only regret in all my years with Sam is that I started a row with him about showing off my ring before he put it on my finger. When I questioned his motives, he was devastated. It took years to get back to where we had been. I was only twenty then. Lilly, you don't have that much time. It just won't be worth it. Besides, when you think about it, it is a silly custom. As Sam explained to me, 'The people who make the ring see it. If it's a unique setting, the Jeweler will show it to everybody who comes into his shop until it is picked up. I was worried that you might not like the ring. I was seeking advice. The only finger that ring will be on is yours. I don't see how I was wrong.' Please don't put Roger through what I put Sam through. I promise you, you'll never regret it."

"Gosh, I guess I never thought of it that way," Lilly responded. "Being first to see the ring is the stuff of fairy tales. How should I handle this?"

"Just the way you have been handling him honey. Shower him with love and understanding," Lori said. "He needs your approval. The ring took a long time because of the setting. It involved a lot of high strength welding. Don't let on that I had this chat with you. My guess is that he will be ripping the ring out of the box to get it on your finger as soon as possible. Don't expect prolonged suspense and a candle light moment."

"Thank you Lori," Lilly said. "You sure can be a life saver."

"My pleasure honey," Lori said. "I must call Sam because I'm suppose to be in our driveway right now. Have a wonderful evening. Actually, have a wonderful life. God bless and good bye."

True to Lori's word, when Roger came home he forgot to shut off his pickup engine. Lilly watched as he put the pickup in park and jumped out to open the garage door. Then, she heard him rush in and push the elevator button to bring the car down from the top floor. But instead of waiting for the car, he must have run over to the stairway. She could hear him thumping up the stairs.

Lilly moved from the south window to the stairway and rushed down to the main floor. She and Roger met in the back hall.

Roger was flushed and very excited. He hurriedly removed the rings from the carton, scattering carton parts on the floor. He excitedly slipped both rings on her finger and passionately kissed her.

"Roger," Lilly laughingly said, "The wedding band isn't supposed to go on yet. We're not married."

"Oh yes we are," Roger said. "We got married when you asked me to share your bed. The ceremony is just a formality. We've been married since we decided we wanted to spend the rest of our lives together. It's our decision that causes that bond. What some preacher puts together any lawyer can split apart. I truly want you for the rest of my life."

"Shut up and undress," Lilly commanded, as she whipped an afghan off of a chair and spread it on the carpet. It's time to consummate this union again." They were soon in each other's arms.

Chapter 5. The Spook.
Spring, 1982

Sheriff Oscar Thompson had reached across his desk to push the intercom button in response to a buzz. "Yes?" he inquired.

"Harley here to see you Oscar," came the reply from his secretary.

Keying the intercom button, Oscar said, "Send him in." They had arranged this meeting over the weekend after Roger had asked both to be groomsmen. Officer Randall Slocum had been chosen to be the third groomsman for Roger's wedding.

Harley Johnson, the Chief of Police, entered and took a chair opposite Oscar. He was a tall man and weighed in at well over two hundred pounds. He had dark wavy hair, nearly curly. He was built like a quarterback; a position he had played in high school and college.

The two men were veterans of their respective positions and had worked together for many years. Oscar was the older of the two. Both were near retirement.

"Well Harley, my concern is with Lilly Larsen," Oscar said. "She's a real nice and smart woman, but probably lonely and vulnerable. She's a good friend of my wife. I just can't find out much about Roger, other than he was suppose to have been in the United States Air Force for about four years. He's a member of the American Legion Club, but not a member of the Veterans of Foreign Wars.

I've checked with Charlie Olson at the Legion club. Charlie said 'Roger showed me ADC form 475. I made a photocopy of it. I'll get it.' I studied the form. It's the Air Force's release and discharge order. However, Roger's was not a discharge order. It was a release order after four years active duty. Charlie said, 'That's all he needed to qualify for the American Legion, but it wouldn't get him into the VFW. He would have to show an overseas transfer order.' The name on the ADC 475 was Roger Jerome Hartec. Roger had told Charlie that he was wounded just before his four years active duty was up. He said he spent an extra six months in rehab.

"After that I checked at the VFW club," Oscar continued. "He wasn't a member over there, but they knew of him. The bartenders told me that he comes in as a guest of Randy Slocum or some of the farmers will bring him in on family night, as their guest. The farmers all say they're treating him for helping them out of tough spots, stuck machinery, birthing calves or ringing hogs. After that beating, by those four bikers, over at Hallston, we found he had three machine gun bullets pass clear through him. Two bullets entered from the front and one entered from the back. The two bullets that entered from the front broke his leg. He sure as hell couldn't have been running away when he got the bullet in the back. Now you figure that one out, Harley, if you can."

"Damned if I can," Harley responded. "I've pondered that a good while. I went to the hospital to see Roger when I heard you had brought him in. Old Doc. Silber insisted I should look him over. Said he was sedated so would never know. It sure looked to me like he had been in a war. Doc. Silber said there was metal holding his leg together. He insisted that a big chunk of bone was completely missing. Doc. said somebody did a damn good job of piecing that leg back together."

"But it gets even stranger," Oscar said. "Since he'd been shot to hell, I figured the Veteran's Administration should be taking care of him. They had absolutely no record of a Roger Hartec."

"Ever since that incident at Hallston, I've looked in every telephone book I could get my hands on," Harley said. "There just isn't any Hartecs."

"Now what the hell can one make of that?" Oscar mused. "I

contacted the National Personnel Records Center in St. Louis, Missouri. They told me the same thing. No Hartec."

"Christ that's creepy," Harley said. "Makes me want to scratch on those scars to see if they're real."

"Oh they are," Oscar intoned. "According to Doc. Sil----," Oscar trailed off as his intercom buzzed. He pushed the button. "Yes."

"Call on line one Sheriff," Oscar's secretary said. " I think you will want to talk to this one."

"Must be a live one," Oscar said, as he pushed the line one button and activated the speakerphone. "Sheriff Thompson here."

"Hello Sheriff. This is retired General Max----, over here in Langley, Virginia."

"Spook town?" Oscar inquired.

"One and the same," came the reply.

"Didn't catch the name," Oscar said. "Just the retired General part."

"Not important," the voice said.

Oscar had become frantic. He began making hand signals to Harley to fetch the tape recorder from on top of a filing cabinet. Harley had understood perfectly and procured the recorder. Snapping it on, he set it on Oscar's desk near the speakerphone. Oscar used this method because an on-line recorder tipped off the caller.

"Well, what is? Sir," Oscar inquired.

"Are you private?" the General asked.

"The Chief of Police, Harley Johnson, is here with me," Oscar replied.

There was a pregnant pause, then the General continued, "Korean War veteran, one Purple Heart, Chosen Reservoir, no problem. This concerns him too. What do you boys know about Roger Hartec?"

"That he gets pissed off when he sees a flag being desecrated," Oscar said. "If his name is Hartec, he's probably the only Hartec on the Goddamn planet."

"His name isn't Hartec," the General said. "That's a moniker we gave him. He took out some big muckity mucks up in North Vietnam. They know his name, rank, serial number and favorite beer. That's the problem. If he keeps making headlines bashing heads and putting park benches through windows, the Communists will eventually figure it out. This is the second incident in less than five years. He's standing out!"

"That war's been over with for ten years," Harley said. "That's got to be some kind of grudge."

"They have incentive," the General said. "Those boys aren't shit in their country until the score is settled."

"How many have been sent for Roger?" Oscar asked.

"Two, that I know of for sure," the General said. "Tell Roger that I think he is standing out too much. He knows his only protection is his name change. He'll understand the message."

"Why didn't you call him up and tell him that yourself?" Harley asked.

"Get a better idea of how he's doing talking to you boys," the General replied.

"Well see here, he's marrying a real nice widow lady in a couple of weeks," Oscar said. "Harley and I and one of Harley's officers are going to be groomsmen. Is that going to be to high of a national profile?"

There was another pregnant pause. "Ah, you should get by with that as long as there's no big deal about war hero in the paper afterwards," the General said.

"Nah, Roger doesn't like talking about that," Oscar said. "He's not one to brag."

"By the way, what's he doing?" the General asked. "How does he make a living?"

"Hell, you know more about him than we do," Oscar chuckled. "We thought you would tell us! Actually, he owns a lumberyard in a little jerk water town north of here. It was about to fold up. He got it cheap. Course, everybody around here thought he would have been screwed if he had paid half the price he did. However, Roger turned it around in short order. He draws up house plans, figures up what customers need and delivers. Several people are working for him. In the fall he cuts, sells and delivers firewood."

"Sounds like he's got both feet on the ground, except for those violent episodes, Mr. Two Purple Hearts, shot in the ass, Battle of the Bulge man," the General said.

"Well by God! Since you seem to have the war Bible in your lap, what can you tell us about Randall Slocum?" Oscar asked.

"Marine sniper, damn good shot. He wasn't my man though," the General said. "My men are slowly picked off. What you gentlemen think is a suicide is actually a communist hit. Not all of them, but enough, to many. We're supposed to be protecting them. Our budget was cut and the protection is gone, totally. All that's left goes to the F.B.I. to harass men like Gordon Kahl."

"Oh for Christ's sake," Oscar entreated. "What about Jimmy Swartz? All we know is that he was discharged early and sent home screwed up."

"I was wondering if you were going to ask about that," the General said." That was a hell of a deal, you having to shoot Jim. He wasn't my man either. I know about him. Army sniper, charged with protecting Westmoreland. Unfortunately, Jim was too good. Westmoreland survived." The General chuckled at his joke.

"No, that poor kid didn't have a chance," the General continued. "He had shot over a half dozen four year old boys carrying a satchel filled with plastic explosives, satchel bombs. When they opened the satchel from the last boy he shot, they found it filled with laundry. Now he's a war criminal deserving of a court martial. Jim wasn't any good any more. They gave him a medical discharge and sent him home. You know the rest."

"Why not a V.A. hospital?" Harley inquired.

"He wasn't wounded," the General said. "Medical discharges cover a broad area. It was a disgrace for a kid like Jim to be lumped into that category. The Army used it to get rid of homosexuals and other misfits. By the way, Randy froze up because he and Jim had been in sniper school together. A man can handle only so much. In that war we constantly pushed the limits."

"Godamn it," an agitated Oscar exploded, "Who the hell thinks up this bullshit? How did you get these men to volunteer?"

"Hell, we didn't know what we were getting into," the agitated General declared. "Vietnam was a new type of war. We went into it with World War Two Japanese mentally. We were expecting the human wave attacks. The Viet Cong and the North Vietnamese didn't cooperate. Those kids didn't know what they were volunteering for and we didn't either. We were breaking new ground. We lost fifty eight thousand good men. Then, we screwed up even more and sent them home. Hell, we practically lost a whole generation of our youth. We should never get in a scrap when Congress refuses to declare war and the President refuses to use nuclear weapons. Damn, those kids didn't have a chance. The early years we were doing okay, but still losing the war. We just didn't have as many casualties. Everything hinged on body count. We had a seven to one kill ratio. We needed a twenty-one to one just to keep up with the Vietnamese birth rate.

That's when the head assholes in D.C. decided to stop the guerrilla action and sniping to go with bigger units engaging the enemy. We just succeeded in getting more of our boys killed faster. They clung to that idiot assed policy until Congress finally cut off the money supply. Then there was that chicken shit Congress who never did declare war and authorize the sale of war bonds. A lot of good men received a court martial for doing things that were okay during a declared war. That was damn confusing when you're on the front lines. The bullets flying toward our boys didn't know it wasn't a declared war. Our boys weren't any less dead because it wasn't a declared war."

There was a long pause. Finally, Oscar calmly asked, "What about Roger? What kind of shit did he fall into?"

"He was my man," the calmed down General answered. "I was a liaison officer with the Central Intelligence Agency. Roger couldn't get V.A. benefits even if he could use his real name. He had only spent two years in the Air Force before I recruited him for the C.I.A. He was given his Air Force pay by the C.I.A. That caused these young fellows a lot of confusion. They and we thought they were still in the military units they had enlisted in. However, the Veterans Administration didn't see it that way. The V.A. said the soldiers were actually on loan to the C.I.A., a civilian operation. Military benefits didn't apply to those wounded in a civilian operation."

"What the hell was the thinking for that kind of claptrap?" Oscar fumed.

"We got some darn good men on the cheap," the General continued. "We would've had to pay a civilian sniper ten times as much and probably had to carry a life insurance policy on him too. That war was getting expensive. Congress was stingy about giving out money for it. The Great Society was eating a big hole in the national budget. That program should have been suspended until the war was won."

"Well I don't recall of anybody every accusing a politician of being bright," Oscar concluded.

"How the hell did you spooks come up with a name like Hartec?" Harley asked.

"That was easy," the General replied. "We bought a half dozen scrabble games and put all the tiles in an ice cream pail. Then we would shake the pail and dump all the tiles out on a large table. When we found something that would pass for a surname; we'd put a common name in front of it. If we couldn't find that name in the New York telephone book; we would throw in a middle name and go with it."

"You're shitting us!" Oscar and Harley said in unison.

"Try it," the General chuckled. "It's the easiest way we found."

"That wars been over with for ten years," Harley said. "If you're retired, why are you bothering with this now?"

"It helps me sleep nights," came the reply. "As I said before, we were breaking new ground. Never anticipated the long-range consequences of what we were doing. We didn't even think about that. We had a war to win. I try to keep track of all my boys, especially since Congress cut off the funding to protect them. Now nobody gives a damn. It's absolutely terrible. They were all damn fine men."

"Why was Roger picked?" Harley inquired.

"He fit the profile." The General replied. "We preferred anybody that looked foreign and was an orphan. Roger's parents gave him away when he was nine. He'd no contact with them since then. Didn't even know how many brothers and sisters he had, but there must've been a passel of them. He didn't get any mail. The mail thing always shot up a green flag for a possible candidate. We borrowed a policy from the Pony Express manual: 'Willing to risk death daily, orphans preferred.' I guess I've been clawing around your tree long enough. Just tell Roger that the spooks want him to maintain a little lower profile. With the budget cuts, he's really on his own."

Oscar and Harley heard the click of the receiver. The speakerphone emitted the buzz of a dial tone. The two men stared at each other in disbelief. "That poor bastard probably hasn't had a decent nights sleep in years," Harley finally said.

Oscar's intercom buzzed. He pressed the receive bar to hear his Secretary ask, "Ready for coffee, Sheriff?"

"Sure am," Oscar replied. Releasing the send bar, he said to Harley, "Darn good woman that Millie is."

"Well Sheriff-shot-in-the-ass, did you get that second Purple Heart on the cheap?" Harley inquired, with a chuckle.

Oscar roared with laughter. "Godamn it Harley. I just knew you would think of that. I've got four holes there, but it wasn't a case of a Purple Heart per cheek. I got the second Purple Heart for some German potato masher damage. That actually left me with fewer holes but more bleeding."

The two men were still chuckling heartily when Millie entered with a tray of pastries, coffee pot and utensils. She set the tray on Oscar's desk, while smiling at their mirth, and then exited the room.

"That is a remarkable Secretary," Harley commented, as he turned the two upside down mugs over to receive coffee from the insulated pot in Oscar's hand. "Yep, in Korea we would cut the buttons off our shirts so we could get closer to the ground."

Both men chuckled. "It wasn't the buttons that got me in trouble," Oscar intoned. "I dreamed about Jenny the night before and it was the hard on I had all morning that got my ass punctured."

Both men broke into a hearty laugh with Harley slapping his knee and shaking his head from side to side. When their laughter subsided, Harley said, "Damn, that General sure was spooky."

"Yeah, but he sure made our job a lot easier," Oscar said. "Sure as hell filled in a lot of blank spaces. Didn't have much respect for Westmoreland though."

"Randy cusses him for the one run in he had with him," Harley stated. "Some of the other veterans got Randy a little lit at a force party and pumped him for information. None of them seemed to have much respect for Westy."

"Guess I never heard much about the grunts point of view," Oscar said. "The press sure liked to put his picture in the paper every day."

"Well it seems Randy got sent to an army supply area for a short R and R over the Thanksgiving holiday," Harley said. "Of course that was still in-country and a combat area. However, Randy being a marine sniper considered any real estate behind his foxhole the rear. Anyway, as Randy tells it, he had just sat down with his mess kit loaded with Thanksgiving dinner when Westy and his entourage dropped in. All the men had to form up and parade for Westy's grand entrance. When they got back to their dinners, a sudden down pour had washed their mess kits and Thanksgiving dinners down the hill they were on. Randy said that would've been his first hot meal in four months."

"That would piss a man off," Oscar snorted. "So old Westy was a dipstick."

"Now we know why they're inviting most of the police and sheriff's departments to their wedding," Harley said. "Roger doesn't have family and most of Lilly's family has died out."

"There weren't many from her side at her late husband's funeral," Oscar said. "Lilly always says her family tree is growing upside down. I've got to call Jenny. She was going to find out about wedding clothes; where we are suppose to rent tuxes. You might just as well sit tight and get this information too." Oscar dialed his home number and put the system on speakerphone.

"Hello," came the reply, "Sheriff Thompson's residence."

"Jenny, Oscar here. What did you find out about tux rentals?"

"No tuxes," Jenny replied. "Roger doesn't approve of formal affairs in rented clothes. They want a rainbow wedding. Lilly said we should all wear our Sunday best or the men can wear their department's dress uniforms."

"Thank you sweets," Oscar said. "I'll see you tonight."

They heard a "touché," as Oscar snapped the telephone off.

"Hot damn!" Oscar exclaimed, "Now that's sensible. Always hated those monkey suits. Always felt like a French butler. Well Harley, you can clue Randy in."

Chapter 6. The Warning. Spring, 1982

Oscar had walked into the kitchen and swooped Jenny up into his arms. Then he planted a kiss on her lips. Setting her down while still holding her he said, "I love you dear."

"And to what do we owe this jolly mood?" Jenny had asked.

"Oh we got a lot of answers about things that were bothering us from some Langley spook," Oscar replied.

"Who are we?" Jenny inquired.

"Harley and I," Oscar replied. "We were concerned about what Lilly was getting herself into, trying to make a life with Roger. We couldn't find any record of him being in the military. The only record we could find was that copy of an ADC form the American Legion had. Heck, we weren't even able to locate another Hartec."

"I guess I've never heard the name before," Jenny mused.

"The spook said Hartec is an alias and Roger was as good as an orphan," Oscar said.

"What's a spook and who is this guy?" Jenny inquired.

"We'll never know dear," Oscar replied. "Just like we'll probably never know Roger's real name. A spook is somebody who works for the Central Intelligence Agency. This fellow was also an Air Force General, or so he says."

"Was Roger C.I.A.?" Jenny asked, her eyebrows shooting up in surprise.

"Darling, could you put dinner on hold and mix us a couple of drinks?" Oscar asked. "I'll meet you in the living room. I've got to wash the salt from my face."

"Sure, I can do that," Jenny replied.

Oscar went to the bathroom to wash his face and hands. Normally he would take a shower, but this evening he wanted to talk first. Jenny was a good listener.

Jenny prepared their drinks in tall cooler glasses, and joined Oscar on the sofa. Oscar took a long drink of his cocktail and set the glass on the coffee table. He licked his lips and said, "Ah, that's good. Thank you dear."

"You're welcome dear," Jenny replied. "I had asked you if Roger was C.I.A.?"

Oscar chuckled, "Yes and no," he replied. "Actually he was a mechanic in the Air Force when he was recruited for sniper work. Now honey, you have to keep all this under your hat. Roger could still be in danger if the wrong people connect him with his real name."

"Heavens! Poor Lilly. She's so in love with him," Jenny said. "Will she be okay?"

"Oh she'll be okay," Oscar said. "Roger will have her up on a pedestal. The best part of his life began with Lilly. With lots of love- the first part of his life could fade into distant memory."

"But, could he get violent with her?" Jenny asked.

"I don't believe he will," Oscar stated. "Everybody he got violent with actually had it coming. There were those four motorcycle riders he put in the hospital when he caught them urinating on the American flag at the Legion Post in Halston. Remember that?"

"Yes I do," Jenny said. "That's when you went out to his place to arrest him."

"Lord, that man had taken a beating," Oscar said while shaking his head from side to side. "It still amazes me that he survived. They had whipped him with chains. Doc. Silber admitted to me later that he didn't think Roger would make it. He had lain out at his place for three days without medical attention. The only place Roger wasn't black and blue was where there was scar tissue from when the machine gun bullets had passed through his body."

"Are you sure it was bullet holes dear?" Jenny inquired.

"Course they were honey. I've got four holes myself. Course, I have to back up to a mirror to see them," Oscar replied, with a chuckle.

"I'm sorry," Jenny chuckled, while pulling on Oscar's arm and laying her head on his shoulder. "I'd forgotten."

"Anyway this Spook was a Bible of war information," Oscar said. "He even knew about Harley's service in Korea and my getting shot in the butt as well as the hand grenade wounds from the Battle of the Bulge."

Oscar paused to take a sip of his cocktail. "We pumped him for information about Randy Slocum and Jimmy Schwartz," Oscar continued. There was a catch to his voice when he said Jimmy Schwartz.

"Now dear, maybe you shouldn't talk about this anymore," Jenny soothed.

"It's hard Jenny, but people really should know about this stuff," Oscar said. "Remember that Anderson boy west of here? He committed suicide. In the letter he left, he confessed to allowing members of the South Vietnamese forces to torture and kill prisoners. He said he had lost half of his men to booby traps without ever engaging the enemy. When he allowed the torture and used the information gained from it, his losses stopped. However, at the time he allowed this to go on, he was convinced he wasn't coming home alive. Once he had come home to the taunts of 'war criminal,' 'baby killer,' and 'Genghis Khan,' he decided the rest of his natural life wasn't worth living."

"Those were horrible days," Jenny said, as she dabbed at her eyes with a tissue.

"The Spook said Jimmy Schwartz got a raw deal," Oscar continued. "Said he knew Jimmy was lost."

"That was a terrible situation," Jenny agreed.

"You don't know the half of it," Oscar said. "Harley and I made some terrible mistakes that day." Again, there was a catch to his voice. He took a couple of deep breaths and another drink of the cocktail.

"Randy had been on duty all night," Oscar said. "He had stayed over to clean up some paperwork. He had been on shift about eleven hours when Harley told him we had a situation." Jenny slid her cocktail in front of Oscar as he drained his glass. "Randy was completely clueless as to who we were dealing with. After he had gotten Jimmy Schwartz in his scope, he realized his target had been a neighborhood playmate. They had been fellow students in sniper school. He broke."

Oscar paused to rub his face while Jenny rubbed the back of his neck. "Jimmy was about to shoot two of my deputies," Oscar continued. "He had the drop on them and they weren't even aware of it. That is some real rugged terrain. Jimmy was holed up in that old fort the kids had made in that rock pile years ago, when they spent their summers playing war. Anyway, when Randy broke, I grabbed my ought-six and shot Jimmy through the heart." Oscar felt himself choking up. Looking at Jenny through moisture filled eyes, he continued, "Maybe the good Lord intended it that way. Randy always did head shots."

"You know the Lord must be looking after you," Jenny said, as she dabbed at her eyes with tissue. "Especially if some of this is starting to make sense. Maybe these young men will start getting the help they deserve. Everything about that war has always been so confusing."

"There certainly was plenty of confusion that day," Oscar said. "I stood up and yelled, 'Medic.' The E.M.T.'s started to run over to the fort. Then I guess I kind of lost it. I started cussing and yelling at them. I remember yelling, 'get your butts over here.' They came over and just stood in their tracks looking at Randy in the fetal position, weeping. I guess I really jolted them when I yelled, 'For Christ's sake, sedate him and get him to the hospital.' Couldn't blame the poor chaps though. I doubt if their training included a war scenario. Just then Harley arrived and took over. He got the E.M.T.'s settled down and into action. I walked over to the fort. I knew Jimmy was dead. Then I discovered the weapon he had was a plastic toy," Oscar choked up.

"They looked so real dear," Jenny said, as she rubbed her husband's back. "And they were only a little smaller than the real ones. You had no way of knowing at that distance."

"Fortunately the Doctor's gave Randy a clean bill of health in just two weeks," Oscar said. "Course, it will be on his record. It will always be there. Harley and I've agreed we would still take Randy, over anybody else, in situations like that. However, we will make sure he knows everything we know about the target. We should never have put Randy in that spot. But as that Spook said today, 'We were breaking new ground.'"

"Yes we were," Jenny said. "Thank God Emil and Ellie Schwartz were so kind. I'm so glad I went to their house with you to inform them about their son. It was nice of them to talk you out of retiring. You didn't have enough years in to get full retirement benefits. Ellie confided to me that they knew something like that was going to happen. Jimmy just wasn't himself anymore since he had come home. Emil took solace in knowing you had fired the shot. He said, 'I know Oscar did that without malice. He was always looking after Jimmy and took him fishing a lot.'"

"He was a spunky little devil all right," Oscar chuckled, as he remembered all the trouble Jimmy had gotten into as a kid. "Emil and Ellie were both fifty years old when they had this only child. And was he spoiled."

"But he never was malicious," Jenny said. "And he enjoyed fishing as much as you did. It was a good thing you two got to be fishing buddies. It gave Jimmy something to do and curtailed his mischief."

"Yeah, those were the days," Oscar sighed. "A time of innocence, I guess. No drugs. No marauding punks. No poolroom rapes. None of the radical divisiveness we have now. I guess wars do that. Well dear, I'm hungry as a bear. Let's have dinner."

Oscar had contacted Roger the day before and had set up an appointment to discuss the Langley Spook with him. He wanted to talk to Roger in person so he could study Roger's demeanor.

Roger had offered to come to Ashland Falls, but Oscar informed him that he needed to get out of his office. Oscar had suggested that if Roger had a place where the two could talk in private, Oscar would meet him there. Oscar wanted Roger to be on his own turf. He felt Roger would be more comfortable and reveal more information. Roger had offered his office and a morning appointment had been made.

Oscar walked across the county sheriff's parking lot to a patrol car in the frigid morning air. He was a large heavy-set man with a thick neck. At five foot eleven inches he looked much taller, since he usually wore western style boots.

The sun was shining brightly and the air was sparkly with hoarfrost hanging in the atmosphere. Removing sunglasses from his shirt pocket, Oscar put them on. The extreme brightness was painful to his eyes. As he started the car's engine, he gave thanks for this beautiful day in early April. The spring had come early. The farmers had already been in the fields planting wheat. This sudden cold snap had put a halt to that process. However, it would be a short lived halting. Soon they would have weeks of overcast and drizzle. Oscar pulled the Sheriff's cruiser into the parking lot at Siding Lumber Yard. Siding was a small town that had been a railroad stop in the early days. It was an area where the railroad had constructed a siding to accommodate the loading of firewood and farm produce destined for the Twin Cities. A ticket agent had made the trip from Ashland Falls, with horse and buggy, several times a week. He would handle waybills and deliver checks. Eventually a small town had sprung up around the first business, a saloon and house of ill repute. The town was simply called Siding. Entering the store part of the operation, Oscar greeted Lori, "Good morning gorgeous," he said.

"Morning Sheriff," Lori said, with a smile. "I'll buzz Roger." Lori pushed an intercom button and said, "Sheriff Thompson here."

"Be right out," came a reply. A door in the wall, between rows of shelves, holding hardware opened and Roger stepped through it. "Good morning Oscar," he said, as he extended his hand out and the two men shook hands. "Come on in."

As Roger followed Oscar into his office he said to Lori, "We'll have coffee a little early this morning." Then he stepped inside and took a chair behind an oversized desk cluttered with house plans.

Lori took a tray loaded with an insulated coffee pot, mugs and cookies into Roger's office. She closed the door behind her as she went back to her desk.

"Well Roger, I wanted you to know that this Spook from Langley filled in a lot of blanks," Oscar said. "However, he's concerned about your high profile of late. Our local scandal sheet is big enough to subscribe to wire services. So, anything they print is available to the National News Media. If it looks like a hot item, it will spread. The Spook was obviously getting his information this way. He said that due to budget cuts your supposed protection is non-existent. Were you aware of that?"

"Yes I was," Roger replied. "The last I knew, my identity would be protected so well that I wouldn't receive my discharge papers from the Air Force. I haven't"

" This Spook insisted that we warn you about high profile incidents," Oscar said.

"Ho boy!" Roger said, as he tapped a wooden pencil up and down on his desk, bouncing it on its eraser. "Did he have knowledge of any specific person on my trail?"

"No, just that he knew there were some out there," Oscar replied.

"Well, I think I've taken care of the one assigned to me," Roger said.

"Oh!" Oscar's eyebrows shot up on his forehead. "When did this happen?" he inquired.

"Sometime back," Roger stated. "It was my second fall cutting firewood. Must have been the fall of seventy four."

"Out in your woodlot? East of Siding? In the Siding hills?" Oscar inquired, in disbelief. He was becoming more comfortable talking with this strange individual. However, He realized Roger was getting uncomfortable about volunteering more information than what was required to answer the questions.

"Roger, the whole county is my jurisdiction," Oscar said, as he poured both their mugs full of black coffee. Grasping a cookie and napkin in one hand and a mug of coffee in the other, he leaned back in the comfortable swivel chair and said, "Mind filling me in on what happened out there?"

"Are you sure you want to know?" Roger inquired; as he rolled his eyes up to look at Oscar over the high edge of the coffee mug he was about to take a drink out of.

"Roger, it's only been recently that Harley and I came to realize that that Godamn war continued for some people long after it was over with in Southeast Asia. Christ! It was long enough over there. The Spook said some of what we think are suicides are actually hits. It's important for Harley and I to understand what the hell is going on. I understand that what happened to you in the woods was a continuation of the war. It would be nice to know what we're up against when we investigate these suicides and accidental deaths. We've certainly have had our share of them in this county."

Oscar paused to take a drink of coffee, and then continued, "Some of the deaths just didn't make sense. It was a stretch to call them self inflicted or accidental. According to what we get out of our conventions, it's a problem all over the country, wherever there is a concentration of veterans. Statistics tell us you Vietnam veterans have a higher suicide rate than the norm. It seems to me, you're getting some help." Looking across at a silent Roger, Oscar continued, "It would be nice to know how the hell your hit planned to stage your death. What the hell was he going to do? Drop a tree on you?"

"Been easier to cut off my leg and let me bleed to death is my guess," Roger said. "I left the lumber yard shortly after lunch to spend the afternoon cutting firewood. I was still on my first tank of fuel blocking up a large tree I had felled the night before. I was bent over the saw, almost through the log, when this cold chill went up my spine. The chill shot up between my shoulder blades and into my brain. I thought my brain would freeze solid. That chill was so cold."

"Ah, That's what we called, 'The Death passed over,' chill," Oscar said. "Had a few of them myself in Europe."

"I guess that's what happened alright," Roger continued. "That Echo chain saw weighs over thirty pounds with the thirty inch bar on it. You don't just straighten up right away after being crouched over to cut several blocks. The chill was a warning. No danger was in front of me. So I whirled around, still in the crouched position, the chain saw still in my hands and running. I rolled my eyes up to see a Vietnamese man rushing at me with a garrote in his upheld hands. As he looped the garrote around my neck, I squeezed the throttle on the chain saw and rammed the bar up into his belly. The bar continued its upward motion and the end came out between his shoulder blades. The chain saw stuck in his spine and it killed the engine. The impact of the saw sucking itself into his body knocked him down. It pulled me down on top of him, since the garrote was around my neck. I went through his pockets and found a car rental receipt and an airline ticket for a return trip to Minneapolis from Fargo. According to the rental receipt the car was supposed to be turned in before midnight. The flight was to leave a little after ten P.M. I figured things could get real complex if I didn't handle this by myself. I had a shovel in the box of the pickup that I had driven to the woods with. So I buried him in the woods. It was tough getting the chain saw out of his body. It was jammed in his spine. I had to start the engine and use the engine to power the bar out. I buried him where a large tree had uprooted during a windstorm. It was easy digging in a spot like that. I put his personnel effects into a large plastic sandwich bag. I laid them in the grave under his body. After I had buried him and disguised the grave; I went in search of his vehicle. He hadn't followed me into the woods with it. I suspected he had left it on the highway. I had his key. According to that key it was a Ford rental. I hiked out to the road and there was a Ford Torino parked on the edge of the road, where my trail went into the woods. I drove the car home. Then I took a shower and ate the lunch, which I had taken to the woods for my supper. I had plenty of time to get to Fargo. Later, I drove the Torino to Fargo in time to catch the flight to Minneapolis. I dropped the car off in the rental company's return lot and walked to the terminal. At that time of night, there isn't much going on. I didn't think anybody even seen me drop the car off. I sat in the terminal until they announced the boarding. Then I went through the boarding line and surrendered the ticket. However, I didn't board. I slipped away after going outside the terminal to board. I hiked over to the freeway entrance and hitched a ride to Ashland Falls. I figured if anybody was keeping tabs of the assassin, they could only conclude that he dropped out of sight on the flight. I figured my identity was still safe and that the assumption would be made that the assassin had successfully completed his job. He couldn't have discussed what his exact plans were for my termination. The procedure would be different for each job."

"How do you suppose he thought he could garrote you without us knowing how you had died?" Oscar asked.

"Darnest thing," Roger said. "He had laced the wire cable on the garrote through a length of surgical tubing. It wasn't his intent to kill me with the garrote."

"Christ! That's spooky," Oscar said, with a shiver. "We have enough war veterans on the police force and in the sheriff's department to pay attention for future assassins. The Spook said he knew of two for sure. Harley and I will quietly get the word to the veterans to keep an eye on you and Lilly. We can check out anybody who looks Vietnamese as soon as they come into this area. As for this other incident back in seventy four----, well I think we may just as well leave a sleeping dog sleep."

"I do believe it's over with," Roger said. "However, there's no way of knowing for sure. I appreciate your offer, especially where Lilly's concerned. I don't think I would be able to handle it if something happened to her because of me."

"It's tough when your country sends you into battle with one hand tied behind your back," Oscar said. "We should never allow our men to fight, if Congress won't declare war."

"We really shouldn't get into a scrap if we're not going to use our nuclear weapons," Roger said. "No point in having them if we won't use them to protect ourselves. Whoever thought we would allow fifty eight thousand men to die without dropping a big one?"

Roger was staring off into space as he continued, "Those of us who were determined to match our enemy blow for blow are survivors. Now we are asked if what we did can be justified by a civilized society? Shucks! The biggest question on our minds is was it worth the effort?"

"Was it Roger? Oscar asked. "What the hell makes you tick? Why haven't you given up?"

"Oh, it isn't as if I've never thought about it," Roger answered. "But then I ran into somebody worse off than I was. Taking on the task of helping them has kept me going. Also, I think it could have a lot to do with family, honor and the burden of shame. I've never been burdened with that in the past. The only person who ever loved me died when I was eighteen. Now that I've met Lilly, I can see a whole new world ahead of me. In my life there's no such thing as the good old days. It's all ahead of me. It's funny how life works."

"Lordy, lordy. You've said a mouthful there, Roger," Oscar agreed, while shaking his head up and down.

Chapter 7. The Wedding.
Spring, 1982

The late April day had broken warm with a bright sunny sky. It definitely portended the possible high of low eighties that the weather bureau was forecasting. The warmer temperatures were going to be welcome after the cold snowy winter and cool spring.

Lori and Sam were going over their checklist of wedding preparations. Lilly and Roger were hosting their own reception at their country home. They had asked Lori and Sam to lock up their place after they left for the honeymoon. Oscar and Jenny were going to help.

Roger had wanted to hire Clayton Shore and his five-piece band for the reception. However, Clayton insisted there would be no charge. Clayton would put out a jar for donations and requests. All of the band members were veterans with alcohol problems. Clayton insisted they could stay sober for two days in a row. They would all get drunk on Thursday night before the Saturday wedding.

Lori and Sam met the other four couples, of the wedding party, early at the church for a short rehearsal. Now all five couples were gathered outside in front of the church. Soon the rest of the invites began to arrive.

"Oh! Look at Janice," Lori exclaimed. "She's absolutely stunning. Who knew such a beautiful lady existed inside those bib overalls and flannel shirts she always wears?"

"She appears a little awkward in those heels," Lilly giggled. "Probably the first time out of the brogans she normally wears."

"Lordy, lordy," Jenny said. "She sure is a gorgeous looking young woman, and just fifteen! Good thing there will be lot of law enforcement people at the reception."

Harley chuckled, "Yeah, Smitty couldn't understand why he had gotten an invitation. He said, 'Gosh, I only talked to Roger once. That was to write him a tail light ticket on his old truck.' I asked him, were you respectful? Smitty had only been on the force for a couple of months. He had moved here from Wisconsin. Anyway, Smitty says, 'I don't know if I was respectful or not. I just know that when I realized whom I had pulled over, I almost crapped my britches. When I finished giving Roger the ticket, I had to red light it to the nearest restroom.'" The members of the wedding party were laughing as they separated to take their respective positions for the ceremony.

Lilly looked stunning in a beautiful blue pastel dress with a white lace cover that she had made. The ladies had coordinated their dresses with Lilly's. The men wore their best suits. The ceremony was short and there was rice throwing outside of the church. Then it was back inside to sign the marriage certificate.

Sally Watkins, Lori and Sam's daughter, was the wedding photographer. She quickly took several pictures of the certificate signing and the wedding party, at the church, before they all left for the reception.

Lilly gave the Pastor a set of instructions that had been included with each invitation. Their place was secluded and could be hard to find. In short order, everybody proceeded to the reception. By the time Roger, Lilly, Lori, Sam and Sally got there; the party was in full swing. A large keg of beer had been on ice for two days. One of the church tables had been made into a bar with hard liquor, punch and other soft drinks being served.

It was a mild day. The doors of the two-stall garage were wide open. The party had moved out to the concrete apron in front. The spring nights had been to cold for an insect hatch. That had eliminated any problems with the flying pests.

Clayton Shore and his band had set up outside on a corner of the apron next to the outside door. They needed to be able to get power to their instruments.

It was almost noon. The ladies decided to serve lunch right away before the men had to many drinks on empty stomachs. The women were amused by the elevator and soon worked out a relay system to transport the food from the kitchen to the garage.

Lilly had put together the main courses. Several of the church ladies brought side dishes, condiments and deserts. There was sliced ham, turkey, sloppy Joe mix and Lilly's specialty, Beef AuJus. There was plenty of food for a ten-hour party. It was suspected the dance would go well into the night.

The wedding party had been the front of the line. They were done eating while many were only getting through the line for the first time. Oscar and Harley found this an opportune time to catch Roger off to the side and solve one more mystery that had been bugging them. Drinks in hand, they drew up chairs next to Roger. He was a short distance down the slab from where Clayton had set up the band. Roger had a large plastic cup full of beer in his hand.

"Say Roger, we have a question for you," Oscar began. "Now if you think we're out of line, just say so. No hard feelings. We'll just forget it."

"Shoot," Roger said, with a chuckle, as he took a drink from his glass of beer.

"Well," Oscar said, "We've been wondering about those three bullet wounds on your body. Two bullets entered from the front and one bullet entered from the back. Now we figure you sure as hell couldn't have been running away when you got the bullet in the back. The two that entered from the front shattered your leg. Must have been impossible for you to run. How the hell did that happen?"

Roger chuckled again. "You fellows are a lot smarter then the investigation team that reviewed that fiasco. There were some who insisted that that operation had failed because I had turned tail and ran. Actually, I was flying butt over pie hole when that slug went through my shoulder. I was upside down and in the air." Roger bent over and pointed to the top of his head, "See that scar on my scalp?" he asked.

Oscar and Harley bent in closer to look. Finally Harley brushed some hair to the side with his pinky finger, "There it is Oscar," he said, as they looked at the wide scar about two inches long, that started just inside the hairline.

"I'll be damned," Oscar replied. "It was the same bullet that went through your shoulder that caused that scar?"

"One and the same," Roger replied. "I never lost consciousness that I can recall. I remained conscious until the medic sedated me." Roger took another drink from his glass. "It wasn't an ordinary mission for me. I was near the end of my second year in Nam. My hitch in the Air Force was over with. I was on an Army base waiting processing when I was tapped as a go-along. It was supposed to be a piece of cake mission. Actually, it was a reconnaissance mission during a holiday truce. Anyway, the Viet Cong weren't paying any attention to the truce either. They were out setting a trap for us. There were forty or fifty of them and only six of us. It was pitch black that night and we walked right into them. Both units were on top of a dike walking toward each other. They were as surprised as we were. I was point man and I slammed into their leader. When I realized we weren't alone out there, I took a step back and swung the stock of my shotgun upward and caught their leader under the chin. I'm sure I broke his neck. Both parties flew off the dike to their left. We ended up on the opposite sides of the dike. Then we started pitching grenades at each other. Our grenades went off. Most of their grenades didn't. The men following the man I killed really didn't know where we were anymore. Most of the grenades that did go off exploded in front of us. We started to fall back into the jungle on the edge of the rice paddy. We got back into the jungle some distance before the Viet Cong got their act together to pursue us. Course, they knew the terrain better than we did. We were able to find some dense jungle with a heavy canopy to make our stand. The B.A.R. man behind me was badly wounded in the grenade attack. When the medic moved him to shelter, we traded weapons. I was providing covering fire for the fallback when I took the two bullets in my left leg. Then a mortar round landed behind a big rotten log in front of me before I could fall down. That whole mess looked like a gigantic manure pile coming at me. The concussion, of the mortar, flipped me up into the air and rolled me over. Then a stray bullet found me. I say stray because nobody would have purposely fired that high. They and we would rake the jungle floor if a specific target weren't in view. It was more effective that way."

Oscar shook his head from side to side. "Damn, that must've been one hell of a mess," he said.

"It sure was," Roger replied. "We were pinned down and about to be annihilated. Had not our radioman a good vocabulary of cuss words, we probably would have been. We couldn't get any covering fire, from our artillery, because of the truce."

"Holy shit!" Harley exclaimed. "You mean they sent you out there knowing they were violating a truce? Then, when the shit hit the fan they wanted to abandoned you?"

"That was it," Roger replied. "Nobody in the chain of command wanted to take responsibility for violating the truce. Our radioman made some real serious threats as to how many officers he was going to shoot, if he got out alive. He was pretty bold with the cussing and bluster. We were all convinced we wouldn't be able to withdraw without artillery cover. We were in a pocket and the night was still pitch black. We were fairly safe until we ran out of grenades or ammunition. However, with the coming daylight, the Viet Cong would find a way of dropping a mortar in on us. That was going to take them a while since we had a heavy jungle canopy over us. I also think we killed most of their mortar crews when we first made contact. I suspect I killed their last mortar crew with the B.A.R. right after they had launched the mortar."

"Did you get covering fire?" Oscar asked, as he reached out and grasped Roger's knee with his right hand.

"I passed out from the pain killer about then," Roger said. "The Radioman came to see me in the field hospital while I was waiting transport out-country. The Radioman was still in a foul mood. 'You laid there four hours before those candy ass sons-a-bitches gave us covering fire to pull out,' he said. 'Talk about a bunch of shitty panted, candy ass officers. Not three balls on the whole Goddamn bunch. Scuttlebutt has it that they had to call all the way to Washington D.C. to get President Johnson to make the decision to violate the truce.'"

"My God! That's what happened on the Chosen Reservoir," an excited Harley retorted. "Don't those bastards ever learn? We were killing the Chinese for a week before Old Mac believed they were in the fight."

"How times have changed," Oscar agreed. "During world War Two we kept killing until they cried uncle. The only truces were to clear the wounded and dead off the battlefield. Course, Old Harry had been an artillery Captain. Few people are willing to give him the credit he deserves for using overwhelming force to defeat Japan. We could have lost a half million more men if he hadn't dropped the big one."

"Well Roger," Harley said, "We're supposed to get together for pictures before we loosen up our suits and take off our ties. I'll inform the women and the photographer we're ready."

The band had struck up wedding tunes as guests started getting props for the picture taking from automobile trunks. There was the ball and chain and a white shotgun. The women and Lilly came out onto the garage apron. Lilly had suddenly grown plump, with a large pillow fastened around her waist and covered by an apron.

There was much laughter at the antics of the wedding party. The band played melodies about have to weddings. Several officers and deputies had changed into their uniforms to act as extras in the shotgun wedding.

The merriment had lasted nearly an hour. Everybody was shouting advice for poses. Roger and Lilly were taking it all in good spirits. Sam ushered Roger onto the scene with the white shotgun.

Lori whispered to Lilly, "You certainly look pregnant."

"Oh Lord, how I wish I were," Lilly whispered back.

Sally Watkins had shot a lot of pictures of the mock wedding. Then she informed the guests to get comfortable for the dance. "I'll catch any humorous shots the rest of the day for the wedding album," Sally said to Lilly. "If you give me a couple of months, I'll put together a nice album and bring it with me when my husband and I come back here to see Mom and Dad this summer."

"That will be nice," Lilly said. "A couple of months will be fine. Roger and I will be to busy until summer to look at the album anyway."

After the picture taking, the dance had gotten lively with several fast tunes. Clayton Shore had left his position with the band to do a Jitterbug with his daughter, Janice. When their dance was done, Clayton had rejoined the band and urged others to try the Jitterbug. Jackie Slocum moved onto the dance area with her son, Willie. Her husband, Randy, paired up with Janice Shore. It was obvious the Slocums could Jitterbug with the Shores. Other couples had joined them for the rest of the dance.

Finally Clayton had declared one last Jitterbug before they slowed things down. Then, Clayton joined Janice on the dance floor. Jackie was paired up with her son, Willie. Clayton was trying to communicate to Jackie without either of the young people catching on. Finally when the couples were in the right position, with Jackie and Clayton back to back, they whirled and left Willie and Janice facing each other. Then Jackie and Clayton danced away together. After a surprised pause, Janice and a very red faced Willie took up the beat and continued dancing, much to the delight of the audience.

After that dance, there was a break for the dancers to catch their breath. Danny, Janice and Willie took refreshments to the band members, who were big on thanks and compliments about the dancing ability of the youngsters.

The afternoon had continually grown warmer with a light south wind off the prairie. That wind kept the humidity down. It had made for a very pleasant day. When the dancing began again, Janice became the most popular request of the day. She was a good dancer and full of energy. However, it was obvious she dotted on her father. She begged time out to take lemonade to him and the other four band members. Her brother, Danny, helped her. Willie Slocum, a tall, slender, painfully shy, tow headed youth with a terrible case of acne was quick to help Janice deliver lemonade and snacks to the band also.

At eight p.m., Roger and Lilly had changed clothes and left the house with two small bags to depart on their honeymoon. Roger's pickup sat beyond the end of the garage apron decorated with crêpe paper and shaving cream. There were long strings of tin cans fastened to the rear bumper.

When Roger and Lilly had approached the pickup, Janice drove along side in Lilly's car. She stepped out of the car leaving it running. "Thank you Janice," Roger said, as he handed her a ten-dollar bill. He threw the two bags into the back seat and helped Lilly in.

Then sliding in along side of her, he drove away. Amid catcalls of "Traitor" and "Suck Up," directed at Janice, the crowd was equally divided about the contest that had just unfolded.

Janice took all the ribbing in stride. She waved the ten-dollar bill in the air and said, "Roger pays well. You turkeys didn't even make an offer."

Oscar, Harley and Sam were slapping their knees and laughing uproariously. "You kiddies will have to learn to get up a lot earlier in the morning if you expect to get ahead of Roger," Oscar said.

The weather had stayed mild throughout the rest of the evening. About half past nine the wind shifted to the east and a chill set in. Everybody started helping clean up. They folded all the tables and chairs and moved them into the garage.

It was a little after ten when Lori and Sam locked the door. Together with Oscar and Jenny they had gone to their respective vehicles for the drive home.

"It sure is chilly," Sam said, with a shiver, as he slid in under the wheel. "It's supposed to get down to thirty by morning."

"We sure had a beautiful day for the wedding and so early in the year," Lori said. "I hope this is a good omen for Lilly and Roger. They both could use a little normalcy in their lives. Lilly wants children. However, she's gone through the change. There's no chance that way. I hope they find happiness."

"Funny how things work," Sam said. "Lilly always looked to you for advice after her mother died. Then Roger moved here and became our surrogate son, a replacement for our Chester. It seemed as if he was looking for parents and accepted the role of our son. Now our two surrogate children are married-to each other. Any idea where they went for their honeymoon?"

"They plan on spending a week at home," Lori said. "They've

rented a motel room for tonight. But they will be home by noon tomorrow. Lilly said all she wanted to see was bedroom ceilings."

"Funny thing," Sam replied, "I remember you telling me the same thing just like it was yesterday." They looked at each other and chuckled.

Chapter 8. Settling In.
Spring, 1982

L illy and Roger had been in high spirits as they spent the remainder of the honeymoon at home. Lilly had painted and repainted everything before the wedding. Now it was a matter of furnishing the rooms and deciding what to get rid of and what to keep. They were bringing two households together. They needed to reduce the supply of furniture.

All of Lilly's furniture was either in the basement or the storage shed behind the house. Lilly had sold her house.

Roger had insisted she invest or spend the money however she wished. He had said, "I'm a male chauvinist pig. That means I'll support my wife. You use your money however you wish."

"I'm going to use some of it for a real fancy bedroom set for the master bedroom," Lilly proclaimed.

Roger chuckled. "By the time we get everything settled in, we will need a new bed. We'll have your old one worn out."

Lilly hated paper work. She was more than happy to turn that part of her life over to her husband. Roger had gotten her two credit cards in her new name. He had also gotten her a new checkbook with carbon receipts. Now she wouldn't have to deal with registrar entries. He had a basket on his desk that she would throw credit card receipts and checkbook carbons into.

Their planning periods were interrupted with regular trips to the bedroom and then to the shower. It was a Roman shower that accommodated two people, which Lilly found delightful. She couldn't get enough of Roger. While in the shower, and clinging tightly to Roger, Lilly said, "I wish you had a zipper on you front side. Then I could unzip you, crawl inside and zip you back up again. Then maybe I could get close enough to you."

Roger chuckled, "We would probably find we still couldn't get close enough. I truly love you, Lilly. I want to be very close to you for the rest of my life. I appreciate the way you let me touch you anywhere and I'll never get enough of that. That first time in your bed was the absolute best day of my entire life. I just knew you loved me too." Roger planted a long passionate kiss on Lilly's lips.

They extracted their bodies from each other's arms and completed their shower. While they were drying off the telephone rang. Roger picked up the receiver. He had been expecting to have to go to the lumberyard. A lot of material was coming in for the building season.

"Lori here," came the response to Roger's hello. "We need to know where to put the extra material you ordered. I know you talked about stacking more out in the parking lot. How should we do it?"

"I'll be there in an hour," Roger said.

"No, no. That's not necessary," Lori insisted. "Danny's on furlough and he's helping out. We need to know if you want the stuff stacked on the edge of the lot or just off the edge."

"On the west edge," Roger said. As soon as I can get some fill and gravel in, we'll move it off the lot. Can't get the dirt until the road restrictions are lifted. I ordered a bunch of cheap tarps. Tell Danny to cover the material with those tarps. He can staple the tarps to the material. The tarps should be in soon, if not already there."

"The tarps are here," Lori said. "We were wondering what all the tarps were for. You two kids keep honeymooning. We have everything under control here. Now may I speak to that gorgeous bride of yours?"

"Sure, but will Danny still be on furlough when I get back?" Roger asked.

"Yes he will," Lori stated.

"Good," Roger said. "Here's Lilly." He handed the receiver to his wife.

"Hi Lori," Lilly said.

"Hi honey," Lori said. "Are you getting the sight seeing tour you were wishing for before you left?"

"Oh yes," Lilly giggled. "It's wonderful."

"Well thank you honey," Lori said. "I told Sam what your wish was and he remembered it was my wish also. That old buck has been trying to do a replay of our honeymoon. It's simply grand. I'll be looking forward to retiring if this keeps up. Well honey, enough of my gab. I'll let you get back to your man. Love you dear, goodbye."

"Love you Lori. Goodbye," Lilly said

Lilly and Roger spent the rest of the week drawing sketches of room layouts, looking through catalogs, and running to town to furniture show rooms to pick out furniture. There were also drapes and curtains necessitating trips to look at hardware and fabrics.

"Which do you like best?" Roger asked Lilly, one day.

"What are you talking about?" Lily asked, "Furniture or fabrics."

"Neither," Roger said. "I'm talking about our love making sessions."

"Oh, I guess I like the night ones when we first go to bed," she replied.

"I like the morning ones best," Roger said. "I do my best work after a good nights sleep."

"That you do," Lilly agreed. She hadn't thought much about making love first thing in the morning. She usually couldn't go to sleep early. So she had a tendency to be slow to wake up in the morning. However, she had to admit that even though the affair started out with her asleep or half asleep, Roger was always careful to make sure she experienced an orgasm. "I find the mornings very enjoyable too."

"Tell you what," Roger said, "Why don't we just do it morning, noon and night?"

"Darling! That's what we're doing now," Lilly exclaimed, as she took her husband in her arms.

"Soon the busy season will be upon us and we will have to forego the nooners," Roger said, as he kissed Lilly while they were still embraced.

"We can always try to make up the lost ones on weekends and holidays," Lilly said, as she squeezed Roger hard. "Wish I had that zipper now."

"I better show you where the safe is," Roger said, as he helped Lilly get dressed. They had gone to the bedroom for some, "Afternoon Delight" after Lilly had wished for the zipper.

Taking Lilly by the hand, Roger led her to the elevator and they rode it to the basement. Sylvester had popped into the elevator with them for the ride. He hadn't been around much. He was very contented with the spacious view from the top floor family room. He spent most of his time there. He had normally slept on the bed with Lilly. Now, after Roger had come into her life-he seldom did. "Maybe we make to much noise," Roger had said.

"I suspect that's probably it," Lilly said, with a chuckle. "Remember how he shot out of the bedroom, that first time, when we both screamed?"

"Lord, I'll never forget that first time," Roger said. "I never knew anything could be so good."

"Thank you dear," Lilly said, as she laid her head on his shoulder and the elevator bumped bottom.

Taking Lilly's hand, Roger led her around to the back of the chimney. In the base of the chimney was a safe with a combination lock. "The combination is my birthday," Roger said, as he spun the dial. He opened the safe to reveal a cigar box full of cash with a tally sheet on top. "Just deduct what you take out from the total and write the new total on the tally sheet." He peeled off a fifty-dollar bill and reduced the total accordingly.

"We have to be careful how we spend this money," Roger said. "I call it my piss away money. My firewood business is about ninety per cent profit and my accountant warned me that I would get in trouble if I reported a ninety per cent profit to the I.R.S. He told me to reduce it down to forty per cent. Naturally, he didn't want to know how I did it. I use the money for bonuses and going out to eat. I dated you with money from this box. If you want to take Lori or Janice out to lunch, just get some money from here."

"Why would I be taking Lori or Janice out to lunch?" Lilly asked.

"Female companionship dear," Roger said. "In the summer we will get so busy that I can't leave the yard at noon, especially when Danny or Janice aren't there. Now that Danny's in the Army, he won't be with us once his furlough is over with. We'll go to lunch as often as I can get away, which won't be often. You're welcome to go with Lori or Janice or both if that works out. You won't want to be out here all by yourself week after week through the busy season. It could get very lonely."

Lilly felt anger rising. She didn't like the fact that Roger was planning her life this way. Then she remembered the heeding of Lori Gustafson. She decided not to say anything. After all Roger could be right. Things would probably be different now that she would be more or less reentering society. "That's very thoughtful of you, Roger," She said.

Roger grabbed her and planted several kisses on her lips. "I love you, Lilly," he said.

"I'm going up to start supper now," Lilly said, as she pulled away from Roger, while still clasping one of his hands in hers. She walked to the elevator with Sylvester in pursuit. They would ride up to the kitchen together.

Lilly was feeling dizzy about this latest revelation. *There had to be thousands of dollars in that box. Roger was certainly placing a lot of trust in her. There was still a lot she didn't know about this man.* "I've never been loved like this before," She said to Sylvester, as the elevator stopped. "At least I hope that's what this is." She scooped up Sylvester and buried her face in his fur as she began to cry. *Was this man truly this kind and trusting, or was this the beginning of control?* The thought scared her.

Lilly had regained her composure by the time Roger arrived in the kitchen. She was busy unthawing hamburger in a frying pan to make tacos. Roger loved tacos. "Supper will be a little late," Lilly said. "I lost all track of time this afternoon."

"That's so easy to do," Roger said. "I'll set the table."

An idyllic summer was speeding to an end. It was early September and the foliage was turning to color. Lilly was nervous about an appointment she had with Doctor Sybil Taylor. Again, a reputation based on gossip contributed to her nervousness. Many women insisted Doctor Taylor was unfeeling and abrupt. Many others insisted she was the best.

Lilly had spent the summer interacting with Roger's employees. Roger had been right about her getting out of the house. She ended up taking Janice to dinner more often than Roger or Lori. Lilly suspected Lori made excuses to allow Janice more time alone with Lilly. Soon Lilly and Janice's lunch date became a once a week ritual.

"I'll bet a lot of people mistake you for mother and daughter," Lori said, with a smile. "A couple of strawberry blonde bombshells hitting the town at noon must have people talking."

Lilly chuckled, "I don't know if anybody who didn't see her at our wedding would consider her a bombshell," she said. "The bib overalls, brogans and baseball cap hide her beauty. Of course, many waitresses think she is my daughter. Janice doesn't bother to correct them, so I don't either. She is truly a wonderful girl. She keeps reminding me to teach her how to be a lady. I've never had a daughter before. We have a most enjoyable time."

"Well Janice needs that," Lori said. "Her mother died when she was just nine. Danny was just thirteen. He kept riding his bicycle out here from Ashland Falls. I think he did that to hide from some other boys who were doing drugs. Roger finally put him to work. Of course when Roger started paying him, it just caused more trouble for Danny. Now the toughs started roughing him up to get money for drugs."

"That must have been terrible," Lilly said. "How did Danny deal with that?"

"Well those punks got so brazen, they started coming out here to extort Danny's money," Lori said. "One day, Roger caught them in the act. Then there was hell to pay. Roger got each one by an ear and slammed their heads together. Then he had them walking on their tiptoes to their car. We never saw them again. Later Danny told me that Roger had threatened to kill them both. Roger told those boys that he better not hear about them coming within a hundred feet of Danny. One of them was the Markham boy. His parents are well to do. I thought sure there would be repercussions, but nothing came of it. That was one of Roger's violent episodes that went unreported by the Journal, or as Janice says, 'The Urinal.'"

Lilly chuckled at Janice's description of the local paper. She knew the paper had taken a lot of cheap shots at Clayton and his problems with alcohol. Clayton Shore had been an engineer at the power company, until his drinking had cost him his job. His only means of support was the band he had. He managed to stay sober on Friday and Saturdays. The band was good and always in demand. Danny and Janice were pretty much on their own. Clayton was seldom sober on weekdays.

"Well I must get back home," Lilly said. "I won't be by tomorrow since I have an appointment for a physical."

"Anything wrong honey?" a worried Lori inquired.

"No, just a routine physical," Lilly said. "Love you Lori. Goodbye."

"Love you honey," Lori said, as Lilly went out the door.

Lilly had sent Roger off to work with his lunch in hand. Then she showered before dressing for her doctor's appointment with Doctor Taylor. The instructions the clinic had sent out said the visit would require a couple of hours. Most of this time would be spent filling out questionnaires. The instructions asked that the patient use no perfumes or deodorants and to bring something along to read. There would be up to a thirty-minute wait after the questionnaires were filled out. The Doctor would need time to study the background information.

Lilly was at the clinic shortly before nine a.m. She had approached the door as the Janitor was unlocking it. "Good morning," Lilly said to the Janitor, as he had held the door for her to pass through. "Thank you."

"Good morning, your welcome," the Janitor had replied. Then he picked up a doormat and threw it outside for cleaning.

Lilly was escorted into a back room where a nurse took her vital signs and started her on the questionnaires. After almost two hours of answering questions, she was escorted back to the waiting room and advised of a long wait. "The Doctor must study your profile," the nurse said.

After reading for about twenty minutes, Lilly was escorted into an examination room and told to remove her clothes and put on a gown. This she did. Then she sat on the exam table and began reading her book. After about five minutes, Lilly heard the door open. A tall, dark haired, statuesque woman wearing a white gown over street clothes walked through the door. A retaining cord that was attached to the eyeglasses she was wearing hung down the back of her neck. Holding a clipboard and completely oblivious of Lilly, she was intently reading the paper work Lilly had filled out.

The woman, realizing she wasn't alone, looked up from the clipboard with a start. "Sorry," she said. "Very interesting profile. I was doing some double-checking. I'm Doctor Taylor."

"Hi, I'm Lilly Hartec," Lilly said.

"Yes," Doctor Taylor said. "And you want to know if you're healthy enough to have children. Also, you would like to know if it's possible for the change to be reversed. Am I correct?"

"Yes, that's about it," Lilly confirmed.

"According to your testimony you hadn't experienced sexual intercourse for nearly ten years," Doctor Taylor said. "You went through the change about age forty-five. That's early. It's probably more of a mental than physical thing. Naturally, it becomes physical too. Now that you're sexually active again the process could reverse itself. At age fifty it's highly unlikely. Have you considered adoption?"

"I've been to Social Services," Lilly said. "They slammed the door because of my age."

Doctor Taylor chuckled, while evoking disgust. "It's completely nuts," she said. "They will shove six to eight children into foster homes managed by seventy and eighty year old couples. Yet, they will slam the door on people like you who would raise the children at no expense to the county. Unfortunately, what comes out of these foster homes joins the ranks of the criminal element." She shook her head from side to side.

"Well Lilly, I'll put the back rest down and you can slide back on the table and put your feet in the stirrups," Doctor Taylor said.

"I'll call a nurse in and we can get the exam out of the way." The nurse came in as Lilly slide her feet in the stirrups and laid flat on the table. Then she hiked up her gown. *I wonder if she will be able to tell how much sex I've been having,* Lilly thought, as she suppressed a giggle.

The exam lasted about a minute. Doctor Taylor dictated to the nurse who wrote what the doctor said on an examination form. "You may get up and put your clothes on," Doctor Taylor said, as she removed the latex gloves.

When Lilly was done putting herself together, the nurse left the room. Lilly took a seat in a chair and Doctor Taylor drew up a chair across from her. "If you should get pregnant you shouldn't have any problem delivering," Doctor Taylor said. "However, as soon as you know you're pregnant get in for prenatal care. We will want to keep a close watch on you. I don't want you to construe this as meaning you can get pregnant. What I said before still stands."

Doctor Taylor picked up her clipboard and paged through the papers. Stopping at one form she studied it for a while. "I think you need to talk to your husband about this. According to your statements here you don't know for sure that he's capable of siring a child. A lot of Vietnam veterans can't or won't chance it."

"I guess we never talked about that," Lilly admitted. "I know he loves children. I was hoping to surprise him."

"Not a good idea," Doctor Taylor said. "With your age and his background, a pregnancy could be a very high risk."

"Do you know my husband?" Lilly inquired.

"We've spoken a few times," The Doctor said. "My husband was Roger's first firewood customer when he started that business. Vernon always invites Roger in for coffee when Roger delivers. Vernon is a one man cheering section whenever Roger's antics make the headlines. He's always in full agreement with Roger's letters to the Editor. Vernon says they're kindred souls. Vernon was on the Chosen Reservoir. We both were subpoenaed to testify against Roger after the theater incident about six years ago. The County attorney wouldn't pursue a criminal case. Of course he was under pressure from both Oscar and Harley to leave well enough alone. The Strands hired an attorney to pursue a civil case."

"Oh yes, I've heard about that," Lilly said. "All rumors of course."

Looking at her watch, Doctor Taylor said, "You should know more than the rumors. We'll be into lunch break soon. If you have the time, I can tell you first hand what happened."

"Oh I've plenty of time," Lilly said, with intense interest.

"Vernon and I were going to attend a matinee at the theatre one Sunday," Doctor Taylor said. "We found parking about a block down from the entrance. As we got out of our car, we saw three punks leaning against the hardware store wall. When people would approach them, they would slide down the wall extending their legs out in front of the pedestrians. Then the pedestrians had to line up single file to get around them. After an episode, they would stand back against the wall to wait for the next bunch to approach.

Vernon got angry. I had to pull him around the boys and hustled him to the entrance to prevent an incident. Just before we went through the door Vernon pulled me back onto the sidewalk. 'Watch this,' he said, 'Roger did a half step. He's up to something.' Sure enough, when Roger got next to George Strand he swung his left foot up under George's legs knocking them out from under him. George slid down the wall and cracked his head against the concrete sidewalk. The other two boys quickly stood up to let Roger pass. Then they started laughing at George and jeering him. About the time Roger got to the front door, a city patrol car pulled up and an officer stepped out to investigate. Roger was chuckling as he went into the theatre. He greeted us and then said, 'The Devil made me do it.' I thought I would never get Vernon to stop laughing."

"Roger was exonerated at the trial, wasn't he?" Lilly asked.

"Well, not exonerated," Doctor Taylor said. "The Judge threw the case out. He said his court wasn't a comedy act. The Strands had no trouble lining up witnesses to testify about the obvious changes in George. They were trying to get compensation for permanent brain damage. The third witness had the jury and the audience laughing so hard, the Judge lost his temper and ended the proceedings."

"Goodness," Lilly said, "What did he have to say?"

"Under cross examination the witness insisted that George must have suffered permanent brain damage. That witness insisted that

George was a much better fellow after the incident. He suggested that the city should grant Roger a Doctor's license and run a bunch more toughs by him for therapy. Of course everybody knew George as a trouble maker."

Lilly was laughing. "Roger, a doctor. Pity the poor fellow who comes in faking."

After the women regained their composure, Doctor Taylor said, "Now back to your situation of having children. One way or another there are ways to accomplish that. There are plenty of waifs to be picked up, especially in the larger cities. There even is a system to obtain birth certificates once you have procured a waif. It's being done even as we speak. The permissive culture is causing a lot of unwanted children."

"That's so sad," Lilly said.

"I can see your maternal instincts are strong. What you've done for Janice Shore is truly amazing. When I first saw you, I couldn't believe you weren't her mother. She carries herself just like you do. Such excellent posture she's developed. That came about after she met you."

Lilly gasped, "But I didn't do that much. I told her about the exercise my father made me do when I was about to become a teenager. He would pull my shoulders back and put a book on my head. Then I was supposed to walk around the living room three times. If the book fell off my head before three rounds, I had to start all over. I hated it. Dad insisted it would give me good posture. He said that was important for females."

"Good posture is important for everybody," Doctor Taylor said. "Janice is sharp. She watches your every move, how you handle your purse, how you interact while conducting business. She is observing you and learning all the time."

"I worry about all the attention she receives from the men coming to the lumber yard," Lilly said. "She's such a flirt."

"She's a good head on her shoulders," Doctor Taylor said. "She told me she isn't interested in any of the men she meets at the yard. She said, 'If I flirt with all of them, it makes it a lot easier to do my job.' I know she's still a virgin, an oddity in these times. This is confidential information. But as her surrogate mother you ought to know."

Doctor Taylor stood up. "I believe we're done here," she said. "I'm sorry I couldn't be more help to you."

Lilly stood up also. "You've probably been way more help than either of us realizes right now," She said. "Thank you Doctor Taylor."

Chapter 9. Rainy. Fall, 1982

The nights had become chilly. The construction business had fallen off at the lumberyard as winter approached. Roger began spending afternoons in the woods. Lilly was in her glory. She had her husband home for lunch everyday. Then there was their, "Afternoon Delight" as Roger referred to their love making sessions before they went to the woods.

Lilly enjoyed the afternoons in the woods. The autumn days were usually sunny and cool. She could help Roger by throwing all the smaller blocks into piles where they would be easy to load. She would also serve her man lunch whenever he was hungry, which was often. Roger burned a lot of calories doing the hard labor of a woodcutter. In spite of all the lunches, he lost weight during the autumn season.

"We'll haul from the woods on Saturday," Roger said during one lunch break. "We can make the deliveries we have orders for and stockpile the extra wood at the lumberyard."

"What about those big blocks?" Lilly asked, "Won't you have to split them?" Some of the trees were gigantic. After Roger had cut them into sixteen-inch lengths, he would split the large blocks lengthwise into six pieces with his chainsaw. Then the blocks were small enough for one man to lift.

"Getting to be less splitting every year," Roger said. "I'm getting business from more and more commercial operations. They want the big blocks. They bring skid steer loaders along and load into dump trucks or onto implement trailers. Also, more and more people prefer to do the hauling themselves. This will give us more leisure time and provide Janice with more weekend hours during school. I've shown Janice how to calculate cordage. She'll measure the load and charge by the cubic foot. She will be able to take care of sales all day Saturday and Sunday afternoons from the lumberyard office."

"You'll make a wonderful Father, Roger," Lilly said. "You've looked after the Shore children when they really needed you. Have you thought about us having children of our own?"

Roger's face darkened as his demeanor changed. Sitting on the ground and leaning against a large tree trunk, with his arms extended across his knees, he stared off into space. He was speechless and in deep thought. Finally he turned to face Lilly. She could see the moisture in his eyes. "I'm sorry Lilly; I can't do that for you. I would in a heartbeat, if I could."

Lilly reached out and took his hand. Then she pulled him down beside her on the tarpaulin she had spread on the ground. Placing her hands on either side of his face, she said, "Roger, I can't conceive any children for you either. Lord how I wish I could have your child, but it cannot be. However, there are other ways for us to have children. Do you know why you can't sire children?"

"No, I don't," Roger confessed. "All I know is both my ex-wives got pregnant after they left me. I think the last one was pregnant before she left. That was probably her reason for leaving me."

"I'm sorry Roger. I shouldn't have asked," Lilly said.

"No, you have a right to know," Roger said. "All I know is I can't sire children. I don't want to know why because I believe knowing won't change the situation. Any news can only be bad news. I've read the Ranch Hand Report and I don't think I need to know anymore than that."

Lilly had heard of the Ranch Hand Report, commissioned by the Veterans Administration. It basically condemned a lot of Vietnam veterans to produce no children or deformed children because of a defoliant used during the war. The Chemist who developed the formula thought the defoliant was going to be sprayed on enemy troops. However, that was rarely the case.

"Darling, will it be okay if I looked into acquiring a child?"

77

Lilly asked. "I've been to Social Services and they've slammed the door on me because of my age. They're willing to let us be foster parents. However, that's not what I want. I want them to be our own children."

"I want them to be our own children too," Roger said. "That foster care looks a lot like warehousing to me. Those kids must feel like prisoners. Sam certainly did. That's why he kept running away. I think we will have to pray that God rewards us somehow."

"I want to thank you for shoving me out the door last spring." Lilly said. "Your suggestion that I take your employees out to lunch was right on target. I truly love Janice. Her flirting scares me though. At first, your suggestion scared the dickens out of me."

"I thought it would be good for you," Roger said. "Your motherly instincts are strong. I thought Janice was at an age where she would need to be asking questions of a woman. I didn't have that problem with Danny. He was able to confide in me. He also had Clayton, whenever he could catch him sober."

"You are truly amazing Roger," Lilly said. "I'm so glad you fell in love with me. I'll do my best to keep you happy."

"Your loving me makes me extremely happy darling," Roger said, as he kissed her. "Let's take a little walk and I'll show you my secret lake. It's about ten acres in size and about fifty feet deep on one end. It's spring fed. Above the spring there's open water all winter."

The two of them stood up and started hiking up a logging road, which went deeper into the woods. The trail rose ahead of them as they hiked up a steep hill. When they reached the crest and Lilly caught her first view of the lake, she gasped with delight. At the crest of the hill the trail turned into a long, gentle, downward sloping, ravine that ran to the lake's edge at the bottom of a deep basin. The deep azure, placid surface of the water mirrored the images of the clouds, sky and the birds in the sky above. As a flat land girl, Lilly was feeling a little giddy from the elevation. She turned and clung to Roger. "Lord this sure is beautiful," Lilly said. "Are there any fish in this lake?"

"Sunfish," Roger said. "Mostly pumpkinseeds, but a few bluegills. The pumpkinseeds are the best."

"Can we fish here?" Lilly inquired.

"It's our own private fishery," Roger stated. "Beyond the hill on the other side is eighty acres of private land, mostly marsh. Then there's a county highway and State Park on the other side of that."

"Why didn't we come fishing here last summer?" Lilly asked.

"The mosquitoes would have carried us away," Roger replied. "There's a narrow window of opportunity in the spring; before the first mosquito hatch. But if you recall, I was to busy making love to you to think about fishing." Roger gave Lilly's hand a squeeze as they smiled at each other.

"I came out here one winter when there wasn't any snow and fished through the ice on the deep end," Roger said. "I had a fantastic fishing day. We can try fishing next spring. However, that window of opportunity is narrow. This deep valley warms up early. It gets lots of sun when the foliage is missing. The mosquito hatch is about two weeks earlier than elsewhere. I've tried fishing this time of year. The sunfish don't seem to respond as the air grows colder."

"How in the world do you suppose fish ever got into this lake?" Lilly asked.

"One end has a sand bottom and the water is shallow," Roger said. "That makes for an excellent rearing area. The fertilized eggs are transferred to this lake on the legs of wading birds."

" The Lord always finds a way," Lilly sighed, as she nestled into Roger's torso.

The year was coming to an end. The shorter colder days were tugging on the waning summer days trying to over take them. Roger watched the forecasts intently. He was trying to milk the milder weather to the last drop. One Monday morning he said to Lilly, "winter will probably hit with a ferocity by next weekend. I believe we should go to St. Paul next Thursday. Friday morning we will load up a year's supply of auto batteries. We should be able to get home before the weather deteriorates."

"But, it's been such a beautiful fall," Lilly protested. "You don't think this weather will last?"

"That's why it's called an Indian summer," Roger said. "The early settlers said these late summers were as treacherous as an Indian when the end comes. Thanksgiving is next week. Winter can't hold off much longer."

Thursday morning had broken warm and sunny. Lilly couldn't understand Roger's tenseness. He kept insisting he was pushing summer to its absolute limits. He had instructed Lilly to pack for an overnight stay in St. Paul and a thermos of black coffee for the drive. They were going to leave right after lunch.

"Roger, why are we leaving so early?" Lilly asked. "We'll be in St. Paul by four."

"We need some time to cruise the town so you can pick out a restaurant," Roger said. "But first, we can take a quick jaunt through the museum at the capitol."

"Do I dare let you get that close to a politician?" Lilly inquired, with a sly smile.

"You have a tremendous soothing effect on me darling," Roger said, with a sideways glance and a smile. "If he doesn't make a move on you-he's safe."

It was a beautiful scenic autumn drive into St. Paul. There was plenty of color because the red oaks don't drop their leaves until spring. Lilly didn't enjoy traveling much, but she was enjoying this sunny day and being able to serve her man coffee and snacks. She had thrown some beef jerky into a bag with a half dozen of Roger's favorite home made cookies. He needed to gain back some of the weight he had burned off cutting firewood.

Lilly had become alarmed when she realized all his ribs were showing. Roger had laughed about her concern. "Happens every year," he said. "My weight can fluctuate up to thirty pounds during the year."

Lilly had picked out a nice looking steakhouse for dinner that night. There were a lot of cars in the lot when they drove in. Roger had made reservations for the meal and the motel room from a public telephone at the museum.

"Looks like you made a good choice dear," Roger said. "I want a big old broiled T-bone with lots of fried onion rings and a couple of beers."

Lilly chuckled. "So that's how you put your weight back on

when you come out of the woods. Are you sure you're not part grizzly bear?"

"Could be dear," Roger said. "What do you think?"

"Well, I can't say for sure," Lilly replied. "If you are you're my first." She was enjoying this trip. She didn't want to go when Roger first suggested it. He had insisted that he had a talk with Sylvester and Sylvester said he wouldn't mind a night alone.

After dinner Roger asked, "Any suggestions for the rest of the evening?"

"How about a replay of our honeymoon night," Lilly said.

"You got it gorgeous lady," Roger replied.

Friday morning broke sunny and clear. By the time Lilly and Roger had finished breakfast the deterioration of the weather situation was definitely in the air. A brisk wind was blowing and giant clouds were racing across the sky. "The storm is supposed to hold off until midnight," Roger said to Lilly as he boosted her into the four-wheel drive pickup. "It's balmy yet. I hope the forecasters got it right." There was some concern in his voice.

They drove over to the battery warehouse and Roger took his order into the office. A warehouse employee followed Roger out of the office with Roger's order on a clipboard. Roger crawled into the pickup and backed over to an open door where the man was waiting with a forklift. There was an empty pallet on the tines. He and Roger unloaded all the old batteries from in the box. Then Roger drove into another section of the warehouse where there were pallets upon pallets of new batteries.

The two men spent nearly two hours selecting different batteries and loading them. Placing pallets on the bottom layer of batteries, they carefully stacked more batteries on top. Then they placed several cartons of sulfuric acid into the box. The warehouse man said, "Eighty seven batteries and four cartons of acid," as he wrote on the order fastened to the clipboard, "She's all there." He handed Roger the clipboard and wandered off.

Roger drove back to the office and went in to settle the account. When he returned to the pickup, light raindrops were flying around in the wind. "The air is still warm but I think this sucker is coming in faster than they forecasted," Roger said, as he started the engine.

"Hopefully we can slide home before it hits." Looking at his watch he continued, "We should be able to grab a quick lunch on the west side of the cities before we head home."

With the west side of the Twin Cities in their rear view mirror, Roger said, "I'm hungry. Start looking for a McDonald's sign. I've got a couple of discount coupons. Please remind me to use them."

In about five minutes, Lilly said, "You got your wish. There's a couple of arches on top of that hill about a mile ahead on the right." They took the exit and went into the restaurant. Roger ordered their choices and presented the coupon for the discount. They sat by a sunny window. Sunny when the sun could poke through the clouds. As was his habit, Roger said grace. Then a dark cloud passed over. Small drops of rain exposed themselves on the plate glass window.

After they had left the building, the cloud cover had increased greatly and the warm wind was picking up. When Roger turned onto the freeway, the rain became heavy. A short distance down the road hail began to pelt the windshield. The storm was getting progressively more violent and the hail heavier.

"I'm going to pull off under that overpass," Roger said, as he turned on the headlights and four way flashers. He eased the pickup up the angled concrete apron that sloped up to the underside of the overpass. He went forward until the hood almost extended into the storm. "Better leave room for others too stack up behind us," he said. Looking into his rearview mirror he continued, "The rest of the folks at that exit must be smarter than me. Not a headlight in sight."

"Look!" Lilly exclaimed, as she grabbed Roger's arm. "There's somebody out there. He's behind that last post, in the center, between the roadways. That person has to be getting wet."

Roger looked out his side window, "All I can see is the roadbed. The pickup is on to high of an angle."

"Look out the front windshield," Lilly had instructed. "That person has crossed the far road and is crawling up the apron. He's probably trying to seek better shelter away from us. Roger! It's a small boy. He's certainly not dressed for this weather. Roger, we've got to try and help him."

"I'll see what I can do dear," Roger said, as he got out of the pickup. He crossed over both roadways and got to the bottom of the far apron. As Roger started crawling up the apron, the small boy inched out from under the bridge and appeared ready to bolt into the storm. Roger had stopped all forward motion and lay on his left side. All the while he kept an eye on the boy. Lilly could see he was trying to talk to the very nervous boy. Finally he came back to the pickup leaving the boy behind. The boy moved back under the bridge.

"Lilly, I think you might be able to coax him down," Roger said. "I think my deep voice is scaring him." He helped Lilly out of the cab and they crossed over the two roadways. Lilly stood at the edge of the apron talking to the boy. Roger retreated to the center of the overpass and concealed himself behind a post.

In about five minutes the hail stones got bigger and started coming down faster. The huge hailstones bounced across the apron and shattered. The small fragments sprayed the boy. The frightened boy scampered down the apron and into Lilly's arms. He was quaking with fear. Lilly calmed the boy enough to get him to let go of her. Then taking his hand she led him back to the pickup. As they passed the center post, she said to Roger, "Wait until we go past you and then follow us to the pickup."

When Lilly got the pickup door open, Roger joined the two. The small dark haired boy looked up at the two of them, his dark brown eyes searching. "Don't speak," Lilly ordered Roger. She took one of Roger's hands and placed it onto the boy's shoulder. With one of her hands on his other shoulder, she squatted down in front of the boy. "This is a good man. He won't hurt you. Roger, I'm going to crawl into the cab and then you hand him to me." Lilly put Roger's other hand on the boy's other shoulder. She appraised the situation, then crawled up into the high side of the cab.

Once Lilly got herself into place, she extended both arms and said, "Hand the boy to me." Roger handed the silent, wet, dirty, frightened child to her. "I've put a small blanket behind the seat on your side. See if you can pull it out," Lilly instructed.

Roger dug the blanket out and handed it to Lilly. Then he crawled into the cab and struggled to close the door, made heavy by the steep angle of the parked pickup. About that time a tractor-trailer rig pulled under the overpass from the other direction. The windshield was cracked and chrome trim was peeling off, due to the effects of the vicious hailstorm.

Lilly was busy drying the boy with her sweater. Then she wrapped him in the blanket, all the while talking to him. He had bright brown eyes that were constantly darting around observing everything in the confines of the cab. "What is your name?" Lilly asked.

The boy smiled and mumbled something inaudible.

"What did he say, Roger?" Lilly inquired.

"Sounded like hay owl on itch, to me," Roger replied.

Lilly talked to the boy as the storm's ferocity tapered off. Finally the heavy hail stopped and the rain, although heavy, was not nearly as severe as before.

Roger looked into the rear view mirror as he started the engine and commented, "Traffic is coming out of the rest stop." He turned off the four way flashers and put on the left turn signal before pulling back onto the roadway to continue home.

Lilly talked to the boy all the way home. He wasn't dumb because he could say some words clear as ever, such as Big Bird or Miss Piggy. Lilly had the boy playing Patty Cake and doing the Itsy Bitsy Spider routine, while he chewed on the beef jerky leftover from the trip down to the cities. He appeared to be a bright happy boy. He also appeared very hungry.

After putting the pickup away, Lilly had Roger supervise the boy in the bath while she washed his clothes. "Make sure he washes his hair several times," She coached. "I'll take him to town tomorrow and get his hair cut and some clothes."

After an early supper, because the boy was still hungry after devouring the left over jerky, Lilly found some flash cards she still had from her days as a schoolteacher. The boy's lessons began that evening. "Oh Roger, he appears to be bright. How old do you think he is? What shall we name him? I used to like Larry, until that incident with Lawrence at the museum. Maybe we should name him Leonard and then we will call him Lennie. What do you think?" Lilly asked.

"Whoa Lady! Slow down," Roger said. "Why not name him Rainy? We found him in the rain."

"But that's not a Christian name," Lilly protested. "I guess we could give him a Christian middle name. Rainy Hartec does sound nice. How old do you think he is?"

"Could be anywhere from six to ten is my guess," Roger replied. "He's been undernourished, skinny as a rail. First, I think we should find out if he has a name." Roger pulled a footstool up to the sofa in front of Lilly and the boy. In spite of obvious malnutrition, the boy's brown eyes were bright and his hair was a shinny brown almost black in color.

Roger thumped his own chest with his index finger and said, "Roger." Then he touched Lilly with the same finger and said, "Lilly." Then he would put the same finger on the boy's chest and the boy would respond with what sounded like a very long name. After repeating this process several times, Roger broke into laughter.

"What is it?" an excited Lilly asked, as a huge smile spread across the child's face. . "Watch this dear," Roger said. Again he pointed at himself and said, "Roger." Pointing at Lilly, he said, "Lilly." Then, he pointed at the boy and said, "Hey you little son-of-a-bitch."

The boy was all smiles as he shook his head up and down in ascent. Finally he said, "Yes."

"Oh Lord! That's horrible," Lilly said, with disgust.

"Not really dear," Roger said. "No one is going to be looking for him. He's ours. Our prayers have been answered in short order. You must have a lot of pull with the man upstairs."

"You must also," Lilly replied, with a smile.

"I think I used up my ration when he gave you to me," Roger said, as he stood up and kissed her on the forehead. "I don't think we have to worry about anybody wanting to reclaim the boy. They didn't even bother to name him."

"Roger, what are we going to do?" Lilly asked. "We can't just keep him, can we?"

'The Doctor you went to hinted at something like that," Roger said. "Maybe you should get in touch with her. How are we going to handle tonight? Our bedroom is on the top floor and the other two bedrooms are in the basement."

"I have that rollaway cot," Lilly said. "We can set that up in the library next to our room and use that until Rainy gets adjusted."

The three of them went up the elevator to set up the cot. When they got to the library, Sylvester, who had remained hidden, was seen peeking around the corner of the stairwell. Rainy became excited and pointed at the cat, "Sylvester, Sylvester," he said, with a big smile, while looking up at Roger and Lilly.

Lilly gave Roger a puzzled look. "Well, he is a dead ringer for the cartoon cat, Sylvester," Roger said.

When they got to the large open room that the library was a part of, it was obvious that the weather had deteriorated. The rain had turned to snow and it was accumulating rapidly. "Looks like you won't be going to town tomorrow." Roger said.

Rainy crawled up on a large stuffed chair to watch the storm. Sylvester hopped on the cushion and up to the back of the same chair. He curled up on the back next to Rainy's face and started purring. Roger flipped a switch to turn on the outdoor floodlights set to light up nature's scenes. Rainy was delighted. He remained there with Sylvester while Lilly and Roger prepared the cot.

When bedtime arrived, Lilly and Roger tucked Rainy in. Lilly had found some small boy's pajamas among her quilt making materials that fit Rainy perfectly.

Later, when Lilly had gone to check up on Rainy, she found him curled up in the quilt on the floor along side the cot. Lilly woke him and explained that he should sleep on the cot. She tucked him back in and then crawled in beside him. Rainy smiled at her. He laid his left arm around her neck and was soon sound asleep. Lilly carefully extracted herself from the cot and slid Rainy closer to the center. Just then, Sylvester hopped up on the cot and tucked himself in next to Rainy.

Lilly walked into her bedroom as Roger was finishing his shower. "Rainy was curled up in the quilt on the floor beside the cot," She said. "Do you suppose he doesn't know what a bed is?"

"Probably not," Roger replied. "You ready for some sleep? It's been a long day."

'I'll be checking on Rainy several times tonight, I'm sure," Lilly said "Don't worry if you wake up and find me gone. I'm going to shower now."

That's the way that first night with Rainy went. Lilly must have checked on him a half dozen times. Each time she found Rainy and Sylvester sound asleep. Her adrenaline rush didn't allow her to sleep much or for very long stretches.

The extra energy was applied to Roger. "It's necessary for a woman to reward a good husband, " Lilly said, as she pulled his pajamas off and attacked him. Her energy was boundless.

Chapter 10. The Storm.
Winter, 1982

The morning broke with a blizzard in full force. Roger turned on the radio. The weatherman reported fourteen inches of snow and still accumulating. He also predicted that the storm would be over sometime during the following night.

Lilly went to check on Rainy. She found him still fast asleep, with Sylvester curled up next to him on the bed. Roger came in and stood behind her with his hands on her shoulders. "Cute pair," he said.

"I think we'll let him sleep a little longer," Lilly said. "Come, I'll make breakfast."

After dressing, they went down to the kitchen and Roger set the coffee maker to brewing coffee. The kitchen radio was providing them with the business closings. The announcer informed them that nothing was moving and nothing would move until the plows could do their thing. All plows had been pulled off the road until sometime tonight. That's when the storm should end. Until then, the plows would only go out for emergencies.

"You better check on Rainy," Lilly said. "I washed his clothes last night but they were still grunge. I think we'll leave him in his pajamas until we can get him some different clothes. Remember those three big cardboard barrels you moved here from my basement? There should be plenty of clothes in them, toys also.

We have to get them in from the storage shed after breakfast. Lord, I can't burn fast enough what he was wearing."

Roger found Rainy sitting on the edge of the cot with one arm around Sylvester. He was rubbing the sleep out of his eyes with his other hand. "Ready for some breakfast, big boy?" Roger asked.

"Breakfast?" Rainy inquired, with a look of puzzlement.

Roger pointed at himself and said, "Roger." Then he pointed at Rainy.

Rainy responded, "Rainy."

"Good," Roger said. "Let's get your face washed and your hair combed."

Roger showed Rainy how to get downstairs using the stairway. The elevator was designed with high buttons to prevent unsupervised children from using it. At the bottom of the stairway was the main floor bathroom. Roger took Rainy inside and said, "Wash up for breakfast."

"Wash up," Rainy said, while looking up at Roger with a big smile. Then he turned both taps on part way. He took the soap off the edge of the basin and lathered his hands and scrubbed his face. Then he wet his hair and dried his face and hands.

Roger pulled a top drawer out, on the vanity, and selected a comb. He gave it to Rainy. Rainy promptly began combing a head of hair that looked like it had been cut with a hoe. Roger escorted Rainy to the kitchen.

When Rainy saw Lilly, he walked up to her and put his arms around her waist. "It looks like you've become a mother again," Roger said.

"Good," Lilly said, as she hugged Rainy. "The first barrel you should bring in is the one with the scribbling on top. It's the toy barrel. Let's have breakfast."

They sat down. Roger and Lilly said their prayers while Rainy looked on with a smile. Sylvester was under Rainy's chair playing with Rainy's feet.

After breakfast, Roger began dressing to retrieve the barrels from the shed. "If I remember right," Roger said, "one of those barrels was really heavy. I always called it your barrel of bricks. I suppose that's the one you want first."

"Sorry honey, but you're right," Lilly said. "I only want two of them today. One has the boy's clothes and the other is toys and teaching material. I know I have a big strong husband who can deliver."

"Yeah, but how's the best way?" Roger inquired. "There's over a foot of snow out there. It would be tough balancing them on a snowmobile."

"It will probably easier to roll them," Lilly said. " A steal band locks the lid on. Make sure it stays locked when you roll it. The second barrel I want is the one with a rough top, where a shipping label has been torn off."

Roger went to the shed and found the two barrels Lilly had identified. He cut short pieces of wire to secure the locks on the bands and rolled one of them down to the garage door. Upon reaching the garage door, he spun the barrel around and through the door. Then he stood the barrel up and pushed it into the basement where Lilly, Rainy and Sylvester were waiting.

"Let's put it in the elevator and take it right up to the top floor," Lilly said. "I think Rainy and I can handle that, if you want to fetch the other one, Roger."

"Okay," Roger said. "But first I'd better call the Shore residence to make sure they're alright." He tipped the barrel on its side so Lilly and Rainy could roll it into the elevator.

"Hello," Janice Shore answered the telephone.

"Roger here. You survive the storm okay?"

"You bet," Janice said. "Dad and I are playing cards. He has a gig tonight. But it will be cancelled unless the storm suddenly clears off."

"That's the breaks," Roger said. "Well, keep warm."

"We will," Janice replied. "Oh Roger, you better get your load of batteries to the store as soon as you can. We took at least a dozen calls from people wondering when you would be back with the batteries. They all admitted to procrastinating because of the nice weather."

"Okay Janice," Roger said. "Talk to you later. Thanks for the tip. Goodbye."

When Roger got back to the garage with the second barrel,

Lilly was alone in the open doorway. "Rainy dived into that tinker toy set like it was a bucket of ice cream," Lilly said. "He found the instructions for that big dragline and he's hard at it."

"Is that set big enough to build that one?" Roger inquired.

"My boys assembled it several times," Lilly said. "They had the deluxe instruction manual. It's all pictures. That's what Rainy is using."

Roger rolled the second barrel into the elevator and set it up right. He removed the wire he had installed in the locking band. "I'm going to start filling batteries with acid," Roger said. "Janice said I should get to the lumberyard with the batteries as quickly as I can. They received a lot of calls on them yesterday."

"But Roger, tomorrow's Sunday," Lilly protested.

"I shouldn't have waited so long to pick them up," Roger said. "The weather was so nice and we were enjoying being in the woods. There's sixty cords of firewood piled in the lumberyard. The big rush on that will come with the battery rush."

"Well, do what you must dear," Lilly said. "Rainy and I will go to church."

"Be careful dear," Roger said. "The roads will be really slick. Better take the Blazer."

Sunday morning when Roger had unlocked the door of the lumberyard, shortly before eight, the first customer pulled in. Fortunately, the battery he wanted was on the top layer and ready to go. Roger had managed to fill all the batteries on the top of the pallet and all those on the bottom that could be slid out from under the pallet.

Roger handled the sale and then parked the load of batteries by the front door. He used the forklift to remove the top pallet of batteries, setting it on the ground next to the pickup. Putting an empty pallet on the forks of the lift, he parked it nearby to receive the old batteries brought in for exchange.

It was a little after ten a.m. when Roger got a break from selling batteries and firewood. The lot had seen no snow removal. The snow was packed down by traffic. Roger decided to call Janice Shore for assistance.

"Hello," Came the jaunty greeting from Janice.

"Janice, this is Roger. Can you work today? It'll be double time."

"Sure Roger," Janice said. "Dad and I just got back from church. I'll get into some warm clothes and be right out."

"Good," Roger said. "I've already been swamped."

"Should I bring Dad along to help?" Janice asked.

"That would be great," Roger said. "He won't need warm clothes. I've turned up the heat and we'll keep him behind the cash register. I'll sell batteries and you can sell firewood."

"Sounds like a plan," Janice responded. "We'll be right out."

It was shortly after twelve when Lilly called the lumberyard. Clayton Shore shoved the receiver between his shoulder and chin as he continued transacting business at the till. "Hello," he said.

"Hello," Lilly said, with a puzzled tone of voice. "This is Lilly. Is Roger there?"

"Ah, he's outside filling and selling batteries right now. This is Clayton Shore. I'm handling the phone and till. Janice is selling firewood. We're busier than a one armed paper hanger right now."

"Goodness, you folks must be hungry," Lilly said. "I'll put together some lunch and bring it over."

"Good idea," Clayton responded. "Bring us something we can eat while we work. It doesn't look like this is going to let up for a while."

"Got you, Clayton," Lilly responded. "See you in a short."

Lilly trooped in with Rainy. She had a huge sack of sandwiches and a gallon thermos filled with hot chocolate. Rainy was carrying a large bag of cookies and a sleeve of large foam cups.

Lilly grabbed a new roll of paper towels from the store room and served Clayton a sandwich, cookies and cup of hot chocolate. Then she put together two more bundles with cups of chocolate and gave one to Rainy and instructed him to take it to Roger, who was just outside the front door. She took the other bundle to Janice at the far edge of the lot.

Janice had parked Clayton's Blazer next to the huge woodpile. The woodpile was surrounded by pickups backed in. Sometimes, whole families were loading wood. "You can put my food on the hood of the Blazer," Janice said. "I'll be right over as soon as I finish measuring this load."

Rainy walked over to Roger and stood in front of him with a big grin on his face. He was enjoying all the excitement. Roger had heard Lilly instruct him to put his bundle and cup on the tailgate. "This is a tailgate Rainy," Roger said, as he patted the tailgate with his hand. Rainy set the bundle and cup down. "Thank you Rainy. Want a cookie?" Roger handed Rainy a cookie while he grabbed a sandwich for himself.

Roger wolfed a sandwich washing it down with the cup of chocolate before going back to work. Rainy, munching on the cookie, wandered over to where Janice was helping load wood. Janice would help any old people load between measuring loads and calculating cubic feet. She would write down the cubic feet on a slip of paper and instruct the customer to present the slip to Clayton for payment.

"How are you, young man?" Janice inquired, as Rainy approached. Rainy stopped and looked at Janice. Then he gave her a big smile. "What's your name?"

"Rainy," he said.

"Want to build a snowman Rainy?" Janice asked.

"Yes," he said, but just stood smiling.

Janice looked around to see if anybody needed her attention. It was a beautiful sunny day and the snow was becoming soft. The parking lot was turning into slush because of the heavy traffic. "Here's how you do it Rainy," Janice said. "First wad together a big snowball nice and round like this. Now you make one." Rainy followed her instructions. Janice set her snowball on the ground and instructed Rainy to do the same. "Now we roll them on the ground to make them bigger." They rolled their snowballs side by side until Rainy couldn't roll his any further. "Now we stack them," Janice said, as she put Rainy's snowball on top of hers.

Taking Rainy's hand and walking back to where they started, Janice said, "Now roll three more snowballs and I'll lift them up for you. I've going to eat my lunch, while my chocolate is still warm." Rainy started packing another snowball.

That's the way the afternoon went until about four thirty when the lot started to empty out. Most of the customers were farmers. They needed to be home at five to take care of livestock. With Janice's help, Rainy had constructed three snowmen. Janice showed him how to put faces on with crushed stones from the parking lot. Rainy was proud of his work.

After putting the equipment away, Roger took a bundle of cash from the register. He counted out two piles on the counter. He gave one to Clayton and the other one to Janice. "No need to share this with the governor," he said. "He didn't show up for work this morning."

"Janice, how about we go to the Steak Barn and I'll buy you the steak of your choice." Clayton said.

"Sounds great Dad," Janice replied. "Let me take off these coveralls and freshen up. I didn't change clothes after church. We can go from here." Opening the bathroom door, so that the mirror fastened to the inside of the door was in better light, she freshened up.

After Clayton and Janice left, Lilly said, "She certainly is a beautiful young woman. There's going to be a lot of broken hearts when she makes her choice of a mate."

"Should we dine out too?" Roger asked.

"No, not yet," Lilly said. "Rainy is to tired. Look at him." Rainy was fast asleep on a bench that was a floor display. Stroking his head, Lilly continued, "I gave his hair a quick trim before we went to church."

"Well dear, let's go home then," Roger said, as he scooped Rainy up.

Monday morning had broken sunny, clear and cold. "There aren't any sun dogs," Roger said. "Should warm up pretty good today. At this rate we could get rid of the ice cover and not have to deal with it until next spring," Roger was getting ready to go to work. "The forecast is for the low forties. What's your plan dear?"

"I think I may see if I can get Rainy some new clothes to supplement the used ones we found for him," Lilly replied. "I have to take him to Doctor Taylor's house for an exam tonight at seven. Doctor Taylor said it was a good thing I called her at her house last night instead of waiting to call the clinic in the morning. I meant to ask her advice about which children's doctor I should use. She insisted I should bring Rainy to her house for the first visit."

"Well, wait until after dinner to go shopping," Roger advised. "The city will be a demolition derby until some of this ice melts."

"I've driven on ice before," Lilly said, while making a face at Roger.

"I know you have dear," Roger said as he kissed her. "I won't worry all day if you wait until later."

After Roger went into the elevator, Rainy and Sylvester appeared at the kitchen door. Rainy was rubbing sleep from his eyes and Sylvester was purring and rubbing himself against Rainy's flannel pajama leg.

"Well little man, are you ready for some breakfast?" Lilly asked.

"Un huh," came the reply.

"Here's some juice," Lilly said, as she set a glass of juice in front of him. "In a couple of minutes I'll have some pancakes done. You can eat this bacon with your juice. After breakfast we'll get back to your schooling. I've found some more flash cards and reading books for us to use. I've also a black board with the alphabet on it. We'll get you started with that first."

Rainy looked at Lilly and smiled, as he munched bacon and drank juice.

Lilly worked with Rainy all day with the alphabet. She decided to forgo the new clothes-shopping trip since his lessons were going so well. Rainy was an apt student. She was in her element-teaching again. She alternated the alphabet with numbers and found he could count to one hundred.

After supper Lilly left Roger to his reading and took Rainy to see Doctor Taylor. Vernon Taylor met them at the door. "Good evening, you must be Lilly Hartec. I'll bet this little man is Rainy," Vernon said, as he bent over and took Rainy's right hand and gave it a shake. "Come right this way," he said, as he led them down the steps to the basement of the split-entry house.

They proceeded to a brightly lit waiting area with magazines and stuffed chairs. "Take a seat," Vernon said. "Sybil will be right with you as soon as she gets off the phone." Vernon left via the stairway they had just come down.

Very shortly, Doctor Taylor appeared. "Come, bring the boy into the examination room," she said, with a smile. "The Lord was good to you. This one didn't even take nine months and no labor pains." Doctor Taylor offered Lilly the only chair in the small exam room. Then she lifted Rainy up and set him on the edge of the examination table. The Doctor sat down on a stool in front of Rainy. She took his blood pressure, checked his throat, listened to his lungs, checked his reflexes and felt of all his muscles. Then she removed blood drawing paraphernalia from a drawer, and said, "This will hurt a little, young man." She unwrapped a tootsie pop and put it in Rainy's mouth. "I'll draw four vials of blood and we will get a lab analyses."

Rainy winched a little when Doctor Taylor put the needle in, but was hard at work on the sucker. It appeared to be the first sucker he had ever had.

After the vials were filled with blood, Doctor Taylor started conversing with Rainy. He repeated back almost every word the Doctor used in clear distinct English. After these conversations with Rainy, Doctor Taylor spun around on the stool to face Lilly.

In amazement, Lilly said, "You were talking with him."

"Yes I was," Doctor Taylor replied. "It appears the only words he knows are what he's learned watching children's programs on television. He's underdeveloped, under nourished and needs good food, exercise and fresh air. I suspect that the reason he's so bright eyed is because he's been eating cat food. If he'd had access to more of it; he would be in better health. He's been slowly starving."

"My goodness, that's horrible!" Lilly exclaimed.

"I'd guess him to be about eight years old," Doctor Taylor said. "What are your plans for his education?"

"I want to home school him," Lilly replied.

"Good," Doctor Taylor replied. "Here's a place that you can order school material from." She handed a business card to Lilly. "We'll need a birth certificate. I'll get that in the works. We'll just make him eight years old today. You'll know how close we are in three or four years. He'll start growing pubic hair at ten or eleven.

His voice will change, and he will need deodorant at eleven or twelve.

"How long will it take to get the birth certificate?" Lilly asked. She was a little mystified by some of what she was hearing.

"Birth certificates like this take time," Doctor Taylor said. "One day within a year you will receive it in the mail. The same with the blood screening, you will receive a copy in the mail within two months. If there is any thing you don't understand, just give me a call at home. I will have seen it before you get your copy. Actually, I'll have a copy on file down here."

"Thank you, Doctor Taylor. How much do I owe you?" Lilly asked, as she extracted a checkbook from her purse.

"The Lord rewards me for this type of work," Doctor Taylor said. "You'll be doing the heavy lifting. Expect some problems with child services. However, with Roger's reputation, I think any problems there will be minimal."

"Oh," Lilly said. "I never thought about that. Roger said no one would be looking for Rainy because they hadn't even bothered to name him."

"I wouldn't worry about that," Doctor Taylor said, with a chuckle. "That's what husbands are for. Well congratulations and good luck." Doctor Taylor extended her hand to Lilly and the two of them shook hands. "Any other medical problems with Rainy before you get the adoption papers call me here."

As Lilly turned to go, Doctor Taylor said, "Oh by the way, I need to give you two more cards. She reached into the card drawer again and selected two more business cards. "This card belongs to the adoption agency who placed the child with you. They will have all the information they need by the end of the week. This card is the local family physician you take Rainy to for routine medical care. Wait until you have the paperwork from the adoption agency before scheduling an appointment. It will be necessary for Rainy to receive certain inoculations to be currant under state law. After the first visit to this Doctor, he will be entered into mainstream society. You may want to call your health insurance provider after you get the adoption papers to have him covered. Use the information from the paperwork you receive from the adoption agency. It won't be

necessary for you to contact the agency. That will be taken care of."
Laying one hand on Lilly's shoulder, Doctor Taylor said, "Good luck
and God bless you."

"I think he certainly is blessing me right now," Lilly said, as
they walked up the stairway to the front entry. "Thank you ever
so much."

Lilly was visibly shaken when she and Rainy returned to
their house. She had planned on doing some evening shopping
for clothes that she didn't shop for during the afternoon, because
Rainy's lessons had gone so well.

"What's the matter dear?" Roger asked, as he took her in his
arms.

"I, I didn't realize I would need to lie so much to have a child,"
Lilly said.

"Whoa dear, whoa," Roger said. "Back up a little here. Just what
have we done that would displease God, since you spotted Rainy
under that bridge. If we turn Rainy over to Social Services, he will
be placed in a foster home until somebody adopts him. That's not
going to happen because of his age, health and mental state. After
he turns eighteen, he will end up in prison and probably on death
row. Don't you think we can do better than that for him?"

"Yes, I'm sure we can," Lilly admitted.

"Whom are you lying to, and for what purpose?" Roger asked.
"I believe there's a difference in God's eyes. Is the lying for a moral
purpose? Are you breaking God's law or man's law? Sometimes you
can't honor both. God's law must be obeyed."

"Oh dear," Lilly said, while shaking her head. "I never thought
of it that way. I guess this is the first time I've come in contact with
the State in a moral conflict. Let's go up to the family room and I
will tell you what happened tonight."

Rainy and Sylvester were frolicking around the kitchen. "Take
Rainy and Sylvester upstairs and get them started with the tinker
toys," Lilly said. "I'll mix a couple of drinks, pop some corn and be
right up."

"I'll have a glass of chilled Manischewitz wine," Roger said.

"You got it dear," Lilly said. "Now shoo,"

Lilly followed a short time later with a tray loaded with two glasses, a bottle of wine on ice, a large bowl of salted and buttered popcorn and three serving bowls. Setting the tray on the coffee table in front of the sofa, she took a seat next to Roger who was watching Rainy and Sylvester selecting tinker toy parts for assembly.

"Doctor Taylor has a completely furnished examination room in her basement," Lilly said. "She's arranging for us to get a birth certificate in the mail. She said Rainy is eight years old and today is his birthday."

"How does she know he's eight and today's his birthday?" Roger asked.

"Roger! She's making all this up," Lilly exclaimed. "Here's three business cards she gave to me. One is for school supplies, one is for a local family doctor, and get this! The third card is for the adoption agency that placed Rainy with us. We're suppose to wait a while before taking Rainy to the family doctor, but we can use information about the adoption agency when needed starting next week."

Lilly handed the cards to Roger. Roger studied the cards for a while. Then he began to chuckle. "Sybil Taylor, the high stepping fashionable lady doctor is part of an underground orphan placement operation," Roger said. "Who would think it?"

"Is that what is going on?" Lilly asked.

"Course it is," Roger replied. "There's even two addresses on the agency card, one in Florida and one in Texas. The cards they use down there probably have a Minnesota and Montana address on them. It looks like next week we'll officially be Rainy's parents. You can't beat that."

Chapter 11. The Twins.
Spring, 1983

Lilly was tending her flower gardens on a fine spring day. She had taken Rainy over to the lumberyard to spend the afternoon with Roger. His lessons were usually completed by noon. Lilly began to muse. *Rainy was nearing the completion of the second grade. The people supplying the courses recommended slowing his progress with some off time. The schedule they had helped Lilly set for Rainy would have him at the proper grade level, for his age, in three more years.*

Lilly's thoughts were interrupted by Sylvester scampering in and through the hedgerow, on the north edge of the lawn. She thought she heard giggling. Walking over to the hedge, she peered over it to see Sylvester playing with two small brown haired girls. Their clothes were filthy and tattered. Their exposed skin was covered with brown spots. "Hello girls," Lilly said.

Both girls took off on a run down a trail, through the uncut grass, that ran through some lowlands north toward the city. Lilly told Roger about the girls that evening. She said, "They've been coming for some time because they've a pretty clear trail worn into the grass."

"After supper, I'll follow the trail to see where it leads," Roger offered.

Lilly, Rainy and Sylvester were waiting at the hedgerow when Roger emerged from the tall brush and walked the last hundred yards of grassland trail to the hedgerow. "The trail goes to that big apartment building just beyond the city limits," Roger said.

"My goodness," Lilly said. "They were such little girls. That has to be a very long walk."

"Yep," Roger said. "Got to be a little over two miles. It appears they've been doing it for a while. Must come to play with Sylvester."

"He's been spending a lot of time outside," Lilly agreed. "He's usually out most of the morning after Rainy begins his lessons."

"Fickle cat," Roger said. "Our son has been thrown over for a couple of dames. The air is getting chill. Frost tonight I'll bet. Let's get inside."

Early the next morning Lilly let Sylvester out. Then she placed a plastic milk crate upside down on the other side of the hedge. She placed a plate of cookies, covered with plastic wrap, and two covered plastic beverage containers, filled with milk, on the crate. As Rainy's lessons came to an end, for the day, there was a crash of thunder. Lighting lit up the dark overcast sky. Then the sky opened up and a hard rain quickly engulfed the entire landscape.

By the time Lilly and Rainy had finished packing the lunch to take to the lumberyard, the rain had subsided. The sun produced a beautiful rainbow. As Lilly and Rainy left the house they took time to admire the rainbow and check on the milk crate table, Lilly had placed on the other side of the hedge. The plastic beverage containers were lying in the grass. The lids were on but the containers were empty. The empty plate was covered with the plastic wrap that held a pool of water.

"Well Rainy, we must keep working at this and maybe we can make friends with a couple of playmates for you. Now we must go to the lumberyard, but first I must get some money." Before leaving, Lilly quickly grabbed some cash from Roger's stash and the ad section from the daily paper. "I'm going to check some garage sales for playground equipment," she said to Rainy. "Maybe we can get those two girls to spend some afternoons playing with you."

After the workers finished lunch, Janice grabbed a roll of plastic wrap and said, "Rainy, do you want to help me wrap an order?"

"Yes," Rainy enthused. He liked spending time with Janice. The two headed out to the yard to be about their task.

"I'm going to garage sales to see if I can purchase some playground equipment for the children," Lilly said to Roger. "I put out cookies and milk for the two girls. They cleaned up the food sometime before the rain this morning. We never got a chance to see them. Sylvester must have because he was outside all morning until the rain began."

"You better take my pickup and leave your car for me," Roger said.

"Good idea dear," Lilly said. "The keys are in my car."

"Here's the keys for the pickup," Roger said, as he handed her the keys and gave her a kiss. "Good luck."

Lilly had a good day shopping. She drove the pickup home with a swing and slide set, a sand box with lid and several pieces of children's lawn furniture. She was elated with the five-piece cast iron table and chair set. Also, there was a croquet set that Lilly anticipated teaching the children to use.

Lilly called Roger at the lumberyard. "Can you bring home enough sand to fill a four by eight sandbox?" she asked.

"You bet," Roger replied. "Have a good day shopping?"

"Yes I did," Lilly replied. "The pickup box is full. I even got a few toys for the sandbox."

When Roger and Rainy got home, they immediately went to work setting up the playground equipment. After supper all three Hartecs finished the project.

Lilly worked for weeks enticing the two girls to become comfortable with her. After a week of empty cookie and milk containers, Lilly moved the makeshift table to the inside of the hedgerow. She added two of the cast iron chairs to the arrangement.

For another week, Lilly and Rainy observed the two girls sneak through the hedge to play with Sylvester and consume the food. On nice days their stays grew slowly longer. Finally during the third week, Lilly got up early to make up the lunch basket for Roger to take to work. She planned to send Rainy outside to attempt a meeting and suspected it might disrupt their normal noon routine.

"Now talk to them and approach them very slowly," Lilly instructed. "Why don't you take another pitcher of orange juice along?" She had added orange juice and toast to the menu.

"More orange juice?" Rainy asked, as he held the pitcher of juice up for the two girls to see. Both girls smiled as they held up their juice glasses. Rainy poured their juice glasses full and set the pitcher on the milk crate between the girls. "What's your names?" he asked.

The stouter of the two said, "I'm Marcy and she's Darcy," while pointing at her sister. "What's your cats name?"

"That's Sylvester," Rainy said. "He's my Mom's cat. Do you want to meet my Mom? She's a real nice lady."

Both girls giggled. "We have to get back home," Darcy said. "Our Mom gets off work at five."

"It's a long time until five. I know how to tell time," Rainy said. "You can have lunch with us and still make it home before five."

"Okay," Darcy said as she stood up and took Rainy's hand. Marcy scooped up Sylvester and the three walked toward the house.

Lilly met the three at the garage door. Rainy was still holding Darcy's hand. He was grinning from ear to ear-very much the conquering hero. "Hello girls. I'm Lilly Hartec," Lilly said. "And what are your names?"

"I'm Darcy," said the girl holding Rainy's hand.

"I'm Marcy," the stouter girl replied, still cradling Sylvester in her arms.

"They stink Mom," Rainy said, still smiling.

Lilly walked around the three children sniffing the air. There was a definite odor. "Let's wash some of that dirt off," Lilly said. "Come into the bathroom." The girls and Rainy followed her into the basement bathroom.

Lilly filled the basin with warm water and soaked a washcloth with water. Then she began wiping the girl's faces. The girls were the same height with brown eyes. Their clothes were tattered and their sneakers worn out. Their hair looked like they had cut it themselves with a dull scissors.

After a couple of rinses of the washcloth, the odor became stronger. "Oh my God!" Lilly gasped. She realized that the brown she was soaking off wasn't dirt. It was feces. It was also matted in the girl's hair. The girls and Rainy were startled. Sylvester shot out of Marcy's arms. "Rainy! We must give the girls a bath. Girls, would you like to take a bath?"

Both girls shrugged their shoulders. "Okay, that's what we will do. Rainy, will you please go upstairs to the sewing room and get some clothes from the closet for Darcy and Marcy?" Lilly asked. "Do you remember where we put all the clothes that were to small for you?"

"Sure Mom. I know where they are," Rainy said, as he left.

"Okay girls, I'll fill the tub and you can get out of those clothes," Lilly said. "I'll be right back." Lilly went to a storage locker and grabbed a plastic garbage bag to put the girl's clothes and shoes into.

The girls were undressed and waiting for the tub to fill. Lilly put their clothes and shoes into the garbage bag and threw it onto the floor outside of the bathroom. Then she washed her hands and arms, and put on a pair of long latex gloves.

"Okay girls, into the tub," Lilly instructed. Both girls crawled into the tub and Lilly started with hair shampoo. She instructed both girls to dip their heads into the water. Then she helped them scrub their heads and all the brown off their bodies. The water was a brackish muddy brown.

"Okay girls, out of the tub," Lilly instructed. After they had crawled out, Lilly wrapped each in a large towel. "Wait until I drain the tub and refill it. Then it's back into the tub you go."

After both girls were back in the tub and scrubbing their hair again, Rainy showed up with his arms full of clothes. Two pairs of shoes, tied together with their laces, were dangling around his neck. "I've got all the clothes they need, Mom," Rainy said, with a big smile.

"Thank you Rainy," Lilly said, as she scooped the pile of clothes out of his arms and spread them out on the laundry table. Rainy had put together everything they needed, including underwear and socks. It was all boys' clothes. However, Lilly didn't think anybody would notice or care.

After two more times in fresh water, Lilly helped the girls get toweled off and inspected their bottoms. There was some rash but nothing serious. The girls giggled at each other as Lilly applied ointment and helped them get dressed.

"Goodness! It's lunch time," Lilly said. "Come up to the kitchen." She took a hand of each of the girls and led them to the elevator where Rainy and Sylvester were waiting. "Okay Rainy, take us up."

Standing on his toes and reaching as high as possible, Rainy was able to reach the elevator buttons. The girls smiled as the elevator went into motion. They appeared to be familiar with its operation.

"Here we are, first floor," Rainy announced.

"Rainy, please get a comb and oil from the bathroom and bring it to the kitchen." Lilly instructed. "You girls may sit at the table until Rainy gets back. I'll make some sandwiches."

Lilly had the ingredients spread on the counter when Rainy got back. "Okay girls, I'll rub some oil into your scalps and hair. Rainy can show you how to comb it." After completing the task, Lilly turned to wash her hands in the kitchen sink. Then she said, "Okay Rainy, help them comb their hair."

When she finished making the sandwiches, Lilly became aware of soft giggling growing slowly louder. Turning around to face the table, with a plate full of sandwiches, Lilly was surprised to see the three children standing in line. Darcy was combing Marcy's hair and Rainy was combing Darcy's hair. All were giggling and having a good time.

"Time to sit up to the table and eat," Lilly said. All three children took a place, while Lilly poured four glasses full of milk. Looking at the girl's hair, she asked, "Who cuts your hair?" Marcy pointed at Darcy and Darcy pointed at Marcy, while they were taking bites out of their sandwiches. "Oh dear," Lilly chuckled, as she shook her head.

That evening, Lilly informed Roger of their progress. "I hated to send them home in the clean clothes. Their apartment must be filthy. I had Rainy pick out another change of clothes for them. After their bath tomorrow morning, the four of us can go back to their apartment with some cleaning supplies."

"Be careful," Roger instructed. "Make sure you leave before momma bear gets home."

The next morning when the girls had come to the garage door, they were still quite clean. Lilly served them breakfast and set them about their bath. She tossed the clothes they had taken off into the washing machine. After the bath, hair wash and toweling, Lilly applied ointment to their bottoms and helped them get dressed.

It was a beautiful sunny day as the month of May was ending. Rainy's lessons had been completed until the school term started again in the autumn. Lilly had found small latex gloves for the children. Roger had purchased a box of gloves for Rainy to use for fish cleaning and other dirty projects. The four set off down the trail to the girl's home. The trail led through abandoned farmland that was now part of a wildlife refuge. It curved off to the northeast. Then it curved back toward the northwest as it skirted the edge of a slough. Here the trail forked for a detour that moved it further east. *Must be the route they use when the water is high,* Lilly suspected.

Lilly's suspicion was confirmed when Marcy said, "This is our short cut, when the water is down." The four continued on across the hilly terrain until they reached the edge of a crushed rock parking lot, next to a large apartment building.

Lilly and Rainy followed the girls into the building. They walked to the center of the building and stopped in front of an elevator. Reaching up, Marcy pushed the up button. When they all were inside, Marcy pushed the button for the third floor.

Upon reaching the third floor, they followed the hall to a corner apartment on the west end. The door wasn't locked so they all walked in. The kitchen was messy. However, it showed signs of having been cleaned in the recent past. The living room was bare. Proceeding down the hall, Lilly opened the first door and looked in. It was the master bedroom and obviously the main living quarters of the occupant. A full bathroom was enclosed within the room. Everything was clean and in good order.

"We're not allowed in there," Marcy and Darcy said in unison. "Our bedroom is this way." They walked further down the hall to a third door. That door opened into another bedroom.

Lilly gasped when she looked inside. There was an air mattress on the vinyl tile floor covered with filthy sheets and blankets. The same terrible odor she experienced when Rainy first brought the girls to the house met her nostrils. "Is there a laundry room in this building?" Lilly asked the girls. They looked at her with puzzlement in their eyes.

"Yes there is. On the ground floor across from the elevator," said a voice from the entry door.

Lilly retreated down the hall to find a little, gray haired, old lady standing in the door way to the main hall. "Hello, I'm Lilly Hartec," Lilly said. "We met the girls about a month ago when they hiked to our place. It's over two miles southwest of here."

"Yes I know," the old woman said. "I'm Lydia Sanderson. I'm in one-o-one. It's the northwest corner apartment on the first floor. I watched the four of you hike across the refuge. There is a large commercial machine in the laundry room. Let me show you. I can help you with change for the machines, if you find yourself in need."

"Come children," Lilly said, as the five moved toward the elevator. "This looks like it was a nice building. The grounds obviously haven't been maintained for years. The pool area is a disgrace. It doesn't help that it's in full view whenever one uses the elevator. Why has it been let go?"

"When it was built seven years ago, it was thought the city would grow out this way," Lydia said. "Then the State bought up all the adjacent land and turned it into a wildlife refuge."

"Oh yes, Roger complains about that too," Lilly said. "He had tried to purchase all this land when it was up for back taxes. However, the State wanted it so Roger lost out."

"Some wild life refuge," Lydia snickered. "All we got was pocket gophers and skunks. The pocket gophers would bore right up through the crushed rock parking lot and leave huge mounds of dirt all over. My husband and I were the managers when the unit's first opened for leasing. The skunks and gophers killed all prospects of renting. Some of these apartments have never been lived in. The city grew north and we became the low rent district." The elevator bumped bottom and the door opened.

"I'm the only management staff left. My husband passed away

107

two years ago," Lydia continued, as she escorted the group to the laundry room. "The owners take turns doing lawn mowing and snow removal."

The five entered a large laundry room with the finest of appliances. "The change machine is out of order," Lydia said. "It's always vandalized so the owners gave up on it."

"I didn't bring my purse," Lilly said. "I guess we'll have to go back home."

"I've got five dollars in my pocket, mom," Rainy said.

"Come to my apartment with me young man. I'll give you change," Lydia said. "Also, you can use my vacuum cleaner and I have a mop pail with a ringer." The two left to get the change and equipment.

"First we'll deflate the air mattress and bring it and all the bed clothes down to the laundry room," Lilly said, to the girls. "We must hurry if we're going to be done by five." Once they got all the bedclothes, towels and washcloths from the girl's bathroom washing, they set to scrubbing the bedroom and bathroom. The bathroom had a shower and tub combination. The mechanical drain plug for the tub was gone. The shut off valve in the waterspout was broken. This made the shower inoperable.

Lilly conveyed this information to Lydia, when Lydia and Rainy came back with the equipment and change.

"Do you think you can screw the spout off and screw another one on?" Lydia asked.

"It would be worth a try," Lilly said. "Do you have another spout?"

"No, but I have all the apartment keys," Lydia said, "We'll take one from one of the other apartments. I can help you change the mechanical drain plug, if you want to try that too. I use to change those things my self. Now I'm to old."

That's what they did. The spouts turned off easy enough. With Lydia's instructions, Lilly was able to replace the drain plug. Soon the bathroom was once again in working order. Lydia had taken a greater interest in the project. She peeked into the bedroom, where the children were scrubbing the walls and floor. When Lydia had seen the filthy pillows on top of the chest of drawers, the lone piece of furniture in the room, she had gasped, "throw them into the dumpster behind the laundry room. I've got two good ones with covers you can have."

Lydia shuffled out of the room and met Lilly in the hall. "At noon sharp please come down to my apartment for dinner," Lydia said. "I just had a fresh supply of groceries delivered yesterday. I baked a fresh batch of whole-wheat buns this morning. We'll have a tossed salad and summer sausage sandwiches. Right now, I need a little rest."

"Thank you, we'll be there," Lilly said. "We'll need the rest of the day to do this job correctly."

As the five sat down for lunch, Lydia kept up a commentary on the girls. "This all happened in the last year. I would go in and help the girls before that. I made sure each got a multivitamin caplet five days a week. Last winter, I slipped and fell in the parking lot. Broke my hip. I spent six months in rehab. Just now starting to get around good, but still tire easy. Bones don't heal so fast when you're eighty."

"What do you know about the girls?" Lilly asked.

"Janet Olson, their mother, has never been married," Lydia said. "George Strand courted her. I'm sure he's their father. He was a decent enough fellow after that run in he had with your husband in front of the theater. However, his parents were so against Janet and the children that George ran off a couple of years ago. Even his parents don't know where he is. Whenever he argued with Janet, he always threatened to go south to Florida or Louisiana and join the Merchant Marine. He never had a whole lot of ambition."

"Does Janet pay any attention to the children, at all?" Lilly inquired.

"I don't think so," Lydia said. "When George was still here, he would help her with them. In fact, I thought he was a decent Father. They were potty trained before he left. I doubt if that would have happened without him. He never made enough money to suit Janet. His parents cut him off when they found out he was spending money on Janet and the children. After George left Janet made sure there was cold cereal in the cupboard and milk and juice in the refrigerator."

"We haven't found any clothes in the bedroom or bathroom," Lilly said. "There is some cereal in the cupboard and milk in the refrigerator, but no juice. I believe the girls were starting to slowly starve, before they found their way over to our place."

"Well I've overheard Janet talking to her boyfriend on the telephone in the laundry room," Lydia said. "Her phone has been disconnected. Her boyfriend is due to get out of state prison soon. He's been doing a year for drug dealing. They're planning on running off to the west coast when he gets out. I suspect they're planning on abandoning the girls."

"Oh no!" Lilly gasped. "That's terrible. May I leave my phone number with you so you can call if you think the children are in any danger or need any help?"

"Sure," Lydia said. "I'll also let her know she can abandoned the girls with you, if you wish. I do run into her in the laundry room often enough."

"Oh, that would be great," Lilly said. "In the meantime, I'll make sure they're clean, clothed and fed."

After drying off the air mattress and putting the two rooms in order, Lilly and Rainy got ready to leave. Lilly hugged the two girls and said, "Please come visit us every day that you can. You can take baths at our place and I'll feed you and give you sandwiches to take home. We'll also go shopping and purchase some new bed clothes for you."

Both girls hugged Lilly and started to cry. "I love you," they said in unison.

"I love you both," Lilly replied. "Some day soon, both of you will be mine. Now we must go. Come see us tomorrow, if you can."

Lilly stood up and turned to look at Lydia. There were tears in the old woman's eyes. "Well Lydia, I believe Rainy has everything down in front of your door. I can help you get it all put away. Then if you have pen and paper, I'll write down my address and telephone number."

"Rainy knows where everything goes in my apartment," Lydia said. "He dug it all out for me. That is one wonderful boy."

"Yes," Lilly agreed, " and to think we found him under a freeway bridge."

"God bless you," Lydia responded. "I've called Social Services several times and the same woman always came out and stood in the hall talking to Janet. I suspect she's one of Janet's partying buddies, a gal by the name of Mizzzz Hargrove," Lydia said mockingly. I quit calling when I thought Janet was starting to suspect it was me making the complaints," Lydia said.

When they got to Lydia's apartment, they found Rainy finishing up putting Lydia's equipment away. "Here's your keys," Rainy said, as he handed the apartment door keys to Lydia.

"Thank you Rainy," Lydia said.

"God bless you Lydia," Lilly said. She left the pen and paper, with her address and telephone number, on the table. "Please call me, if you need help with anything. Now we must scoot before Janet gets home. It's after five already."

Chapter 12. The Confrontation. Summer, 1983

L illy had been apprehensive about the coming weeks. The girls had come everyday that the weather was fit, even on weekends. They had never come on weekends before the apartment cleaning.

Lydia Sanderson had kept in touch. "I met Janet in the laundry room on the weekend," Lydia said. "I told Janet that her daughters were visiting a lady in the country who would like to adopt them. I told her it would be an option for her to consider if the girls were getting to be a hardship to support. Janet just grunted. When I left the laundry room, I noticed Janet laying out a bunch of quarters at the pay phone. I popped around the corner and out of sight. Then I turned up my hearing aids. Janet's boyfriend is getting out soon. I overheard her say, 'some old biddy has taken an interest in the girls. They've been spending almost every day with her for the last couple of months. We can dump them with her when we blow town. No Curt, I've been saving a lot more money since the girls made friends with the old biddy. I don't have to buy them food or clothes anymore. They even bring sandwiches, cookies and fresh fruit home with them. The old biddy makes a damn good sandwich.' I think you'll be getting your girls soon," Lydia concluded, "In about two weeks."

Then it happened. On the third of July, early in the morning, the girls came through the hedgerow. A piece of paper was safety pinned to Marcy's dress. "They yours," was the simple message on the paper.

Lilly was ecstatic. *She had to call Lydia. It was too early, no; she would wait awhile to call. In the meantime she needed to get the twins settled into their own room. She needed to call Roger. She must call Doctor Taylor and get appointments for physicals. She must get orders placed for their school materials. Classes would resume in September.* Lilly found herself turning in circles, as she tried to do everything at once. "Settle down girl," she ordered herself, as she thought of Lori Gustafson. *I must call her too!*

Lilly decided to have the girls sleep in the library for the next few nights. *This would give them time to get accustomed to the house. They could sleep on the rollaway cot, as Rainy had for the first week. After that, they can share the bedroom next to Rainy's on the first floor. In the meantime, I must redecorate that room to reflect two little girls. Girls! Not just one girl, but two girls. Finally, daughters.* "The Lord sure has been good to me," she said aloud.

Taking the girls over to the stairway, Lilly said to Rainy, "I'll show them how to use the stairway. They won't be tall enough to reach the elevator buttons for a while. I'm going to have them sleep where you did the first week. Then we'll move them down to the room next to yours."

Lilly took Marcy's hand and together they started up the stairs. Right behind them, Rainy followed holding Darcy's hand. Sylvester always wanted to be first to arrive at any destination. As usual, he shot ahead of the group.

Lilly got the rollaway out and she and Rainy got it set up. Rainy and the girls got the bedclothes out of a closet, while Lilly used the telephone in the library to make calls. Roger was still in the office, so she got through to him right away. "Congratulations, Roger. You're father to twin girls."

"Is that so. How did that happen?" Roger asked.

"They came through the hedgerow this morning, right after you left for work, with a note pinned to Marcy's dress," Lilly said. "The note said, 'They yours.'"

"Good," Roger said. "Now you have daughters for the first time in your life. That's great."

"Dear heart, I'm putting them in the library for the first week," Lilly said. "I'll redecorate the room next to Rainy's." "Do you suppose you could install one of those baby monitors between the first floor and our bedroom, before we move them down stairs?"

"Good thinking, you bet," Roger stated. "I'll bring one home with me tonight."

"Okay darling," Lilly said. "Can you transfer me to Lori? I must tell her the good news."

"Will do dear." Lilly heard buttons clicking and Lori picked up. "Lori, Lilly wishes to make an announcement," Roger said. Then he hung up his receiver.

Lilly gave Lori the news. Then she dialed Lydia Sanderson. "I saw the girls leave this morning with a note pinned to Marcy's dress," Lydia said. "Curt and Janet are gone. They packed all her stuff and gave me the keys. The owners were desperate for renters so no deposit was involved.

"Now that the girls are safe, I've decided to move into that new assisted living high rise down town," Lydia said. "I've given my thirty days notice. There will be very few people left in this building."

"You must let us know your new address when you move," Lilly said. "Better yet, be sure to call me so we can help you move, when the time comes."

"I will dear," Lydia said. "God bless you."

Lilly and the twins had redecorated the girl's bedroom. Rainy usually went to the lumberyard with Roger every morning. Lilly and the twins took lunch to them every day at noon. One day a week, Lilly and the twins took Janice out to a restaurant for lunch, after they had delivered the men's food basket. The twins quickly accepted Janice as their big sister.

Then one day Lilly picked up the mail from the mailbox on her way to the lumberyard. Among the daily paper and assorted envelopes was a six by nine manila envelope addressed to Roger and Lilly Hartec. There wasn't any return address. It was postmarked Ashland Falls.

"Look at what was in the mail," Lilly said to Roger, as she handed the envelope to him. "What do you suppose is in there?"

"Let's find out," Roger said, as he reached into his pocket for his jack knife. He slit the envelope, returned the knife to his pocket and removed two pieces of paper, which were folded in half. "It's the twin's birth certificates. George Strand is listed as their father. Small world. Hey! They were five years old on the third of July. That's the day they became ours."

"Doctor Taylor will be happy to know we have the certificates in our possession," Lilly said. "I'm suppose to take the twins to her place next week for physicals. She knew of the twins and insisted that I should bring them to her private clinic for the first doctor's visit. She wanted to see them sooner, but couldn't. She and her husband were all packed and ready to head to Glacier National Park, for a two week vacation, when I called."

"It looks like the loose ends are all tied up," Roger stated. "You are a gorgeous looking momma." Then he kissed her.

Shortly after Roger and Rainy left for work the following Friday morning, there was a ringing of the doorbell. Lilly and the twins were in the basement so they weren't aware of a vehicle coming up the long driveway. Upon opening the door, Lilly found herself face to face with a chunky, sluttish looking woman in a miniskirt. She was about Lilly's height. She had dark bobbed hair and an over abundance of make up, which she must of spent hours putting on. *I'll bet automobiles are painted is less time than is required for that paint job*, Lilly thought.

"Good morning, I'm Miz Susan Hargrove, the county Social Services Director. I understand you have in your possession the Olson girls."

"Yes I do," Lilly firmly stated.

"Well I must put them in a foster home until we can arrange placement with an adoption agency," Susan said. "Are you folks interested in being foster parents until I can arrange an adoption? Foster parenting pays well. At their age they'll probably be snapped up quickly."

"Look Missy, you had plenty of opportunity to take custody of those twins when they were being starved by their mother," Lilly said. "They'll be removed from my care over my dead body and probably yours. Now scoot and never darken my doorway again. You will cast a damn short and prone shadow if you do."

At noon Lilly told Roger about the confrontation, while the lumberyard crew were eating lunch. They were all howling with laughter after hearing her story.

"Where oh where did you come up with that 'damn short and prone shadow?'" Lori inquired.

"I, I don't know," Lilly stammered. "It just came out of my mouth. I was so angry. I don't talk like that! You know that. It just came out. I was so angry because Lydia Sanderson had told me Social Services wouldn't help the twins, when Lydia had reported the neglect."

"I've a Colt pistol stashed away somewhere," Roger chuckled. "I'll dig it out if you want to start packing heat. It will make a more authorative figure out of you."

Lilly was a little perplexed by all the amusement at her expense. However, it was obvious they all supported her. They were proud of the way she had handled the Social Services Director.

Janice smiled and gave Lilly a big hug before going back to work. "You're a champion," She said. "You and Roger certainly belong together."

———

It was the beginning of a new week and Sheriff Oscar Thompson had just sat down at his desk to start on paperwork.

Millie, his secretary, buzzed him on the intercom. "Yes?" Oscar inquired, as he levered the bar on the intercom.

"A Mizzzz Susan Hargrove here to see you, Sheriff."

"Send her in," Oscar replied. *I wonder what that slut wants now. Probably wants to lodge a complaint because one of my deputies couldn't make her squeal.* He stifled a snicker.

Getting out of his chair and walking around to the front of his desk, he greeted Susan as she entered the office. Then offering a chair in front of his desk, he retreated to his chair behind the desk. "And what's on your mind this fine morning?" he asked.

"I want to lodge a complaint against Lilly Hartec," Susan said. "She threatened me."

"There must be some mistake." Oscar said. "That certainly

doesn't sound like the Lilly Hartec I know. Just what is it you construe as a threat?"

"She told me never to darken her doorway again, or I would cast a damn short prone shadow," Susan replied.

Oscar couldn't control his mirth. He laughed until tears came to his eyes. "That doesn't sound like Lilly. You must have done something to piss her off. Did you threaten to take the Olson twins away from her?" Without waiting for an answer, Oscar continued, "Didn't anybody ever tell you not to get between a momma bear and her cubs? Lord, lord, that's a good one. I can't wait to tell Jenny this one. You know, I've never heard Lilly or Jenny use language like that. I suspect Jenny would be up to it too if you tried to take her kids away from her."

"They're not her kids," Susan snapped. "They're wards of the State."

"Whoa there sister. Wards of the State you say," Oscar fumed. "Well I'll have you know that a bunch of air headed legislators make those rules and then expect the counties to pick up the tab. In this county we don't operate that way. Legislative mandates have to be paid for. We want the cash up front or we don't cooperate. The State pays your salary-that's why you're here. However, they don't pay for the foster care program. That has to come out of the county budget. We avoid that program like the plague."

Oscar leaned forward across his desk to better get into Susan's face. "Further more, It's up to the State to separate children from abusive parents," Oscar continued. "That was your job. Once the kids are abandoned, it's up to the county to see that they have a good home. The County Attorney, the Board of Commissioners and I are real satisfied with the present arrangements. You are probably the lone dissenter in the whole county. Well tough shit!"

"What about all the children in foster programs in this county that have disappeared?" Susan retorted. "You haven't recovered any of them."

"I'll have you know that's your responsibility," Oscar fumed. "I know that you've done your best every night, looking for those children, by visiting every Honky Tonk in three states. Well I happen to know where each and every one of them is, including the Jackson boy who ran away with the circus. They're all doing just fine. No thanks to the foster care program."

Leaning back in his chair, Oscar continued, "If you want to make something of it, talk to the Attorney General if you can find him in his office. He's probably out harassing the Indians and trying to steal from their casino operations. His State run lottery isn't doing so well after he got sued for cheating with it. That was a hell of a boon for the Indian casinos."

"Well," Susan huffed. "We'll see about that. I went to college with the Attorney General. He's a friend of mine. You religious freaks think you can run everything. Well, you'll find the State has something to say about that." Susan got up and left. The wall shook as she slammed the door.

So he's a Friend of her's. That nymph probably screwed his brains out. Probably what makes him so lame. Grabbing his coffee mug, Oscar went to the outer office to refill it with coffee.

"Pleasant engagement?" Millie intoned.

"Right amusing," Oscar replied. "Can you believe that Lilly Hartec? I knew she could be bossy and nosey, but not such a spitfire!"

"One would have to be a saint to contend with that Hargrove woman," Millie confided. "She insisted I address her as Miz. Miss isn't good enough for her. I sure wish I could have been a fly on the wall when Lilly told Susan, 'They will be removed from my care over my dead body, and probably yours.'"

"Lilly said that too?" Oscar asked, as his eyebrows shot up.

"That's what Susan told me," Millie replied. "What did she tell you?"

"She said Lilly told her not to darken her doorway again, or she would cast a damn short prone shadow," Oscar replied.

"Whew," Millie whistled. "I guess she can be a spitfire."

"Well those twins had been in a frightful condition when Lilly met them," Oscar said. "She had worked with them for over two months getting them cleaned up while feeding and clothing them. Now their mother has abandoned the children with her. Lilly gave my wife a blow-by-blow account on how things were going every

Sunday at church. Those twins couldn't be in better hands than they are right now, with Roger and Lilly as pa and ma."

"Lydia Sanderson called here several times to complain about conditions at the Olson apartment," Millie said. "I contacted Susan and she always promised to investigate. However, Lydia was never happy with the results from Social Services."

"Well, I guess we'll just sit tight and see what the Attorney General will try to do," Oscar said. "I can't picture much more than a short sharp letter. That pup is long on socialism and short on brains. Now his pappy, Old Flannel Mouth, was a little more principled when it came to dealing with the electors. The pup thinks he's Caesar. He's fed on the taxpayer's dime virtually ever second of his worthless life."

Godamn Christians, Susan thought. They're always so high and mighty. They've been causing trouble since the beginning of time. Well she would see about that. She had screwed the Attorney General at least a hundred times while they were in college. Why she didn't have a job in St Paul was beyond her. Well now it was time to call in some markers. It's time for the Attorney General to return some favors. That smart ass Sheriff will get his.

Susan went to her office to compose a letter to the Attorney General.

Chapter 13. Wheels for Janice. Winter, 1984-85

Lilly's life had taken on a much faster pace. Roger's business was growing and Lilly had three children at home and one surrogate daughter working at the lumberyard, who needed her counsel.

Janice Shore loved her father, Clayton. She remained with him in his house to take care of him. Clayton would sober up for Friday and Saturday nights, since his band was in big demand. Most of the rest of the week he was inebriated.

One morning at breakfast, Roger said, "The business is changing rapidly. Selling firewood from the yard and stopping deliveries has worked great. There are always a few dirt contractors who are willing to do deliveries with their gravel trucks. They load the wood with skid steer loaders. The wood hauling extends their work season, 'Christmas money,' one of them called it. This fall, Rainy handled most of the limbs with that little chain saw we gave him for Christmas. We had a good wood season. Good thing too, because the recession hurt the construction business."

"When do you think the construction business will pickup?" Lilly asked.

"Next season," Roger stated. "There's still a lot of substandard housing through out the country. A lot of buildings weren't properly ventilated when the heating contractors converted them to central heating. The moisture that collected in the walls rotted them away."

"You certainly see some good in all bad," Lilly said. "The eternal optimist. Well, I hope you're right."

"I think so," Roger said. "But what I wanted to talk to you about is the fact that businesses are planning for next year. The Ford Motor Company is suggesting a banner year."

"Pray tell, what has that got to do with us?" Lilly asked.

"The Ford dealership in Ashland Falls wants to purchase Old Red. That's what it's got to do with us," Roger replied.

"Heavens! Whatever for?" Lilly inquired.

"They want to restore it this winter and use it as a display and sales tool," Roger said. "There's papers in the cab showing it was put on the road during October, nineteen fifty two. A private contractor used it to build breakwaters in Lake Michigan. I drove it here from Chicago. That old truck has seen thirty-two years continuous service. That's something to brag about."

"What did they offer to pay for it?" Lilly asked.

"We're in the proposition stages yet," Roger said. "That's what I want to talk to you about. They have a nineteen eighty American Motors Eagle wagon on their sales lot. It was in a fender bender and they had to rebuild the right front. They did a beautiful job of repairing it, but everybody knows it was in an accident. Seems nobody wants to take a chance on a four-wheel drive that's been in an accident. They're ready to take it to the cities for auction."

"And what would we do with it?" Lilly inquired.

"I thought we should get it and give it to Janice for Christmas," Roger said. "She has her driver's license and it would save us chauffeuring her to her commitments."

"Roger, that's thoughtful of you!" Lilly exclaimed. "Janice certainly deserves more independence. Clayton's Blazer is an accident looking for a place to happen. What is an Eagle like?"

"It's a midsize station wagon with an inline six cylinder engine. Its full time four wheel drive," Roger stated. "There really isn't a safer vehicle to be driving in foul weather."

"Well if you can swing a deal, let's do it," Lilly enthused.

Lilly had taken the twins and Rainy to the lumberyard at noon for their family lunch. Rainy would stay with Roger and the twins would go back home with her. The children usually had their lessons completed by noon, so they had their afternoons free.

Janice was in school now. After school, she would ride the school bus to Siding and worked at miscellaneous tasks until closing time. Then, Roger or Lori would drive her home.

"Where should we have the Eagle delivered to?" Roger asked. "Here or home?"

"You got it dear?" Lilly quizzed. "What kind of deal did you get?"

"Straight across trade," Roger stated. "Course, they want all the papers that were in the glove box too. The original order and bill of sale were there. I was the second owner. They knew about the papers, because I had it to their shop to have a new oil pump installed a couple years back."

"What is that Eagle worth?" Lilly asked.

"They tried to get three thousand for it all summer," Roger said. "Then in the fall they marked it down to seventeen hundred and still no takers. I popped over this morning and took it for a road test. It's in tip-top shape. The sales manager told me the owner's son is in the Army with Danny Shore. The owner knows the family. When the owner was told the Eagle was for Janice, he insisted on giving it a good cleaning inside and out. He said they would hang an air fresher inside and some of his office staff would fashion a big red bow to put on the steering wheel. He asked to put the dealership's bronze plaque on the back, rather than the stick on logo. The bronze plaques are usually reserved for management cars. I told him to go ahead. I have to call him and let him know where to deliver it."

"Oh! Have him deliver it to the house," Lilly said "I'll bring Janice out after church on Sunday and we'll give it to her then."

"Okay," Roger said. "Selvin is driving Old Red over to the dealership right now. His wife will pick him up and take him home from there. He only works mornings, since there isn't much to do afternoons. A couple of the salesmen will deliver the Eagle on their way home from work shortly after five."

"I'll be sure to be home then," Lilly said.

Sunday morning broke cold and sunny. The sun was welcome because they rarely seen it during December. At this latitude it had a tendency to go into hibernation until after the New Year.

Lilly was preparing to take the children to Sunday school and church services. Roger had made arrangements with Janice to spend the afternoon with the Hartecs. Lilly would pick her up after church.

Clayton would be sleeping off the effects of the party his band had after their Saturday night gig. All of the band members, like Clayton, had bottle problems.

Rainy and the twins had been bubbling over with excitement all morning. Lilly was afraid they would spill the beans before they got home. The Eagle was parked in the far stall of the garage, so they couldn't get to the elevator without seeing it. When Lilly pulled up to the garage door, it started up before she could push the button on her remote. Roger was standing off to the right side. Lilly pulled in and stopped. Roger opened Janice's door and said, "welcome," while standing between her and the Eagle. He was blocking her view of the large red bow on the steering wheel.

Waiting for Lilly to come around to the right side, Roger and Lilly stood on each side of Janice and said, "Merry Christmas. This is your Christmas present."

Janice threw both her hands over her open mouth in astonishment. Then she gave Lilly a big hug and said, "thank you, thank you." Turning to Roger, she gave him a hug and said, "thank you Roger. It's the nicest gift I've ever received."

"Take us for a ride, take us for a ride," the twins chimed in together. Rainy stood with his hands in his pockets and a big smile on his face.

"Not until after dinner," Roger said. "The oven must be beeping now as we speak. Come on in everybody and dinner will be served."

"Dinner will be unusual," Lilly whispered to Janice. "Roger was on his own and he can come up with the strangest combinations."

Sure enough, there was the pan salad Lilly had made the night before. Then there was Banquet chicken with home made corn fritters that could be ate with pancake syrup or rolled in powdered sugar. For a vegetable there were boiled peas.

All through dinner Rainy and the twins discussed where they would go for a ride.

"I think we should go to the cinema at the mall," Janice said. "They're showing a couple of Walt Disney movies this afternoon. We must agree on one."

"Good idea," Roger said. "It's kind of cold to be doing anything out side. Look at those sundogs. More cold weather coming."

"You young people figure out which movie you want to see, while I get some money from my purse," Lilly said. "Let's see, two fifty apiece for the twins, four for Rainy and six for Janice. That's fifteen dollars for tickets. I'll give you another ten for treats." She gave the money to Rainy. "Which movie have you decided on?"

"No Time For Sergeants, No Time For Sergeants," Rainy piped up.

"Is that all right with you girls?" Janice asked.

"We've seen the other one," Darcy said. "I guess it will have to be No Time For Sergeants."

"It's a real good movie," Janice said. "Very funny. I've seen it a long time ago but I won't mind seeing it again. Mostly what I remember is how funny it was."

"No Time For Sergeants it is," Rainy concluded.

"We better hurry," Janice said. "The movie starts at two and it's almost one thirty now."

As Lilly handed Janice the keys, Roger yelled from the kitchen, "Be sure to use your seat belts."

"Yes children, be sure to buckle in," Lilly said. "That means you two also." Lilly tapped the twins on their heads with her index finger. "Be sure to mind Janice."

The four filed through the kitchen and said goodbye to Roger, as they headed for the elevator.

Lilly and Roger watched the Eagle cruise down the driveway from the kitchen window. At the end of the driveway, it turned left on the township road and headed toward the city.

"Goodness, this house hasn't been so quiet since we got the

twins last July," Lilly said. "Roger, what will we do for the next two hours without our family?"

"Let's do a rerun of our honeymoon night," Roger suggested, as he gave Lilly a hug and a kiss.

"You conniving fox," Lilly teased. "I'll bet this is what you had in mind when you thought about trading Old Red for the Eagle."

"Oh no," Roger chuckled. "I'm not that bright. But you have to admit, it sure worked out nice. Sylvester is taking a nap in the sun. So there's nothing to interfere with some afternoon delight."

And delightful it was.

After a short nap, they cuddled into each other's arms. "Oh, Roger, I wish I had a zipper on your front. Then I could crawl inside you and zip you back up," Lilly said. "I just can't get close enough to you."

"You would probably find you still weren't close enough," Roger chuckled. "I know you are the most wonderful thing that ever happened to me in my whole life. I love you Lilly." He planted a kiss on her lips.

They spent the rest of their free time reminiscing on what had brought them together. Before long, they were hit with the realization that it was time to prepare for the children's home coming.

Lilly was knitting and Roger was reading in the living room when the twins arrived.

"Janice has a boyfriend, Janice has a boyfriend," the twins chimed, as they came running into the living room from the elevator.

Janice and Rainy followed the twins in. Lilly could see Janice was flushed. She didn't know if the twin's announcement or the cold winter air caused the flushing.

"And whom might this young gentleman be?" Lilly inquired.

"It's Willy Slocum, Ma," Rainy said.

"He met us in the lobby and asked if he could sit with us, since he was alone," Janice said.

"Here's your ten dollars Ma," Rainy said. "Willy paid for all our treats."

"And he sat right next to Janice all through the whole movie," Marcy announced.

"Now Marcy, no need to tattle," Lilly said, with a smile.

"Want to play a game of chess, Janice?" Rainy asked.

"First I have to call home to check on Dad," Janice replied. "If he's okay, I can play a game before going home." She went into the kitchen to make the call.

"Lord, how I wish this was her home," Lilly commented. "But I know Clayton needs her. He just can't seem to get over losing Elaine. I guess I probably wouldn't act any different if I lost you dear. And to think he never even drank before Elaine died."

"Good morning dear," Jaclyn Slocum said as her husband of sixteen years entered the kitchen. "The French toast is ready. Coffee and juice are on the table."

"Morning love," Randy said, as he grabbed a handful of her butt.

"Not on the kitchen table honey," Jaclyn said. "Willie will be down soon for breakfast."

"We'll have to put it off until tonight," Randy said.

"Your son's smitten," Jaclyn said. "He met up with Janice Shore at the matinee yesterday afternoon. She had the three Hartec children with her. She told Willie they were driving the nineteen eighty Eagle wagon Lilly and Roger gave her for Christmas."

"Quite a Christmas gift!" Randy exclaimed, as he sat down at the table.

"Word is that Roger got a heck of a deal at the Ford dealership," Jaclyn said. "Traded his old red truck for the Eagle, even up."

"Is that so?" Randy queried. "Course, I guess that AMC was on the lot all summer. Was marked down to seventeen hundred, last I heard. Loren bought it last winter to give his body man something to work on. Nobody repairs a car in the wintertime. They wait until spring. I suppose he'll do the same with Roger's old F-5."

"He's going to use it for a display," Jaclyn said. "There were papers in the glove compartment that prove it's been in service for thirty two years."

"That's impressive all right," Randy agreed.

"But I've got even fresher news," Jaclyn said. "Our son was holding hands with Janice through most of the movie yesterday afternoon."

"That grapevine of yours must have been running hot for you to get that information so quickly," Randy snorted.

"The girl is sixteen and has her own car," Jaclyn said. "Poor Willie is only fifteen and can't get a driver's license for another year. You better give him another talk about the birds and the bees because he will be at her mercy."

"Janice has a good head on her shoulders," Randy replied.

"You had a good head on your shoulders when you were sixteen," Jaclyn said. "However, that didn't stop you from picking my flower when I was just fifteen."

"Ho boy!" Randy exclaimed, with a chuckle. "Those were the days. I had to get another part time job to pay for all the condoms we needed. We were going through a dozen a week. Course, we'd already had been engaged for four years. It was bound to happen."

"Yes, I suppose it was," Jaclyn said, as she looked down at her ring finger. There were three rings welded together. Two were stainless steel rings. Then there was a silver band with three diamonds set in it, in between the steel bands. The two steel rings cost Randy thirty-five dollars when he was twelve years old. He had proposed to her on her eleventh birthday.

Chuckling, Jaclyn said, "I still remember our first date. You stuck your head through that old board fence and asked me if I would go swinging with you."

"Yep," Randy said. "We started going steady after that. You're the only girlfriend I ever had."

"And you're the man," Jaclyn chuckled. Just then Willie entered the kitchen "Good morning son. Ready for breakfast?"

"Yes Ma, I'm hungry," Willie said. "Can I go to public school next year?"

"And what is wrong with the academy?" Randy asked.

"Janice Shore can't go to the Academy, but I can go to the school she goes to," Willie explained.

"Sorry son," Randy said. "We have it all arranged. You'll be taking courses at the Junior College next year. The year after that you'll be able to get into a university, either the University of Minnesota or University of North Dakota, your choice. You'll be able to have a Masters by the time you're twenty one."

"Your Father's right, Willie," Jaclyn agreed.

"Goodbye dear," Randy said, after kissing Jaclyn and sneaking another grab of her butt.

"Have a good day honey," Jaclyn said. "You sure look handsome in that policeman's uniform." Then whispering in his ear she said, "look even better without it."

"Without a driver's license, it will be a whole year before I can ask Janice out," Willie complained. "She'll forget me by then."

"Not if she really likes you," Jaclyn said. "Besides, she has a car. Let her do the driving until next year."

"Oh Ma, girls don't drive their boyfriends around on dates," Willie protested.

"Well I can chauffer the two of you around if you wish," Jaclyn said.

"Gee Ma, I think I would rather have Janice drive me around than my Mother," Willie moaned, while eating his French toast.

"Last night, you told me Janice took your hand and held it through the movie," Jaclyn said. "She's clearly interested in you. You made such a lovely couple at the Hartec's wedding."

"Yeah," Willie agreed. "We sure found the same rhythm quick."

"Well, did you let Janice know that you would like to see her again?" Jaclyn asked.

"I didn't have to Ma," Willie said. "Janice told me she would call me and let me know when they would be at another matinee."

"Willie! What in the world are you worried about?" Jaclyn asked. "She's your girl. She knows you're a year younger than she is. That didn't matter yesterday afternoon. You just concentrate on getting good grades and get your Masters. You're going to marry that girl one day. Now get your books. We have to get you to the Academy."

Jaclyn was happy about the relief Willie seemed to experience after she told him he would marry Janice one day. He was such a well meaning boy-just like his father. He wasn't very athletic because he was tall and skinny. He stood six inches taller than his Father and was three inches taller than she was.

Jaclyn chuckled as she recalled their height problems. Randy had left high school at the beginning of his senior year and joined the Marines. He got his high school diploma through the G. E. D. program. He was discharged in the fall of sixty-seven, at the age of twenty. They had been separated for eighteen months. When Randy had come home, they were horrified to find Jaclyn three inches taller than Randy.

There had been a nine-month break up in their halcyon courtship, while they sorted out this problem.

Jaclyn loved to wear spike heels. The heels made her tower over Randy. She tried to make up for it by walking with a slouch to appear shorter. Randy hated it and a breakup ensued, followed by a make up and another breakup.

Grandma Muir, Jaclyn's maternal Grandmother, had solved the problem. "Burrr it's cold out there this morning," Granny had said, as she came in the front door. "Would never know it was May."

"It's going to warm up a lot today," Harold, Jaclyn's father, had said. "Suppose to hit seventy five degrees for the high."

"Did you walk all the way from the drugstore?" Jaclyn's mother had asked.

"No. That nice young police officer, Randy Slocum, picked me up half a block from the drugstore," Granny said. "Good thing too. They had my prescription ready and hadn't started the coffee yet. I didn't stay around long enough to get warmed up after the cold walk to the store." Granny hung her heavy wool sweater on the hall tree. "Of course, Randy would be my grandson now if I didn't have such a foolish, stubborn granddaughter," Granny Muir continued. "She doesn't know a good man when she sees one."

"Mother! That's none of our business," Judy said. "Besides he's so short. What could Jackie do?"

"He's not short where it counts," Granny Muir retorted, her temperament declining with each passing second.

"Mother! How you talk." Judy fired back.

"Jane and Florence are wheel chair bound," Granny said. "That puts them at eye level with the plumbing department. They say the big gun isn't the one in his holster."

"Mother!" a horrified Judy repeated while her husband, Harold, was choking up, trying to hold back laughter.

"Well just ask her," Granny said, while accusingly pointing at Jaclyn with her cane. "I'll bet she knows."

Jaclyn remembered how hot her face had gotten after Granny's accusation. Randy was the only man she had had sex with. From what her catty girl friends had said about their sexual escapades, she suspected Granny was right.

"You're partially responsible for this Judy," Granny had stated. "You never did like him."

"It's not that I don't like him. I just thought Jackie could do better," Judy protested.

"Do better?" Granny's disposition deteriorated further. "A war hero with a bunch of medals and scars to prove it. He's an up and coming officer on the police force. What's wrong with that, may I ask? I should have a great grandchild by now. Don't know if I'll live long enough anymore."

"Oh Granny, I'm so sorry I disappointed you," Jaclyn said. "It's just that we were always fighting after Randy came home. I still love him. It just seems we can't get along."

"What do you fight about?" Granny asked. "You two were like two peas in a pod ever since you were four years old. You were always getting into trouble together. But, you never fought about anything. What happened?"

"Randy doesn't like it when I slouch to make myself look shorter," Jaclyn said. "You know how much I love my spike heels. Randy thinks I shouldn't wear them when we're together. He says I wouldn't be so self conscious then."

"That's asking to much?" Granny had fairly screamed. "You look like hell when you slouch. Stand up straight and be proud. That young man is nothing to be ashamed of."

"Oh Granny, what should I do?" Jaclyn had wailed.

"If you really love him, quit slouching and only wear the heels when you two aren't together," Granny said. "He just got off duty.

He doesn't go back to work until Sunday night. Get over to his place and screw his socks off."

Jaclyn remembered looking at her parents. Her father had nodded in agreement.

It was only five blocks to Randy's house. Jaclyn had taken off on a run, shedding her spikes on the way to the door. Jaclyn had been half way across the front lawn when she heard Granny Muir yell "And this time get yourself pregnant."

By the time Jaclyn had gotten to Randy's door, her panty hose had worn through on the bottoms and crawled half way up to her knees. When Randy had opened the door and seen her barefoot and breathless, he burst into laughter.

"I'm sorry Randy," Jaclyn had gasped. "Please make me pregnant, right now."

"Whoa lady, slow down a little," Randy had said. "I'll do everything you ask if you promise me one thing. Never walk along side me slouched over. Stand up straight. You can wear your heels. I don't care."

"I will, I will, I promise," Jaclyn said. "I'll never wear heels when we're together. I'll always carry a pair of flats with me to work. I can slip them on for any unplanned meetings."

"Well dear, let's get busy on a family," Randy had said, as he escorted Jaclyn to his bedroom. Willie had been conceived that day.

"Well dear, what do you know about Willie Slocum?" Lilly asked Roger, after supper Monday night. "It seems our surrogate daughter is smitten and now she has wheels. A little scary."

"I've only seen Willie twice," Roger replied. "The first time was on a county road, where I broke down with Old Red. It was early on a Sunday afternoon. I was delivering a cord of firewood to an old couple in Bend. Old Red started misfiring and I could hear compression leaking. I thought the head gasket had blown. When I got the truck stopped and raised the hood, I found a spark plug had blown out of its hole. I had a wrench to screw it back in but the spark plug was gone. Just the wire was hanging there. I figured the plug had to be on the side of the road somewhere. It was a blacktop road so the white porcelain would stand out like a sore thumb. But it was nowhere in sight.

"About that time a pickup towing a boat came over the rise behind me. It was Randy and Willie. They were headed home from a morning of fishing. I knew who Randy was because I'd done a lot of deliveries in Ashland Falls. Whenever I delivered to old folks, Randy always seemed to show up to chat with them. I overheard him say, 'my son is in the boy scouts earning merit badges. If you folks need any help stacking this wood, I'll let my son know and some scouts will come over after school. They don't accept money for the work, but it's okay if you feed them.'

"I've had a few beers with Randy from time to time. We always treated each other depending on which of us saw the other one first. But back to the truck-I'd searched quite a while in vain before the two of them came. Randy and I reasoned that the plug should be stuck in the gravel or in the grass near the gravel. We also figured we would need to search about fifty yards of road edge. Meanwhile, Willie was walking back and forth across the whole ditch-like he did to pick up rubbish. He found the spark plug half way up the outer edge of the ditch. It was several yards behind the truck. There was rubber seared on the porcelain end and it was broken. It had landed on the road and the outside dual went over the end and popped it across the ditch. The Slocums had waited until I got the truck running. They had wanted to make sure the broken porcelain wouldn't be a problem. Then they took off. The next time I saw Willie was at our wedding."

"Why did you pick Randy as a groomsman?" Lilly asked.

"I guess it was because he gave me a two thumbs up after I threw that park bench through the window at the museum," Roger said, with a chuckle. "I figured we had to be kindred spirits. If Willie was in the scouts, you must know something about him."

"He never was in my unit," Lilly said. "However, I did get a chance to talk to leaders who did work with him. He really didn't stand out. He was extremely shy. However, near the end of their projects he was always in big demand. The slower boys would go to him for help. The leaders said helping the slower boys was a tremendous boost to his self-esteem. I suppose that self-esteem took a hit when he became a teenager and developed that horrible case of acne."

"Well it seems Janice has made a good choice," Roger said.

"Yes," Lilly agreed. "Apparently she can see beyond the acne. I suppose he will be a handsome boy when he grows through that stage."

Chapter 14. A Tangled Web.
Winter, 1985

"**D**amn that ungrateful S.O.B.," Susan Hargrove muttered. "I've written four letters since the summer of eighty-three. Here it is eighty-five. All I've gotten is a bunch of sorry ass excuses. That bastard owes me."

She decided she should try calling the Attorney General. Since it was early Monday morning, this would be her best chance to speak to him personally. Dialing the telephone number, she got a secretary after the second ring.

"Attorney General's office. How may we help you?" came a male voice.

In her most pleasant voice, Susan said, "Good morning. This is Miz Susan Hargrove. May I speak with Bogey?"

"Do you have an appointment sweetie?" came the reply.

"No I don't," Susan cooed. "Bogey and I are old friends from our U of M days." Susan suspected the male she was talking to would have been told by Horatio to send any call from a Miz through. Horatio had always kidded her that Miz was a code word for, "I love to screw."

Susan was right. The familiar twang of Horatio Bogarth's voice came on the line. "Hello Susan, how are you doing these days?"

"Not so good," Susan said, sweetly. "I'm not getting screwed nearly enough. Why don't you make more trips out-state? You have an expense account. You would get laid more often."

"I also have a wife," Horatio said. "A person can't be to careful when he holds an elected office."

"Must raise hell with your libido," Susan replied. "I can remember needing all night to get you down loaded. How do you suppress that?"

"Well I'm married. I'm not totally without," Horatio replied. "One must make sacrifices for his country," he chuckled.

"Yes I know," Susan replied. "That's why you kept getting deferments until you got lucky on the lottery draw." Susan giggled. "Course, having a Pappy in high office didn't hurt either."

"Well that's the natural pecking order," Horatio chuckled. "Can't change nature. Peons make good cannon fodder. Somebody must stay behind to lead."

Susan could detect some impatience in Horatio's voice. Thinking she better get down to business, she said, "I'm calling about the Hartec's taking three children illegally. I'm sure the older boy isn't adopted. I heard they picked him up along the freeway."

"You're sure he wasn't adopted?" Horatio asked.

"He couldn't have been," Susan replied. "Lilly had come to my office to apply for adoption. I turned her down because of her age and her husband's violent tendencies. Now that old biddy is picking up girls off the streets. They should be in foster homes. I offered to set her up in the foster care business. She threatened me and run me off her property. That pissed me off."

"Yes dear, I'm aware of all that," Horatio replied. "However, this problem is a lot bigger than one of our subjects not bowing to your wishes. We had a run in with Roger Hartec during my first year in office. The situation was handled poorly. Now we must tread lightly where he's concerned. Also, it doesn't help that he ended up in Sheriff Oscar Thompson's jurisdiction. That old bastard is popular. He's been in office forever and is tenacious as a bulldog. If he gets wind that something's wrong; he could start checking records. We have an attorney in this office that's a weak link. He has doubts about the liberal agenda. He's the one who prosecuted Roger."

"You mean you can't make that old problem with Roger go away?" Susan queried.

"Don't dare," Horatio replied. "After President Nixon got caught, we can't trust anybody anymore. A lot of people handle public records. Destruction of routine records would give somebody a heads up. It seems every goddamn clerk or paper shuffler wants to be the next deep throat. Every fucking journalist envisions himself another Woodward or Bernstein. Times are tough toots."

"What the hell kind of stunt did your office pull on Roger that makes you people so fucking scared?" Susan asked.

"It wasn't my doing," Horatio protested. "I had just gotten into office and my staff was trying to enforce my campaign rhetoric. Roger had protested an OSHA violation where he worked. He wanted the decision reversed and the fine refunded to his employer. Our office subpoenaed him to appear at an administrative law hearing in St. Paul. Roger complained to his Congressmen. He found a state Senator that agreed with him. We had to reschedule the hearing closer to his home. That should have clued some of our people in, but it didn't. Combative foes should be silently appeased. Unfortunately, Roger wasn't handled that way."

"He must have had some high powered attorney," Susan said.

"No he didn't," Horatio replied. "Even though we had charged and subpoenaed him, the same as we would have a common criminal, the court didn't have to provide him counsel. OSHA regulations didn't allow for the provision of counsel. This was intended to intimidate and scare people away from protesting. Roger had picked up on that and used it against us. That caused even more problems. The courts are required to show leniency of protocol when this happens."

"And he slipped those dumb fucks a Mickey Finn?" Susan queried.

"Did he ever," Horatio agreed. "First he called the prosecuting attorney on the witness stand. The Judge put the attorney under oath and Roger presented him with a hypothetical case. Then Roger said, 'You're the Judge. What's your conclusion?' When the attorney rendered his verdict; Roger applied that verdict to the case at hand. He proved conflict of interest. He did a damn good job of it."

"He won the case?" Susan asked.

"Oh no," Horatio said. "If that asshole Judge would have had an I.Q. in the double digits, he would have thrown the case out right then and gone home. However, they went into this situation with the intent of crushing upstart taxpayers. Also, they didn't want anything to interfere with the revenue stream created by the fines being imposed."

"Well, how did they screw up?" Susan inquired.

"After Roger got through embarrassing the Attorney, he put the Administrative Law Judge on the witness stand. The Judge refused to take the oath. He insisted his high office precluded it. Damn good thing he didn't take the oath because he committed perjury. He would have had to admit to conspiracy. Those boys were lucky there weren't any members of the press there. Had there been, there would've been hell to pay."

"You've managed to keep this quite all these years?" Susan asked.

"Oh yes," Horatio replied. "But it could break any time. The prosecuting attorney admires Roger and his grit. Says Roger is a modern day Patrick Henry. However, it was that same Attorney's quick thinking that saved the day."

"And what was it he did that was so grand?" Susan inquired.

"He was recording the trial for the records," Horatio said. "Roger thought he was entitled to a copy of that tape. The prosecuting attorney knew the Judge had perjured himself and it was on the tape. But he had to agree that Roger was entitled to a copy. He told Roger, "I'll send you a request form in the mail. You fill out the form and send it back with a check. It will cost somewhere between fifty and a hundred bucks."

"Roger wouldn't spend the fifty bucks," Susan said.

"That's right," Horatio said. "At that time he couldn't afford to hire an Attorney. Fifty bucks was a lot of money back then. However, he was entitled to a copy for eight dollars. That included the cost of the cassette and postage. We're not supposed to profit from public records. The prosecuting attorney insists he won't carry any more water to douse departmental fires. Says it cost him to much sleep."

"Oh, what a tangled web we weave, when first we practice to deceive." Susan quoted Sir Walter Scott.

"That's not the worst of it," Horatio said. "The Judge was so embarrassed and pissed, he found in the State's favor. Roger lost his case. That dumb ass Judge compounded perjury with gross misconduct. Roger was young, without financial means back then. It will be a whole different ball game now. He won't make the same mistake twice."

"Shit! So we're going to have to let him get away with snatching children off the streets," Susan sighed.

"Not necessarily," Horatio said. "Oscar is near retirement. Usually when a sheriff of long standing retires half his deputies aspire to the job. You just need to find out which one has the best chance and educate him to the New World Order."

"How do you propose I do that?" Susan asked.

"Are you telling me you've lost all your seductive powers?" Horatio asked. "I can remember a time when you could handle more hose than a volunteer fire department."

"Fuck you," Susan said, as they both laughed. "When you come through this area; look me up. We can reminisce about the old days. In the meantime keep in touch. Let me know when we can go after the Hartecs. Goodbye sweets."

"Goodbye dear, I'll keep you in mind," Horatio said, as he hung up the telephone.

Horatio buzzed his secretary, Daniel.

Daniel came into the Attorney General's office. "What's up Chief?"

"We need a contingency plan for Miz Susan Hargrove," the A.G. said, "in case the elections in Ashland County don't go our way."

"What do you have in mind Chief?" Daniel asked.

"We must get together with the head of Social Services at the Capitol," Horatio said. "We must prepare to have Susan transferred if she can't swing that Sheriff's election our way."

"Like to Bum Fuck, Egypt?" Daniel asked.

"No, no!" Horatio exclaimed. "We don't dare punish her; especially after what I had to tell her today. We certainly don't want her and Roger Hartec becoming asshole buddies. It's got to be an advancement, or a move she will like."

"What do you suggest Chief?" Daniel asked. "I'm all ears."

"Can we find a college town?" Horatio asked. "Maybe a town with a University of Minnesota campus. We need an area that's mostly male with ugly women. Susan will be happy if she's in an area with a lot of horny males. She's a nymphomaniac. We've got over two years to set it up. We must be prepared to make a move right after the election."

"I'll get some men right on it," Daniel said, as he left the Attorney General's office, closing the door behind him.

Horatio leaned back in his large, plush swivel chair and kicked his feet up on his desk. Clasping both hands behind the back of his head, he was soon lost in thought. *It was ironic the way the people they thought they would be helping were becoming their biggest obstacles. Take Roger, for instance-, it had been their intention to help people like him when they conceived the Occupational Safety and Health Administration. However, it hadn't work out the way Roger had anticipated.*

It had been Congresses' intent to find a large source of revenue by fining employers and corporations to raise the money. It had worked great. An inspector would go in and write up deficiencies left and right. Then the inspector would levy fines according to the manual OSHA provided him. The employer was automatically guilty. They kept the fines low enough so the businesses would just consider them a nuisance and pay them.

However, When Congress authorized the OSHA department, several members actually anticipated there would be follow-up inspections to insure corrections had been made. Many members of Congress actually wanted employees to be safer. That wasn't how OSHA operated. Right out the gate, it started as strictly a revenue raising operation.

Roger's trial had changed all that. Almost single handed, Roger had destroyed that revenue source. He had made a convincing argument that the fines actually worked against the employee. The government was taking money that the employers needed to do the repairs and give the workers raises. He had also made a convincing argument that no employer should be fined for the deficiencies found during the initial inspection.

Roger had said, "The employer should be given ninety days to correct the problems before being fined. They shouldn't be fined unless it's found the problems haven't been corrected, after a follow up inspection, three months later."

The Prosecuting Attorney had been convinced that Roger was right. That attorney had the Legislator's ears. The changes had been made and the quick, easy source of revenue had dried up. The Prosecuting Attorney's conversion had come about because of the OSHA Inspector's testimony. Roger had put the inspector under oath. *That Hartec must be one intimidating bastard. That dumb ass inspector admitted he had never done a follow up inspection, during the three years he had been an inspector. The dumb shit had admitted that he seen his job as a collector of revenue. Roger got him to admit that it made his job a lot easier if he didn't do follow up inspections. That way he would have the same defects to write up again and again. Lazy bastard!*

Yes, "Oh, what a tangled web we weave, when first we practice to deceive." Susan certainly got that one right. *Good thing I was there to clean up that mess,* Horatio credited himself. Horatio had told the Administrative Law Judge that he was wide open to charges of malfeasance, misfeasance, gross misconduct and a host of other charges.

"Damn good thing I was able to get him a professorship at the University of Minnesota. Good thing I had Daddy to help." Horatio spoke his thoughts, as he dropped his feet to the floor.

Chapter 15. Clayton's Passing. Spring-Autumn, 1985

L illy had finished packing the family dinner in a large picnic basket. The children had finished their lessons. Lilly had planned to take them to the lumberyard for dinner with their father. She would take Janice to dinner alone.

Lilly thought Janice was experiencing depression. She had hoped to help her. Lilly was fearful that Janice was pregnant. She knew Janice and Willy were spending a lot of time together, especially during the summer. Lilly loved Willy and Janice. She hoped Jaclyn had the presence of mind to prepare Willie for the male female relationship. Sometimes she had her doubts.

Roger loved stage plays. They attended every play that they were able to, especially if Jaclyn was acting in it. Lilly truly enjoyed the dinner theatre the local actors started putting on each summer. However, Lilly feared if Jaclyn was anything like the characters she portrayed in the plays, Janice could be in big trouble.

If Lilly and Janice could get away today, some of the help at the lumberyard would have food to take home. Lilly always packed the full compliment of food, even if she had plans to eat out. There was always somebody at the yard who could make use of the extra food. Sometimes, Roger would give the food to a customer, whom he thought might be struggling. Lilly and the children entered the lumberyard office. Lilly set the lunch basket on the picnic table that the employees used for breaks. "Janice dear, I think we should go out for dinner today," Lilly said.

Rainy and the twins loved being at the yard, especially if Roger was there. Roger was usually there in the afternoons, having taken care of customer meetings in the morning. Roger had said that first thing in the morning was the best time to find a farmer at home. Most of the farmers want to discuss business over breakfast. "Can they ever eat a breakfast. I'd really fatten up if I shared breakfast with them every morning."

Janice wasn't her usual self, that was for sure, Lilly had observed. They drove to their favorite restaurant on the west side of Ashland Falls, in silence. After Lilly had parked and they both had gotten out of the car, Janice turned to Lilly and said, "I don't think I can eat today. I'm not feeling very good."

Lilly rushed over to the other side of the car and embraced Janice. "What's the problem dear?" Lilly asked.

By now Janice was sobbing. "It's Dad," She said. "He's dying. Willie and I got him to the V.A. Hospital, in Fargo Friday night. He's not doing well. I should be with him. He can't last much longer."

"You certainly should be with him," Lilly asserted, as she opened the car door for Janice to get back in. "I'll take you to your place and you can change clothes. While you're changing, I'll call Roger and let him know our plans. *My Lord, that poor child certainly has had her problems.* Janice would sob from time to time as they drove to the hospital.

After checking in at the front desk they proceeded to the third floor where Clayton's room was. Lilly stopped short outside the door wanting to give the Shore family their privacy.

"No, no, please come with me," Janice insisted, as she took Lilly's hand. The two entered the room together.

A nurse was in the room with Clayton. "He'll be awake soon," she said. "He's had a busy day. His son called from Italy and they talked for nearly an hour. That was about twenty minutes ago. He should wake up soon."

Lilly and Janice pulled two chairs up beside the bed to wait. Then Janice said, "I need to go to the bathroom. I'd better do that before Dad wakes up." She left Lilly sitting in the room alone with Clayton.

Shortly after Janice left, Clayton woke up. He was a ghost of the person who had played music at Lilly's wedding. All the paraphernalia he was hooked up to didn't do anything to help his appearance.

After blinking several times, Clayton recognized Lilly. "Is Janice with you?" he asked.

"Yes she is," Lilly replied. "She had to find a bathroom. How are you doing, Clayton?"

"Not well," Clayton replied. "But it will be over soon. All my organs are failing. Danny called me this morning. We had a good long talk. I hope my children can forgive me. They were so much like Elaine. Both were way more my wife than they were me. They were a constant reminder of my dear wife. It was like a curse for me. I didn't want to live after Elaine died. I would have taken my own life, if it hadn't been for the children. God provided us Roger at the right time. The medications the Doctors had provided didn't work and I lost my job. I don't blame the power company. A lot of people can be killed when an electrical engineer makes mistakes. Getting drunk and passing out was the only way my body got any rest. I haven't slept in years. I never drank before Elaine died. I didn't have to with her by my side. She was the light of my life."

Just then Janice had entered the room. When she saw her father was awake, the tears started flowing. She rushed to the bed and kneeling on the floor she hugged her father while sobbing. "I love you Daddy," she repeated several times.

"I love you Janice," Clayton said. "Danny and I had a good talk this morning. He's engaged to be married. His fiancé lives north of Rome."

"Oh Daddy, is he still angry with you?" Janice asked.

"No, he's forgiven me," Clayton said. "Danny said, 'Now that I'm in love, I understand what you've been going through. Dad, if something like that happens to me, I don't know if I could handle it any differently than you did.'"

"Oh good, " Janice said. "I'm so glad the two of you got back together," Janice was sobbing and hugging Clayton.

Shortly, Clayton fell asleep. Lilly decided to make a trip to the restroom while he slept. On the way to the restroom she met the nurse who had been in the room when they arrived.

"It won't be long now," the nurse said. "His organs have failed and his body is shutting down."

Lilly returned to the room to find Janice crying softly and a jaundiced Clayton in a fitful slumber. Then Clayton opened his eyes. It took him a while to focus on the two women. "Elaine," he said, addressing Lilly.

"No Dad, this is Lilly Hartec with me. Mom died years ago," Janice said.

"That's right. Lilly and Roger," Clayton said. "They're your parents now. Be sure to obey them and they will take good care of you. You and Danny must promise me that you will be good children." Clayton closed his eyes.

Opening his eyes again, Clayton said, "Danny wants you to have the house. It's all paid for, but it does need a lot of work." Then Clayton closed his eyes again and soon afterwards stopped breathing.

Lilly took Janice home with her that night. She didn't want Janice to be alone. Besides, she and Roger would be helping Janice with the funeral arrangements. Danny had secured military hops all the way to Fargo. They would pick him up in Fargo late on Wednesday.

Willie would take Thursday and Friday off from his studies at UND to be with Janice during the funeral service. Military honors were arranged for the funeral service on Thursday.

Clayton's funeral had brought Danny home on emergency furlough. Danny had always admired Roger since they had first met. He had a tendency to think of Lilly as his mother ever since she had married Roger. Sometimes he even addressed her as Mom. Now, he was adamant. They should come to Italy for his wedding in the fall. "We can plan the wedding for whichever week you folks feel you can best get away," Danny said. "Stephanie is dying to meet you folks and I can arrange military hops for you."

"Oh, that won't be necessary," Lilly said, "We'll fly commercial."

"And we'll bring Janice with us," Roger said. "You two are part of our family now. Yes, we'll be there. I'll tell you which week will be best before you return to Italy."

"Then it's settled," Danny said. "I'll let Stephanie know. She's impatiently waiting to tell her parents. Her parents are looking forward to meeting you folks. I'll warn you right now; they'll throw a big party with you folks as guests of honor. The whole neighborhood will be there to meet you. That's just the way the Italians are. The parties are simple. Lots of wine, cheese, homemade sausages and dozens of homemade bread recipes. They will all be jabbering in Italian, so you won't understand a word they say. Only Stephanie and her Grandmother speak English. Granny struggles a little with her English because she learned to speak it as a child, during World War Two. She was taught English by an American soldier who befriended her. However, she has been speaking more English again, ever since Stephanie took me to meet her family."

It was early afternoon of that late September day, when Lilly and Roger drove to Oscar Thompson's place to pick up their children. Oscar and Jenny had insisted that the Hartecs leave the children with them, while the Hartecs were in Italy for Danny Shore's wedding.

The Hartecs had dropped Janice Shore off at the university campus in Fargo. Willie Slocum would bring Janice back to Ashland Falls during the evening. Janice was taking classes at the Junior College in Ashland Falls. She needed to be at those classes in the morning. She still worked at the lumberyard around her college schedule.

Lilly rushed to the Thompson's front door and rang the doorbell. She was anxious to see her three children.

"Good afternoon dear," Jenny said, as she opened the door.

"How are the children," Lilly breathlessly inquired.

"I'm sorry, they're not here," Jenny said. "I wasn't sure when you folks planned on arriving home. Had I known, I would have made sure Oscar had them here for the occasion."

"They're somewhere with Oscar?" Lilly asked.

"They're at Mosquito Lake," Jenny said. "Please come in and sit.

I'll try to raise Oscar on the radio. I doubt that I'll be able to get in touch until suppertime. They'll be out hiking or fishing now.

"The fishing was so good, the first day, that Oscar took vacation time and set up our camper out there," Jenny continued. "They've been out there all the time you folks have been gone. I've spent several nights out there myself."

"The mosquitoes haven't carried them off?" Roger asked.

"Oh no," Jenny responded. " It's been a cool northeast wind all the while you folks have been gone. Oscar thinks that is what is keeping the mosquitoes away. Northeast winds in this country are unusual. Oscar says the wind sweeps right up the length of the valley and blows the slopes clean of mosquitoes. I guess mosquitoes can't handle much wind."

"No they can't," Roger agreed. "Can't handle the sound and exhaust of a chain saw either."

"It gets real cool in the evenings so they always have a campfire," Jenny said, as she tried the radio. "His radio is shut off. Would you folks like a drink, the usual? She started putting ice in three glasses as she looked to them for their answers.

"The usual works for me," Roger said.

"Same here," Lilly added.

"When I get these finished, we'll go into the living room," Jenny said. "If Oscar goes into the travel trailer before supper time, he'll call. As beautiful as it is out today, I rather doubt I'll hear from him before then."

"Have the children been well behaved?" Lilly inquired.

Jenny chuckled, "As well behaved as Oscar," she said. "When you called about staying the extra days, Oscar extended his vacation. He hasn't taken many days off since the incident. He's having the time of his life. The kids were all questions and one night the subject of families and grandparents came up. Oscar explained what grandparents were and then the children took to calling Oscar Grandpa and they called me Grandma. The children reasoned that if you folks adopted them and they didn't have grandparents, they should be able to adopt grandparents of their choice. I'm afraid Oscar might have gotten a little carried away. As you know, all our grandchildren are in France. We seldom see them." Jenny was dabbing tears from around her eyes with a tissue. "We were so caught up in their enthusiasm, we accepted the offer of being their grandparents. I suppose we should have talked to you folks first."

"Oh gracious no," Lilly said. "I guess grandparents hadn't crossed our minds. My parents are dead and Roger has lost all track of his original family. I feel honored that you and Oscar wish to take on that responsibility. How about you Roger?"

"I think it's great," Roger said. "But they should have two sets of grandparents."

"Good," Jenny said, as she chuckled and dabbed at some tears of joy from around her eyes, "because Oscar suggested the same thing. The children made a second selection."

"And who did they select?" Lilly asked.

"Let me guess," Roger said. "Lori and Sam."

"Yes! That's who," Jenny said, as tears of joy started flowing again. "I hope you don't mind. I just had to tell Lori. One thing led to another and Lori talked with Pastor. He wants to conduct a special adoption service some Sunday. Is that okay with you folks?"

"Why that's fantastic," Lilly agreed. "I don't know why we didn't think of it. Let's have the ceremony as soon as we can." *It'll probably be one of the few times I'll get Roger into a church.*

"That's where we left it," Jenny said. "Pastor is waiting to hear from you."

"How's Oscar managing in the wilderness with three wild kids?" Roger asked.

"They're having a grand time," Jenny said. "They came back here one morning for more equipment. Oscar and Rainy had loaded a big water tank on the pickup. Also, a shovel, pick axe and transfer pump and more gas for the generator. They run to a small store out side of the State Park entrance, where they purchase drinking water and ice. They seem to keep busy all day, with fishing, hiking and camp chores. They had to dig a wastewater pit for the travel trailer. They fry fish every day over a campfire. The fishing has been good."

Again, Jenny started to cry. "Lord, you don't know how good those children have been for Oscar," she said as she wiped tears from her face. "This is the first time he's been fishing since that horrible incident with Jimmy Schwartz. This has truly been a blessing for him. I hope you will be able to share your children with us even more after Oscar retires."

Regaining her composure, Jenny said, "Why don't you folks stay for supper? You'll be here when Oscar calls."

Looking at Roger for his nod of approval, Lilly said, "We can do that. We won't have the children until tomorrow, so we'll have all evening to prepare for their homecoming."

"Good, I've some pork roast I can heat up to make some hot pork sandwiches," Jenny said. "Tell me, how were things in Italy?"

Lilly chuckled, "Grandma Calderone idolized Roger. When she learned he had been an American Soldier, she wanted to talk to him as much as she could. She had a lot of memories to share about the soldier she made friends with during World War Two. Actually, the whole neighborhood did. The old people all remembered the American soldiers who ran the Nazis out in nineteen forty five."

"I don't think I've ever eaten so much cheese and drank so much wine in my life," Roger said. "I didn't know what we were toasting most of the time. They were all jabbering in Italian. They sure were a friendly bunch. Good thing this vacation was a break in the wood cutting season. I believe I gained ten pounds. I needed to put a little weight back on. However, I'll burn that off again, before the cutting season is over."

"Stephanie's parents were very gracious," Lilly said. "Their villa has been in the family for centuries. The whole countryside is vineyards and populated with vintners. It had been a good season for them. They were very festive."

"They were really pleased with their new son-in-law," Roger said. "Of course, being an American Soldier doesn't hurt in that part of Italy."

The radio started buzzing and Jenny answered it. "Jenny here, over," she said.

"Oscar here sweets. We just got in from fishing. The kids have started cleaning fish. I got a fire going, over."

"Their parents are here to pick them up," Jenny said. "You ready to relinquish parenting? Over."

"We thought we would stay out here until winter drove us in, over."

"They need to get back to their studies dear, over."

"Always something, always something," Oscar complained. "Okay, we'll break camp and be in before noon tomorrow, over."

"Okay dear. We'll see you in the morning. Love you, over and out."

"I love you," Oscar replied. "Over and out."

"Well you should have your family back by noon tomorrow," Jenny said, "Come, let's have supper."

Chapter 16. The Complaint. Spring, 1986

olice Chief, Harley Johnson was perplexed about the forthcoming special meeting of the city council. The council had called for this discussion at their regular meeting to address complaints about officer Randy Slocum chauffeuring people around in his squad car.

Harley knew Randy's Boy Scout days had never left him. Harley considered Randy his best officer. It was Randy who always helped with detective work. Harley suspected the complaint originated out of jealousy. Randy always volunteered for police workshops and was a model officer. However, Randy's chances of being appointed to the Chief's position were almost impossible. He had required psychiatric care after the Jimmy Schwartz incident. Randy was aware of the problem. The city council would have to make the promotion and their decisions were highly subject to prejudice.

Thankfully Randy didn't have to attend this meeting. There had been complaints like this before. They always seemed to come after the council had hired some new officers. One of the councilmen was onto the farce. He insisted that the council would not drag Officer Slocum through these unnecessary hearings until some validity had been established.

"Chief, there's an envelope for you on the night desk," the Desk Sergeant said, as Harley walked into the police station that morning. "You probably want to check it out before the big pow-wow this morning."

"Thanks," Harley grunted. "When did this show up?"

"Sometime last night," the Sergeant said, "Tom said he got up to get a cup of coffee and a doughnut. When he got back to the desk, it was lying there. Tom ran to the front door to see if anybody was in the street. All he saw was traffic. There were no cars parked at the curbs on either side and no pedestrians." The Desk Sergeant chuckled. "Tom said, 'I don't believe in ghosts. But, if something like this happens to me again; I'm going to start believing. Hell, I wasn't gone long enough for somebody to walk in here, drop off the envelope and then go back to the street and drive away.'"

"Well, I guess I'd better check it out before the meeting," Harley replied.

"Have a good day Chief," The Sergeant said.

"Thank you," Harley replied. Then he took the envelope to his office and looked at the contents. *It was obvious somebody had done a lot of research to defend officer Slocum.* Harley rose from his desk to go to the Records Section to check out the validity of the statistics in the report. He had very little time to verify before the meeting.

"Good morning sweets," Harley said to Ellen, as he handed her the report. "Can you verify what's in this report?" he asked. "I don't have much time. Only twenty-five minutes before the council meeting. Start with Randy's record of handling complaints and writing citations. I'll be back in fifteen minutes."

Harley went to the restroom to drain off some morning coffee. Then he went back to his desk for a stick of gum. He went by Records on his way to the council chamber. "What did you find, sweets?" Harley asked Ellen.

"I didn't get through it all," Ellen said. "I did get to check the stats in regard to work load and citation writing. Those stats are dead on. I've checked some of the other stuff and found it all to be accurate. Somebody did some good research."

"Thank you Ellen," Harley said. "Who would have access to these statistics?"

"The information comes in here daily," Ellen replied. "We put it on a monthly work sheet. You get your own copy. A copy goes to each council member, and a copy goes over to the Sheriff's department. We mail that copy to the County Courthouse."

"Thank you again and have a good day," Harley said. "I've got to scoot over to the council chambers."

The number of citizens at this meeting surprised Harley. There were usually one or two, sometimes half a dozen. This morning there were about two-dozen in attendance. Most were older people.

The chairman called the meeting to order. "The agenda is complaints about Officer Slocum using public property, a squad car, to chauffeur people around town. First we will hear from the Chief of Police, Harley Johnson."

Harley moved to the microphone. "This is nothing unusual for Randy," Harley said. "He's always giving rides to citizens, whether he's in a squad car or his own vehicle. That's just who he is. I've considered it part of community policing that's coming into vogue. I Believe Randy could be ahead of a trend."

"If he's buzzing people around town, how does he keep up with complaints and citation writing?" asked a councilman. "How much revenue do we lose because of citations not being written?"

"This report mysteriously showed up at the station last night," Harley said, "I gave it to Ellen to check over. She got about half way through it. She said everything so far is dead on. The report shows that Randy's record of handling complaints and writing citations is well within the average for the force."

The Chairman recognized a lady from the floor. She introduced herself as the Assistant Hospital Administrator. "I wish to comment on some of our statistics since Officer Slocum was hired," she said. "Although our population is aging proportionate to extended overall life spans, we've seen a drop in broken hips and other fall related injuries. The old folks attribute it to Officer Slocum and other nice officers who give them rides, especially during inclement weather. Another anomaly-I can't explain-is that for the last ten years incidents of purse snatching are way down."

"That reminds me of an anomaly in this report," Harley said. "It coincides with what Mary just told us. Over the last ten years, complaints of police harassment and police brutality are way down. They're well below the state's average. These charges usually came up after the physical apprehension of a purse-snatcher. Don't ask me to explain that. I can't."

Jerry Samuelson, one of Harley's officers, asked, "May I see that report?"

"Sure thing," Harley said, as he had the crowd pass the papers back to Jerry.

The Chairman recognized an elderly woman from the floor. "As a member of the Biddy Brigade, I can tell you that helping old folks shouldn't interfere with citation writing. If our ride takes fifteen or twenty minutes longer because the officer has to write a ticket-so what? We old folks always leave for our doctor appointments an hour early; we're just wired that way. Shucks! The officer could write two tickets and still get us there in plenty of time."

There was cheering and clapping from the old folks and several amen's.

While the Chairman was gaveling the meeting back to order, during the clapping and amen's, Jerry passed the papers through the crowd back to Harley.

"Well Jerry, have you figured it out?" Harley asked.

"Yeah I think so," Jerry answered. "That was a couple years after Roger Hartec started delivering fireplace wood throughout the county. He can't be charged with Police-Brutality."

All the police officers in the room quickly tucked their chins down against their chests. They were trying to hide their laughs of amusement inside their open shirt collars. However, the bouncing of their shoulders gave them away.

At the mention of Roger's name a hush fell over the room. Most of the old people knew about Roger from hearsay and rumors. Not much of that was good. Then Vernon Taylor projected both of his arms straight out from his shoulders, toward the Chairman, and gave the two thumbs up signal. There were elbows poking and whispers of "Randy and Roger are friends." Soon, all the old people were silently sitting with both arms projected forward and both thumbs pointed up.

Harley broke the tension with a hearty chuckle. "That makes

sense Jerry. In Roger's line of work, one would never know where he'd show up and when."

The Chairman suggested that they had all the information they needed to make a valued judgment on the complaint. He thanked the crowd for their participation.

Jaclyn Slocum finished putting the breakfast dishes into the dishwasher. She wiped the table and counter tops and made sure everything was in the refrigerator. Randy had left for work after his habitual grab of a handful of her butt.

Removing her apron and glancing at her watch she thought, *I've plenty of time to freshen up and change into heels before my appointment with the Auditor.*

The County Auditor kept track of the vacation schedules for the county employees. As a substitute, Jaclyn would receive a calendar showing who she would replace and when for the whole summer.

Jaclyn had worked two days the week before for a clerk who had an out of town funeral to attend. The county staff had kept her busy with typing, which they would save up for her anytime they knew she would be working. Jaclyn was a speed typist and the courthouse staff all agreed that the only thing that clicked faster than her spike heels was her typewriter key.

Throwing a pair of flat-soled sandals into a tote bag, Jaclyn headed for the door. It was their plan that Randy would pick her up at the courthouse and the two would go out for lunch. The schedule arranging usually went past noon.

"Good morning Jim," Jaclyn said, as she entered the County Commissioner's conference room, where the meeting was to be conducted. There were three other women who would receive schedules for the assortment of offices.

"Morning Jackie," Jim responded. "Lot's of requests this year for your typing skills. I hope you'll be able to give us more time this summer."

"Just summer theatre to interfere with my schedule this year," Jaclyn said, as Jim left the room to answer a page.

"I thought you've ditched the shrimp and gone professional by now," Joyce said.

"No intentions of doing that," Jaclyn said. "It's not work if you're an amateur." *Catty bitch.*

"You probably would have made it big in New York, if you could've gotten Randy to move there," Ann said. "Was he worth it?"

"I think so," Jaclyn responded. *Eat your heart out, bitch. You'll never get a shot at him.*

"How come you always play the parts of a flighty, flirty, bimbo?" Irma asked.

"Because those parts are the most fun to play, and the easiest lines to memorize," Jaclyn said. "If I forget some lines and ad lib, nobody knows the difference."

"Well playing a slut is easy," Joyce commented, as the other two women giggled.

You would know bitch. You've been married and divorced three times before you were twenty-five. "I didn't think you were going to work this summer," Jaclyn said. "I figured that jailhouse lawyer you've been shacking with would get your three alimony checks increased enough to support you both in style." *That ought to shut the bitch up.*

Just then Jim returned and gave the four women copies of calendars and blank schedule forms. "Jackie, I've got your calendar marked when we would like you to work. I've tried to make sure none of those dates interfere with the dinner theatre. I believe I haven't scheduled you for the day after any of the performances. I know there will be hell to pay with the public if we interfere with their dinner theatre."

"Yes, it's really became popular," Jaclyn agreed. "We may have to add another night this year. That would be the only interference with my work availability. We won't know for sure until we start selling tickets."

"Let me know as soon as you find out. I'll scratch you off the schedule," Jim said.

"A lot of easily entertained people in Shumuckville," Joyce said.

"Yes, and their pleasant dispositions are delightful," Jaclyn stated, as she shot a glance at the smiling and approving Jim.

"Okay, lets get the rest of the open days discussed and designated," Jim said. They worked on the schedules all morning. "We'll have to break for lunch and come back in at one p.m."

"You coming with us for lunch, Jackie?" Irma asked.

"Sorry dear, Randy is coming to pick me up. We're having lunch together," Jaclyn said, as she slipped into the flats from her tote bag.

Just then Randy walked in. "Ready honey?" he asked.

"Oh Randy, can you come over here and help me get my necklace clasp closed?" Jaclyn asked. "It came open when I bent over to change my shoes. I can't seem to get it shut again."

Randy walked across the room to help her with the necklace. "Doesn't seem to be anything wrong with it," Randy said. "It closed right up."

"Thank you sweets," Jaclyn said, as she bent toward him to give him a peck on the cheek. Since his backside was out of everybody's view, Jaclyn grabbed a handful of his butt and shot her tongue deep into his ear. Jaclyn suspected her actions would have the desired effect on Randy's policeman's uniform. Out of the corner of her eye, she observed the stares of the three women. They were looking at the bulge in Randy's pants. She had purposely steered Randy so they would walk across the room in front of them. As the two of them exited the room she said to Randy, "I think it's going to be an interesting afternoon dear."

"Lord, I sure wish I had the afternoon off," Randy said.

"Just keep wishing dear. Then we can make up for lost time tonight," Jaclyn said, with a giggle. *Hot damn, that was fun. She had given up a chance at a career in acting to marry Randy. She had decided a long time ago, that that was the smartest thing she had ever done in her life. She truly loved Randy and their son Willie. She and Randy had been life long pals. It still scared her to think she had almost let Randy slip through her fingers. Jaclyn had the better of two worlds, catty bitch by day and loving housewife by night.* She chuckled thinking about it.

"What's so amusing dear," Randy asked.

"Oh, I was just thinking of all the fun I'm going to have with Joyce and Ann this summer. Irma is a natural innocent straight man!" They both laughed. Randy had helped her with her tricks in the past.

"Did you remember to order the package in the plain brown wrapper for our son?" Jaclyn asked, as Randy proceeded out of the parking lot and into the street.

"Yes I did. It should arrive any day now," Randy said. "I wonder how many parents purchase condoms for their sons."

"Smart parents do," Jaclyn said. "How would you've liked to have gone without until you were twenty?"

"You know we could never have done that," Randy said. "You would've gotten knocked up."

"That's exactly what we don't want to happen to Willie and Janice," Jaclyn said. "Willie has one more year at the university and then they will be married."

"Janice sure knew how to get rid of his acne," Randy said, with a chuckle.

"Yes, Willie is a handsome boy and Janice is an absolutely gorgeous looking girl," Jaclyn said. "We're going to have some beautiful grandchildren. I hope there are lots of them."

"We should've had more children," Randy said.

"I agree with you dear, but that's water under the bridge now," Jaclyn said. "We were both having so much fun with our son; we didn't realize how time was slipping away and I wasn't getting pregnant again. Time just flies when you're having fun." Jaclyn playfully punched Randy on the shoulder.

"I told Willie to make sure Janice tells the Hartecs they're planning on getting married before they announce their engagement," Jaclyn said.

"Good, I'm sure Roger and Lilly will want to be involved," Randy said. "They took Janice with them to Italy for Danny's wedding three years ago."

"Yes, Janice still talks about all the fun they had," Jaclyn said. "The Italians loved the Hartecs. Even talked them into staying over for three more days."

"Janice is concerned about them paying for their wedding," Jaclyn said. "That's why I told Willie to make sure the Hartecs know about the engagement. I think Willie should ask Roger for Janice's hand."

"Not a bad idea," Randy concurred.

"I cautioned Willie that he was marrying into strange circumstances," Jaclyn continued. "The Hartecs have done a lot for the Shore children and must consider them their children as well. After all, none of their children are natural born to them. They certainly don't know the difference, or at least Roger doesn't. I told Janice that I think she better be prepared to accept the position as Roger's oldest daughter. Danny has no problem crediting the Hartec's role in his life. Janice said that Danny introduced the Hartecs to the Italians as their surrogate parents."

"Ho boy, things can get complicated around the Hartecs," Randy said. "Good People, though. Roger's business has grown by leaps and bounds. He had his cliental from the north and east sides of the county and then when he married Lilly they gained her friends and neighbors from the south and west. By the way, Willie told me he'd be working for Roger this summer. He's actually working for him now. He's drawing house plans and calculating materials lists. He took several projects with him to Fargo to work on in his spare time."

"I'm not sure if he wants to work for Roger or just be close to Janice," Jaclyn said.

"Oh, Willie's interested in the business all right," Randy said. "Willie said Roger has taught him a few things they didn't even talk about in his business classes. Of course Roger is cautious. Right now, Willie only gets paid for what he produces. Willie says with his education and expertise it translates into good money."

Jaclyn chuckled. "Sounds like two capitalists sparring away."

"I understand Roger owns that business lock stock and barrel," Randy said, "That's no small accomplishment in the time that he's had it. Here we are," Randy said, as they pulled into the restaurant parking lot. It was a long drive to the Country Buffet. However, it was the Slocum's favorite restaurant because of the drive and the quickness of the meal. At noon it was a soup and sandwich buffet and in the evening there was a more relaxed barbeque rib or prime rib meal.

As they were leaving the restaurant, Jaclyn stuffed a dinner roll in her purse. "Still hungry?" Randy asked.

"No," Jaclyn chuckled. "When I get back to work, I'll nibble on this roll and tell the girls we had an emergency stop at a motel and this is my lunch."

"You're something else," Randy chuckled, as he took her arm and escorted her to his car.

"What do you know about Roger's war experiences?" Jaclyn asked. "You two buy each other drinks whenever you meet at a club. You must have had a little shop talk after all these years."

"Well dear, Vietnam Veterans don't talk very much about the war," Randy said. "Not nearly enough."

"But, you both were snipers," Jaclyn protested. "Surely you must have compared notes."

"There were different kinds of snipers," Randy replied. "All things weren't equal."

Jaclyn realized her husband was choking up. As she observed the moisture becoming apparent in his eyes, she said, "We don't need to talk about this anymore."

"No we don't," Randy said. "And it's hard, but it does help. Jimmy Schwartz and I volunteered to be snipers. We were sent to sniper school for training. Then we were given an opportunity to volunteer for where we would prefer to serve. I chose the front lines and Jimmy chose personnel protection. He liked the idea of flying around in the officer's aircraft. Now with Roger it would have been a whole different deal. He was recruited by the Central Intelligence Agency. Then he was run through their special program. He probably was treated more like a civilian after he was recruited. The mystery about Roger is-why did he leave a relatively safe job as an aircraft mechanic to become a sniper. It just doesn't make sense."

"Well why would the C.I.A. pick Roger in the first place?" Jaclyn asked. "You said he was recruited."

"No family," Randy responded. "That's why he invited mostly police officers and sheriff's deputies to be his guests at his wedding. He's probably an orphan. A hell-raising orphan."

"Well he certainly raised enough hell around here when he first arrived," Jaclyn chuckled.

"Don't judge him to harshly," Randy cautioned. "Every incident he was involved in was an act of meting out justice. Our only problem with him was we couldn't allow him to assign himself as Judge, Jury and Executioner; even though we agreed with his verdicts." Randy was chuckling over his last statement and Jaclyn joined in.

"Our son appears to admire Roger very much," Jaclyn said. "Lori Gustafson told me Roger is contemplating offering Willie the office manager's position. Lori will have time to train him before she retires. Lori said, 'With office manager's salary and drawing of house plans, Willie will be hard put to find a more lucrative career.'"

"It does sound like a heck of an opportunity," Randy agreed. "There's good money in the construction business right now. Roger says that when all those old houses were converted from space heating to central heating, they weren't ventilated properly. Now the walls are rotting out. He figures the building business will be good for years."

"And Willie will be marrying the bosses' daughter," Jaclyn chuckled. "Willie really likes Roger," she added.

Chapter 17. Janice's Engagement. Spring, 1988

Lilly was walking with Janice from the far side of the parking lot at their favorite restaurant. They were later than usual and the parking lot was full.

Another car pulled up and parked, partially on the grass and partially on the entranceway, leaving just enough room for other vehicles to get by. It was Jaclyn Slocum and her three girl friends. Lilly observed Jackie getting out of the car. Then recognizing her and Janice, Jackie threw both of her arms in the air in a gleeful gesture. She started click clicking across the concrete surface of the parking lot, in her spike heels, as fast as her tight skirt would allow her.

Upon reaching Lilly and Janice, Jaclyn gushed, "Oh please let me see your ring." Lilly observed the other three women keeping their distance. She suspected they didn't want to be seen with any woman in bib overalls, brogans and a baseball cap.

"Willie wanted me to help him pick out a ring," Jaclyn said, as Janice extended her hand. "I said, no, no, Willie, you must do this yourself. Lord that is beautiful. That's some rock. Willie took his Dad's advice. Randy told Willie to ask the jeweler the price of the setting and the price of the stone. He said to Willie, 'Put the most money into the stone.' Men! They always have to be so practical. Just look at my ring," Jaclyn gushed as she extended her hand. "The two rings on the outside of the center band, with all the stones, are actually stainless steal. Randy spent a whole thirty-five dollars on them. Of course, he was only twelve and I was eleven."

"And what did your parents have to say about that?" Lilly asked.

"Oh that was our secret," Jaclyn said. I was always wearing custom jewelry, as a little girl. They thought my engagement ring was just a toy. After we were married, and Randy had more money, he wanted to replace the two steel rings with something nicer. I wouldn't hear of it. I had never taken the engagement ring off except to have it enlarged. The Jeweler, bless his soul, suggested the center ring with all the diamonds. He told Randy, 'you buy this ring and I'll weld all three together into one ring, no charge. We'll put the two stainless on either side of the silver band for a two-tone look.' So, for the second time I've had those rings off my finger to get them welded together. Oh! My friends are getting antsy. Jaclyn grabbed Janice into a big hug and said, "Congratulations dear, I just know you'll be perfect for my Willie." Then she click, clicked back to her friends who had spent the time smoking.

Lilly chuckled and said to Janice, "I'll bet those other ladies cringed when they saw Jackie hugging you."

Janice chuckled, "That certainly is a strange bunch. Jackie isn't like the others at all, when she isn't with them. I think she enjoys acting catty. I know she loves the theatre she's involved with."

"Roger always says her whole public persona has to be an act," Lilly said. "He says, 'I think she does it to keep up her image as a actress, which she's darn good at.' That's why Roger likes plays better than movies. He insists stage players have to be a lot better than movie actors."

In the inn they chose an alcove for two. It was Lilly's favorite place to dine. Besides a large dinning room, the perimeter was divided into private dinning alcoves of various sizes. It was patterned after an Irish inn with subdued lighting. The alcoves had three different levels of lighting controlled by the diners.

While they were looking at their menus, Janice said, "Jackie loves doing comedies. She is a riot when practicing."

"I'll bet," Lilly responded. "Is she ever serious?"

"She was real serious when she insisted that Willie should ask

Roger for my hand," Janice said. "Willie took me to his house for dinner one Sunday after church. Randy and Jackie knew of our plans to get married. I was feeling guilty about you and Roger paying for my wedding after all that you've done for me. Jackie insisted that Willie should ask Roger's permission to marry me. Then she said to me, 'don't hurt him by ignoring him. You may not think of him as your Father. But, I'll bet in God's eyes Roger is. Darling, you were just lucky enough to have two Fathers.'"

"Randy agreed with Jackie," Janice continued. "He said to Willie, 'when it comes to these kinds of things, your Mother's always right. You kids must understand that the Hartecs are your family also. God works in strange ways. Don't ask me to explain it, I can't.'"

While the waiter was bringing their iced tea, Janice began giggling. "Willie told me what it was like when he asked Roger for my hand. He said Roger stared off into space for what Willie thought was at least three days. Finally Roger looked at him and smiled. 'I presume she's agreed to be your wife. Well Willie, you're one lucky man to win her heart. I know I couldn't have been blessed with a better daughter. Let Lilly and I know the date so the four of us can plan the reception.' Willie told Roger that he was proud to become a member of your family. Then they shook hands."

In the short wait between the salad and the main course, Lilly said, "Once, you told me you knew how to clear up Willie's acne. I've noticed it has disappeared. Did you have something to do with that?"

Janice's face became very flushed and she started giggling again. Finally she sheepishly replied, "Oh yes, I just screwed his socks off!"

Lilly couldn't help herself. She burst into laughter and felt a hot flushing as she thought of herself and Roger.

"Sometimes I worry that we do it to much," Janice confided. "How does one know?"

Lilly felt the flushing growing warmer and spreading. Laying her right hand on Janice's left hand, she said, "It's never to much as long as it doesn't interfere with your ability to make an honest living." Looking into each other's eyes and holding each other's hands, mother and daughter enjoyed a hearty laugh together.

Growing serious, Janice said, "I have a problem that maybe you can help me with."

"Shoot," Lilly said.

"I don't have any problem addressing you as Mother," Janice said. "You've been like a mother to me ever since you became Roger's wife. I always had a father at home so Roger was more like an uncle. I just feel uncomfortable calling Roger Dad. Maybe that will change someday. I suspect it will when our children are calling him Grandpa. But right now, I, I think it's to soon after my Father's passing for me not to feel like somehow I'm being disloyal to him. I've wrestled with this problem for sometime. I'm sure, in time, this will all change. Dad thought very highly of Roger after the way Roger had helped Danny. It was Dad who took me to the lumberyard at closing time, when only Roger was there. Dad told Roger that he was incapable of being a good Father. He wanted to know if Roger would hire me to replace Danny who was going into the Army. Dad said, 'she's as smart as Danny and I'm sure she can earn whatever you wish to pay her. I've a bachelor brother working in the aircraft industry out in Washington, but I think Janice would be better off with you'".

"What about your mother's family?" Lilly asked.

"Mother was an only child and the end of her family," Janice continued, as she began to cry. "I was so frightened. Danny had told me how Roger had threatened to kill the two punks who had been harassing him and stealing his money. Danny said, 'Roger grabbed each boy by an ear and slammed their heads together. Then, Roger told the punks they would disappear off the face of the earth if he ever heard of them coming close to Danny. I guess that's why Dad wanted me in Roger's care instead of Uncle Dave." Janice hesitated, as she wiped away the tears caused by the unpleasant memory. "But for me the stories about Roger were frightening. Especially since Danny had witnessed that incident at the lumberyard where I'd be working. Danny admitted that he was scared to death of Roger. But he continued to work for him because he didn't know what else to do. When he never saw the two punks again and even stopped having trouble at school, he felt safe again. Then he came to admire Roger. It was then when the distance between Danny and Father grew."

"What was Roger like back then?" Lilly asked.

"Roger was different in those days," Janice continued. "As a businessman he was all business. Otherwise, he didn't talk much and was kind of moody. He was really a sad, sad man. Then he met you at the museum and that all changed. I'm glad I'd only worked for Roger a short time before he met you. I would try to joke with him but he didn't seem to respond. After he started courting you he was happy. Then he was just like a father to me. He even made sure I got to basketball games and other school functions that I wanted to attend. That was the first winter after Danny left home. The next winter you were there. The problem is, I was Daddy's little girl even before Mom died." Janice started sobbing. "About a year after Mother died, Father crawled inside a bottle and only came out long enough to play on weekends. Most of the rest of his band were the same way. The only partial sober member was the business manager. I hope Roger can forgive me," Janice was in tears.

Lilly's heart went out to this young woman. She was glad to gain this insight into Janice's childhood. Until this day, Janice had been almost as much of an enigma as Roger was. Wiping the tears from her own eyes, Lilly took both of Janice's hands in hers. "I'll speak to Roger about this tonight dear. Trust me, if anybody in this world will understand your dilemma, its Roger. I know he loves you dearly and is extremely proud of his role in your life. Roger has a very strong faith in his Creator. He insists that ours is not necessarily to understand, but to have the faith to play the hand the Lord deals us. Once Roger confided in me that if it hadn't been for the responsibility of taking care of you and Danny, plus the acceptance of Lori and Sam-he probably would've screwed up like he had in the past. He thinks that he would be in prison now. He said you two children gave him the time he needed until he met me. How could I not love a man like that?" Lilly asked, as she dabbed the tears from her eyes. I better call Roger and tell him we'll be late getting back," Lilly said, as she got up to go up front and use the telephone.

"I'll ask the waiter to reheat our meals while you're on the phone, " Janice said.

Lilly returned to the table as the waiter was returning the reheated plates. "I told Roger we were having a mother daughter thing and needed more time. He said, 'Good, take all the time you need,' I think you should continue addressing him as Roger until the day comes when you're comfortable relinquishing Clayton's role in you life," Lilly said. "I believe you're right. That day will come when you hear your children constantly calling Roger Grandpa. Roger is always a little unsure of himself in relationships of this nature. He will need some time too. I was ready to marry him a month after I'd met him. But he was afraid to ask me. It's funny, most of our new customers think you are our natural daughter."

"I know, and none of the other workers or even our older customers, who know better, ever bother to correct them." Janice concluded. "So I don't either."

After they had completed their dinner, Lilly and Janice departed to a near empty parking lot. "Since Roger said take your time, I think we should go to the party store and pick out some decorations for your reception," Lilly said.

"We won't be busy at the yard this afternoon because it rained the last two days," Janice said. "All the contractors were picking up stuff during the rain and now that the sun is shining they'll be trying to make up for lost time. It's always that way when it rains."

"Rainy will be glad to fill in for you," Lilly said. "He loves waiting on customers."

"He has the whole yard memorized," Janice chuckled. "Even Roger will ask Rainy where something is. The customers love him. He has such a winsome smile and such bright shiny brown eyes."

"Yes, his growth was stunted because of the malnutrition," Lilly said. "But his eyes were always shiny, right from the day we found him. Doctor Taylor said, 'he's in all probability been living on pet food. My guess, it was cat food. That would explain the bright eyes.'"

"Oh that's horrible," Janice gasped, clearly shocked at the thought.

"He wasn't in as bad a shape as the twins were when we found them," Lilly said. "For them the malnutrition wasn't as bad, but were they ever filthy. Of course the rain could have cleaned Rainy up some. He was completely soaked when we got him into the pickup."

"Oh, oh, look who's at the Strip Mall," Janice said, as she pointed toward the far end.

Lilly pulled into a parking slot near the party store, shut off the car engine and looked up. "Mizzz Susan Hargrove, what a thrill."

Susan arrived in the vicinity, as Lilly and Janice were about to enter the store.

"Ah, Mrs. Hartec, it's been a while since we've had the opportunity to chat," Susan said.

"A very pleasant while indeed," Lilly agreed.

"Well it won't be so pleasant once Oscar Thompson's term as sheriff is over with," Susan responded. "Seems it's mostly progressive police officers and deputies running for his position. In fact, I don't know of one conservative in the race."

And you're probably screwing the whole bunch. "Is that so?" Lilly stated.

"Don't you think it's just terrible you're such a dying breed?" Susan asked.

"Don't start shoveling dirt just yet," Lilly retorted. "There are still plenty of good people around."

"If by good you mean conservative, you're right. It's just to bad they're all a little long in the tooth," Susan said. "The generation coming into power is all progressive. You'll see. The Attorney General promised me he would revisit your issue once Oscar retired, if I could be sure the new sheriff is a progressive," Susan said.

Lilly could feel her heart sinking. Rainy would be sixteen before they could do much, but she could lose her twins. "We'll see about that," Lilly said. "I've bested you before and my husband has bested your precious Attorney General."

Lilly and Janice entered the store leaving Susan standing speechless on the sidewalk, with her mouth hanging open.

The two women found a lot of potential decorations but couldn't concentrate on plans for using them. Finally Janice said, "I'm not enjoying this at all. I'm afraid I'll lose my two little sisters. It just isn't fair."

"I agree, we should do this another day," Lilly said. "In the meantime I think we must pray. But mind you, we're not going to remain on the defense. We'll watch for an opportunity and attack!"

Chapter 18. Lilly's Offense. Summer, 1988

Sheriff Oscar Thompson had just sat down at his desk on a hot July day. *It's going to be a scorcher,* he thought.

"A gentleman here to see you," Millie's voice came over the intercom system.

Pressing the return bar, Oscar said, "Send him in."

A stocky man a little under six foot, Oscar guessed, dressed in light weight slacks and a Hawaiian print shirt entered his office.

"Kelly Callahan, of Alabama," The man said as he extended his right hand, while flashing an Irish smile.

Oscar stood up and while taking Kelly's hand in his, he noticed the last two digits were just stubs. "Oscar Thompson, take a chair. How may I help you?"

After sitting down, Kelly said, "I thought I should introduce myself to you and the Chief of Police. I'm going to be campaigning for the job you're retiring from. I figured I better check in with you fellows before your telephones start ringing off the hooks. This being a Scandinavian community, a southern Irishman is likely to stand out like a sore thumb."

"What ever brings you up to this neck of the woods to run for sheriff?" Oscar asked, while staring at Kelly's missing digits.

"I've a wayward son incarcerated in a Minnesota State Prison east of here," Kelly said. "I've heard this is a fractious race with eleven candidates seeking the position, and no clear favorite. I thought it would be worth the shot-to be closer to my boy. Maybe I'll be able to visit him enough to help him."

"That's an admirable goal. Do you have any other children?" Oscar asked.

"Oh yes," Kelly enthused, as he reached for his wallet. Flipping through picture windows, Kelly selected one and removed it. He flipped it on the desk in front of Oscar. "That's the rest of our children."

"Holy cow!" Oscar exclaimed. "There must be two dozen kids in this photograph. Doesn't look like an Irishman in the bunch." Both men chuckled.

"They were all orphans," Kelly explained.

This is the man for Lilly, Oscar was thinking. *She's worried about problems with Susan Hargrove after I retire. Well she ought to be. Mizzz Hargrove was screwing at least half the candidates; some were married.* "Ah, ah, just what are your plans for the campaign?" Oscar asked. "You've only a few weeks before the primary. You're going to have to work hard and fast."

"I planned on traveling the whole county and talking to the folks door to door. I'll be doing a lot of hand shaking." Holding up his right hand to display the two stub fingers, he asked, "Do you think this will be a problem?"

"Depends on how you lost them is my guess," Oscar said.

"Froze them off on the Chosen Reservoir," Kelly said. "I cut those two fingers off my glove and used them to line the slots for my thumb and forefinger. By doubling up the fabric, I was able to save my thumb and forefinger to hold the weapon and pull the trigger. It may sound like a dumb ass move, but it saved my life," Kelly grinned.

"The Chosen! You say. Harley Johnson was on the Chosen," Oscar said. "He's the Police Chief. You said you were going to see him."

"Yes, that is my plan," Kelly affirmed. "Thought I would try to catch him this morning."

"I'll have my Secretary call over and set up an appointment," Oscar said, as he keyed the microphone. After Millie came on the line, Oscar said, "Millie, would you please call Harley Johnson and tell him I'm sending a Kelly Callahan over to introduce himself. Find out if this morning will be convenient, please."

"Will do," came the reply.

"As you probably know, Harley and I elected to stay out of the coming fray," Oscar said. "We've publicly stated we will not endorse any candidate for office. It's mostly members of our staffs that are running. Truth be told, none of the eleven impress either of us."

"Is that so? Maybe I've a better chance than I thought," Kelly said. "I didn't think I could pull this off. But a man's got to try."

"Those two missing fingers prove you believe that," Oscar said. "Tell you what, just north of here is a little town called Siding. It really should be your first stop after meeting Harley. You must get out there around noon. Don't worry about eating lunch before you go out there. You'll be well fed. Lilly and Roger Hartec are the people you want to meet. They own the Siding Lumberyard."

"Made contact with Harley," came Millie's voice over the intercom. "He said anytime this morning will be fine. He's busy cleaning up paper work. He said he will be in his office all morning."

"Thank you Millie," Oscar replied. "I've got to scoot over to the courthouse."

"The two men stood up and shook hands. "Thank you for your consideration," Kelly stated.

"Oh, make sure you show Lilly Hartec that picture of your children," Oscar said. "It'll be easy, with her, to get an opportunity to do that."

After visiting with Harley, Kelly had headed north out of the city to Siding. Harley had assured him that Oscar had a good plan. Harley had drawn a map for him and made sure he left so that he would arrive at the Siding Lumberyard at the proper time.

Walking through the door, Kelly saw a beautiful lady in overalls and baseball cap behind the cash register on the counter top. A long blond ponytail was poking through the hole formed by the rear of the cap and the size strap.

"Lilly Hartec?" Kelly inquired.

"No sir," Janice said. "Mother will be here in a few minutes.

Roger will be too; it's near lunchtime. If you haven't had lunch yet you're in for a treat. Mom puts together a fantastic lunch. Is there anything I can help you with?"

"I stopped by to introduce myself," Kelly said. "I'm Kelly Callahan. I'm going to run for Sheriff Thompson's position. I introduced myself to the Sheriff first thing this morning. He suggested I should pay a visit to the Hartecs."

"You're obviously not from this locality. Where do you hail from?" Janice Slocum asked.

"Alabama," Kelly replied. "I've a sheriff's position down there. I've spent most of my life in law enforcement. I also have a son in prison east of here. I thought if I won Sheriff Thompson's position, I'd be closer to my son."

"Do you have any other children?" Janice asked.

Kelly reached for his wallet and pulled out the picture he had shown Oscar. He proudly showed it to Janice. "Here's the whole kit and caboodle," he said.

Janice took the photograph and studying it she displayed a huge smile and whistled. "That's a passel," she said. "Willie and I want a bunch, but I don't think we'll have that many. We just got married last month."

Kelly heard a car pull up just outside the door he had entered through. "Here's Mom now," Janice said.

Kelly turned to observe a tired and worried looking older lady walk through the door with a huge wicker basket. The younger woman set the photograph on the counter and rushed around to help the older woman. She grabbed the basket and set it on a picnic table in the display area.

"Mom, this is Sheriff Kelly, from Alabama. He's going to run for Oscar's position," Janice said. Rushing back to the counter, she grabbed the picture of Kelly's children and took it over to show her mother. "This is a picture of his family."

Kelly noticed the distress of her features slowly fading, as she studied the picture, to be replaced with what appeared to be a thoughtful smile. He couldn't get over the striking resemblance of the two women. Both were gorgeous looking strawberry blonds, and displayed nice figures and very good posture. The posture was apparent on Lilly, but was a little harder to detect on her daughter because of the loose fitting overalls.

"That's a beautiful family," Lilly declared, as she handed the photo back to Janice. "Be sure Roger sees this. Here come the rest of mine." A man, a boy and twin girls walked through the door. "You must share lunch with us." The man and children went to the restroom to wash their hands.

"What would you like to drink, iced tea or soda?" Janice asked.

"Iced tea will be just great," Kelly responded.

After her family had finished washing up, Lilly lined them up for introduction. "Sheriff Kelly, ah, is Kelly your first name or last name?" Lilly inquired.

Kelly chuckled, "I'm Sheriff Kelly Callahan, from Alabama," He said. "I'm planning to run for Oscar Thompson's job."

Noticing Rainy staring at his two stub fingers, Kelly held up his hand and said, "These two fingers got froze off on the Chosen Reservoir" Then looking at Rainy he continued, "so when your mother tells you to put your mittens on, during cold weather, listen to her."

Rainy flashed his winning smile as Roger stepped forward and extended his hand. "Roger Hartec," He said, as he and Kelly shook hands. "This is my wife, Lilly, and our oldest daughter, Janice Slocum. Janice just got married last month. Our oldest boy, Danny, is in the Army. This is our next son, Rainy, and last but certainly not least, our twin daughters, Marcy and Darcy."

"Pleased to meet you folks," Kelly said, as he started down the line shaking hands. *Janice was the spitting image of Lilly and obviously of Scandinavian descent. She's probably a daughter from a previous marriage. The other three children look more like Roger. Probably eastern European stock-German or Polish. They all had darker hair and brown eyes. Roger's eyes were green. Those three younger ones must have a different mother. The two women are much lighter and have blue eyes.*

"Come, sit down for lunch," Lilly said, as she opened the picnic basket. Janice fetched a pitcher of iced tea from a refrigerator, and a sleeve of Styrofoam cups from a box on top.

When they were all seated, and Roger had said the blessing, Janice handed Kelly's photograph to Roger. "This is a picture of Kelly's family," she said.

"After studying the picture, Roger chuckled. He looked over at his wife and said, "We have some catching up to do if we're going to keep up with the Callahan's."

Kelly noticed Lilly smiling. Then she said, "Yes, we have our work cut out for us. Where are you staying and how long will you be in the area?"

"I'm staying at that old hotel on the river," Kelly said.

"Oh my goodness," Lilly said, "the top two floors have been condemned. We must get you out of there."

"Yes Ma. Get Kelly out of there before the rats carry him away," Rainy chimed in.

"Rainy!" Lilly exclaimed, with a smile, as the twins giggled and Roger chuckled.

"We have a room you can use while you campaign," Lilly said. "Roger has a good office at home that you can use. You can call your wife every night if you wish. You are married, aren't you?"

"Oh yes, I've been married to the same Irish lass for over thirty years," Kelly said.

"I believe my headstrong wife is volunteering to be your campaign manager," Roger said, with a chuckle. "If you want to win this race, I suggest you accept her offer. No point in you wasting your money at the rat box. We'll put you up and feed you so you can concentrate on campaigning. Yours is going to be a tough row to hoe. You're going to need all the help you can get."

"Well sir, since you put it that way, you and your wonderful family have convinced me," Kelly said. "I'll accept your offer. What time should I show up on your door step?"

"We're usually home by five-thirty," Roger said. "When we're done with lunch, Rainy will draw a map for you. Won't you son?"

"You bet pop," Rainy said. "Our place can be hard to find. But I draw good maps."

"I'll bet you do son," Kelly replied, while flashing the boy a smile.

Kelly couldn't believe his luck *If he was successful in his run for sheriff, he was going to have to have a long talk with Oscar Thompson. Oscar obviously knew something when he sent me to Siding.*

When they finished lunch, Lilly said, "I'll be home in about an hour. You can come anytime this afternoon. The twins and I will do a little rearranging to get you set up."

Lilly hadn't told the twins about the threat to lose them. She was elated that Kelly was running for sheriff. *The picture of his family was a story in itself. Just about every race on the planet had to be represented in that photo. He obviously procured his family the same way she had procured hers. After they get Kelly settled in, she would invite his wife up to help Kelly campaign.*

"That has to be some remarkable women," Lilly said to the twins. "There must have been over twenty children in that photo. I'll show Mizzz Hargrove a thing or three," Lilly said to the bewildered twins. "I'll bet she gets no further with Kelly than she did with Oscar. Janice said Grandpa Oscar sent Kelly to see us."

Chapter 19. The Sheriff's Race.
Autumn, 1988

Kelly had moved in with the Hartecs. True to Roger's word, Lilly had thrown herself into the fray. The whole family was on board to get him elected sheriff. Kelly had volunteered for a "Meet the Candidate," night and felt he'd made a good impression. In just two weeks a run off election would be held to narrow the field to just two candidates for the General Election.

Lilly had conversed with Kelly's wife, Colleen, on several occasions when Kelly had called home. Although the two women had never met they really hit it off. Lilly had convinced Colleen that it was imperative for her to come to Minnesota and help the campaign. One night Kelly overheard Lilly tell Colleen, "This is a suspicious Scandinavian community. It takes these people a while to warm up to an outsider. The women can be convinced easier than the men. Once you gain the women's confidence, the men will fall into line." There was a pause and Kelly suspected Colleen was protesting the fact that she didn't have a clue about campaigning. "You don't need to know anything about politics. Just have pictures of all your children with you. Be prepared to answer a lot of questions about cooking and home making. This is a rural agriculture community. You just need to win their hearts. I think you can do that."

After Lilly hung up the telephone, she said to Kelly, "The run off probably won't be as tough as winning the general election. But we must throw full effort into the run off, or we won't get to the general election. Also, we want people's curiosity piqued after the primary, or runoff, to garner bigger crowds for our 'Meet the Candidate,' meetings. Your clear Irish ancestry and Southern accent are going to be handicaps we must surmount. These are good conservative people. However, we must overcome a strong preference for a local over an outsider. Colleen can be a big help here. She's very charming and if the women find her interesting and like her, you'll get their vote and most of their husbands as well. I think all she'll have to do is be her natural charming self. These people subscribe to the proverb, 'Birds of a feather flock together,' If they like Colleen, they'll like you. If we survive the primary, and we will, we're going to want to host long Saturday afternoon and late Friday night meetings. We'll want to give Colleen as much exposure as possible."

Colleen had agreed. Kelly would drive to Fargo to pick her up at the airport.

The Hartec's living room had become control central. Maps were marked and strategy charted. Cases of brochures were stacked behind furniture. The telephone was in constant use as somebody was calling people and setting up appointments for personal visits.

These meetings were charted so that the person making the call could make maximum contacts with minimum miles. Rainy was an organizational whiz when it came to plotting routes. The twins took turns with the rest, campaigning on the telephone.

Kelly was really proud with the way his wife fit in with this family. The children were already addressing her as Aunt Colleen. Colleen was the same height as Lilly and Janice, but much stockier. Light brown wispy hair framed a freckled face with bright green eyes and a pert Irish nose. Having watched the three women together gave Kelly some idea of what Lilly was talking about. Their Irish ancestry would definitely make them stand out in this community. He chuckled to himself as he thought about their children. *They had twenty-three, and not an Irishman in the bunch.*

This particular Saturday afternoon Kelly and Colleen had

finished their rounds early. Rainy had set them up with in-city routes. Lilly and Janice were working the south and west sides of the county, each with a twin in tow. Roger and Rainy worked the north and east side of the county, while Willie ran the lumberyard. Kelly and Colleen were in the living room putting together more brochure bundles for Sunday afternoon calls.

"Do you have any idea why this family has chosen you for Sheriff?" Colleen inquired.

"It seemed everything came together when I showed the picture of our children to Oscar Thompson," Kelly said. "Oscar insisted that I show the picture to Lilly. Then Harley Johnson, the Chief of Police, told me Oscar's plan was solid. Harley also made sure I set out for the Siding Lumberyard at the right time."

"This family can't be working this hard for us unless it means that our success will create success for them, somehow," Colleen stated. "What do you suppose their ultimate goal is?"

"I got some idea from Rainy," Kelly said "Lord, that is a lovable boy. You know, he's suppose to be fourteen."

"He sure is small for fourteen," Colleen said.

"He must be fourteen," Kelly said. "His voice has changed."

"But Roger is a big man," Colleen protested. "Maybe those aren't his biological children."

"Janice is Lilly's daughter by a previous marriage, or so it would seem," Kelly mused. "She doesn't call Roger dad. He must not be her father. A case could be made that the other three aren't their biological children either. Rainy made an offhand comment when I suggested he might be working to hard. He certainly was tired that night. He said to me, 'I'm going to do this last bundle because I don't want to lose my sisters.' I suspect he was talking about the twins."

"They do look like they are brother and sisters," Colleen said. "Same dark hair and soft brown eyes. Do you suppose some of the children are waifs that they don't have adoption papers for?"

"Could be," Kelly answered. "This is a rather cold climate for homeless children to survive. Can't be more than three months that they wouldn't die of exposure. However, they only have two or three, not twenty three like we have."

"You must check on Minnesota's abandoned children's laws as soon as you get a chance," Colleen said. "This state may not be as lenient as Alabama."

"Well, it's known as a socialist state," Kelly said. "They don't even recognize the two major political parties. It's Independent Republican or Democratic Farm Labor up here. It doesn't matter which party a Minnesota politician is in; they all lean toward socialism. The state constitution lists their citizens as subjects. It's the only state constitution that does that, as far as I know."

The first Hartecs to come home that afternoon were Lilly and Marcy. Next, Janice dropped off Darcy and went home. The twins came into the library to help Kelly and Colleen put together brochures in bundles for tomorrow's calls. Colleen went down to the Kitchen to help Lilly get supper for the hungry campaign workers.

"Roger and Rainy will be late," Lilly said. "They both can get tied up talking with the farmers. Rainy loves animals and Roger grew up on a farm. He could even be helping deliver a stuck calf as we speak. He's taught a lot of farm boys how to deliver calves that try to be born with one leg folded back. In the past, the farmer would call the veterinarian, and the vet would cut the calf out. Roger showed the farmers how to push the calf back. Then they can unfold the leg for a normal delivery. The farm boys have saved a lot of calves since Roger moved into the county. It goes better if a boy does it because their arms are smaller. One farmer, who only had daughters, couldn't do it himself because his arms were so large. One of his daughters wanted Roger to coach her. She insisted that several boys in school talked about how they delivered calves and she knew that she could do anything they could do. Roger told that girl that he was an equal opportunity instructor who was impressed by results. Jane handles the difficult deliveries on that farm."

"That's remarkable," Colleen said. "That's why you assigned that area to Roger and Rainy?"

"Oh yes, Roger is much better known on the north and east sides of the county in the hill country," Lilly said. "I, on the other hand, grew up and farmed with my late husband on the western side of the county in the prairie country, or 'The Valley,' as they say here.

Janice grew up in the city and knows kids from all over the county. They all go to high school in the city."

"That looks like Roger and Rainy turning into the driveway now," Colleen said, as she returned from setting the table in the dinning room.

"Good thing supper is done," Lilly said. "I'm sure the men will be hungry. Tomorrow will be the last day to campaign. Roger was suppose to secure a place for a 'Meet the Candidate' meeting tomorrow afternoon, somewhere in the northeast townships."

As they were eating, Lilly inquired about the meeting place for the next day.

"Orville Swanson offered his new machine shed in case it rains," Roger said. "It happened to be our first stop. I knew he was chairman of the township board. I inquired about a place. Orville said, 'Use my shed and I'll even furnish you a crowd. We're going to have a tub grinding demonstration tomorrow afternoon. The machine dealer and I are both unhappy with all the candidates. We heard you were supporting some new fellow from out of state. If he's your man he's probably our man. We would like to meet him.'"

"Heavens," Lilly said, "Did the Lord smile on you today or what?"

"The best part is, it was our first stop," Roger continued. "Every stop after that we got to tell the people about the meeting tomorrow afternoon. Orville said the tub grinder demonstration would draw up to thirty farmers, and generally lasted thirty to forty-five minutes. Orville said, 'be there before one-thirty p.m. before the crowd disperses. Maybe you telling folks about the sheriff candidate will bring more men for the grinding demonstration.'"

The following day, the Kelly Callahan campaign staff broke off passing out brochures to gather at the Orville Swanson farm. To their amazement, they had to park almost a half a mile from Orville's driveway. They had to park behind the cars that were lined up along the narrow township road. Then they had to walk about three quarters of a mile to get to Orville's shed. The farm lawn, all around the shed, was filled with parked cars.

By the time the campaign staff got to the new shed, the tub grinder demonstration was just concluding. It was an unusual crowd for a machine demonstration. A lot of women and children were there.

Orville came out of the crowd to meet Kelly and Roger. Roger introduced Kelly to Orville and Orville, with haste in his voice, said to Kelly, "Quick, get into the loader bucket and I'll lift you up a few feet over the crowd. It's a nice harvest day and the men all want to get into the fields this afternoon."

Orville lifted Kelly about four feet above the ground. Then from his perch on the tractor seat he yelled to the crowd, "This is the new sheriff candidate you folks been hearing so much about."

"Don't dump him into the grinder until we've had a chance to hear him speak," came a voice from the crowd, as everybody broke into laughter.

With the crowd in a jocular mood Kelly began his speech.

"Good afternoon folks. My name is Kelly Callahan. I've been in law enforcement ever since I got out of the Marine Corps after the Korean War. I've been the sheriff of the same district in Alabama for twenty-four years. I've been reelected five times. Now, you may be wondering why the heck does that crazy Irishman want to be sheriff up here in the Snow Belt. I'm going to give it to you straight. My wife, Colleen and I, she's the Irish lass standing next to Lilly Hartec over there." Kelly pointed toward his wife in the crowd. "Give them a wave of your hand, honey."

Lilly rose up on her tiptoes and pointed down toward a blushing Colleen, who smiled and waved to the crowd.

Most of the people yelled, "Hi, Colleen," and gave a cheer.

"Let's see, where was I?" Kelly asked.

"Why you want to move up to refrigerator land," came a response from the crowd.

"Yes, that's right. Thank you sir," Kelly continued. "We want to relocate here because we have an adopted son incarcerated in a Minnesota prison near here. No, we don't mean to spring him." Kelly had to wait for the laughter to subside. "However, he's still our son. While we can't save him from a lifetime in prison, we still have his soul to tend to. That would be impossible to do if we can't relocate here to Minnesota. The election is this coming Tuesday and I will sincerely appreciate your vote. I hope I've kept my speech short enough so you folks don't vote to have Orville dump me into the grinder."

The crowd broke into laughter. "Set him on the ground Orville. He'll do," several voices from the crowd, yelled in unison.

Orville set Kelly on the ground and escorted him over to a spot where most people would file by on the way to their vehicles.

Lilly escorted Colleen over to stand alongside Kelly. Most of the families lined up to shake hands with the Callahan's and take bundles of brochures from the Hartecs. Then they rushed home to work on the harvest.

Lilly had walked toward the far end of the line. She greeted people waiting to meet the Callahan's. She answered any questions the people wished to ask. She had overheard several people say, "He's just like Oscar Thompson."

"Well, what's the prognosis of my Campaign Manager?" Kelly asked Lilly at supper that night.

"I think our campaigning is done until Tuesday," Lilly said. "I believe you and Colleen can go home for some much needed rest. We've had those two other meetings in the western and southern townships. There are very few voters in the southeast. That's state park and a lot of lakes and lowland. Now all we can do is sit tight until the primary is completed. Then we'll see if we're still in the race."

"If that crowd today is any indication, we should make it through the primary," Roger said. "Almost everybody there got in line to shake hands with Kelly. The ones who didn't wait for the hand shake made sure they picked up our brochures as they rushed out."

"We'll rest up for a while and then start planning anew after the primary," Lilly stated. "I think Kelly and Colleen should spend the last two weeks before the general election up in this country. In the meantime, we'll keep the Callahan name on the front burner with signs and newspaper ads. The farmers don't appreciate campaigning when they're trying to wind up the harvest. We can get together with them the last two weeks in October. They're usually celebrating the harvest and receptive to campaigning."

"We should be able to line up meeting places at their familiar water holes," Roger said. "So, oil up your dancing shoes. I hope you folks like to play Bingo. Out on 'The Flats', it's dancing on Saturday night and Bingo on Sunday afternoons."

"We believe for the rural folks it will just be a matter of you folks rubbing elbows," Lilly said. "A short speech like the one you made today will be all that's necessary. By the way, that speech was a hit. The rural folks like to see the person they're going to vote for. They also appreciated your frankness in regard to your son. However, in the city it will be different. That's where we'll have to pick up the new votes spent on the other candidates. We'll want to program at least three meetings and those will be on Thursday nights. I think you must figure on three Thursday nights campaigning in the city just before the election."

"Are you going to be able to get that much time off?" Roger inquired.

"No problem," Kelly said. "I've got more vacation time than that coming. The County Board is happy to see me taking it. My Under Sheriff is running the shop now. He is running for my position. I've endorsed him."

"So, it is this job or no job," Lilly stated.

"That's about it," Kelly replied.

"We've put all our eggs in one basket on this one," Colleen agreed.

"We'll do our best to see that Kelly stays employed," Lilly stated.

Monday afternoon Lilly took the Callahans to the airport. The twins rode along. For the twins it was a tearful goodbye. Kelly and Colleen had won their hearts.

As Kelly and Colleen settled back in their seats for the ride home, Kelly said, "Orville Swanson told me I should make a good showing in that area. Roger Hartec helping me campaign is a big plus. He said, 'All the folks around here know it was Roger who saved most of our calf crop during the spring of seventy-six. I'd called Roger to work up an estimate and materials list to repair my calf barn. Roger showed up with the paper work when I was gone. My son, Teddy, had just brought a cow into calf when Roger arrived at the barn. Teddy could see that one leg was folded back and had headed to the house to call the vet. Roger told Teddy he would lose the calf if he called the vet. He told Teddy that he could show him how to save that calf. Roger and Teddy got a couple of buckets of warm water and they had the cow drink one bucket to help her relax. Then they used the other bucket to disinfect their arms. Roger showed Teddy how to push the calf back just a couple inches. Then Teddy reached in with one arm and cupping the calf's hoof in his hand, to protect the walls of the womb, he pulled the leg forward. Then he helped the cow with the delivery. Teddy showed me how to do it the next time, but Teddy was a lot better at it because his arms were smaller. Between the two of us we saved five calves that spring. That sure beat paying two hundred dollars to have them cut out. We also taught our neighbors how to do it.'"

"Orville also told me what the Hartec's interest in our winning is," Kelly said. "It seems the Social Services Director wants to take the twins away from the Hartecs. Oscar Thompson has prevented her from doing that. Orville said the Director was screwing over half of the other candidates running so that they would owe her, if any one of them became sheriff."

"Good gracious, politics can be confusing," Colleen said. "Will you be able to help Lilly keep those two lovely girls?"

"Well if I'm elected, I'll just have to find out how Oscar did it," Kelly said. "In the meantime, I'll have to crack the books on Minnesota's laws." Grasping Colleen's hand, the two leaned back in their seats and were soon asleep.

Lilly compiled the election results on paper. Kelly won by a wide margin. However, if all the votes cast for the eleven other candidates were to go to Kelly's opponent, Kelly could lose by a wide margin.

With the information printed in the newspaper, and a couple of calls to the Auditor's office, Rainy was able to map out areas that needed to be worked. Lilly and Roger formulated a strategy from Rainy's map.

The north and east side of the county went almost exclusively for Kelly. Lilly planned an elbow rubbing party as a courtesy to the voters of that area. A new supper club was opening up and the owner was a Kelly supporter. He wanted to host a 'Meet the Candidate' party in conjunction with his grand opening. Lilly scheduled that party the third Friday evening before the election.

The southern and western edge of the county had mostly gone for Kelly. Lilly set up meet the candidate parties with tavern owners. They scheduled elbow-rubbing opportunities in conjunction with Saturday night dancing and Sunday afternoon cards and Bingo games. These were set for the third and second weekends before the election.

Rainy had done the math and the charting. The city of Ashland Falls was Kelly's weak area. It also had the largest concentration of votes. In spite of the heavy support in the rural areas, Kelly would have to get seventeen per cent of the vote from the city just to break even. In the primary election he had only gotten three per cent of the vote.

"We've got our work cut out for us," Lilly told Kelly during a telephone call. "We planned on having three Thursday night meetings. We can get the meeting rooms at my church and Janice's church for two of the meetings. Roger is a member of the American Legion club, so we can get a couple of nights there. Rainy thinks we should spend the last Saturday night and Sunday afternoon in the city. We rented the college theatre for a Sunday afternoon blitz. I think we have everything under control here. You folks don't need to worry about anything. Just be here to hit the campaign trail the third Thursday before the election."

"You folks certainly have been wonderful," Colleen said. "I don't know how we'll ever repay you for all the help."

Lilly chuckled, "We've got a long way to go yet. Kelly can polish his charisma and speech making. The people up north are still talking about how Kelly packed so much information into such a short speech. They loved it. In the meantime, we'll keep your name in the news and on the street corners."

"We really appreciate all the hard work you're doing," Kelly said.

"Oh by the way, you'll be getting some forms in the mail to sign," Lilly said. "Then get those forms back to me. We started getting donations from the country folks. We had to form a campaign committee to spend the money."

"I'll get back to you with our arrival time at the Fargo airport," Kelly said. "God bless you folks and goodnight."

"Wait a minute," Lilly quickly stated. "We've been getting some rather large donations from down your way. Quite a few using the Callahan surname on the checks. I also got a letter from a Dallas, Texas law firm on some very prestigious-looking stationery. Enclosed were instructions on how the money could be spent and reported. There were six business cards enclosed also. I was instructed that if any officials question the reports I file; I was to give them a business card and tell them that that was the law firm representing Kelly. The law firm would handle all questions. I noticed one of the partners listed on the business card is a Callahan."

Kelly chuckled, "I understand that all our children are on board, especially since we got through the primary. They want to honor our wishes to be near Irvin."

Chapter 20. The Transition.
Winter 1988-89

The General Election was over. The Hartec family, with the Callahans, followed the election returns at the lumberyard the following Wednesday morning. The children had brought their lessons along. There were two laundry baskets full of food prepared by Lilly and Colleen. They planned on feeding the whole crew and any customers that might drop in throughout the day.

Rainy had gotten up early to get his schoolwork done. He wanted to follow the election returns when they started announcing them on the radio. Just after lunch it was announced that Kelly Callahan was the new Sheriff with forty nine per cent of the total vote. There was jubilation and hand shaking.

Later that afternoon, when the returns were final, Rainy finished his calculations. "We only got fourteen per cent of the vote from within the city," He said.

"How could we have won?" Lilly asked, as the rest of the group looked on in astonishment.

"Kelly got forty nine per cent of the total vote. Jordan got forty five percent of the total and the other six per cent, almost all of which were cast in the city, went to others in the write in section," Rainy explained.

Roger chuckled. "Some of the die-hards insisted on writing in the name of the one they voted for in the primary. Congratulations

Lilly. You just busted the favored lousy local boy over the efficient outsider syndrome. You're quite a General." He planted a kiss on her lips.

The Callahans had headed home the next day to sell their house and prepare for the move to Ashland Falls.

Lilly's life had settled back to a much slower pace. Kelly's compact but hard-hitting speeches had generated enthusiasm and many small donations. Also, there had been the larger donations from members of the Callahan family. The Elections Commission had inquired about those donations. Lilly had sent The Dallas law firm's business card to the Elections Commission in St. Paul and heard no more about it.

Per instructions, from the Dallas law firm, the considerable balance left over was donated to the Battered Women's Shelter. The reports had been filed with the State and the campaign committee's books were closed.

Horaito Bogarth had been expecting the call. His staff had done some preemptive work just for this contingency.

"Miz Hargrove on line one," His secretary said over the intercom.

"Hello Miz Hargrove," Horaito said, in his most pleasant voice.

"Well! You must have heard that red neck S.O.B. from Alabama was elected sheriff," Susan ranted.

"Yes I've heard that," Horaito replied. "I can't believe the Hartecs were actually able to pull that one off."

"Oh those two fancy stepping blonde bitches were out dancing with all the horny farmers in the county to pull it off," Susan continued her rant. "God damn it, I got out maneuvered. I was screwing the candidates and they were screwing the voters."

"Now, now, dear, calm thy self. It's water over the dam," Horaito said. "How would you like a professorship on a University of Minnesota campus?"

"Why would I want to leave this job?" Susan asked.

"Well----, this job would be more money, and you would be away from the Hartecs," Horaito soothed.

"It would be nice to get away from this bunch of ignoramuses who would actually elected a red neck sheriff," Susan whined. "Where is this campus located?"

"Torrance, it's down in the southwestern corner of the state," Horaito said.

"For Christ's sake! I know where the hell it is! That's even more rural than this fucking place," Susan screamed. "At least this fucking place is on an interstate highway."

"There's an interstate down there too," Horaito soothed. "Of course you will be a little further away from it."

"How far?" Susan snapped.

"Oh, it's less than thirty miles," Horaito cooed. "They'll be putting in another interchange soon. That will only be ten miles from the campus. That city is a little larger than where you are now. You only have a Junior College where you are."

"Now that's interesting," Susan begrudgingly admitted. "Tell me more. What subject will I have to teach?"

"Math, History, English or Social Studies. Which would you prefer?" Horaito asked.

"Huh, I had to screw my Math and English professors for grades," Susan mused. "I did well in Social Studies. I had a female professor there, so I had to study." Susan giggled.

"Well I hadn't realized you were that discerning," Horaito chuckled.

"Fuck you. You know damn well I'm not lesbian," Susan retorted.

"That's why you'll like this campus," Horaito cooed. "The boys outnumber the girls two to one. I've heard the male population is so desperate that most of them lose their virginity to heifer calves."

"Yech! That's supposed to be a good thing?" Susan asked.

"Well the last time I was through the area, I noticed a lot of happy heifers," Horaito said, "That's got to say something for the plumbing stature of the male population."

"And when would I start this job?" Susan inquired.

Good, she's starting to show interest. "Oh----, I could get you started right after the year-end holidays," Horaito said.

"Good, I'm ready for something different," Susan said. "It'll be good to get back to a U of M campus. When your wife starts having headaches, you can always come to the campus to make a speech."

"Well I'll certainly keep that in mind," Horaito said. *Not on your life, bitch,* Horaito hung up the telephone. *Still----.*

Buzzing his secretary, Horaito said, "Daniel, please come to my office."

Daniel stepped through the door, closing it behind him. "Did she go for it?" he asked.

"Hook, line and sinker," Horaito replied. "Is your kid brother still horny enough to fuck a rattlesnake?"

"If he can get somebody to hold its head," Daniel snorted.

"Jeez, does your brother have any redeeming qualities?" Horaito asked.

"Oh yes, that's why I selected him," Daniel assured. "He's a very sharing kind of guy."

"How's that a good thing?" Horaito quizzed.

"Well Chief, they don't allow calves in the dorms," Daniel explained. "Susan will get miles of country sausage." Both men chuckled. "Also, there are a lot of cowboys from the western side of the Dakotas. They all think of themselves as Rough Riders. I hope your Susan is smart enough to have them remove their spurs." Both men laughed.

Horaito suppressed a winch at the "Your Susan" comment. Daniel had a tendency to tie the two of them together. Horaito didn't know if it were intentional. He thought it would be better not to broach the subject right now. Daniel was much too valuable and smart to risk upsetting.

The Callahans had moved to Ashland Falls and rented an apartment. Kelly had taken on his new responsibilities and spent a lot of time studying Minnesota's statues, and County ordnances. He met several times with the County Attorney.

Kelly had also spent a lot of time with Oscar Thompson during the transition phase. The two men had become good friends. They were able to conduct a couple of business meetings with, Chief of Police, Harley Johnson. Consequently, Kelly and Harley were able to get to know each other. After Kelly had taken office, he asked Oscar Thompson to meet with him at the Sheriff's office.

"Damn, it sure feels good to sit on this side of that desk," Oscar said, as he sat down in the stuffed swivel chair opposite Kelly.

"I would like you to fill me in on the Hartecs," Kelly said. "Colleen and I know that it was their efforts that got me elected. The twins call my wife Aunty Colleen and me Uncle Kelly. We do fill like part of their extended family."

"The Hartecs have a way of doing that," Oscar chuckled. "Welcome to the family. Jenny and I are the Hartec children's Grandparents. The children adopted us. We had an adoption ceremony at our church. The Hartecs threw a party afterwards. The other set of Grandparents are Sam and Lori Gustafson. You must have met both of them on the campaign trail."

"Let me guess," Kelly said, "Janice and Danny are Lilly's children by a previous marriage. We thought Rainy and the twins were Roger's children, but were told those three were waifs Roger and Lilly picked up."

Again Oscar chuckled. "Partially right. Actually, Janice and Danny are Roger's wards. Their father, who was an alcoholic, was a friend of Roger's. His band played at the Hartec's wedding. Clayton Shore died during the spring of eighty-five. Years before he died, he had left the raising of Danny and Janice to Roger. Clayton had crawled into a bottle about a year after his wife died."

"I'll be darned," Kelly said. "Colleen will be interested in knowing that."

"Anyway, the major problem the Hartecs were having seems to have solved itself, right after the elections," Oscar said. "The Social Services Director meant to take legal action to remove the twins from the Hartec family. After the election she took a teaching position at U of M Torrance. She transferred during the holidays. I understand she was spending a lot of time at the YWCA exercising right after the elections. Was supposed to have lost twenty-five pounds."

"That's a relief," Kelly said. "I've been boning up on Minnesota's laws. Pardon me for saying so, but this state is really chicken shit when it comes to abandoned children. Shucks, Colleen and

I just picked up all twenty-three of our children. If we had any extraordinary medical expenses, we just sent the bills over to the welfare department and they took care of it."

"Well it's not that way here," Oscar said. "The state gets more intrusive every year. The politicians have the citizens fooled."

"Subjects, according to Minnesota's constitution," Kelly corrected him.

"Well we were admitted into statehood by a bunch of socialists," Oscar confirmed.

Kelly chuckled. "It shows."

"However, the national attention this election drew has changed the climate in this county," Oscar said. "There's been a slight pull back. It's like somebody in St. Paul wants to sweep this election under the rug and out of the headlines."

"What makes you think that?" Kelly inquired.

"The first day the new Social Services Director arrived in town, he came to see me," Oscar said. "He's a family man. He informed me that his primary concern was that the children were being properly cared for. He asked me if the Hartec children were being properly cared for, and how did I know that. I told him those children are in excellent hands. I know that for a fact. Those children have adopted me as their Grandfather. I interact with them all the time. He slammed his folder shut and said, 'Case closed, have a good day, Sheriff.' Then he left."

"That's certainly a relief," Kelly said. "Thank God that's over with."

"But, there's something you need to know about the Hartecs," Oscar said. "The first thing you need to know is Roger's name isn't Roger Hartec. Nobody knows his real name. His identity was changed by the C.I.A. after the war. He took out some big shot in North Vietnam. They're still after him."

Kelly chuckled. "When we were campaigning, some old fellow said to me, 'yep, in the old days, Roger was a real artist when it came to pissing people off.' He hinted at a scrape that Roger had with the Attorney General's office."

"That would explain the efforts coming out of St. Paul to get this year's election news off the front burner," Oscar said. "You won't experience much dull time in office with Roger in your bailiwick. You see, Roger killed one would be assassin in his wood lot, with his chain saw. That was the second year he lived here. Lilly knows nothing about any of this. Several war veterans on both forces are privy to this information. We suspect there will be another attempt on Roger's life. They quietly watch and check out any new Asians that move into the area."

"You have any suspicious ones right now?" Kelly asked.

"Actually we do," Oscar replied. "There's a fellow running several laundries in the area. We suspect he is forcing new Asian immigrants to work for him. Our background checks revealed he worked for the C.I.A. as a double agent. He was granted citizenship after the fall of Saigon."

"And I suppose, like all double agents, it's hard to determine which side he was the most faithful to," Kelly said.

"Exactly," Oscar intoned. "We're sure this one is into white slavery and who knows what else. We've collected nearly enough evidence for the white slavery charges. Once we can charge him and do some questioning, we'll find out what he knows about Roger. But I guess that's your problem now. Deputy Anderson will be able to fill you in. It's time I got home. Jenny says she can't tell that I'm retired yet. I'm going to take her to the Florida Keys before the end of January. We tried leaving earlier, but that blizzard delayed our plans."

Standing up, Oscar reached to shake Kelly's hand. "Best of luck to you, Sheriff. Deputy Anderson will fill you in on the Asian Connection. He'll introduce you to the other deputies and officers involved. There are only a select few actually involved. We want to protect Roger's family from the publicity."

After Oscar left, Kelly inquired into the where about of Deputy Anderson.

"He's on patrol," The Dispatcher said. "Want me to call him? Chief."

"No, just get a message to him that I would like to meet with him in my office at the end of his shift," Kelly said. "It shouldn't take long, probably fifteen minutes. He can try to come off patrol a little early if possible."

Kelly spent the rest of the day handling routine paper work. He also inspected the rest of the department while chit chatting with the employees on duty. Near the end of the shift, he went back to his office to receive Deputy Anderson. Earlier, Kelly had pulled Anderson's personnel file and studied it. He had done this with all the personnel after being sworn in as sheriff. Anderson was a veteran of the Vietnam War. His college education had been interrupted when he was drafted in nineteen sixty-six. He had spent two years in the Army-one year in combat.

"Come in," Kelly said, in response to the knuckle rap on his office door. Getting out of his chair, Kelly walked around the desk with his hand extended to greet the deputy.

"Good afternoon chief," Deputy Anderson said, as he shook Kelly's hand.

Gesturing toward the guest's chair, Kelly said, "Have a seat. Would you like a soda or a cup of coffee?"

"No thanks," the deputy said. "I'm saving space for a beer. I always have one beer after getting off shift."

"Not a bad idea," Kelly chuckled. "Let's see, your name is Donald Anderson. You've been with the department since shortly after your discharge in sixty-eight."

"Yes sir, will have twenty years in this summer," Donald said.

"You're married, three children, all in high school," Kelly stated. "Hobbies include woodworking."

"Yes, I make and sell furniture, doodads, gizmos and puzzles," Donald said. "Sell all my stuff at craft fairs. Made almost all the furniture in our house. My wife sees a picture of something she likes; she gives me the picture and tells me about how big she wants the piece to be. I draw it on graph paper and make it."

Solid, both feet on the ground, Kelly thought. Donnie was of slender build, dark blonde hair nearly brown. He was over six feet tall, and in a neatly tailored uniform. *His wife probably did the tailoring of the uniform.*

"I understand you're the person in charge of collecting information about the Hartec-Asian Connection," Kelly said.

"Yes I am," Donald said. "We don't get a chance to get close to Dong because he's mostly within the Police's jurisdiction. Officer

Randy Slocum keeps me up to date constantly. Randy's got a dog in the fight, so to speak."

Kelly's eyebrows shot up. "Oh! How's that?" he asked.

"Randy's son, Willie, is married to Roger's oldest daughter, Janice," Donald said. "The kids both work for Roger."

"Um, that's right," Kelly said. "Janice told me she was married. I don't believe I had ever heard mention of her last name, although I must have. We were busier than one-armed paperhangers back then. I understand you had a suspect."

"Still have," Donald said. "But we lost our witness, an old Vietnamese woman. She got lost in a blizzard week before last and froze to death. She almost made it to her back door."

"Suspect any foul play?" Kelly inquired.

"Randy didn't think so," Donald said. "She had a routine. That routine would have put her walking home from the market at the time of the blizzard. The frozen groceries were found next to her body."

"So it's back to square one?" Kelly inquired.

"That's about it Chief," Donald said. "However, her death may enhance our case."

"How's that?" Kelly asked.

"Now that the old woman is gone, three other women and a man have stepped forward," Donald said. "Randy speaks some Vietnamese. They contacted him when they realized their only contact wasn't available to us anymore. It's going to take a while to put a case together again. Randy thinks we'll end up with a much stronger case than we had with the one old woman."

"How's this case affect Roger?" Kelly asked.

"Randy suspects Dong is actually after Roger," Donald said." But Dong doesn't know who Roger is. Dong apparently suspects Roger lives in this area. Dong has three laundries, one here, one in Fargo and one on Grand Forks Air Force base. His head quarters are in Fargo."

"But Dong spends most of his time down here," Kelly speculated.

"That's it," Donald said.

"How many men on the two forces are privy to the Asian Connection?" Kelly asked.

"Four deputies, six police officers besides Randy," Donald said. "Sidings off the beaten track between here and Fargo. However, it's on a truck route. Fortunately, what little lumber Dong uses he gets from a yard in the city. Nobody has ever seen him on the truck route. He always takes the interstate to Fargo where he lives."

"Let's hope it stays that way," Kelly said.

"We'll nail the little bastard," Donald said. "Randy's small in stature. We suspect that's why the Vietnamese looked him up. Larry Hansen speaks better Vietnamese, but he's a big black fellow with a deep voice. We suspect the Vietnamese find him scary. We've got four of them jabbering to Randy. We only had one old woman before."

"I'm glad to hear that," Kelly said. "Keep me posted on your progress, will you?"

"You bet Chief," Donald said. "I'm happy to know you're on board."

"You bet I am," Kelly said.

"Good, we'll have a chance to even the score a little," Donald, mused aloud.

"How's that?" Kelly asked.

"Well we figure we weren't allowed to win the big war. If we can make sure Roger dies peacefully, of natural causes, it'll be a huge victory for our small force here," Donald said. "All the men privy to the Asian Connection are dedicated to that. Some haven't even met Roger yet. They're all combat veterans though. They'll carry the load for the long haul."

That evening Kelly took Colleen in his arms. "Do I ever have a story to tell you," He said. "Our friends, the Hartecs, have bigger problems than any of them even know about."

"And I have some news for you," Colleen said, "But you first."

"I need a beer to wet my whistle first," Kelly said. "Would you like one also?"

"Sure," Colleen replied.

With their beers the two settled down in their recliners in the living room.

"It seems Roger was recruited by the C.I.A. to be a sniper in Vietnam," Kelly said. "He was in that business for two years, and was highly successful. Since the communists won, and took over all of South Vietnam, they have the resources to retaliate against those they feel inflicted the most damage."

"Their version of the Nuremberg Trials?" Colleen questioned.

"That's about it," Kelly answered. "As with any war, vengeance belongs to the victors."

"Oh Lord, is the whole family in danger?" Colleen inquired. "I've gotten so attached to them."

"Donald didn't think so," Kelly said. "Donald is going to arrange a meeting with Randy Slocum at a tavern some evening. Randy Slocum is the police officer in charge of what they refer to as the Asian Connection."

"Pray tell, what is the Asian Connection," Colleen asked.

"It's about a dozen law enforcement personnel on both forces," Kelly said. "All are combat veterans. They've taken it upon themselves to make sure Roger isn't assassinated. Harley Johnson, the Chief of Police and Oscar are part of the group, and now I am."

"What do they do?" Colleen asked.

"They birddog all the Asians that move in or come through the area," Kelly said. "They do some real in dept investigations without the person knowing about it. Roger doesn't even know about the one they're tracking now. Lilly and the rest of his family don't even have a clue that he's a hunted man."

"Does Roger know he's a target?" Colleen inquired.

"Roger killed the first would be assassin in his woodlot with a chainsaw," Kelly said.

"Oh my Lord! Why isn't the C.I.A. protecting him?" Colleen asked.

"They are," Kelly responded. "They've changed his name and his real identity appears to be totally lost. There's absolutely no record of his military service, other then an Air Defense Command form saying he spent over four years in the United States Air Force. However, after the war the C.I.A.'s budget was cut and that's the extent of his protection."

"What kind of chance does he have?" Colleen asked.

"Hard to say," Kelly said. "The boys of the Asian Connection think a would be assassin is operating a business just eight miles from Roger's lumberyard. The assassin's been there for twelve years and hasn't made the connection yet. What's your news?"

"When Maureen and her husband were here for Christmas, we went house shopping," Colleen said. "We found this big old mansion on the south side of the city. It has twenty two rooms."

"Oh Lord," Kelly chuckled. "We can't afford a twenty two room mansion."

"You're right dear," Colleen said, "but our children can. They want to do this for us. All we have to do is sign the papers and move in, when they finish restoring it.

Chapter 21. Harley's Dilema.
Spring, 1989

P olice Chief Harley Johnson sat at his desk bouncing a long wooden pencil, on its erasure, as he rotated it between his fingers. *This should be it,* he thought, as he looked at the notes he had prepared. *Not much to talk about.* He got up from his desk to go to the monthly strategy session he held the first Monday of every month.

Harley entered the conference room to find all the officers, he could expect, already assembled. The officers working the night shift had stayed over.

"This being the month of May, it's the usual spring stuff," Harley said. "High school kids acting rowdy, and the usual drinking parties to deal with. Some of you younger officers will be tempted to join the party, but don't." Several of the men chuckled.

"Next item is the influx of fisherman with the season opener during the middle of this month," Harley continued. "Remember, they bring revenue into the county for our paychecks. Be polite, courteous and helpful. Boat trailer taillights are always a problem. Write them a repair ticket and direct them to the nearest business that offers repair service. They will appreciate spending their money on a repair rather than paying a fine. We still get the money, just have to wait a little longer for it, and we've made a friend."

At this point in the meeting one of the officers coming on shift threw a newspaper on the table in front of the Chief. "Have you seen this?" he asked.

The top half of the front page was a full color photograph of a group of people repairing the old Wright Mansion.

Harley was aware of the hard feelings generated by last fall's election of Kelly Callahan for sheriff. Several of his officers had run for the job and prejudices still ran high because an outsider had been elected.

According to the story, the city had sold the mansion to the Callahans for five hundred dollars. The Callahan's had to agree to restore it while remodeling. It was on the register of Historic Homes, so there were strict rules involved in the remodeling.

Harley suspected that the picture was full color, which the newspaper seldom ever used, because it would expose the races of Kelly and Colleen's children. There were all colors of the human race represented.

Harley held the paper up so all could see the picture, and chuckled, "Look at that group of kids. There's not and Irishman in the bunch."

"Yeah, makes you wonder what all Kelly's been sticking his dick into," Carl Schneider sneered.

The room fell silent. Then Randy Slocum picked up his cap and equipment and walked out. Following Randy were Larry Hansen and the other two black officers on the force. Then about a third of the officers present did the same.

Harley recognized the ones leaving as veterans, orphans or both.

"What did I say? What did I say, that got them so pissed?" Carl asked. "I was just trying to make a joke. What did I say that was so wrong?"

"Not a thing, son. Not a thing," Harley chuckled.

"What about those men who left the meeting early?" Chuck asked. "Will they get demerits?"

"Meeting was over with," Harley responded. "We can't force them to listen to crap. The rest of you can skedaddle."

Smiling, Harley returned to his office. He figured Carl's remark would have repercussions throughout the law enforcement community. *In all bad there's some good.* He suspected that before the end of the day, something was going to be done to welcome the Callahans to the community.

An hour later, as Harley was finishing his reports, his secretary forwarded a call from Randy Slocum. "Hello," Harley said into the receiver.

"Hello Chief," Randy said. "I got in touch with Donnie Anderson about a welcome aboard party for the Callahans."

"What do you fellows have in mind," Harley asked.

"We thought a barbeque and beer bust this Saturday at noon," Randy replied. We'll invite that whole crew remodeling the Wright Mansion over for dinner. We'll invite all officers and deputies not on duty that day via the bulletin board. We need to do it this Saturday because the fishing opener is next Saturday."

"Where are you planning on having it?" Harley asked.

"Well," Randy hesitated, "here's where you come in. We thought we should have it at the Hartecs. There're a lot of law enforcement personnel who should meet Roger as well as Kelly. After all, Lilly and Roger are responsible for Kelly being here. We're kind of hoping that we could get you to set that up for us."

"Kind of short notice for Lilly," Harley said. "However, it's a fantastic idea. I'll get in touch with Lilly as soon as I get off the phone with you. Maybe I can get her to take care of getting the construction crew out there for dinner."

"Tell Lilly we'll take care of everything else," Randy said. "We'll bring the food, tables and chairs. All we need is real estate, bathrooms and a little electricity."

"Gottcha," Harley responded. "I'll get right on it."

Lilly had jumped at the chance of helping host the party, especially since her burden would be so light.

Furthermore, she welcomed the chance to visit with Lennie Callahan. She had been over to the remodeling project many times with Colleen. Of all the Callahan children, Lilly enjoyed talking with Lennie the most. Lennie was tall, thin and black as the ace of spades. He had a flashing white-toothed smile, and was a happy youngster full of jokes and jibes-a practical joker. His wife, Camille, was equally pleasant.

About ten Saturday morning the deputies began to arrive with the tables, chairs, picnic utensils and a keg of beer on ice. They set up a couple of tables inside the garage along the north wall. That wall had several electric outlets for the roaster ovens. Two more tables were set up in the center of the garage to form a serving line. Two deputies tied a banner over the garage door that proclaimed, "Welcome aboard Sheriff Callahan". By eleven-thirty they had everything set up and ready. Soon after members of the building crew began to arrive.

About the time Lennie and Camille approached Lilly, all three heard the plaintive wail from the police officer, Larry Hanson, inside the garage.

"Oh Lord, I should have know better than to try a new recipe for this party," Larry said.

"What's wrong with it dear?" his wife, Jean asked.

"Just taste it," Larry said, as he held a forkful of shredded beef for her.

"You're right dear, it's tasteless," Jean agreed.

"No zip at all," Larry wailed. "I didn't think there were enough spices in that recipe."

"You better help the poor man," Camille said, to Lennie.

As Lilly and Camille followed Lennie over to the table, Camille said, "Lennie has won several barbeque cook offs in Atlanta. He doesn't have a recipe. He just slops stuff together."

"There's a barbeque in distress here?" Lennie asked.

"Yes, it's flat, no zip," Larry said. He held a forkful of shredded beef out for Lennie to taste.

Lilly was amused at the sight. Lennie and Larry were the same tone of black. However, Larry was a giant of a man-especially standing next to skinny Lennie.

"This can be made into something good," Lennie said, after having sampled the beef. "It's well cooked and shredded to just the right texture. Shredded meat is much better than ground meat. It takes more time to do it this way, but well worth the effort."

"It's the first time I've tried the shredded meat," Larry said. "This recipe was quite a bit different from others I've used."

"Well Miss Lilly, if I can make use of your kitchen for about ten minutes, I'll put together a sauce," Lennie said. "Thankfully, what Larry has here is dry. I can add about two quarts of my sauce and we'll be in business."

"Sure thing," Lilly said. She knew it was no use trying to persuade Lennie into calling her just Lilly without the Miss. He had insisted that she looked just like a Miss Lilly.

"Can Larry have a copy of your recipe?" Jean asked.

"Sure," Lennie said, with a chuckle, "but he'll need a pencil and paper. It'll be the first time it's ever been written down."

Lilly escorted both men into the basement and to the elevator that took them up to the kitchen. "Nice," both men commented as they stepped out of the elevator.

"I'll need a bowl that will hold about a gallon that I can put in the microwave," Lennie said.

Lilly got the bowl and a mixing whip for Lennie. Then she opened the door in front of her spice supply. She gave a couple of recipe cards and a ballpoint pen to Larry.

Lilly and Larry watched as Lennie was putting ingredients in a bowl. Brown sugar, flour, an assortment of spices, tomato paste, Worcestershire sauce, a lot of vinegar and some taco sauce and seasoning. "I'm subbing the hot taco sauce for pureed jalapeno pepper I would normally use," Lennie said.

Lennie had added water and combined all the ingredients into slurry. He put it into the microwave oven and heated it to a near boil. He had to stop the oven several times to stir the mixture. "Did you get all that?" Lennie asked Larry, who was finishing writing on the back of the second card.

"Yes I did," Larry said as he tucked the two cards into his pocket. "Thank you."

"You can take this down and stir it into the meat," Lennie said, as he handed the bowl to Larry. "I'll help Miss Lilly put this stuff away and clean up her kitchen."

"Not much cleaning to do here, Lennie," Lilly chuckled. "You didn't use any measuring utensils. Just a matter of putting everything back in the cabinet, and a quick wipe of the counter top will do it."

"I'll take this down and get it stirred into the meat," Larry said, as he headed for the elevator with the bowl of sauce.

It's really wonderful what you folks are doing for Kelly and Colleen," Lilly said, as she put the different containers into the cabinet and Lennie wiped the counter top.

"It's time we started helping back," Lennie stated. "If it weren't for Mom and Dad, we kids probably would never have had the chance they gave us. Probably none of us would be where we are today. Shucks, at least six of their children are millionaires."

"You're kidding!" Lilly exclaimed.

"No, it's true," Lennie said. "Mom and Pop don't even realize it. I know because I'm an investment banker and I handle their accounts. Years ago, we children set up a retirement account for them. We could see that they would just keep raising children. They just didn't seem to ever contemplate the consequences of old age. Ten years from now, when it's time for Pop to retire, their youngest will just be leaving the nest. Mom and Pop have never given any thought to themselves. It's always been the children. Not only that, there's Grandma and Grandpa who they take care of. They're living with Mom's sister now. They will be coming up when the mansion is finished."

"How many children are still in school?" Lilly asked.

"Six," Lennie said. "Seventeen of us are on our own-all doing well except Irvin. The millionaires are among the oldest. We've architects, contractors and lawyers in about every field in our family. One of my sisters is handling the planning and scheduling. We hope to have the old house ready before school starts in the fall."

"That's wonderful," Lilly said. "How has Kelly been doing in his efforts with Irvin?"

"That's not going so good," Lennie said. "Sometimes Dad thinks it was a mistake to move up here. Irvin is bitter and reluctant to allow to Dad see him, but he does. Dad really would be heartbroken if he didn't. Irwin was the oldest child Dad and Mom tried to help. He was almost a teenager when they got him. He had been running with a gang who were all sent to prison. The rest of us tried to convince him how lucky he was to be in our family. However, he preferred stealing to working."

"How old were you when they took you in?" Lilly inquired.

"I was left on their door step in a cardboard box as an infant," Lennie said. "I kid my older sister, she's the one handling the planning and scheduling, that she came from affluence. She was left on their doorstep in a wicker basket."

Lilly chuckled at Lennie's joke. "All of our children are adopted to," She said. "In spite of rough beginnings, they've all developed a sense of humor. Of course, Roger sees some humor in just about everything. The humor is wonderful."

"Yes, it is," Lennie agreed. "There's so much in the world to be really thankful for."

"There truly is," Lilly said, as auto horns began honking. "The guests of honor must've arrived. We must go down to greet them."

As they entered the garage they both looked over at the end of the table where Larry had his barbeque. He had just finished stirring it and was putting the lid back on the roaster. When Larry saw Lennie and Lilly, he smiled and gave them the two thumbs up signal.

Roger was drinking beer with Oscar, Harley and Sam. Lilly went over to greet him. "It was really slow at the yard this morning," He said. "The weather is so nice; everybody must be doing lawn work."

Just then a bunch of deputies broke into a rendition of, "He's a Jolly Good Fellow," and the rest of the crowd joined in.

Oscar Thompson said the blessing and a prayer of thanks. The Hartec's extended family had picked up on Roger's policy of saying the thanks up front. Then the people lined up behind Kelly and Colleen to dish up their lunch.

Later, Lilly noticed Lennie, Larry and their wives dining together and in animated conversation. The men were pulling out their wallets to display pictures. Soon the wives were into their purses and even more pictures came out.

Lilly nudged Roger with her elbow, "I believe this party is going to be a huge success. The police officers and deputies and their families are interacting well with the Callahans," She said.

"Yes they are," Roger agreed. "I over heard several making arrangements to take members of the construction crew fishing on the opener next weekend. I hope it wasn't in their plans to work on the mansion next weekend."

"According to Lennie, this crew has one more week to work," Lilly said. "Then, they will be replaced by another crew. There are sixteen families involved in the project. Colleen said that all She and Kelly had to do was sign the paper work. They will move in, once the project is completed. Their Children insisted that it was time they accepted this gift from them."

"There's a bunch of building contractors in the family," Roger said. "They seem to know the business well. They're ordering and purchasing everything through our yard. Willie has been writing special orders left and right. They aren't sparing any expense. They pick out what they want and order it. If Willie hasn't heard of something they want-they give him the name and address of the company to order from. Willie insists he's developing a lot of new sources for materials."

"Colleen said they only paid five hundred dollars for the mansion, because it was owned by the city and was on the Historic Register," Lilly said. "They have stringent rules to follow in the remodeling of it. However, one of their daughters is in the restoration business out east. That daughter said that the midwestern jobs were a piece of cake."

"They're buying materials to make it maintenance free as much as possible," Roger said. "They're allowed to use steel siding as long as it resembles the original wood siding. The windows are all special order, because the originals were divided lights. The new ones they ordered are all insulated glass-expensive!"

"It sounds like the good Lord's decided to shower favors on the Callahans for all the sacrifices they've made all their lives," Lilly said. "All those children they took in wouldn't have had much of a chance, if they hadn't landed on the Callahan's door step, literally."

And so it went. The law enforcement community rallied around the Callahans. As one bunch left and the next bunch arrived, a picnic was arranged and weekend activities were planned between individual families, according to family interests.

Lilly and Roger had paid calls to different family members at the campground where they set up their vacation vehicles. "There is no doubt that there is affluence in that family," Lilly declared. "But you would never know it by just meeting them on the job site. They're all so down to earth and industrious."

Chapter 22. Roger's Revelation. Summer, 1991

Early on a Monday morning, Police Chief, Harley Johnson had puzzled as to how he could put a meeting together between Roger Hartec and himself. He would need Oscar Thompson and Sheriff Callahan present. He didn't want Roger's family to know about it.

Finally, Harley decided to make a personal call on Sheriff Callahan at the Sheriff's office. He didn't want to use the telephone system. Hot news always became public information. Together, the two men had decided Kelly would pay a visit to Roger at the lumberyard. They thought this wouldn't raise any suspicions. The yard was in the county and in Kelly's jurisdiction. Also, deputies stopped in for coffee on a regular basis. A Sheriff's squad car at the yard wouldn't be anything unusual.

"I'll call on Roger sometime today and make arrangements," Kelly said.

"Oscar says we can meet in his travel trailer on Mosquito Lake," Harley said. "He had left it set up out there for fall hunting. He didn't plan to travel with it this summer."

"Okay, I'll see if we can make it work," Kelly stated. "We're all going to have to come up with excuses to keep this private."

Harley received a visit from Kelly the next afternoon. "Roger suggested next Sunday afternoon," Kelly said. "He was supposed to have a meeting with a family about a new house at Trenton Mills.

The party called and cancelled, but Roger hasn't told his family about the cancellation yet. They were all disappointed because of the water ski show being held Sunday afternoon. I believe that would be the best time. We must come up with good excuses to miss the show ourselves."

"That shouldn't be hard for me," Harley said. "My family is use to being disappointed because of my job. I'm usually on duty for high profile weekend activities."

"Oscar says he hasn't been to the last few shows since he started fishing again," Kelly stated. "Jenny usually goes with some friends while he goes fishing."

"Well Kelly, if you can make it, it's a go," Harley said.

"I can make it," Kelly said. " I'll get back to Roger."

The following Sunday, the four men met at Mosquito Lake on Roger's private property. Oscar brought a can of gasoline for the generator and a cooler of iced beer for the men.

"Seems retirement is agreeing with you real well," Harley said, as he observed Oscar gassing up the generator.

"Well enough not to be without air conditioning," Oscar chuckled. "The mosquitoes have our scent and are moving in." He set the gas can down and swatted at a mosquito. "Hope the battery is still good." Oscar pushed the starter button and the engine roared to life. "Hurry, let's get inside." Both men were swatting mosquitoes as they rushed for the door. Once inside, Oscar closed four air vents and got the air conditioning going. "Not bad in here yet, but it's early." Cracking four beers open and setting them on the table in front of the four of them, Oscar said, "meeting called to order." All the men chuckled.

"Roger, this is about you," Harley said. "We've put the Ding Dong Gang away. However, there's been a slight hitch. Dong only got ten years and could be out in four. We believe he's after you."

"Where the hell did you come up with the moniker Ding Dong Gang?" Oscar snickered. "Sounds like a venereal disease."

The other men laughed. "I suppose I better fill you in first," Harley said. Looking at Kelly, he continued, "Oscar and Roger probably haven't heard much about Dong and his slave business. Dong is the old man's name. My officers took to calling his son

Ding, because his real name is long and hard to pronounce. Both are in prison. Ding probably for life. We had a laundry list of charges against him." Kelly, Harley and Oscar chuckled at Harley's last statement.

"That's the outfit that had all those laundries around the country," Oscar explained to Roger.

"Yeah, Ding had extended the business onto Grand Forks Air Force Base without his father knowing about all of the details," Harley said. "He created more laundry business for the firm by providing prostitutes for the G. I.s in the barracks."

"Well! That was damn noble of him," Oscar joked and all the men chuckled.

"When we interrogated them, Dong tried to separate himself from the prostitution part of the business," Harley said. "He insisted he had little knowledge of the North Dakota part of the operation. We convinced Ding that his old man was trying to throw him under the bus. He would take the fall for the slavery part of the operation. Boy did that kid sing! The old man handled the hiring scams and human traffic part for labor. Dong maintained that his part was limited to cheap labor for his laundries. Ding had extended into the prostitution aspect without Dong's knowledge. Ding ran that business off the books and kept all the profits. Dong was pissed when he realize how much money he'd been screwed out of. Ding also had a drug business going as well. That's why he got such a stiff sentence," Harley concluded.

"How does Roger figure in all this?" Oscar asked.

"When we were interrogating Ding, he kept hinting that his old man was into the snuffing business as well," Harley explained. "He bragged that the old man was going to be paid from two sources on the next hit. Ding had this picture because he was supposed to help his father locate the target. Here it is," Harley pulled a picture out of his shirt pocket and slid it across the table to a spot between Oscar and Roger. "Kelly's seen it."

"Holy crap! Roger! That's a damn clear picture of you," Oscar exclaimed.

It was a picture of Roger in jungle fatigues. He was standing next to a pole with his left hand extended up on the pole. In his right hand he held an M-1. He was wearing bandoliers of ammunition and hand grenades.

"That picture was taken at a firebase overlooking no-mans land," Roger said. "That's the flag pole you see my hand on. I did not pose for that picture. It was taken without my knowledge. I was standing there talking to the firebase Commander."

"Obviously, somebody on that firebase took the picture," Oscar said.

"We found a picture of you just like this one in Dong's office," Harley said. "He also had a picture he had cut out of the newspaper. It was a picture of you standing at the job site, where Kelly's kids were renovating that mansion. Here it is." The color pictures the newspaper printed were very fuzzy and poor quality images. Roger was barely recognizable and at the very edge of the photo.

"Dong had connected the two pictures," Harley said. "However, he insisted he hadn't discovered who you were."

"How the hell did you do that, Roger?" Oscar asked. "I thought the enemy had the name, rank and serial number of all our snipers over there."

"I kept a low profile," Roger answered. "I didn't worry about getting credit for all the kills I made. Besides you would need a spotter to verify count. I didn't like working with a spotter. I couldn't get comfortable in a two-man team situation. I insisted on working alone." Still fingering the picture of him on the firebase, Roger continued, "I never wore any clothing that would help identify me, nor did I wear my dog tags. I couldn't see the point. There was nobody at home to claim my body. I was only concerned about my soul. I put that in God's hands. I figured anybody trying to put an identity on me would be searching the records of the Army or the Marines. I was Air Force."

Oscar couldn't help himself. With a hearty chuckle, he said, "Damn it Roger, you sure as hell had that figured right. Nobody knows who the hell you are! But those boys must have made the Air Force connection."

"Are you saying some of those fellows allowed themselves to stand out to much?" Harley queried.

"Well, a lot of them got cocky, especially the high numbers

guys," Roger said. "One even wore a feather in his cap, on the front. I wanted to survive. After I'd become a civilian, I displayed my ribbons and medals for a while. But I never displayed any certificates or anything with my name on it. Course, that small bit of showing off came back to bite me in the butt. So I got rid of it."

"Here's the problem Roger," Harley said. "We couldn't connect Dong with actually intending to snuff you. We couldn't make a case of that to get him a stiffer sentence. We couldn't even nail him for taking people across state lines. His attorney successfully proved that Dong actually live in Moorhead, Minnesota. Everything on the other side of the border was actually Dings operation. We didn't see that one coming and he stiffed us. He had lived in Fargo. He moved to Moorhead when Minnesota's housing market collapsed. He'd gotten a big beautiful house dirt-cheap. He'll spend about four years in prison and then he will be up to his old mischief again."

"That's the same prison Irvin is in," Kelly thoughtfully said.

"If Dong was going to be paid by two sources to snuff Roger, who was the other outfit?" Oscar asked. "A domestic outfit? And why?"

"That's what we're thinking," Harley said. "Roger, did you piss off anybody in the states?"

"Is the Pope Catholic?" Oscar interjected, as the four broke into laughter.

"Well, at my court martial. Only after I found I was going to be framed," Roger replied.

"You were the subject of a court martial?" Oscar asked in disbelief. "What the hell for?"

"They were trying to blame me for that fiasco when we got ambushed during the holiday truce," Roger said.

"How did you fare at the court martial?" Harley asked.

"The charges were dropped right in the middle of it," Roger replied. "Charlie showed up and kind of busted things up."

"The Viet Cong?" both Harley and Kelly asked in amazement.

"No, no, Charlie was our foul mouthed radioman on the ill fated mission during the holiday truce," Roger said. "He had a very threatening presence about him. He was a civilian when he broke up the court martial proceedings. I had spent a lot of time in rehab so the court martial came much later. Anyway, Charlie heard about it. He walked up to the two security personnel out side of the trial room. He was in lightweight civilian clothes and obviously not armed. Both guards had M-16s slung over their shoulders. Charlie politely greets them and then said to them, 'they're sticking it to my buddy in there. I'm going to walk through that door and into that room. If you hear a ruckus in there, just ignore it and stay out here. If you chaps do come in, I'll be forced to shove those M-16s up you asses.' Then he turned and walked in on my court martial."

Oscar chuckled. "That Charlie must have been one mean bastard."

"He certainly looked the part," Roger said. "He was a mass of scar tissue from knife fights, from when he was a kid. His mother had remarried when he was a teenager. His stepfather had moved them out of the tough neighborhood. He always said his stepfather got him straightened out. Funny thing was that he was a draftee. He never was wounded in Nam. He was the one who dragged me back to cover, after I had knocked out the machine gunners and mortar men. I had met him just before that operation. Course, after we left the court martial-we went out and tied one on. He was recently married and working as a machinist in a big machine shop outside of Chicago. He gave me his address and told me to look him up after I was done with the military."

"So, you still have a buddy left from the war years?" Oscar quizzed.

"Well, not exactly," Roger said. "Charlie was killed two months later."

"What?" Oscar and Harley asked in unison.

"Well fellows, you said you wanted to know about the strange stuff," Roger answered. "Let's pop another beer. This is as good a time as any to fill you in."

After the men had opened another beer, Roger continued, " I'd finally gotten released from the hospital. I had to sign a lot of waivers to get discharged from active duty. Of course by this time, I had two C.I.A. officers escorting me around the base. They even spent the nights in the barracks with me. They made sure I got the two thousand nine hundred dollar reenlistment bonus. I would have gotten that bonus if I had reenlisted. They got that approved, even though my extension was a forced one for medical reasons. They told me to avoid anybody I'd ever met in the service. That wasn't that hard to do. I was never with any unit for more than two weeks during the last two years I was in. The kind of work we did was dangerous. The survival rate wasn't good. Anyway, after the Air Force released me from active duty, I headed back to the Midwest. I didn't have a clue as to where I was going or where I would end up. When I got near Chicago, I thought about Charlie. I dug out my wallet and retrieved the card he had given me. Course, contacting him could be the worst thing I could do. I now had a new identity. I wanted to see Charlie again, real bad. He was the only friend I had who survived the war. However, I decided it would probably be a mistake. So I took the I-90 exit north toward Milwaukee, Wisconsin. I was tuning the radio trying to find a music station. Then I heard the name Charles Hammer. I stopped the dial. It was a small local suburban station. The announcer said, 'A local boy, Charles Hammer, was found dead in his car early this morning. His wife had reported him missing at ten p.m. last night. She said he was supposed to be home at five p.m.'. The announcer gave the name of the medical center where the autopsy had been preformed. I took the first exit I came to and stopped at a service station. I got instructions to the medical center. When I got there Charlie's family was just leaving. I asked if this was the place Charlie Hammer was brought to. An older gentleman asked, 'who are you?' I said, 'I was in the war with Charlie. He saved my life.' He said, 'they called us down here to see the body and identify it. It's Charles. If you want to see the body-just tell them you're a member of the family. If anybody calls us I'll back you up.' Then the three of them left. Charlie's wife was very pregnant and obviously in a bad state. I went in and found the autopsy room empty except for Charlie's body on a table. I went up close and picked up a corner of the sheet to get a better look. There were two small holes just a little forward and above the right ear. Just then, a young woman in whites came into the room. 'Oh my God, I wasn't suppose to leave the room,' she said. 'Who are you?' she asked. A friend of Charlie's. He saved my life in Nam. She said, 'I've got to tell somebody. I assisted with the autopsy. All we did was follow the path of the bullets. Either bullet would have rendered him unconscious instantly. There's no way he could have fired the second shot, especially with a revolver.' Then she said, 'my boyfriend works in forensics. He just called me and said the death weapon was a twenty-two revolver loaded with hollow point ammunition. He said only Charlie's prints were on it. He also said it had very recently been wiped clean, to clean.' Then she started bawling. 'I just had to tell somebody because we've been ordered to rule it a suicide. Please leave now,' she said. 'I have to stay here.' I thought it would be prudent to leave."

"What did you make of that?" Oscar asked. "Why do you think he was killed, if he was killed?"

"Oh he was killed alright," Roger stated. "Charlie was left handed. His wife kept sobbing 'he didn't do it, he didn't do it.' She should have known. At my court martial Charlie threatened to turn in a lot of top brass if they didn't cease lining up scapegoats. He insisted they were just trying to cover up their screw ups."

"Did he have anything on them?" Harley asked.

"No," Roger said. "That was just Charlie. He was a whole lot of bluff and bluster with a tough guy vocabulary and a whole lot of knife scars for props. That night while we were tying one on-he said that he just happened to be on the East Coast to observe a new machine his boss was planning to purchase. While he was having breakfast that morning he overheard a couple officers discussing my court martial. It pissed him off. He decided to intervene. I told Charlie that my defense attorney had told me it was an open and shut case. The Attorney had said, 'We got Charles Hammer lined up to testify in your defense.' Charlie said, 'like hell they did. I wouldn't have even been in the area. My boss brought me out here to watch a demonstration of the new auto lathe he plans to purchase. We did that yesterday. Than the boss told me to get lost. He wants me back in the room tomorrow morning to catch the flight home. Nobody contacted me. Those bastards were going to hang you out to dry.'"

"What the hell do you make of that, Oscar?" Harley inquired.

"It sure appears to be a domestic job," Oscar said. "Could have been some military big shots getting even for losing their scapegoat.

Or more likely, it was a defense contractor or congressman complicit in some rotten dealings. Always plenty of them in any war. My guess is we'll never know."

"Anyway you slice it, it was Charlie's big mouth that got him killed," Roger said. And he did it to save my butt again."

"What about you Roger?" Oscar asked. "Could the same people be after you?"

"I didn't think so. But, these pictures change all that," Roger answered. "The spooks insisted that they had fixed it so the Air Force wouldn't even know where to find me. I've never received my discharge papers. I should have received them, in the mail, after six years of service. I think Charlie must have struck a raw nerve, with his accusations, and had to be shut up.

"Well gentleman, we've got some time to work on this," Harley said. "Dong will be out of circulation for a little while yet. He's pretty old. Maybe he won't survive the short sentence. He's not a likable chap."

Oscar and Roger shut the generator down and locked it up. They had left Roger's vehicle at the lumberyard and rode out together in Oscar's suburban.

Harley and Kelly had each driven out in their own pickups. Three vehicles left the secluded Mosquito Lake campsite and maneuvered the winding logging trail to the highway.

Harley was deep in thought as he motored home. *He liked Kelly Callahan and was as close to him as he had been with Oscar, while Oscar was sheriff. While the two men were opposites-he was comfortable with both of them. Oscar was gregarious while a much quieter and thoughtful Kelly would amaze people with how much of a conversation he retained.* Harley had learned that while Kelly was silent, his brain was filing information. Several of Kelly's deputies had made the same observations. *I hope he has a solution for this problem. It would be impossible to protect Roger when Dong got out of prison.*

Chapter 23. Combat's Harvest.
Summer and Autumn, 1992

Lilly had felt the sun warming her cheek when she woke up. Her surroundings were foreign to her senses. She was in a hospital bed and hooked up to tubes. When she tried to speak-she found she couldn't. Then she realized she was restrained.

Just then a nurse walked into the room. "I see you're awake. I'll take the restraints off and we'll stand you up and see how well you can move. You won't be able to speak because we have your fractured jaw immobilized. You're also wearing a full neck brace."

Then Lilly remembered Roger had had one of his violent nightmares. He had told her he was anticipating a violent episode. He had begged to sleep in the library by himself. She would have none of it. "We've shared a bed every night since we first slept together," Lilly had said. "Besides, I have that broom handle to poke you with and wake you up, if you have a nightmare. I've done that many times before."

Lilly felt panic. She protested as best she could.

The nurse said, "Now calm down. I'll get a pad and pencil and you can ask questions when I get the restraints off."

After the nurse had removed the restraints, she got Lilly sitting up on the edge of the bed, than standing. She helped Lilly walk around and swing her arms to get the blood circulating again. "It would be nice if you weren't restricted by the I.V. tubes," the nurse said. "However, we should have you limbered up enough so you can write. I'll run your bed up to the sitting position. Then we'll get you back into it." With that done, the nurse handed Lilly a tablet and pencil.

Lilly quickly scrawled on the page, "What's happened to Roger? This wasn't his fault. I love him."

He's under a doctor's care also," The nurse said. "He had called the ambulance and they brought you here. Later this morning, Doctor Taylor found Roger wandering the corridors with a handful of roses bawling his eyes out. He was looking for your room. He was on the wrong floor. Doctor Taylor is treating him for shock. Right now he's sedated and sound asleep. We'll bring him to visit you as soon as he's rested."

"How long have I been here?" Lilly wrote on the pad.

"Since about two a.m.," the nurse said.

Responsibility and guilt began to vex Lilly. Roger had started having more frequent and violent nightmares as the years wore on. He had been reliving combat episodes. Lilly had always been able to poke him awake with a broom handle. This last episode must have been particularly violent. Roger hadn't even gotten out of bed to sleep walk. Instead, he stood up on the bed and the last thing Lilly remembered was his bare foot coming at her head. Lilly started to cry and the tears were flowing across her neck brace. *I should have listened to him. I hope they don't arrest him. I hope we can get help.* Lilly cried herself to sleep.

When Lilly awoke again, a very tired looking Roger was sitting in a chair next to her bed. She reached out to touch Roger's face. Her tears started to flow again.

Roger turned out of the chair and knelt on the floor beside her bed. Hugging Lilly and burying his face in her shoulder he said, "I'm sorry Lilly. I love you darling. I love you."

Lilly stroked his head with her left hand while encircling him with her right arm. Then grabbing a handful of hair, on the back of Roger's head, Lilly pulled his head back and looked into his eyes. She tried to smile as best she could. She pulled the note pad out from under her pillow and gave it to Roger, so he could see what she had written.

Roger read her notes and smiled at her. He said, "I love you, Lilly. I'm so sorry this happened to you."

Lilly moved her face closer to Roger so he could kiss her on her lips. Then taking the note pad from him she wrote, "The Children?"

"They slept through the whole thing," Roger said. "Randy and Jackie were out there for them when they woke up this morning. Jackie told them you fell and I had to take you to the hospital. Rainy took the twins along with him to the lumberyard. They'll spend the day there. Randy filled Willie and Janice in. I'll be discharged later this afternoon, so I'll be home tonight. Janice offered to cook supper tonight. I told her to pick up supper for all of us at Kentucky Fried Chicken and I would pay her for it. Janice and Willie and our two grandchildren will be eating with us tonight."

"Good," Lilly scribbled on the pad. "You shouldn't be alone."

"I've got more medicine to take," Roger said, as he shook the prescription bottle. "I have to take one of these every twelve hours. It's a drug that is supposed to keep me from dreaming. Doctor Taylor wants to see me again in three days."

"Oh, I see you're awake," a nurse said. "It's time for new bags on your I.V. What would you like for supper tonight? How about ham and eggs, or would you prefer a steak and baked potato? Actually, it'll be sugar water regardless of what you order."

Lilly smiled while Roger chuckled. "They served dinner just before I came over here," He said. "You slept right through noon. Rainy and the twins are going to pick me up and take me home after they close up the yard. I hope you're up to seeing them."

"I am honey," Lilly wrote on the pad. "Wake me up if I'm asleep."

"I will," Roger promised.

———————————

Sheriff Kelly Callahan had talked with Doctor Taylor after she had sedated Roger. "In cases like this I have to order a mental evaluation," Kelly said. "This will show up in the records as domestic violence. We know Roger isn't guilty of something like that, but he does need help. Can you just, out of hand, suggest an appointment at the Mental Health Center and schedule him for it? He may just cooperate and we won't have to order it."

"I'll do my best," Doctor Taylor responded. "Roger insists that it must have been him who fractured Lilly's jaw. However, when I questioned him for details, he had very little recollection of what happened. He only remembers finding Lilly unconscious and then his calling for an ambulance and calling the Sheriff's Department."

"Good," Kelly said. "He did exactly the right thing. I'm going to beat the bushes for some financial help. The mental health bill will be a big one."

As Kelly left the hospital he thought, *I could have a couple of big problems on my hands. The bigger problem will be the barroom rapes making their way west toward this county.* They had started over by Madison, Wisconsin, and slowly moved across the border into Minnesota. The last one occurred in a little town north of St. Cloud. They were getting to close for comfort.

The perpetrators of the rapes had all been illegal immigrants. Most couldn't speak English. The rapes had taken place in bars with pool tables. Under the scrutiny of crowds, the rapists had been cheered on. Kelly couldn't help reflecting how sick society had become.

Kelly had ordered stepped up surveillance at all bars and poolrooms in the county. He had instructed his men, "Especially, check on Middle Eastern and Mexican men. That's not profiling. That's telling the world you're smart enough to know somebody's Norwegian or Irish grandmother didn't perpetrate the rapes. Just ask the waitresses or managers if some Arab or Latin types are showing signs of rowdiness. If they have any rowdies-bring them in. If the manager or owner doesn't cooperate-slap cuffs on them and bring them in too. We can hold any suspect for twenty-four hours without charging them. Those twenty-four hours may well prevent a rape from happening. We don't want any rapes in this county. Be sure and call for backup. Harley says to call on his officers if the other deputies are tied up. They can assist in the county."

Sheriff Callahan had called Roger on the morning of Roger's first appointment at the Mental Health Clinic. "You'll spend about four hours filling out paperwork on this first visit," Kelly said. "You'll be done at one p.m. If you can come over to the American Legion club right after you're done, I'll buy dinner for you."

"Gotcha," Roger replied.

Kelly had been relieved when Doctor Taylor had informed him that Roger had been eager for the help she had suggested was available to him. "The people at the University of Minnesota are looking forward to working with him," Doctor Taylor had said. "They were really impressed by the fact that he took full responsibility for the incident, and had the where withal to call for an ambulance and notify the Sheriff's department. I've informed Roger that he is suffering from Post Traumatic Stress Disorder. Make no mistake about it, these violent nightmares he's been experiencing are caused by that war. It's time we got to the bottom of it."

Kelly and Roger took a booth in a semi-private location at the back of the clubroom. They ordered dinner. Then Kelly asked, "How did it go Roger?"

"All right I guess," Roger replied. "Sure was a lot of writing. Some of the questionnaires were very repetitious. I'm supposed to go back tomorrow afternoon and talk with some Doctors."

"That's what I wanted to talk to you about," Kelly said. "This is going to be very expensive. I've gotten the County Board to agree to kick in five hundred dollars. I've talked with both service clubs and they said they'd support you. They want you to know that they will do much better than the County Board has promised."

"They're only going to charge me according to my income," Roger said.

"You're income is pretty high, Roger, " Kelly said. "You've a family to support and Lilly's hospital bills to pay. If your insurance company has an act-of-war or riot clause-you could very well be stuck with all of that. I advise you to be ready to accept any help offered. Your country owes you this. That twenty-nine hundred dollar reenlistment bonus wasn't much in comparison to your service. Two years in constant combat. They overloaded your donkey, Roger."

"If you think I should, Kelly, than I guess I will," Roger said. "I'm feeling great now. I know that's because of the happy pills I'm taking. I can't take them the rest of my life. Do you have any idea of what's in store for me? With the Doctors, I mean."

"You'll meet with them once or twice a week for about an hour," Kelly replied. "Could go on for a couple of months. What are your plans for the rest of the day?"

"I'm going to the hospital to sit with Lilly," Roger answered. "I'll read to her to help pass the time. The kids will all come by after work."

"How're things going at the yard?" Kelly asked.

"Willie and Rainy are running that," Roger said. "They both told me to stay away from work for a while. They have everything under control. We got a real good man, when we hired Janice's replacement. She's got her hands full with two kids and a third one in the oven."

"She's pregnant again?" Kelly asked.

"Yep," Roger proudly responded. "She insisted she wanted to have her children one after another. She didn't want to have the distance there was between her and Danny."

"Good for her," Kelly enthused. "That's the way to do it."

As they left the club, Kelly said, "If you have any problems after any of the sessions give me a call."

"Will do," Roger assured him.

Sheriff Kelly Callahan was concerned about Roger's sessions at the Mental Health Center. They had gone on for twelve weeks now with no apparent end in site. Kelly had stopped in at the Mental Health Center. They wouldn't give him any information other than to say Roger was doing real well.

"We've four different doctors working with him," the receptionist said. "We've brought in three from the University of Minnesota. He'll be fine."

"That's good to hear," Kelly said. He was still concerned about the cost since he had gone out on a limb about the payment. This was going on a lot longer than anybody had anticipated.

Lilly had insisted that Roger was doing great. She was talking very slowly after having the immobilization equipment removed. "He's responding to the treatment real well," she said. "I can't help but feel a little sorry for those doctors if Roger is baring his soul. His war experiences were horrible."

Another month had passed since Kelly had inquired about Roger at the clinic. Kelly was out in the county in a patrol car wondering when Roger's sessions would end. Then a call came from the dispatcher to interrupt his thoughts.

"Lilly Hartec called," the Dispatcher said. "She said she needed a favor of you. Can you get in contact with her today?"

"Sure can," Kelly said. "Is she at home now?"

"Yes she is," came the reply. "That's where she called from."

"I'll just buzz over there now since I'm close," Kelly said.

Lilly met Kelly at the front of the garage. "Thank you for coming so quickly," she said.

"I was in the area when the Dispatcher called," Kelly explained.

"Let's go up to the kitchen," Lilly said, as she led the way to the elevator. "I thought this elevator was a lot of nuisance at first. Now that I'm nearly sixty I really appreciate it. Roger was truly thinking ahead on this one. We love this place and probably will never leave it."

"It's beautiful out here," Kelly agreed.

After Kelly was seated, Lilly said, "Would you like a cup of coffee or something else to drink?"

"If you have a cold beer, I'd appreciate that," Kelly answered.

"Sure, Roger almost always has one the first thing when he gets home," Lilly said, as she set a bottle of beer in front of Kelly. "Would you like a glass?"

"Nah, I'm a bottle baby," Kelly said, with a chuckle.

"The reason I wanted to see you is because I would like you to go with me tomorrow when the Doctor goes over the results of Roger's treatment," Lilly said.

"They're done?" Kelly's eyebrows shot up in surprise.

"Yes," Lilly sighed. "It's been four months. The receptionist said it should only be family members that have access to their report. I assured her that besides being Sheriff, you're also a member of our family. She said it would be okay."

"Sure, I can do that," Kelly said, after taking a long draught of the beer. "What time is the meeting?"

"Tomorrow, two p.m.," Lilly said. "Will that be a problem?"

"No, not at all," Kelly responded. "I'll have my secretary put it on my agenda as soon as I get back to my squad car."

Kelly met Lilly in the parking lot of the Mental Health Center the following afternoon. Together they went inside and were ushered into an office where they took seats in front of a desk. Lilly placed several tissues in her lap.

Shortly a man in a suit entered the room carrying a manila folder. "Hello, I'm Doctor McLaren," He said, as he extended his hand toward Lilly. "Mrs. Hartec, I presume."

"Yes," Lilly said, as they shook hands. "Lilly will be fine."

"Okay Lilly," the Doctor said, as Kelly stood up. "And you must be Sheriff Callahan."

"That's right," Kelly stated, as the two men shook hands.

Doctor McLaren sat down behind the desk. Looking at Kelly, he said, "I understand you have some concern about the bill, since it was your office that requested the treatment."

"Yes I do," Kelly said. "All I could get the County Board to commit to was five hundred dollars. However, both service clubs have promised to do better than the county."

"We'll only charge you the two thousand dollars that were agreed to at the start; even though it went on much longer than we anticipated," Doctor McLaren said. "Will that be satisfactory?"

"Very satisfactory," Kelly said. "I appreciate that." Kelly knew the service clubs would be willing to make up the fifteen hundred dollars that the county wouldn't pay.

"This was way more than we expected at the outset," Doctor McLaren said. "However, Roger was an excellent subject because of his vast experience and knowledge of what happened in that war. We've garnered a tremendous amount of information from him that we will be able to use to help other troubled veterans and future veterans. Roger signed a release form. We will be able to use the information to produce a program to help future combatants. Our country really dropped the ball with the Vietnam Veterans. The only war that had more men in combat was World War Two.

Vietnam was the longest war our country was ever involved in. There are thousands of men in this country suffering from Post Traumatic Stress Disorder. We lost fifty eight thousand men to combat and nearly twice that many have committed suicide since the war's end.

"We've been commissioned by the military services to come up with a program to prevent this problem," Doctor McLaren continued. "In the future, anybody involved in killing of the enemy will be given treatment. In the past, these men were denied treatment, by the Veteran's Administration, simply because they weren't wounded."

"But Roger was wounded," Lilly protested.

"My dear, Roger isn't even in the system," Doctor McLaren said. "We know he was a soldier who was placed in extreme situations for far to long. This happened because he was good and manpower was hard to get. He's seen, oh, probably three life times of violence. He was being overwhelmed because of the dreams he started having years ago. This was a case of systemic failure of a nation to take care of its veterans. The North Vietnamese did a way better job than we did. It was important to the Vietnamese families to have the bodies of their soldiers returned home. In what we considered a backward society-they did a far better job of taking care of their warriors. Getting back to Roger, we believe his problems could have been prevented. We need to have in place a system for debriefing any soldier who has experienced killing. Mind you, we're only talking about ten per cent of the military work force here. Typically it takes nine troops to support each man involved in the actual killing. Roger really was an open book. He didn't hold back on anything that he could remember. The problem was sorting out what was fact, what was nightmare, what were both and what was actually brain overload. I think we were able to do a good job of helping him sort this all out. We had to categorize everything into these four groups. Then we would pick the episodes apart and do some resorting. After he had a chance to communicate with somebody, more and more of what was in his subconscious boiled to the surface. Even though Roger didn't know what was actually in his subconscious brain-it was still stressing him. We had to prove to him that the standard of conduct he had placed on himself was way to high. Once we convinced him that mistakes are made under ideal conditions, it was possible for him to quit blaming himself for incidents he really had no control over.

"We've learned a lot about modern day combat," Doctor McLaren continued. "We will make use of this information in the future. Believe me, in the future, combat veterans will get help right from the get go. It will not be necessary for them to be wounded either. We can't afford to lose another generation. Roger has all our personal cards if he should need any help. He can call any of us at any time. There are probably still some troublesome experiences embedded in his subconscious that will come to the surface from time to time. Talking about it will help him greatly."

Lilly was in tears. "I've always avoided the subject because it seemed like anything he said was just to horrible to contemplate. I knew he didn't want pity. What can I do?" Lilly sobbed.

"As hard as it may be, you may have to listen to some of his experiences," Doctor McLaren said.

Looking over at Kelly, Doctor McLaren continued, "Roger has a very strong sense of duty to his family, even to the point of defending his wife when she wouldn't allow him to sleep alone in the library. You know of the rape incidents moving west from Wisconsin. If Roger's wife or daughters should be raped, we all think you can expect a blood bath."

Kelly couldn't control his laughter. His body bounced up and down in the chair he was sitting in. "If something like that should happen in my jurisdiction, I probably won't notice the blood bath. I'll be to busy passing ammunition to Roger."

Chapter 24. Renewed Commitment. Spring, 1993

Lilly had awakened on a Sunday morning to the sound of rain and the rumble of thunder. Roger was sound asleep, along side of her, in their top floor bedroom. Roger generally didn't sleep in except on these rainy days.

Lilly propped herself up on a couple of pillows to watch her husband sleep. She amused herself by tickling his nose hair with her fingernail, which caused quirky facial expressions. She knew that when he awoke she would have to be ready for him.

Roger's carnal appetite had always amazed her. However, her own appetite for sex, after she had seduced him, amazed her even more. Roger preferred to make love first thing in the morning. Her preference was when they first went to bed at night.

Once, Roger had suggested they should make love morning, noon and night. "I would rather make love to you than eat," He had said, "and we eat three times a day and never think anything of it." Lilly chuckled, after softly blowing in his ear. She certainly couldn't fault his reasoning.

After a minute more of Lilly's pestering, Roger shook himself awake. The attack was on. Lilly was glad the children's bedrooms were on the first floor. These sessions got noisy. About twenty minutes later they both awoke again, their bodies entangled.

"I love you Lilly," Roger said. "You're the best."

"I love you darling," Lilly replied. "When did you first decide you were in love with me?"

"I think it was when you grabbed my vest and told me to be careful, after I'd delivered that load of firewood," Roger said.

"But Roger," Lilly protested, "it was months after that before you ever told me you loved me."

"Well that love business hadn't been much of a success story for me in the past," Roger said. "Shucks, I don't know why I didn't say anything. I do know I was in love with you, and I was scared."

"A big brave man like you scared of a little thing like me?" Lilly teased. "What was there to be scared of?"

"What if you weren't in love with me," Roger stated. "I would have been heartbroken. I figured I wouldn't have to deal with a broken heart if I didn't stick my neck out and scare you off. I was thoroughly enjoying every minute I got to spend with you. I fondly anticipated the next time I would be with you. Why did you fall in love with me? A beautiful woman like you must've had dozens of offers."

"Not really Roger. I'm way to bossy," Lilly confessed. "Haven't you noticed?"

"What's bossy and what's concerned?" Roger asked. "You always seem to know what's best for me. You've never let me go to the woods alone, to cut wood, since we were married. So you really must care about me. I guess I never experienced that much concern for my well being since Mable died."

"And who was Mable, pray tell," Lilly inquired, while pretending to be jealous.

"She was Thor's wife," Roger replied. "They purchased me when I was nine years old. Thor considered me chattel, just a farm hand. Mable wanted to raise me as their son. That caused them to quarrel, especially about my schooling."

"Why didn't Thor want you to go to school?" Lilly asked.

"Because it cost money," Roger said. "It also was time I couldn't be working on the farm. By law he had to send me through the eight grades. Mable constantly reminded him of that. Before I got through eight grades the law was changed. Thor had to allow me to go through the tenth grade."

"So you were allowed to go to school through the tenth grade," Lilly stated.

"Mable had talked Thor into letting me finish high school," Roger said. "She insisted that I had been a good worker for all those years. She said I had earned the right to a high school education. Thor finally agreed."

"Why did Thor dislike you so much?" Lilly asked.

"Oh it wasn't me," Roger said. "Thor was mad at God. He didn't like Mable teaching the Bible to me on Sundays either. We were convenient scapegoats for his wrath."

"Goodness, Thor must have been a terrible person," Lilly said. "Why was he mad at God?"

"Thor and Mable had lost their three children in a diphtheria epidemic," Roger stated. "Most of the time he forgot his bitterness and was nice. I suppose that's why Mable stayed with him. Of course, a farmer's wife was the only life she had ever known. Thor's anger usually disappeared when Sunday had come and gone. Mable told me Sunday mornings had always been special to Thor. He had always helped get the children ready for the Sunday morning church service. It was his time to be close to their children. Then their last child died, in Thor's arms, on a Sunday morning."

"Was Thor ever nice to you?" Lilly inquired.

"Yes," Roger stated. "Especially after I'd saved a calf. He always seemed to forget his bitterness whenever there was new life on the farm. Even forgot to be mad on some Sundays. He was actually happy then."

"How did you save calves?" Lilly quizzed.

"Some years, for some reason, a lot of calves were born with one leg folded back," Roger said. "The farmer would call the veterinarian and the vet would cut the calf out. I always helped the veterinarian and he told me that I could save all those calves. He said, 'by the time I get here the calf is out to far and has to be cut out. If you shine a flashlight on the water sac, as soon as it appears, you can see if both hooves are under the calf's chin. If they aren't, you must break the sac and push the calf back about two inches. Then, reach in and cup the wayward hoof in you hand and pull it forward. Then quickly pull the calf forward so it won't suffocate.' I followed his instructions and started saving calves. Thor even took me over to some of the closer neighbors to help with calf deliveries. He was proud of me then, although he would never say so. However, he would let me keep any money the neighbors offered. It was during these times that Thor taught me the principles of business. He explained profit and loss and always cautioned about wasting time. He liked efficiency. He really was a good man. But he let his anger at God blind him. Anyway, that's what Mable had always said."

"Whatever happened to them?" Lilly asked, as she thought about Lori's earlier assessment of Sam and Roger's lives. "Damaged merchandise. Yet, both turned out to be good men."

"Mable died shortly after I graduated from high school," Roger said. "Before she died, she had given one hundred dollars to me. She had saved it out of the money Thor gave her for groceries. She told me to go into town and enlist in one of the military services if Thor didn't treat me right, after she died."

Lilly could see the tears in Roger's eyes. "Was Thor mean to you after Mable died?" she asked.

"Oh yes," Roger responded. "He, for some unknown reason, thought I was responsible for Mable's death. We fought a lot. One morning Thor and I argued. I told him he had worked Mable to death. Thor cuffed me on the ear with his fist. So I cold cocked him and ran away."

"And joined the Air Force," Lilly said. "Why the Air Force?"

"All the recruiting offices were in a line down a side street," Roger explained. "The Air Force recruiter's was the first one. They had a busload of volunteers leaving for an induction center that morning."

Lilly remembered how Doctor McLaren had urged her to communicate with Roger about his past. *Roger hadn't had another nightmare since he had put her in the hospital last summer. In fact, he seemed to be a stronger man.* Doctor McLaren had said if his group were successful, they felt the trauma of war would strengthen rather than weaken Roger. He had said, "We call it Post-Traumatic-Growth."

Lilly decided to plunge in. "Roger, what were all those horrible nightmares about? Were they memories of all the people you killed?"

Taking Lilly in his arms and piling her pillows on top of his, Roger lay back on the pillows with her tucked in beside him. Then he pulled the covers on top of the two of them. "It wasn't all the people I'd killed, it was the one I didn't kill that was causing all the problems," he said.

"Goodness Roger!" Lilly exclaimed, "I would think your nightmares would be about all the people you killed, not about a life you spared."

"It wasn't a matter of sparing a life as much as it was a failure to do one's duty," Roger explained. "All through the history of the world, as societies became more civilized they have gotten soft. Consequently, they would be overrun by a more barbaric society. That barbaric society would adopt the easy life style of the conquered. Then another more barbaric group would conquer them. Without a warrior class, a civilized society can't survive. I always thought our Constitutional Republic was mankind's best hope. I'm sure the North Vietnamese thought communism was best for them. The government in the south, that we were supposed to be protecting, certainly wasn't worth the effort. While we were over there fighting an Asian war the sneaky socialists here at home were passing all kinds of legislation circumventing our own constitution. The very constitution we warriors thought we were protecting. But, back to the nightmares. I didn't know it at first because there wasn't much rhyme or reason to the images. After fifteen years of bits and pieces of a picture-the full picture finally emerged. It was a composite of a whole lot of earlier images."

"What happened, Roger?" Lilly softly asked, as she snuggled into his right side while hanging onto his left hand with her right hand.

"I was dropped into a kill zone to take out a North Vietnamese general," Roger said. "I'd been told that if I stayed on the east side of the river, I would be okay. I was inserted at night and got all set up to make the shot after daylight broke. That's when the General would begin to move about the encampment. The shot was a little over a mile. It was my plans to do one shot and remove my self at least one mile to an extraction point. This particular morning, a three-man patrol came walking along the east side of the river. I could see that they would come through my position. I knew I would have to kill them, without making any noise. Once they discovered my position, I wouldn't have time to remove myself far enough for safe extraction. It really was a do or die situation. I left my position and circled around so I would be behind them, when they came upon my equipment. I quickly dispatched two with my knife and knocked the third one down to the jungle floor. He had lost his weapon when I hit him. He was lying on the ground crying and shaking in fear. I could see he had wet his uniform and I could smell that he had filled his pants. He was young, probably thirteen or fourteen, and I foolishly took pity on him. I kicked him in the jaw. But I pulled my kick so I wouldn't kill him. I just wanted to render him unconscious."

"Did you kill the General?" Lilly asked.

"Oh yes, I made the shot," Roger said. "What was precedent in the nightmares is that kid's face, filled with fear, before I kicked him. I've come to realize that the possible reason is because I was supposed to kill him. How many Americans did that boy kill because I failed to do my job properly? I knew I'd made a mistake after I was extracted. "I'd over a year of sniping in, so I could quit anytime. I tried to quit. I thought I'd lost my edge. But as soon as that job was done I was rushed into another job without even being debriefed. I was debriefed on that particular job a full month later. Then it was the same thing. I was rushed into another job."

"Didn't any of this scare you?" Lilly asked.

"No more scared than anybody else in combat," Roger answered. "A lot of men wet their pants, during combat, without even knowing it. I guess it's always been that way. I always thought that as a sniper I had better control of the outcome. I didn't feel comfortable going into combat in a unit. As a unit, where somebody else is in charge, a soldier must follow orders; regardless of whether they are good or bad orders. I wasn't comfortable leaving the thinking up to others. In the end, it was that kind of scenario that got me shot up. What really scared me was that incident last summer. If my nightmares were chiding me for not doing my job, how come I pulled my kick and only fractured your jaw instead of killing you? Why did I repeat the same mistake instead of correcting it? Roger rolled toward Lilly and buried his face into her neck and started sobbing. His shoulders were shaking. His body was wracked with grief. Finally, through his grief, Lilly heard him say, "My God! Lilly! I could never have lived with myself if I had killed you."

Lilly held Roger tight to her body. She stroked the back of his head and neck. "The Lord had to have been watching over us that night," she said. This was the first time Lilly had ever seen Roger cry. Doctor McLaren had warned her that it would in all probability happen. He had said, "Emotions suppressed out of the necessities of combat will eventually resurface. It's part of the healing process."

What seemed like hours, but was actually about a minute, Roger regained his composure. He appeared to want to talk some more. As horrible as his testimony was-Lilly decided that this might be her only chance to get to know about her husband's past.

"Rainy is always watching military stuff on television," Lilly said. "Is that stuff they say about snipers true?"

"What kind of stuff are you talking about?" Roger inquired, as he wiped the tears from his face.

"How they compete and keep track of their kills," Lilly replied. "They all had a record of estimated kills and then a smaller number of confirmed kills. Did you keep track, Roger?"

"No I didn't," Roger replied. "I didn't think those fellows were very smart doing that. I figured my job was to kill as many as possible as quickly as possible so I could go home. I never wore any identification. There wasn't anybody back home to claim my body. There wasn't any point in worrying about that. I figured the notoriety would just be a burden, later in life, if I should survive the war. Survival was really what it was all about for me. I would have needed a spotter for confirmed kills. I thought working with a spotter was cumbersome. When I was in aircraft mechanic school, we learned that Air Force fighter pilots hated side-by-side cockpit configurations. The Air Force refused to purchase combat fighters unless they seated the two men in tandem."

"Why was that?" Lilly asked.

"The men wanted to be able to see out both sides of the cockpit during a dogfight," Roger answered. "In the side-by-side version the pilot could only see out one side and had to depend on his partner to tell him what was happening on the other side. That could prove fatal in a dogfight. I thought the same applied to sniping. Also, there was the nerve level. It wasn't a good feeling having your spotter bug out early when things were starting to get hot. I always thought I was better off eliminating danger rather than trying to avoid it."

"Did that ever happen to you?" Lilly asked.

"Oh yes," Roger replied. "You couldn't blame them though. There wasn't any way for them to know what I was thinking. Even though I thought I had the situation under control, there wasn't any way for me to communicate that with my spotter. When the spotter thought it was time to leave, he would tap me on the shoulder three times and bug out."

"So you became the Lone Ranger?" Lilly quizzed.

"That's about it," Roger replied. "I thought I was more effective that way. I studied the enemy's habits and judged each event on an individual basis. I didn't handle any situation the same twice. That way I was more effective. I could fire more rounds. I really liked to empty a clip."

"You always emptied your clip?" Lilly inquired.

"Not all the time," Roger stated. "It depended on the circumstances. One time I emptied two clips. That was forty shots. It only took about two minutes. I only had three minutes to do the deed and bug out. If a sniper is set up right-it only takes a second and a half per shot. If I got to pick and choose my shots-I could get a little more time before the artillery or mortar rounds started dropping in."

"How did you do that?" Lilly inquired.

"I would take out the radioman first," Roger said. "Then I would shoot the mortar men. After that I could start picking off the riflemen. The North Vietnamese were typically undermanned so there would only be forty or fifty men in a unit. It was easy to destroy most of the unit. I liked to catch them in a wide river crossing, especially when the water was deep. I preferred a close up position for that kind of work. No spotter liked working that close."

"How much time did you have in a situation like that?" Lilly asked. She knew that action in that war was hard, fast and brief.

"Three minutes," Roger stated. "After the North Vietnamese artillerymen lost contact with their radioman for three minutes they started firing. They were accurate."

"How come they never hit you?" Lilly inquired.

"It was a game of cat and mouse," Roger replied. "I out catted them. They had their field pieces sited in to dump the first rounds about five hundred yards from the riverbank. Then they would walk the barrage back for half a mile or more hoping to catch any or all ambushers as they fell back. Since I was close-the first rounds fell behind me. I would follow the river for half a mile or so before moving away from it."

"You let the enemy get that close?" Lilly asked.

"This was all done at night," Roger said, "usually a dark night. If my kill rate were high enough and fast enough the attacking unit would break off. The Vietnamese were good at keeping their promise of returning a dead soldier's body to his family. Even if it were just the bones, they did it. That was very important in their culture."

"How could you possibly kill that many in the dark of the night?" Lilly asked.

"Night scope," Roger stated. "The night scope is limited. It needs ambient light. There had to be some light at the shooter's position. River crossings were good ambush sites because the enemy's mobility was hampered. However, there was moonlight above them when they left the protection of the jungle canopy. That light lit up their faces. I'd made a study of the silhouettes of the soldiers by their assignments. I knew by the silhouettes what that soldier's duties were. A deep-water crossing was nothing more than a turkey shoot. I had to wait until they were almost across. I had plenty of time to study their silhouettes as they spread out in the river. That's when I chose my shooting order."

"Breakfasts ready," Marcy said over the intercom that Roger had connected between the twin's bedroom and the master bedroom years ago.

"Well dear, it's time for us to see what the children have cooked up for breakfast," Lilly said. Donning bathrobes and slippers the two of them went to the elevator to ride down to the kitchen.

Lilly felt a pang of nostalgia. Sylvester was no longer with them for the ride. He had died last year and she was still missing him underfoot for the elevator rides.

The kitchen was filled with breakfast aromas, and the table was all set for four. Rainy had a place of his own that he had moved into last fall. Lilly's family was growing smaller.

Marcy loved to cook and was planning on becoming a chef. Darcy had helped with the table setting and serving. For Lilly and the twins there was an oriental breakfast. Marcy had made blueberry pancakes with bacon and eggs for Roger. Roger disliked oriental food. Roger said grace and the four began their breakfast.

"What's on your agendas?" Lilly asked the twins.

"We're gong to church with Willy and Janice and their kids," Darcy said. "Then we'll spend the afternoon with them. We'll probably take in a movie."

"They do like the movies, don't they?" Lilly said, more of a statement than a question.

"It's romantic for them," Marcy said. "It's where they fell in love."

"I suppose that would give rise to a fondness for that entertainment," Lilly agreed. "Look Roger, the wind is blowing the cloud cover away and the sun is peeking through. Why don't you come to church with me? I'll pack a picnic lunch. After church we can go for a long drive and eat whenever we get hungry."

"It's a date darling," Roger answered.

Lilly was happy about this opportunity to spend the afternoon alone with Roger. They had just celebrated their eleventh wedding anniversary. She was finally getting to know Roger better than she had during the first ten years of their marriage. The violent incident last summer had brought them closer together. This morning had been the first time that she had seen Roger cry. She had been told he cried when he had fractured her jaw, but she hadn't seen it.

Lilly was feeling excitement about this date with her husband this afternoon. She told herself to remember to put a blanket into the pickup cab with the picnic basket.

"We'll get the dishes," Darcy said. "We have plenty of time before Willie and Janice pick us up."

"Good," Lilly said. "Thank you for breakfast. You girls are the best. Your dad and I need to shower. Then I must put together our picnic dinner. Come dear, let's shower." Lilly headed toward the elevator.

Lilly and Roger were hugging and kissing on the ride up. Roger had her completely nude by the time they got to the master bedroom and the shower. Lilly was so thankful for the Roman shower. She and Roger almost always showered together.

After church, Roger boosted Lilly into the cab of the pickup. They always took a four-wheel drive vehicle. They would definitely be visiting Mosquito Lake. If it rained while they were there, a four-wheel drive vehicle was a requirement. It was a favorite spot of theirs. If the timing were right, they would probably eat dinner there. Oscar Thompson had left his travel trailer set up on Mosquito Lake. He had decided not to tow it on vacations anymore. He had made it a point to fish at the lake as often as the mosquitoes allowed it. He was always after one of the Hartec children to accompany him. He was also chomping at the bit For Willie and Janice's children to become old enough to accompany Great Grandpa on a camping and fishing trip.

As Lilly stroked Roger's neck, she hoped they would end up at Mosquito Lake for dinner. She was planning some afternoon delight and would rather it be in the travel trailer than somewhere else on the picnic blanket.

Chapter 25. Futile Effort. Summer 1995

Attorney General, Horatio Bogarth had just settled into his large, plush, swivel, office chair with a steaming cup of coffee and a large pastry on a napkin. Sliding the chair away from his desk, he leaned back and put his feet up on the desk. Withdrawing the writing board for use as a coffee table, he was ready to proceed with his first and most important business of the day. Filling his increasingly prodigious belly was foremost on his mind. There was a rap on his door. "Come in," He said.

Horatio's very excited secretary, Daniel, had entered. "Hey Chief, do you want to settle an old score?"

"What's up?" Horatio inquired, before taking a huge bite from the pastry.

"Calvin, over in records, is a computer junkie," Daniel said. "He spends most of his off-time on the Internet snooping. He's even got his own computer at home. Remember that redneck sheriff the Hartec's got elected to foil Susan Hargrove's plan to take their children away from them?"

"Sure do," Horatio said, as he set the partially eaten pastry on a napkin on the writing board. "What's he got to do with anything?"

"Calvin did some checking and the Red Neck didn't adopt any of those kids," Daniel said. "It seems in Alabama they weren't concerned about that."

"They're not in Bama now!" Horatio exclaimed, as he sat upright in his chair. "How many kids does he have under sixteen?"

"Three," Daniel said. "An eleven, thirteen and fifteen year old. And he's been sheriff for over six years now. He's retiring at the end of this term. We'll have to nail him before he gets a chance to skedaddle back to Bama."

"You're an evil genius Dan," Horatio said. "If we can successfully pull this one off you'll have to choose a deserving pal to inform Susan Hargrove and accept her gracious thanks and reward. I understand she's having the time of her life."

"Yes, she could be way to busy. However, I'm sure a word from you could persuade her to prepare an orgy for a deserving messenger," Daniel said. "Maybe I'll volunteer. It's been a little slow at home since that last baby. My brother said she's a great ride."

"See what Calvin can come up with on our computer here," Horatio ordered. "I hate those damn things. I hope they don't advance any further than they have now. Damn expensive toys in my opinion."

"They can be great if you know how to work them," Daniel said. "A lot of information to be gleaned."

"Get back with me when Calvin has all the information," Horatio ordered, as Daniel went out the door. Horatio went back to his pastry and barely warm cup of coffee. *This will be great. If I can nail that red neck sheriff-that damn Hartec will realize he's not invincible.*

Half an hour later, Daniel called Horatio over the inter-office telephone system. "I think you may want to see what we have in the computer room," he said.

Horatio's coat tails were flying behind him as his protruding belly broke the air in front of him. He moved swiftly through a maze of corridors to the computer room. *Maybe those damn contraptions will prove worthwhile.* Horatio bent over behind Calvin to observe the computer's screen in the dimly lit room. Calvin was sitting at a keyboard. Horatio watched as Calvin flipped through pictures.

"Here's a picture from Ashland County's official newspaper of Sheriff Callahan," Calvin said. "This is a picture of his wife and six children. He moved them up from Alabama. Notice the two youngest ones are black. They can't be Sheriff Callahan's natural born children. His wife is white. We think that in Alabama they don't care. However, in Minnesota he will need proof of guardianship. We couldn't find anything on record."

"Huh," Horatio snorted. "No Grand Jury would touch that argument."

"Maybe not," Daniel said. "But we could keep it in the headlines for years. That would be a blight on Callahan's Administration."

"Yes," Calvin agreed. "We could make it uncomfortable enough for him to skedaddle back to Bamma. Maybe even before his term was up."

"That would be a feather in your cap," Daniel said. "You don't have to worry about losing votes from that area since you hardly get any from there anyway."

"How much information can you get out of that damn contraption?" Horatio asked.

"That county went on line last year the same as the state did," Calvin said. "It depends on how much information they've put on line. Nobody has much history online yet. However, we can get quite a good supply of information from newspaper archives."

"You can get into Ashland County's files from here?" Horatio inquired.

"Oh yes," Calvin assured him. "Anything that's public information will go into the archives and can be brought up by anybody knowledgeable on a computer. They can view all our online files as well."

"Bring up Callahan's political contributions report he would have had to file, after the last two elections," Horatio ordered. "Nobody looks at the damn things. Might be worth checking."

Calvin went into the state archives and came up with the two reports filed with the State Elections Commission. The reports were in order and appeared proper.

"Looks like he had a lot of small contributors on that first election, Chief," Daniel said. "His relatives made some large contributions. Those came through a Dallas, Texas law firm and covered literature expenses. Most of the stuff was even printed in Texas. The Elections Commission said it was legal; something about special privileges afforded a Republic. He didn't need much effort for the reelection."

"What about the reports he filed in Ashland County?" Horatio asked. Do they match these two?"

"Let me bring them up," Calvin said. Rapidly typing on the keyboard, Calvin had the screen doing a lot of flipping and finally the county's web site came on. It took Calvin about ten minutes to get the copy of Sheriff Callahan's first election report.

"Everything appears in order on the first report," Daniel announced. "That's Lilly Hartec's signature on it. She ran the campaign."

"What about the second campaign?" Horatio asked. "Does everything appear in order on that report?" He was getting impatient. *This computer nonsense wasn't yielding anything so far. The two younger men were enjoying all the blitzing around that the computer required of them. Fucking waste of time.*

"Here it is Chief," Daniel said. Again, at the bottom of the report was Lilly's signature. Right below the signature line and in the middle of the page appeared two words, "Scroll down."

Calvin scrolled down and two side by side copies of the Attorney General's Elections Commission's report came into view.

"What the fuck is that?" Horatio asked, in a very agitated tone.

"I can't read it. Calvin, can you enlarge that page?" Daniel asked.

"Sure can," Calvin said. "I'll blow it up three hundred per cent."

After it was enlarged the trio recognized it as Horatio's campaign report. One was a copy of the report filed with the Elections Commission. The other was a copy of the actual report that the filed report was generated from. The filed report had been altered ever so slightly, in a manner that could be argued as typographical error. However, it did change some of the uncommon names. When the names were common, the addresses had been changed.

"How in the hell did they get that fucking information?" Horatio fairly screamed, his huge belly quivering, while he swiveled his head to look accusingly at his two assistants. "You two were the only staff privy to that information."

"Search me," Daniel said, with a shrug of his shoulders. "I gave

Calvin the paper work so he could type up the three copies for the Elections Commission. He was suppose to produce just one copy of the real version for you, Chief."

"Well Calvin?" The Attorney General asked.

"Beats the shit out of me Chief," Calvin protested. "I typed them up on this machine because I didn't have to make carbon copies. I just punch the button and it spits out however many copies I want."

"Did you send the fucking things out?" Daniel asked, "maybe accidentally?"

"No! Hell no," Calvin protested. "You can't send something accidentally. There's to many steps in that process. I don't know how anybody could get copies of anything that isn't sent over the airwaves or put onto a web site."

"Are there copies in this Goddamn machine?" Horatio fairly screamed.

"Sure there is," Calvin said. "They're in its memory. I put everything I type in its memory, in case you want more copies later. If somebody figured out how to suck information out of its memory, they're damn good."

"Is that possible Daniel?" Horatio asked.

"Hell I don't know," Daniel replied. "Calvin's the expert. I suppose anything's possible."

"Go back to the copies Ashland County has," Horatio ordered.

In about a minute Calvin had the two copies of the two reports on the screen. The scene had changed a little. Below the two reports in very small red letters were two words, "Scroll down."

Calvin scrolled down and in larger print appeared the message, "Cease and desist and I will too." Followed by "XXXOOO."

"Fucking bitch knows way more about computers than I do," Calvin complained. "And she's monitoring us right now."

"How do you know it's a female?" Horatio asked.

"The X's and O's," Calvin replied. "That's female jabber for hugs and kisses."

"Or maybe you have a fairy friend you don't know about," Daniel suggested.

"Fuck you Dan," Calvin said, in an exasperated tone.

"Now children," Horatio admonished. "Calvin, can you get into our main records section to see if both copies of those reports are on file there?"

"Sure can," Calvin said. "It will take a while." Calvin typed on the keyboard.

While Calvin and Daniel were jabbering, Horatio was deep in thought. *This computer technology could destroy the good life for the ruling class. Just to damn much information available. He had heard predictions of people getting University degrees without sitting in classrooms. There were enough universities, not accepting government funds, which would be happy to educate using the Internet. This technology could well be the end of an intellectual ruling class. They would no longer be deciding what is best for the uniformed, uneducated masses. If these machines became as cheap as it was predicted-and why wouldn't they? The State could no longer control information. Look at what had happened with satellite television. The State's monopoly with the public education system would be gone. Indoctrination could be a thing of the past.*

"Here it is Chief," Daniel said. The screen lit up with the copy of Horatio's report that had been filed with the Elections Commission.

"Just the report you filed Chief," Calvin said. "Nothing else in their records."

"Well, we better get back to the bitch and let her know we agree," Horatio said. "Unless any of you nerds have any ideas on how else we can handle this."

"No, that's about it," Calvin and Daniel agreed.

Calvin went back to the Ashland County web site and brought up the cease and desist message. "What do you want me to say chief?" Calvin asked.

"Just say it's agreed," Horatio said.

Calvin worked the keyboard to bring up "Reply to Sender." Then he typed in "it's agreed." Clicking on the send bar, he said, "There she goes."

"Good," Horatio said, as he turned to leave. He was thinking, *who the hell would bother rubbing shoulders with these nerds if they weren't dependant on their fucking machines?*

"Hey chief, we're getting a return," Daniel yelled.

Horatio spun around and viewed the screen. There it was-three words, "So be it," followed by three X's and three O's.

"Son-of-a-bitch!" Horatio exclaimed, while shaking his head in amazement.

Chapter 26. Two Down.
Spring, 1996

Lilly had been busy planning a graduation party for the twins. Their high school education was completed. Darcy was nervous and undecided about what she wanted to do. Marcy planned to attend the Junior College in the city.

Marcy had always worked at restaurants and talked about being a restaurateur for a career. She intended to attend a Chef's school in St. Paul after college.

Darcy on the other hand was a problem. She had always liked to baby sit for her spending money. She was a very unsettled young lady. She had been having a terrible time getting along with her brother Rainy. They had been like two peas in a pod when they were little tykes. Lilly sighed, *Why, oh why did that have to change?*

Rainy had purchased a little cottage on the far north side of the city. He had moved into it the first summer after graduating from high school. He had spent an extra year in school because the Home School Provider felt they were pushing him to hard and his grades were suffering. The Provider had contacted Lilly during Rainy's sophomore year. After some discussion, it was agreed that Rainy had experienced some brain damage due to malnutrition. They had stretched out his course material. They thought that by slowing things down his grades would improve. The strategy had worked.

Rainy seldom came to the house anymore. But Lilly saw him

every day at the lumberyard. Willie Slocum was store and office manager. He had replaced Lori Gustafson. He drew house plans during the winter months. Rainy was yard manager and handled all the details in the yard. The two boys got along famously. Rainy also drew house plans during the winter months.

The Hartec house plans were unique in that they would draw all views of the house and the plans came with materials list. There were also cutting instructions and explanations of how the materials were supposed to be used. The Hartecs charged more for their house plans than the local architects. However, they applied all but one hundred dollars of that cost as a credit against materials purchased from their yard.

A lot of contractors doing the actually construction were prone to brag, "If you follow the plans on a Hartec house; you can wheel all your scraps away with one wheelbarrow load. If you follow other plans; you will have a dangerous bonfire."

The business had been expanding consistently. Roger's business philosophy was, "Grow or Die." They had added more lines of merchandise. They had also become a lawn and garden center as well as a home appliance store.

Roger's holdings had grown considerably since the firewood business required more and more timber acreage. The Siding Lumberyard owned over a section of timberland in the Siding Hill Country.

Roger had transferred more and more responsibility onto Willie and Rainy. At age fifty-two he was slowing down and changes in the weather had negative effects on his damaged leg. At the end of a hard week he would develop a noticeable limp. The limp usually disappeared over a restful weekend.

Hearing a car pull up to the garage, Lilly looked out the window to see Lori Gustafson getting out. "Come right up," Lilly shouted out the window. Lori had volunteered to help clean the raw vegetables for the vegetable tray.

"Good afternoon honey," Lori said, as she stepped out of the elevator into the kitchen. "One certainly appreciates that elevator when they're seventy-two years old."

"Yes they do," Lilly agreed.

"What's the food plans for the party?" Lori asked.

"The twins wanted to keep it simple," Lilly said. "It's going to be Lennie's barbequed beef on buns with potato and pickle chips. We'll have this vegetable tray and punch. Roger will have a cooler of beer for the adults."

"That won't take much," Lori chuckled. "Those old bucks have slowed down with the drinking too. I guess it was bound to happen."

Just then Marcy showed up in the kitchen via the elevator.

"Goodness! We didn't even hear you drive in," a startled Lilly said.

"I could hear you people yakking over the noise my little car makes," Marcy said, with a chuckle.

"You're home early," Lilly stated.

"It's such a nice day," Marcy said. "All the kids were out of town. The hamburger joint was dead. A bunch of us volunteered to leave early. I've got about four hours before I start waiting tables tonight. That job pays better. I thought I would try for a nap."

"So you're planning on attending the Junior College this fall," Lori said.

"Yes, then I want to go to a chef's school," Marcy said. "Or maybe I could join the Army and be a cook. I'd learn the trade while being paid."

Lori chuckled. "According to what all the veterans tell me-the only thing you will learn how to make is shit-on-a-shingle. Better go to chef's school, honey."

"Better listen to your Grandmother," Lilly said, with a smile. "Where's your sister today?"

"Over at the yard," Marcy said, "Willie had some displays he needed set up. She's helping him."

"Does Willie manage to keep Darcy and Rainy separated?" Lilly inquired.

"No problem there," Marcy said. "They keep as far from each other as possible."

"Oh Lord, that's not good," Lori said. "They use to be inseparable. They were never more than a shadow's length away from each other. Whatever happened there?"

"Oh it's a case of raging hormones," Marcy said. "They're in love."

"Marcy!" Lilly snapped, "They're brother and sister."

"No they're not Mom," Marcy protested. "I told them as much. I told Darcy to talk to you about it. I've told Rainy to talk to Dad about it. They're both so stubborn and stupid."

"What makes you so sure they're in love?" Lori inquired.

"They told me so," Marcy said. "Darcy thinks it's unfair that she has to be Rainy's sister. Rainy told me all the girls he's dated are starting to think he's queer. He said to me, 'I can't kiss those other girls because I feel like I'm cheating on Darcy.' There were tears in his eyes Mom."

"Lordy, lordy," Lori said, "Lilly, you and Roger are going to have to get a handle on this. Those poor kids are going to be miserable for the rest of their lives. Maybe they're meant for each other."

"Oh!" Lilly exclaimed, as she sat down with a thump on a kitchen stool. "I didn't see this one coming, at all. Thank you Marcy. I suppose there's no reason they can't get married. We can prove they're not related."

"Well honey, I must be getting Sam's supper soon," Lori said. "I'll shove off now, love you. I'll see you again Sunday afternoon."

"Love you Lori," Lilly said, as Lori entered the elevator.

That night Lilly had told Roger about their children's dilemma.

"I think we should find out if we can get them married," Roger said. "I don't know what I would have done if somebody had told me I couldn't marry you. Especially after that night we had seen Brigadoon."

Lilly stuck her tongue out at a smiling Roger. He planted a kiss on her lips.

"What's that for, " Lilly asked.

"I overheard some teenagers talking at the garden center the other day," Roger said. "They had said that when a person stuck their tongue out at you, it meant that they were saying, 'Kiss me quick, and don't slobber.'" Lilly and Roger were chuckling while holding tightly to each other.

The next morning Lilly and Roger met at his desk in their

library. "I'm going to call the Clerk of Court at a County Seat in South Dakota," Roger said. "A lot of people elope to South Dakota to get married faster."

"The court house won't be open today, its Saturday," Lilly protested.

"I think they're still open on Saturday mornings in South Dakota," Roger said. It hasn't been that long ago that the court house was open Saturday mornings here."

Roger dialed Directory Assistance and requested the telephone number for the Clerk of Court in Indian Wells, South Dakota. After writing the number down, Roger hung up and said, "Now we'll see if anybody's home."

Roger dialed the number and somebody picked up after the first ring. "Clerk of Court, Indian Wells Court House," came the reply.

"Good morning," Roger said. "This is Roger Hartec in Ashland Falls, Minnesota."

"How can I help you Roger?" Came the reply.

"We have a son and a daughter. Both are adopted. The boy's twenty two and the girl's near eighteen."

"And they want to get married," the voice interrupted. "Judge Harland Harrington does it all the time. The Judge requires three things: birth certificates, blood tests and the bride to be can't be pregnant. The Judge says if the groom to be is pregnant, he'll marry them right away. However, if the bride to be is pregnant-it doesn't matter if she's forty years old; they have to wait until after the baby is born."

Roger chuckled, "He appears to be a man who knows his mind," He said.

"That he is," The clerk said. "The Judge insists that less than ten percent come back after the baby is born. He figures he's saving the people the price of a divorce."

"And who can argue with logic like that?" Roger asked.

"Well a lot of people do," the clerk said. "But that's the way it is and I don't see old Judge Harland ever changing."

"Thanks for the information," Roger said. "We didn't think you would open."

"This will be the last year for Saturday mornings," the clerk said. "Not much happens on Saturday mornings anymore. In fact, you'll probably be the only person I'll talk to this morning. I feel like the Maytag repairman. By the way, how big of a wedding are you planning? We're known as the Little Las Vegas. If you give me your address, I'll send information from local motels that will put on about any type of affair you wish for. Their brochures are in the lobby. I've got all morning to put them in an envelope and mail them to you."

"Say, that would be great," Roger said. "The Grandparents will want to attend. We'll probably be a party of fifteen or twenty."

"Good. We appreciate the business," the clerk said. "I'll get this information in the mail box today. You'll have all the phone numbers you'll need to make your plans. Have a good day sir. Goodbye."

"Well that was one thoughtful Clerk of Court," Roger said, as he hung up the receiver.

"Do your ears hurt," Lilly asked. "I could hear her plain as day, sitting next to you."

"No, she really didn't sound that loud, but her voice had extreme clarity," Roger said. "Course you could have been picking up the sound as it came through my head and was amplified as it came out my other ear."

"Roger! You can make up the weirdest things," Lilly exclaimed. "Your head isn't hollow. Leastwise, I can't see through it."

"Ah, you're going to need a flashlight," Roger replied. "It's kind of murky in there."

Sunday morning broke sunny and clear. "You know the Lord has really been good to us whenever we have a party," Lilly said. "We've gotten the most beautiful days for our summer parties."

"Yes," Roger agreed. "There was our wedding, Janice's graduation and wedding, Kelly's welcome party and Rainy's graduation. They were all nice days. Hope we don't get rained out today. However, there's rain in the forecast."

Lilly had spoken to Darcy about the situation with Rainy. "Your father called a Judge in South Dakota who will marry you two if you're blood tests turn out okay. You can't be pregnant."

Darcy was giddy with delight. "Oh Mom, I love him so," Darcy said. "I want to have children with him."

"You're not pregnant now?" Lilly asked.

"Mom! How could I be?" Darcy asked. "All we've done is fight for the last three years; ever since Rainy started dating other girls."

"Did Marcy tell you about Rainy?" Lilly asked.

"Yes she did," Darcy said. "It makes perfect sense. Rainy always paid more attention to me than he did to Marcy. For Marcy he was a good brother."

"Well your father paid Rainy a visit last evening to explain the situation," Lilly said. "Rainy will come to the party this afternoon so you two can work things out. However, what ever you do, don't get pregnant. The Judge won't marry you if you're pregnant. The blood test will tip them off."

Lilly and Darcy had gone to help Marcy and Roger take everything down to the tables in the garage, and on the garage apron. Through the space provided by the hinges on the partially opened basement door, Lilly caught a peek of Darcy hugging her sister and thanking her. Lilly smiled at Roger, "This will get interesting when Rainy arrives," she said.

The guests Marcy and Darcy had invited to their graduation party started to arrive. The men all had a bottle of beer in their hands. Lilly took inventory of the crowd because she hadn't seen the list. The twins had only informed her of how many would be there. She had felt the number was sufficient so that nobody was left out. She was especially pleased when the twins informed her that Randy and Jackie would be bringing Lydia Sanderson along with them. Colleen had called to inform her that she and Kelly would be out later in the afternoon.

"Here comes Willie and Janice and the stair step gang," Roger fairly shouted. "Excuse me gentlemen," Roger said as he set his bottle of beer down on a nearby table. "I'll help Janice with the youngums"

Roger rushed across the slab and down the line of cars to where he anticipated they would park. He arrived at the spot before the Eagle turned into the driveway.

The men moved a little closer to where the women stood, "What's with the moniker stair step gang?" Sam asked.

Lilly chuckled. "Watch when Roger lines them up and marches them in," She said.

"They're still driving that old Eagle wagon you and Roger gave Janice for her sixteenth birthday," Lori said, in amazement.

"Yep, it's got nearly three hundred thousand miles on it," Randy said. "Willie and I have put in a new set of lifters, a new transmission and torque converter, one constant velocity joint and brakes. It's been a good old rig. Sixteen years old now."

Willie pulled the wagon into its parking slot. All the windows came down. "Hi Dad," Janice said to Roger.

"Grandpa, grandpa," came a chorus from the back seat.

Roger reached it through the open window and unlocked the door. Opening the door, he said, "Okay troops, fall out." Two boys and a girl tumbled out. The girl who was the youngest and smallest fell to the ground.

Roger quickly picked the little girl up and hugged her. "Are you all right, honey?' he asked.

"Course I am Grandpa," she said. "I'm tough."

"Okay, you're first in line," Roger said. The two boys lined up behind her. "Okay Janice, do you have the packs for the troops?"

"Here they are Dad," Janice said, as she passed out something for each child to carry. Roger gave the children a burden according to their size. "Here Dad, you can carry little Roger," Janice said, as she handed Roger a baby of about six months of age. "And here's your back pack." She handed the diaper bag to Roger.

"I hope these are the clean ones," Roger said, as he sniffed at the bag.

"Of course they are," Janice said. The reason there's so many is because we have two in diapers."

"Oh," Roger said. "Okay troops, forward march. Your left, your left," Roger called cadence.

"Your left, your left," came three small voices.

"Your left, right, left," Roger called.

"Your left, right, left," came the echo.

"Look at the tops of their heads," Lilly said to the adults

observing the scene. "That's why Roger calls them the stair step gang."

The observers began to chuckle when they realized the tops of the children's heads looked like evenly spaced stair steps.

"They're all a bunch of tow heads just like their Grandpa Randy," Jaclyn proudly stated. "And just a year apart, except for the last one."

"I couldn't help but notice that Janice is calling Roger Dad now," Lori said.

"She has been for a while now," Jaclyn said. "I think it came about when Danny and Stephanie got transferred back to the states. They started spending some of their vacations in Ashland Falls. Danny was calling Roger Dad before Clayton died."

Danny and Steph have three of the cutest children," Lilly said, as Roger called halt. "They're so well mannered, just like these three," The three youngsters stomped their little feet to a halt.

"That's quite a gang you have there, Roger," Oscar said, as Roger handed the baby to Lilly and with one foot scooted the diaper bag under a table.

"I'm hoping for a stairway gang," Roger said, with a sly smile, as he took the pans of bars from the small children and set them on the table.

"Troops dismissed," Roger said. The three children scrambled to the playground equipment in the back yard.

"I heard that Dad," Janice said. "The answer is no, unless you can talk Willie into doing the birthing."

All the women laughed. "Good luck Roger," several said in unison.

"You men could never take the pain," Jaclyn teased. "Lord, when I had Willie I thought his head was a watermelon."

"It looked like a watermelon attached to that skinny little body," Randy said, with a chuckle. Looking at the men, Randy continued, "I don't dare repeat the names she called me for the next few weeks. Not in mixed company." All the men had a hearty laugh. All the women chuckled.

"I see the old Eagle is still purring along," Sam said to Willie.

"Yes, it keeps hanging in there," Willie answered. "We're going to get a Suburban. The Eagle will be too small when the children get a little bigger. Of course we're going to need a bigger house too. Which one will come first-I'm not sure-probably the house."

"It's gotten dark in here," Oscar stated, as he walked out of the garage to study the weather.

"It appears to be clouding up," Sam said, as he followed Oscar outside.

"Coming in from the Northeast," Oscar stated. "Looks like a pretty good break in the clouds up there." He pointed to an opening in the cloudbank on the horizon. "We'll probably get a couple more hours of sun before the rain hits."

Lilly banged on a kettle with a large serving spoon. "Time to eat," She yelled. "Roger, will you please round up the children and grand children."

Roger walked over to a small venting window on the back wall of the garage and yelled, "Chow time," to the grand children on the playground. "I'll have to go up to the library to get the teenagers. Rainy and Darcy are out front behind Oscar's pickup."

"I'll get the two out front," Lori said. She had filled the rest of the family in about her grandchildren's dilemma.

After the picnic dinner, the small children went back to the playground. Marcy and her teenage friends went back to the library. Rainy and Darcy disappeared down the trail the twins had used to come to the Hartec's place.

"What's the attraction in the library?" Lydia Sanderson asked. "It's such a beautiful day out here."

"It's that computer that fellow from Grand Forks Air Force base gave to me," Roger said. "How's that one I gave you working out?" Roger asked Randy.

"Oh we have it working real good," Randy responded.

"Yes, it's a lot of fun," Jaclyn said. "The state of Minnesota set up a web site in July of ninety-four. We'll be able to pay bills online by the end of this year."

"So you think it will develop into something more than an expensive toy?" Lilly questioned.

"Oh yes," Randy stated. "The World Wide Web was created in eighty-nine. People in the electronics world are predicting home computers in a couple of years. They'll start out at about five hundred dollars and quickly drop down to about two hundred fifty as sales take off."

Roger chuckled. "I wouldn't give twenty-five cents for that junk. The only reason I got these three is because they were given to me. Some times I think I should take the one I got to the dump, where it was originally headed. However, it is a big improvement over the typewriter and word processor. I haven't used my word processor since I got a printer hooked up to the computer."

"Well, the three you got are obsolete military units," Randy said. "I can get some new boards and tweak your unit like I did ours. I did the same on the one you gave Willie. He purchased some special programs and he and Rainy do jobs on it. That's why they insisted they didn't need another draftsman this spring."

"The computer speeds things up that much?" Roger questioned.

"You bet," Randy stated. "Windows is coming out with a new program all the time. When they come out with something that's an improvement over Windows 95, I'll be happy to upgrade your machine."

"Oh Roger, you should do that," Lilly said. "The twins really love that machine. They can go on the state's web site and get a lot of information from the Capitol."

"Here come Kelly and Colleen," Lori said.

"Roger, I believe we should get all the tables and chairs into the garage," Lilly said, "It's starting to sprinkle."

"I'm going to get a beer for Kelly," Randy said. "We've got to get him going with the Irish jokes."

Lilly could see disappointment in Randy's face when he approached Kelly with an open bottle of beer in his hand. Turning to look at Kelly and Colleen, she could see there was something very wrong. Randy still offered the beer to Kelly, which he accepted.

Lilly rushed to a tearful Colleen and took her in her arms. "I'm sorry dear. Is there anything I can do for you?"

"No," Colleen sobbed. "Irvin was killed in a prison riot last night. That's why we're late. We shouldn't have come. This should be a happy occasion."

"Nonsense dear," Lilly said. "It's times like this that you need your friends. Come with me. Let's get you seated."

Inside the garage the women had all gathered around a tearful Colleen. "Irvin was really rotten to the core," Colleen sobbed. "But we always held out hope. We couldn't just give up on him. He even called Kelly Dad. That was just last week when Kelly went to visit him. That was the first time he had ever called Kelly Dad. I was hoping Irvin would allow me to go with Kelly for a visit. Now he's dead." Colleen's body was wracked with grief.

"Anybody else killed in that riot?" Oscar inquired of Kelly, as he handed another beer, to him and took his empty bottle.

"Yes," Kelly said. "Dong and one of his prison henchmen. Two other henchmen are in serious condition. Probably won't make it." Kelly set his bottle of beer down and pulled out a handkerchief to blow his nose.

"He actually called you Dad?" Jenny inquired, as she looked into Kelly's moisture glazed eyes.

"Yes, his last words to me as the guard took him away were, 'I'll make you proud of me Dad,'" Kelly said.

Looking at Oscar, Kelly continued, "Dong was due a parole hearing at the end of the month. Prison scuttlebutt was that he was going to be granted parole. Irvin held his own real good for being just a street punk."

Oscar clapped a big hand on Kelly's shoulder and said, "There's some good in all bad, Kelly, that's just the way it is."

Lilly suspected that there was something these two men knew that they weren't telling anybody else.

Chapter 27. A New Sheriff. Summer, 1996

I t was a beautiful July Saturday. Business at the yard was unusually slow because of the impending holiday. Darcy and Rainy had agreed to keep the yard open until the noon closing time. They wished to accommodate the housing contractors. The rest of the family and hires took off early.

Roger and Lilly had gone on a long camping weekend. They had left on Friday morning. It had been a busy summer and Roger had wanted to hire more help. However, Willie and Rainy had insisted that the electronic age and computers made it possible to get way more work done with fewer people. They even had parents with computer savvy children placing firewood orders online. Roger didn't understand it all. However, the numbers were impressive. All of his family knew that Roger was a bottom line man.

As Darcy and Rainy made the rounds locking the various doors and gates-they met in a lumber shed near the main gate. Rainy had walked up behind Darcy and placing his arms around her he started kissing her on her neck. Darcy backed up pushing Rainy until he bumped into the end of a stack of lumber. Grasping his right hand and sucking in her tummy, she slid the hand inside her jeans and panties into her wetness. Taking Rainy's left hand, she pushed it under her blouse and inside her bra.

"Will you marry me, Darling?" Rainy whispered in her ear.

"Yes, yes Rainy," Darcy said as he extracted his hands from

inside her clothes and took her in his arms. After much kissing they continued their chores of locking up.

"What would you like to do tonight?" Rainy asked. "Where would you like to go for supper?"

"Your place Darling," Darcy said. "Tell you what Rainy. I'll go to the grocery store and get some groceries for the weekend. You go to Pamida and get a big box of condoms. I can't be pregnant or the Judge won't marry us."

"Okay, I'll see you at my place," Rainy said. "I'll pick up a bottle of champagne to celebrate."

The two had left the yard in their separate vehicles to do their appointed tasks. Darcy knew Rainy was a little slow mentally. She had talked to her mother about it.

"Doctor Taylor believes his mental slowness was caused by malnutrition," Lilly had said. "He's bright enough and learned rapidly at first. It was when we got into complex subjects like Algebra and Geometry that he began to struggle. He was always capable of learning, although a little slow. History was a piece of cake for him. Of course, he and Roger were always watching The History Channel on television.

"What about our children?" Darcy had asked.

"There's no guarantee," Lilly had told her. "Doctor Taylor is certain Rainy's disability was due to malnutrition and not drugs. If that's the case- your children will be normal. Rainy wasn't born that way. His disability came about after he was born."

Darcy had made up her mind that she would take that chance. "I love him and I want to have his children," she said to her reflection in the rear view mirror.

Lilly had had an extremely busy year. First there was the twin's graduation party and then the prospect of another wedding. Rainy and Darcy had gotten back to being two peas in a pod. Darcy was proudly wearing an engagement ring.

Lilly and Roger had made all the arrangements with the Clerk of Court in Indian Wells, South Dakota. An appointment for blood tests was scheduled at the clinic. Judge Harland Harrington would perform the ceremony, once the blood tests determined it was okay.

The wedding would take place on a Friday afternoon in October. Arrangements had been made with one of the motels catering to wedding parties. Besides the wedding, this years elections were on Lilly's mind.

Sheriff Callahan was retiring and a new sheriff would be elected. Minnesota's primary election was on September fourteenth. That was when all the wannabes would be reduced to two candidates in this non-partisan race.

Lilly, Lori, and Jenny wanted Randy Slocum to run. At fifty-two years of age and a veteran of Ashland Fall's police force, he was the perfect candidate. They needed to get Jaclyn and Janice, on the inside, encouraging Randy to file.

"Randy's concerned about the records of his nervous breakdown being exposed," Jaclyn told the women one summer day when they were together for a family gathering.

"Maybe somebody will bring it up," Lilly said, "but I'll bet we can overcome that. Jackie, if you can convince Randy to file, I'm volunteering to run his campaign."

"That just may tip the scales in our favor," Jaclyn had said. "Harley has told Randy many times that he's been passed over for promotions because of that horrible incident. He's suggested that Randy should try different cities. But this is our home. We don't want to leave here. If Randy could retire from the Sheriff's position, it would be a tremendous boost in his retirement check. However, he's pretty sensitive about the time he spent under the care of a psychiatrist."

"What did the doctors tell you Lilly," Jenny inquired. "Didn't they say that the patient returned to society a stronger individual?"

"That's right," Lilly responded. "It certainly has worked that way for Roger. It was terrible-the stress those veterans were put under. They suppressed the bad as long as they could. But eventually it will boil up. Roger's nightmares are gone and he's gotten his confidence back. He's a stronger individual than when I met him."

Randy keeps reminding me of Thomas Eagleton," Jaclyn said. "Eagleton was dropped like a hot potato by George McGovern during the presidential race of seventy-two."

"That's right," Lori said, "old George dropped Eagleton like a hot potato and my Sam dropped George just as fast."

"Yes," Jenny said. "Oscar insists that's what cost George the election. Oscar say's George had the presidency in the bag until he displayed his lack of courage; courage that he had displayed often during the war."

The Vietnam veteran's homecoming didn't help either," Lori said. "After I retired and we started traveling, we went through several towns where there were two American Legion clubrooms. One clubroom was for the Vietnam veterans and another for all other veterans. We stopped into the Vietnam veterans club for lunch. I inquired of the waitress about the two separate Legion Clubs. The waitress told me that the other Legionnaires didn't want to be associated with baby killers. There were enough Vietnam Veterans in that town to form their own club."

"Oh Lord," Jenny said, "How can people be so narrow minded and cruel?"

"Exactly," Lori replied. "The waitress told us her husband lost two limbs because of a four-year-old boy carrying a satchel charge. Of course, I had to tell her about Chester and we had a good cry together."

"Roger always insisted that he was lucky because he never had to shoot any four-year-old boys," Lilly said. "I swear, some days I think that man must wonder if the white stuff in chicken manure isn't vanilla ice cream."

"Boy, that's positive thinking," Jaclyn said, as the entire bunch of women began to laugh.

"Well he always tries to find some good in all bad," Lilly chuckled. "I don't think he's missed a cue yet."

"Randy says the same thing," Jaclyn said. "He was always on the front line. He didn't have to shoot children. He remembers when Jimmy Schwartz volunteered to be in the protection detail for General Westmoreland. Jimmy thought it would be good duty flying around on that big airplane. Randy said 'Nobody knew the job would entail shooting kids.'"

"Roger told me that's why he picked Ashland Falls to settle in," Lilly said. "He ran into too much trouble everywhere else. He even lived in a town with two Legion clubs for a while. After that, he started checking out cities before he moved. Roger would go into a town and put in employment applications at sheriff's departments and police departments. He said that was the quickest way to learn if he, as a Vietnam War Veteran, would be welcome."

"He never got hired?" Janice asked.

"He wasn't looking for a job in law enforcement," Lilly replied. "He just wanted to learn if he would be welcome in the area. He was surprised when he put in his applications in Ashland Falls. All the veterans on the two forces wore their ribbons on their uniforms. That's why he purchased the lumberyard in Siding. He was at his wit's end finding a place where he could do business and not have his military status work against him."

"That was a great policy Oscar and Harley formulated and convinced the County Board and City Council to sign on with it," Jennie said. "Oscar said they got a lot of good men from out of state. There's a stigma attached to being a Vietnam Veteran. The Veterans really appreciate being able to display their ribbons and medals."

"And that brings us back to Randy," Lilly said. "Jackie, if you can convince Randy to throw his hat into the ring, The Biddy Brigade will work to get him elected. That Boy Scout attitude of his has endeared him with the elderly and medical professionals. He certainly deserves the job."

"I'll do my best," Jaclyn promised.

"I'll step up my suggestions too," Janice said. "He would make an excellent sheriff."

"Yes he would," Jennie agreed.

"Oh, by the way Jackie, Lydia Sanderson called me this past week," Lilly said. "She wanted to know if I could convince Randy to throw his hat into the ring. Lydia said they have a group of forty old folks living in the high rise who want to march and campaign as soon as Randy registers. They plan to march from the high rise to the west end of Main Street and back again, while passing out brochures. They've ordered five hundred brochures and have them on hand. They also have banners and signs."

"Ho boy Janice, we better be able to convince Randy to do this,"

Jaclyn said. "I'll tell him how many people he's going to disappoint if he doesn't run."

"The last day to register is this coming Friday," Lilly said. "Is Randy on duty that day?"

"No, it's his day off," Jaclyn said.

"Well," Lilly said, "why don't you and Janice march him out the door after lunch? Take him to the courthouse and register. I'll call Lydia to get the parade started and you can drive Randy down Main Street to see his support."

"That just might work," Jaclyn said. "If he can see he's got a lot of support, we may just get him over to the courthouse to register. I really think he wants the job. It's just that psychiatrist thing that's got him worried."

"I can't fault him for his concern," Jenny said. "After George McGovern dumped Thomas Eagleton, those men have been stigmatized. We supported George until he pulled that stunt. Oscar said, 'Eagleton was smart enough to know he needed help and got it. The rest of those politicians need the same help, but aren't even smart enough to know it.'"

"Well one of the candidates, I won't say which one, needs a dozen psychiatrists working on him," Lori said. "Unfortunately, he isn't even close to admitting it."

Friday morning broke clear and sunny but very cool for August. Lilly had received a telephone call from Jaclyn right after breakfast. Jaclyn had informed Lilly that Randy had agreed to register if he thought he had enough support. "I've agreed to drive him to the court house at two p.m." Jaclyn said. "Can you get the Biddy Brigade to march on Main Street then?"

"I sure will," Lilly replied. "We'll start the march at one-thirty. Thank the Lord it's going to be a cool day. A lot of those old people are in wheelchairs and electric scooters. Their slowness will make the march last a while. Also, there will be three vanloads going over to the courthouse with you to get Randy registered. Oscar and Jenny are in charge of that group."

"Oh good," Jaclyn replied. "Janice and all her kids will be with us as well as my parents. It sounds like we have plenty of the support Randy is looking for lined up."

"Great," Lilly said, "I'll see you at the courthouse this afternoon."

At two p.m. Jaclyn and her family had piled into her parent's Chevrolet-suburban and headed for the courthouse via Main Street. The Biddy Brigade had started down the second block of their route. A lot of pedestrians were lined up on both sides of the street waving banners that the Biddy Brigade had purchased and distributed. The banners proclaimed "Slocum for Sheriff," and had been passed out earlier by more agile members from the retirement home. It was a festive crowd that shouted encouragement to the Slocum entourage as they proceeded to the courthouse.

After arriving at the courthouse, they were greeted by Lilly, Oscar, Jenny and about forty other supporters. Lilly, Jenny and Oscar went to assist Janice with her children. Jaclyn was hanging onto Randy's arm as they walked to the County Auditor's window to register. The group followed behind and waited inside as the registration took place.

When the Auditor announced the registration was complete a cheer went up from the crowd. Jaclyn kissed her very nervous husband on the lips and said, "congratulations dear."

Upon returning to the parking lot, they were stopped by two reporters. One reporter was from the radio station and the other was from the newspaper. The radio reporter got his information first and went inside the courthouse to call in his report. Then Randy answered questions posed by the newspaper reporter.

When the Slocum's got their brood loaded into the suburban, the news of Randy's registration was already on the radio.

"Let's cruise Main Street again," Jaclyn said.

"We sure will dear," Jaclyn's father said. "I wouldn't miss this drive for the world."

As they started down Main Street from the east end, they had to wait as the old folks were crossing the street on their way back to the high rise apartments. The city police were assisting with the crossings. A couple of officers were scurrying about with the wooden wheel chair ramps to help the chair bound up and down the curbs.

When the Slocum group was allowed to proceed, the police

officers yelled, "congratulations," to Randy. The people on both sides of the street were waving their banners and holding up transistor radios. Teenagers in parked cars had their radios turned up so everybody could hear the news about Randy's registering.

"You've seemed to have impressed the whole spectrum of the masses son," Jaclyn's father said. "Heck, those boys in that car aren't even old enough to vote."

Lilly was pleased with the way the registration had turned out. There wasn't any doubt that a lot of people were pleased with the prospects of a Sheriff Slocum. She couldn't help wondering if Randy's nervous breakdown years ago would become an issue. *Well, they would have to surmount that obstacle when it arrived.*

The following Monday morning, the news on the radio was all about the withdrawals of the other men registered to run for the sheriff's position. When Lilly arrived at the lumberyard with her noon lunch basket, she heard the announcement on the radio. The last of Randy's opponents had withdrawn from the race. Randy would be the only one on the ballot.

"Telephone for Lilly Hartec," Willie Slocum announced from behind the service counter. He unraveled the cord and pushed the telephone to the outside edge of the counter. "It's Mom," Willie said, as he handed the receiver to Lilly.

"Did you hear the news?" an excited Jaclyn asked.

"Yes I did," Lilly responded. "The job is Randy's."

"Oh Lord! And he was so worried about his chances," Jaclyn exclaimed. "He's coming home for lunch. Harley told him to take an extra hour."

"Remember, we'll want to do a couple of meet the candidate meetings," Lilly said. "We don't want to appear presumptuous. We've got over a thousand dollars to spend. The old folks solicited donations on their wheelchair run. The people Oscar and Jenny escorted all made donations. Oscar and Jenny also donated."

"Oh thank you, thank you for organizing this," Jaclyn said. "Let us know when you can arrange the meetings and we'll be sure to accommodate you. Thank you again and have a good day Lilly."

The rest of her family was at the lunch table waiting for Lilly to finish on the telephone. As Lilly sat down, she said to Willie, "your mother certainly was excited about the news on the radio."

"Mom was on pins and needles all weekend," Willie said. "We couldn't believe the turnout for the registration and wondered if the enthusiasm would hold up through the weekend."

"It appears the enthusiasm grew over the weekend," Roger stated. "The other candidates were smart to withdraw. Running against Randy would have been a waste of both time and money. Randy's the most qualified for the position."

By the end of the week Lilly was able to line up an auditorium and a dance hall in the rural areas for a meet the candidate meeting. Jaclyn rented the college theater; dates were set and ads placed. Now Lilly was able to get back to wedding plans.

It was the end of October when the Hartec clan with in-laws and grandparents took all the rooms in one wing of a motel at Indian Wells, South Dakota. Judge Harland Harrington was scheduled to officiate at the wedding ceremony at two p.m. that Friday afternoon.

The bride, groom and parents had spent the morning getting the details taken care of before the wedding. They had a nine a.m. appointment at the clinic for blood tests. It was a merry crowd that filled the courtroom that afternoon for the ceremony.

Judge Harland Harrington was a tall bearded man in his mid-seventies. He was quite taken by the charming Darcy in her wedding attire. The two of them spent a lot of time in conversation before the ceremony. They were both showing each other family pictures. Darcy was having quite a time explaining her diverse family.

The guests all filed into the courtroom as the appointed hour arrived. Judge Harrington pronounced them man and wife. "You may kiss the bride," The Judge said to Rainy.

Rainy and Darcy kissed. Then to everybody's amazement, Darcy reached up while standing on her toes and pulled the tall Judge's face down to her level. Then, she kissed him on the lips. "Thank you for making this wonderful man my husband," Darcy said. "We'll name one of our sons Harland."

"Harland Hartec," the red-faced Judge said. "It rolls off the tongue nicely. Ladies and gentlemen, I give you Mr. and Mrs. Rainy Hartec."

While the cheering was taking place, Lilly rushed to invite Judge Harrington to the reception and encouraged him to bring his wife along.

Everybody congratulated the bride and groom and then they all headed to the motel and reception. Roger, Randy and Willie were busy helping Janice with the Slocum brood. Four children only a year apart were a handful, but Janice and Willie loved it. It was what they both had wished for in their childhoods.

Chapter 28. The Exhibition. Summer, 1998

S heriff Randy Slocum was putting the finishing touches on plans for a private shooting exhibition. Five years earlier, Randy's wife had told him about a conversation Roger Hartec had had with his wife Lilly. According to the story, Roger had gotten off forty shots for forty kills in a night river crossing ambush.

Randy had talked to his cousin, Raymond Elmdorf, about this revelation. Raymond was still active in the Army National Guard. He had talked to his commanding officer, Colonel Jamison, who was a sniper instructor.

"I've heard of a man who pulled that off in Vietnam, "Colonel Jamison had said," but I think he's dead. Never knew who he was. We just referred to him as the Lone Ranger. He didn't like working with a spotter. He claimed it cost him to many kills. His killer instinct must have been paramount. Without a spotter he didn't get credit for the kills. He sure as hell wasn't in it for the glory."

"This man is a good friend of my cousin who happens to be the Sheriff of Ashland County," Raymond had said.

"Can you set up a shooting demonstration with him?" Colonel Jamison had inquired. "I can supply any weapon he wants to use."

"I'll see what I can do," Raymond had promised. "I'll have my cousin approach him about the possibility of a demonstration.

He's had a real bad episode of Post Traumatic Stress six years ago. I think he's recovered from that."

Randy had broached the subject with Lilly Hartec. She thought it was a good idea. Together they had suggested to Roger that Randy could arrange a shooting exposition on his cousin's farm, in the Red River Valley, west of Ashland County.

Lilly had urged Roger and he had agreed. "You must get together with your peers and talk about the war," Lilly insisted. "You'll be able to talk to these men who can understand everything you're talking about. It will be good for all of you. Oscar has agreed to drive you and Randy there. Randy and his cousin and Colonel Jamison were all snipers in the war. Their wives all think they need this chance to hash things over."

"How many people will be there?" Roger had asked.

"Six, as far as I know," Lilly replied. There would've only been five but Randy's cousin's dad got wind of it. He insisted he would be there instead of at the Hollis County fair. He's never missed a day at the fair before. He was on the front during World War Two. The Sheriff of Hollis County will be there to handle any shooting reports that may come into the Dispatcher's office. He'll have cell phone contact with the Dispatcher. He was also a sniper in Vietnam. They aren't expecting many calls because most people will be at the fair. Charley Pride will be performing there that afternoon."

"Well it should be an interesting day," Roger had said. "I have to let Randy know what we need for targets. Both county fairs are at the same time. I suppose almost everybody will be at the fairs."

"Yes dear," Lilly said. "And that's where all the women folks will be. You men will have the Elmdorf farm to yourselves, all afternoon."

When Oscar Thompson pulled the suburban into the farmyard, a wiry, short, old man rushed up to the driver's door and pulled it open. "Sergeant Thompson!" he gleefully cackled. "How are you doing? You old war criminal."

"War criminal! Hell! You're the master of the five finger discount," Oscar retorted.

Roger had gotten out of the passenger's seat and walked around the vehicle to where Oscar and Herman were.

"Roger, this is Supply Sergeant Herman Elmdorf," Oscar said. "He was possessor of the stickiest fingers in the U.S.Army. Herman, this is Roger Hartec. Roger's going to show you how to shoot. If you hadn't been in supply-they would've had to put you in artillery. You damn sure couldn't hit anything with a rifle."

"That's a fact," Herman cackled. "Never could make those things work right." Looking up at Roger, as they finished shaking hands, Herman smiled. "Locating beer was my forte'."

"Damned good at it," Oscar affirmed.

Herman signaled the other three men over and introduced them to Roger, Randy and Oscar. There were Hollis County Sheriff, Jerry Axle, Colonel Jamison and Herman Elmdorf's son Raymond.

After introducing Roger, Herman said, "I believe we've met somewhere before. But I'll be hanged if I can remember just where."

Randy looked at Oscar, who had a quizzical expression on his face. *They both knew Roger had grown up somewhere in Minnesota. Neither had thought about old Herman Elmdorf ever having an opportunity to know who Roger was. Was bringing Roger out here a mistake? Would his cover be gone?*

"I keep putting you together with Lilly Erickson," Herman continued. "The Ericksons were our neighbors years ago. Lorraine Erickson was my late wife's best friend. Most of that family died of a scarlet fever epidemic. Those who survived had bad hearts."

"My wife's maiden name was Erickson," Roger said.

"That's it!" Herman exclaimed. "You folks brought that southern sheriff over here for an introduction. We lived in Ashland County then. We lived in that old house on our southeast section. That's in Ashland County. We moved into the new place here, a few years ago, just before my wife passed away. God rest her soul. Well you can tell Lilly the Irishman got our vote."

Randy felt a sense of relief as he and Oscar began unloading supplies from Oscar's suburban. There were a bundle of laths and a package of fifty eight-inch white paper picnic plates, as well as a mechanical stapler.

Randy, Raymond and Jerry were busy stapling paper plates on

the laths, while Colonel Jamison fetched the automatic rifle with two twenty round clips and a supply of ammunition.

At Roger's direction, the stakes with paper plates stapled on them were driven into the ground of a field of stubble, which had remained after the winter wheat harvest. The targets were spread out in a pattern about a hundred yards wide and a half-mile from Roger's shooting position.

One plate had a split lath fastened to the main lath to stick up like a radio antenna. Three of the paper plates had a cross lath stapled across the paper plate horizontally to represent the mortar men, carrying their mortar tubes above their heads, as they waded the river.

Again at Roger's direction, the four special targets had been set up in a row at the far end of the field of targets-since these troops had been the last to enter the water. When the targets were all properly set, Roger walked over to Colonel Jamison to receive the rifle.

Picking up the rifle Roger had tinkered and examined it for what seemed to Randy like an eternity. Roger's face was completely expressionless. Randy looked questionally at Oscar for a second time. Again Randy couldn't help but wonder if they were making a mistake.

Oscar had slowly moved away from Herman and toward Roger. Clapping a big hand on Roger's shoulder, Oscar softly asked, "Anything wrong? Son."

"No, no," Roger stated, as he looked up at the concerned faces watching him. "I was just checking the serial number. I need to establish the characteristics of this weapon. There were some changes in later models. I always committed to memory the serial numbers of all the different weapons I used."

Randy noticed Colonel Jamison's eyebrows shoot up with interest.

"Is this one a later model?" Oscar asked.

"No, well, actually one later," Roger stated. "The serial number is only one digit larger than the serial number of the weapon I used that night in Vietnam."

"Well how do you like that?" Oscar chuckled. "This should be a piece of cake for you Roger."

"Still got my age against me," Roger replied, deadpan serious.

Colonel Jamison was ready with a stopwatch and spotter scope. "Better fire a few practice rounds to check the characteristics," He said.

By now the late morning sun was already hot. All the men were perspiring. The entire landscape was enshrouded in a haze. The humidity was nearing one hundred per cent.

Roger chambered a round and said, "Far left target." Then he slammed the rifle to his shoulder and snapped off the round.

"Dead center on the plate," Colonel Jamison said, as he looked up from his spotter's scope.

"Guess I don't need to do anymore adjusting," Roger said. "Winds calm and it's hot and sticky; just like the night of the crossing. Temperature must be in the nineties."

Raymond nudged Herman with his elbow. "I think you'll lose the bet and be paying for the beer, dad," he whispered.

"I already think it will be well worth the money," Herman whispered back. "Did you see the way he handled that weapon? Like his third arm. Damn! I couldn't make those things work that good."

Roger crawled up on a big round hay bale that was standing on end. Colonel Jamison passed the rifle and loaded clips to him along with a military poncho. The hay bale provided the rise Roger was on when the river crossing occurred. The poncho would prevent the hay bale from igniting, and Roger had used one on the night of the crossing. Oscar and Colonel Jamison took positions beside the bale with stopwatches and scopes.

"When you hear the first shot, start your watches," Roger stated. In less than two minutes the shooting was over with.

"Screwed up," Roger stated. "One plate won't have any hole. But two plates will have two holes. The one I used for the practice round and another that I hit twice. I got confused because all the targets stayed up after being shot. Didn't have that problem in Nam."

"You had well over a minute to skeedaddle," Colonel Jamison

said, as he looked through the spotter's scope. "All your shots are near the centers of the plates. Which target did you double up on? You must have put the second bullet on top of the first one. I can't see it."

"The one just to the right of the clear one," Roger said, as he handed Oscar the rifle and extra clip. Then Roger crawled off the hay bale with the poncho in tow.

"Yes sir, I see it," Colonel Jamison said. "Almost dead on top of your first round. It's less than half the hole off. Damn fine shooting Roger!"

Pulling his sweat soaked shirt away from his body, Roger said, "Now I'm ready for some cold beer."

"That shouldn't be a problem son," Oscar said. "Half the people here brought a case. I've got a twelve pack of MGD. I figured it was your favorite."

"Now we're getting to the part I'm good at," Herman cackled, with glee.

Oscar chuckled. "The only thing Herman was better at than drinking beer was finding it. He had to be good at finding it to practice his original attribute."

"Whew, It's going to be a real scorcher today," Herman said, as he wiped the sweat off his forehead with his bare forearm. "Let's skeedaddle into the screen porch. I closed all the windows and turned on the air conditioner first thing this morning. Follow me with those coolers boys."

Randy, Oscar, Jerry and Colonel Jamison all pulled coolers out of vehicles and headed for the house. The men gathered in the screen porch. The air-conditioned porch felt like a walk in cooler after being outdoors. They shook their shirts loose from their sweat soaked backs and started cracking beers.

"Close enough to noon to eat," Herman stated. "I'll get the sandwiches Mary made. How about some help with the pickles and chips Ray?"

"I'm famished," Jerry stated. "Breakfast was a little light this morning. I better have a sandwich before I start on the beer." Just then his cell phone rang. "Sheriff Axle here." There was a pause, and then Jerry said, "Good answer. If you get any more calls handle them the same way." There was a short pause then Jerry continued, "No, I didn't think about them being so fast either. Forty rounds in about a hundred seconds." There was another pause, "Yes, essentially he did it. I'll fill you in later."

All the men heard a loud "yahoo," of a female voice coming through Jerry's cell phone.

"Have a good day," Jerry said, with a smile. "That was our dispatcher, Jean Thornton," a red faced Jerry explained. "She's all alone there today. I had to confide in her about today because I expected some calls about all the shooting. She's got a good head on her shoulders and like she argued with me, she's got a dog in this fight. Her husband came back from Vietnam without any legs. Jean received one call so far. She told the caller it was an arms dealer demonstrating a new weapon to the sheriff's department. Jean and the caller were surprised at the closeness of the shots."

"That was some mighty fast shooting, considering the spread of the targets," Herman chuckled. "I had to see it to believe it. Damn! That was something."

"Roger, these sandwiches are ham and cheese with mayo and mustard on rye," Raymond explained. "Mary took the liberty of calling your wife to inquire about your favorite."

"That was real thoughtful of her," Roger said, with a smile. "Please tell her I appreciate the extra effort."

"Dive in fellows," Herman commanded. "If you leave here hungry or thirsty, you have an I.Q. problem."

Everybody chuckled as they loaded paper plates. Soon the room was quiet except for the crunching of chips and the popping of beer can tabs.

Chapter 29. Enigma Penetrated. Summer, 1998

After Randy had finished his sandwich he turned to Jerry and asked, "What years did you serve?"

"I was an advisor during the Easter offensive of seventy-two, same as Raymond," Jerry answered.

"Were you able to get the Vietnamese to fight?" Randy asked.

"Oh yes, there were some real good soldiers," Jerry stated.

"Officers weren't much," Raymond interjected. "To much nepotism and politics involved with them. With good leadership, most of their troops would fight hard. Course, they were totally dependant on our Air Force."

"Our leadership, especially the civilian wasn't much better," Jerry said. "Still isn't. When you fellows beat them at the gorilla game, they switched to conventional warfare. We whipped them at that. We won that war. But for some reason it doesn't feel like it."

"We had never won in the press because they were unwilling to print the facts," Raymond said. "The politicians pulled out completely. Never left an occupation force to help the South Vietnamese."

"That's right," Colonel Jamison concurred. "Would Europe or Korea turned out any different if we would have ended those wars the same as Vietnam? We still have Army and Air Force in those countries. Our politicians hung the South Vietnamese out to dry."

"Yep, the press lost that war for us," Raymond stated. "Bunch of self righteous bastards. They only cared about the second amendment. Most of the people in that business were a bunch of Godless socialists and they controlled what passed for news."

All ears perked up when Roger said, "We should never have a commander-in-chief who is afraid to use the big one. We don't have enough people to take on a war against the communists and expect to win without being efficient."

"They were worried about the ruskies stepping in," Oscar said.

"And we couldn't have whipped them?" Randy asked, as his eyebrows shot up.

"I don't think we knew for sure back then," Herman intoned.

"I don't know where our leaders got the idea we couldn't," Randy said. "General Giap said had we dropped the big one on Hanoi early in the war, with the threat of more to come, the North would have had to capitulate. They wouldn't have gotten support from anybody."

"The war was run by civilians and the Joint Chiefs of Staff were left out of the loop," Colonel Jamison said. "General LeMay sure as hell would have bombed them into oblivion. But nobody listened to him."

"I don't know fellows," Herman intoned. "Hindsight is always twenty-twenty."

"It isn't all hindsight," Roger said. "Our leaders, after Eisenhower and Kennedy, just didn't have confidence in our capitalist system. Yet, there had been plenty of evidence there."

"How's that, Roger?" Oscar asked.

"Well, we started out way behind in the space program," Roger said. "However, we caught up in short order and beat the Russians to the moon. Our boys had to ride machinery put together by the lowest bidder. Hardly our best."

"Lordy, lordy, you said a mouthful there, Roger," Herman said, as he took another drink of his beer.

"Our government was just to paranoid and secretive," Roger said. "The Russians put up a beeping satellite, and we had men flying on the periphery of outer space. Nobody knew about it. We were way ahead of the Russians when they launched Sputnik."

"Yeah," Randy agreed. "The space program was good, but not necessary at the time. We in the military took a back seat to the space program and The Great Society welfare state."

"I agreed," Raymond said. "We fought that war by ourselves. Hardly anybody at home was involved like they were in World War two. Had an all out effort been made to win the war, it wouldn't of lasted beyond the end of sixty-six."

"Ray's right," Randy agreed. "At the end of sixty-six we had suffered less than eighty-five hundred fatalities. Thanks to our politicians, who elected to kill off fifty-thousand more of us, our generation is a little skint."

"Yeah, and those who were killed in the late sixties and early seventies died for nothing," Roger said. "Had we pulled out in sixty-six there wouldn't have been any difference in the outcome. However, there would be fifty thousand more Americans today."

"Without all the alcoholism and suicides," Jerry Axle stated.

"That's right. You had them too," Oscar said, as he looked up at Jerry.

"Yes we did," Jerry affirmed.

"Something sure as hell went wrong, big time, with that war," Oscar said. "Our boys won virtually every battle. In the end the North Vietnamese finally overran South Vietnam, two years after we pulled out."

"It damn sure couldn't have been handled right," Herman Elmdorf agreed.

"I can't see that things have changed much," Jerry said. "I'm afraid our boys are going to get hung out to dry in this Middle East fiasco. The Military Industrial Complex has a lot of politicians and newsmen beating the war drums itching for a fight. They can't even agree on an objective. It will be a protracted war. That is our Achilles' heel. The civilians won't stand for a protracted war."

"Politics has become to partisan," Herman stated. "The two major parties are more interested in their own pocketbooks than they are in America or the American people. That's going to have to change. But I'm afraid I won't live to see it."

"You've said a mouthful there," Oscar agreed. "Congress will reject a good idea just because it's offered by a member of the party out of power. The only time they will cooperate is if the bill will delete some of our liberties or increase our taxes."

"Well, I think this bunch here could settle our problems in short order. But we sure as hell won't get that chance," Herman said. "Say Randy, have you told these boys the story about the time you were called off the front line to stand inspection? That's my favorite story."

Randy chuckled. "I believe you and Raymond are the only ones here I've told it to. One morning I came off the front line," Randy began his story. "I was told I would have to stand inspection in five minutes. I only had time to brush my teeth and wash my face. The colonel inspecting us asked, 'Why the hell are you in such a disgraceful condition, Marine? You haven't even shaved this morning.' Sir, I said, 'I've been to busy killing the enemy. Last night, the number of enemy I've killed exceeded the number of times I've shaved in my life.'"

"The colonel tapped me on the shoulder and said, 'Good answer son.' Then he turned to the sergeant accompanying him and said, 'See that this Marine gets some new underwear and fatigues.' Then they moved on down the line."

The men had a good chuckle at Randy's story. "Sure glad we didn't have to put up with that political crap during World War Two," Oscar said to Herman.

"That's the only war that our government has handled right," Herman stated. "Since then we had the Afghan War. However, that war was handled by a renegade congressman and a renegade C.I.A. agent. We did to the Soviets what they did to us in Vietnam."

"Yeah, those two renegades were backed by President Reagan," Oscar added. "First Republican I ever voted for."

"Me too," Herman chuckled, as he reached out with his hand and bumped Oscar on the knee. "He had balls, didn't take any crap."

"We all worshiped Roosevelt," Oscar said. "I guess the politicians wanted to keep it that way. That's why they made everything top secret for fifty years."

"Yeah," Herman chuckled. "Once the documents from the war were declassified and the truth came out; Roosevelt's star wasn't so shiny anymore."

"The Venona Papers pretty much proved Senator Joseph McCarthy was right," Colonel Jamison said. "Out government had been infiltrated by the Communist Party. The communists were either selling or giving away military development secrets to the Russians. Some of Russia's developments, especially in aircraft and nuclear power, were to identical to be accidents."

"Hell! I never even heard about that," Herman exclaimed.

"If it goes against the grain of the political establishment, you won't hear about it," Oscar said.

"Yep, it's just like the suicides that Jerry had to deal with," Raymond said. "He couldn't get any help beyond our local resources. When we wrote to out elected officials, we got the brush off. They just wanted to sweep it all under the rug. Neither political party wanted to deal with it."

"We had one young fellow, Bobby Anderson, who was in charge of a search and destroy unit," Jerry said. "He did some things that he said he couldn't have done if he had known he would be coming home. However, what he did saved the lives of a lot of his men because the enemy ambushes began to fail. After he got home, he decided he couldn't live with himself because of the divisiveness. How does one cope with something like that? Bobby committed suicide."

All attention shifted to Roger when he said, "Bobby Anderson's coping wasn't the problem. It was the collective guilt of our society that put him in the position he found himself in. Even a lot of men who served were critical of him. They failed him when he most needed their help. Bobby called me at two a.m. We talked for five hours. I thought I had talked him out of doing the deed. I guess I'd only talked myself out of it. I tried, but I failed."

Randy noticed tears flowing down Roger's left cheek. That cheek was out of the view of the other men. He wondered if the tears were flowing from his other eye as well. He looked at the other men's faces. He couldn't detect by their expression if that was the case.

"I sure couldn't have done what Bobby did," Roger continued.

"What Bobby did needed to be done and I wasn't the man for the job. But I certainly wouldn't have criticized him for what he did. Yeah, sure, I slammed those two punk's heads together. I clubbed that bunch of biker's with a nine-pound lug wrench. That was personal. There was nothing personal about all the men I killed in Vietnam. It was a matter of ideology. I'll still defend our ideology today. It's capitalism versus communism and too many people in this country aren't capitalists; even though it's capitalism that insures us our highest living standards. People don't understand that for us to win a war we have to destroy an ideology. Any ideology is encapsulated in the brains of human beings, whether they be man, woman or child. That whole group must die before full victory can be achieved. The enemy fights for the same reason we do. They're willing to part with their lives to support their ideology. Only when one side convinces the other side that the burning isn't worth the candle can victory be achieved. We, as a nation, have forgotten that principle. We learned it from the Indians when we settled this country. After World War Two, that principle has been for the most part abandoned with disastrous results. I think when the truth is known, and it will be, most of the people who criticized Bobby Anderson and soldiers like him were charlatans and goldbricks. Right now they're probably running for public office. They gained their national prominence and attention at Bobby Anderson's expense."

There was a long silent pause after Roger finished speaking. Finally Sheriff Jerry Axle said, "I think you're right Roger. It scares hell out of me to think that someday some of that garbage will be running for President."

Four, "Amen's" followed.

"Say Roger, why the hell did you trade a wrench for a rifle?" Herman asked.

Randy cringed. He was sure that everybody but Herman and Roger had quit breathing, as he did. His uncle Herman was never known for tactfulness. However, this was a question that had plagued many of them for years.

Roger hung his head for a while and then began to chuckle. Then he started laughing and went into a coughing spell. After he regained control of his reflexes, he said, "I suppose on the face of it, that looks like a single digit I.Q. decision." Looking up at the men and grinning, he continued, "Shucks, I had turned down the C.I.A.'s offer twice. The last time was that very day of the attack. That night I was working on the flight line. We had all the planes parked in a row. It was about three hundred yards to where our security forces had revetments, to protect us from a Viet Cong attack. We mechanics were issued an M-1 carbine with one ten round clip. I was working alone in the cockpit of a fighter aircraft. I couldn't work in the cockpit wearing the carbine slung over my shoulder. I had leaned it against the front landing gear. Then the rockets started coming in, two at a time. There was an aircraft between the one I was in and the two that got hit. Each plane had about a ton of fuel on it. Two gigantic fireballs lit up the night. The fireballs rolled back behind me toward the hangers. I suspected the next two rockets would be aimed at the next two aircraft. I was sitting in one of them. I didn't think running to the hangers would be safe. I'd watched the fireballs overtake three mechanics. I slid down the ladder from the cockpit, grabbed my carbine and headed for the revetments. Before I got half way there, two rockets went by on either side of me and hit the next two planes. Both went up in gigantic fireballs that rolled back toward the hangers. The fireballs would have caught me, had I tried to escape to the hanger. I ran up to the revetment next to a concrete bunker. There was a master sergeant firing over the wall and rolling hand grenades down the steep slope on the other side. A machine gun was firing from inside the bunker. I peeked over the wall. The whole area in front of me was lit up with kleg lights. A hundred and fifty yards behind the wall was concertina wire. Viet Cong were flowing through the openings they had cut in the wire. I notice two Viet Cong sneaking along the wall toward the sergeant's position. I hung over the wall, with my carbine, and popped both of them. Then I started shooting the closest men and kept shooting at targets. I walked my attack all the way back to the concertina wire. The Viet Cong broke off their attack about the same time that I ran out of ammunition. 'Nice shooting Airman,' the Sergeant said. 'Thanks for saving my butt. I didn't see those two sneaking up on my left along the wall. We're one man short tonight. There should've been another man in the position you're holding.' 'Do you have any more ammo for me? I asked.' 'You bet', he said, while throwing a bandolier of fifty rounds toward me. I pulled out the first stripper clip and realized it was ought-six ammo and wouldn't fit my carbine. I told the sergeant that the ammo he gave me wouldn't work because my weapon was a carbine. 'What the fuck?' the sergeant cursed. 'You mean they issued you knuckle busters peashooters? What a bunch of idiots. Airman, you better fall back. All you have to defend yourself with is your pecker and that empty peashooter.'"

The men, who had been listening intently, broke into laughter at the Sergeant's assessment of the situation.

"Did you fall back?" an excited Herman asked.

"No," Roger continued. "Everything behind us was on fire. The fire trucks were working on the fires and we could see more security forces unsuccessfully trying to get through, to reinforce our position. 'I can't fall back Sarge. It 's not safe. You got anything I can throw at them?' I asked. 'Should be plenty of grenades in the bunker', the Sergeant said. He yelled at the men inside the bunker, 'Hey, bring us a couple cases of grenades.' Two men came out of the bunker. Each was carrying a case of grenades. They set the cases down between the sergeant and I. 'Who's the newby?' one asked. 'A knuckle buster from the flight line,' the Sergeant responded. 'You dipshits let the V.C. blow an airplane right out from under his ass.' The other man looked over the wall and said, 'good thing we did Sarge. Looks like he saved your ass. He's got two right by the wall and eight more stretched out all the way down to the wire.' Both men scampered back to the bunker when the sounds of the V.C. mounting a second charge became apparent. The Sergeant asked if I'd ever thrown a grenade."

"Had you?" an excited Herman interrupted.

"No I hadn't," Roger responded. "But I told the Sarge I could always hit home plate from the outfield whenever we played baseball in basic training. He was relieved to hear that. He quickly explained the finer points of grenade throwing and then gave his colt forty-five to me. 'Empty the son-of-a-bitch and then throw it at em. Keep your peashooter handy because it makes a good club.'"

"Did you get out of there okay?" an excited Herman asked.

"Nah, I got killed," Roger said, with a chuckle. All the men were laughing at an embarrassed Herman.

"Shit! I need another beer," Herman stated. "This takes me back to the old days." Herman popped the tab on another beer.

"Anyway we fought off a second charge," Roger continued. "We killed a lot of the enemy that night. It must have been hard for them to give up on penetrating our perimeter after suffering all those losses. The Sergeant said, 'I doubt they have the resources to mount a third attack. But we'll stay on alert until relieved.' It was morning when we were relieved. I found the liaison officer who had been making the offers to me and said, 'I'm your man.' Pitching grenades and firing a rifle seemed a lot safer than sitting on top of a ton of jet fuel with only a tool bag and a two cell flashlight for weapons."

Looking up at the men, Roger said, through moisture filled eyes, his darkened face quivering, "I lost five good buddies that night in the fireballs. Two of them I had been with since basic training. They were the first real friends I'd ever had."

"You sure as hell were between a rock and a hard spot," Herman said. "I guess I'd have done the same thing."

Randy had heard several "Amen's," including his own.

Chapter 30. Empty Nest. Summer, 2000

L illy was cleaning the kitchen after the morning breakfast. She and Roger were alone again. She missed her children. At age sixty-eight she tired easily. Lilly still went to the lumberyard daily with lunch for Roger. At the yard she was able to see her children and grandchildren.

Darcy had gotten pregnant on her honeymoon and now had two boys. They were two dark-haired, bright-eyed bundles of pure energy.

Just like their mother, Janice and Darcy showed up at the lumberyard each day at noon, with their children and a picnic basket for their men.

Willie and Rainy had added on a large room for the family gatherings and conferences. It was complete with a range, sink, refrigerator and microwave oven.

Oscar and Jenny as well as Sam and Lori put in regular appearances at noon to visit and help with their great grandchildren. Kelly and Colleen also showed up regularly to visit with the family. Lori had started coming less frequently since Sam's health was failing.

Lilly felt a pang of sadness when she remembered Lydia Sanderson's passing. They had kept in touch since that first meeting at the twin's apartment. The ringing of the telephone interrupted Lilly's thoughts. "Hello," She said.

"Hi Mom, Marcy here. I called to tell you that I'll be home for vacation next week."

"Home for good, don't you mean?" Lilly asked. "Your chef's course will be completed."

"No Mom, just a vacation," Marcy said. "My scores were the highest and a Mr. Chin Lee came to the school to interview me. He's made a wonderful offer. I've accepted. It's an opportunity of a lifetime."

"And what makes this such a wonderful opportunity?" Lilly quizzed.

"Mr. Lee owns a very popular oriental eating establishment," Marcy said. "I'll be an assisting chef learning from oriental people. This is a feather in my cap just to get this offer."

"What do you know about the Lee's?" Lilly asked.

"They invited me to spend a Sunday afternoon with them at their home," Marcy said. " I met Mrs. Lee and their son George. They proudly informed me that they named their son after George Washington. Both Mr. And Mrs. Lee are very polite. Their son George is a little snot who exasperates them at times. I'll probably never see him again."

"How old is the son?" Lilly asked.

"He's sixteen and he obviously didn't like me," Marcy said. "He's an Americanized oriental brat."

"You say oriental. Which country are they from?" Lilly asked.

"China," Marcy answered. "I think originally from Thailand. George the snot looks Chinese. However, his parents don't. They're smaller. Mrs. Lee said she was Vietnamese and Chinese."

"Well your father and I will be disappointed that you're not coming home to stay," Lilly said. "Of course we've always insisted that you children apply yourselves well to your chosen careers. I can see where working for Orientals in an oriental establishment will be a boost for your career."

"Oh it will Mom," Marcy said. "I've had four years of chef schooling. Two years of traditional cuisine and now two years of oriental cuisine. I'm eager to get a spoon in the soup and start earning my way in this world."

"We know how much you always enjoyed experimenting with

oriental recipes," Lilly said. "It's to bad your father doesn't like oriental food. Well, you can always throw some pancakes or corn fritters his way and he'll be happy."

Marcy chuckled, "Yes he will. I love you, Mom. Please tell Dad I love him. I must get to typing letters to several other employers who made offers. I need to let them know I've accepted Mr. Lee's offer. Goodbye Mom."

"Goodbye dear," Lilly said, as she hung the receiver back on its hook. *Oh dear, I hope Roger won't be too disappointed.* Roger had encouraged Marcy to go to San Francisco for the oriental chef's school. He had insisted that degrees from two schools would make her more in demand. "You should be able to command a much higher salary," he had said.

They had assumed Marcy would come right back to Ashland Falls. There was a significant oriental population in Minnesota. All the churches sponsored many families, during the refugee program, after the Vietnam War ended. *I'll have something for the family to talk about at noon.*

Lilly sat down in her recliner for a short nap. Soon, she would need to pack the noon lunch. Her thoughts drifted to her husband. *At age fifty-six, he was still very active and energetic. As always, he was very attentive to her wants and needs.* After Roger had turned fifty, he started turning the business over to Willie and Rainy. The business had expanded enough to support three families and several part time workers. Now, Willie and Rainy ran the business and Roger worked for them.

Lilly and Roger still cut fireplace wood every autumn. They would throw the wood in piles and their boys would go to the woods with a tandem axle truck and a skid steer loader and haul the wood to the lumberyard to sell.

Lilly had always enjoyed the firewood-cutting season. She and Roger would spend five days every spring cutting down enough trees to dry for blocking in the fall. The birch had to be blocked and split in the spring. This prevented it from rotting over the summer.

During the cutting seasons, Lilly would always pack a lunch for two plus food and coffee for several breaks. Roger would always eat something after he had burned two tanks of fuel with the chain saws. In spite of the regular breaks, when he would eat caramels or cookies, he lost weight. He would lose up to twenty pounds by the end of the autumn cutting season.

On cooler days, Roger would build a campfire. Then Lilly would make a hot meal. They would roast marshmallows for desert.

Lilly always carried a thick quilt along. Their carnal appetite hadn't abated much. One day Roger summed up their activity with the statement, "If we had been able to procreate, we would've produced a lot of brush colts."

On real cold days, Lilly would sit in the warm cab of the pickup and knit or read. When there were smaller blocks for her to pile, she worked outside with Roger. They had done some woodcutting above Mosquito Lake. They had felt privileged to use the mobile home Rainy and Willie had hauled in with great difficulty. They had removed Oscar's travel trailer. It had required too much maintenance due to its age. The new place had a well, sewer and a bigger generator for electricity. The next generation had aspired to more luxuries. Lilly and Roger felt fortunate to have use of them. They agreed that they had wonderful children.

Lilly had gotten use to Roger's appearance of lacking emotion. Lori had warned her about that. Roger could smile or laugh, but he couldn't display much in emotion after that. There were never any frowns, pouts or other displays of displeasure. Lilly knew he experienced these emotions, but he couldn't manipulate his facial muscles to display them.

The children and grandchildren had Roger wrapped around their little fingers. Roger had often come to her for help, whenever the children had become to manipulative. One day Lilly had chided Roger about enforcing discipline.

Roger had said, "I'm an expert at enforcing discipline. However, whenever I did it, somebody ended up dead." Lilly never chided Roger about that again.

While Lilly had been concerned about her becoming the family ogre, because Roger didn't do discipline, it didn't happen. Roger never let the children forget her birthday or Mother's day. He had personally took them shopping for gifts. Sometimes they would pool their money and purchase a large gift Roger knew she wanted. The whole family treated her like royalty on those two special days.

Lilly knew Roger was having mini-strokes. The Doctors called it Transient Ischemic Attacks or T.I.A.'s. They had Roger taking children's aspirin daily. His war wounds had started to bother him, as he grew older. "I think that steel plate holding my leg bones together frosts up whenever the weather turns cold," Roger had said. "I'm experiencing frostbite from the inside." Lilly chuckled at that memory. Roger always said, "Humor beats complaining. Might just as well have a good laugh."

Lilly had fallen asleep thinking about her Roger. When she awakened two hours later, she realized it was nearly time for her to start packing Roger's lunch. First, she would freshen up and put on a pair of long dangly earrings that Roger liked.

Arriving at the lumberyard, she carried the lunch basket into the break room. All of the staff was either in the store or the break room, but no Roger.

"Where's Roger?" Lilly asked, in an earnest tone.

"Don't get frantic Mom," Willie said. "He's on his way."

Janice grabbed Lilly by the arm and said, "let's go outside and watch for him. He should be coming over the hill any minute now."

Lilly, with Janice and Willie on either side of her walked outside and watched the hill for the delivery truck.

"Roger had just called on the radio when you walked in," Willie explained. "He's a little late because he got confused and took a wrong turn on a township road. He was in E-town when he called. That's only three miles away. Listen, here he comes."

Lilly couldn't hear the truck. Janice and Willie assured her that from the sound they heard, Roger would come flying over the top of the hill.

When the truck came into view, Willie whistled. "He must be doing eighty. I told him you were here before we signed off."

Now Lilly could hear the sound of the truck engine revving as Roger down shifted to slow down.

Janice stood behind Lilly and placed both of her hands on Lilly's shoulders. "You obviously still have the same effect on him that you had when he first met you," she chuckled.

"Yeah, he's a regular Dale Ernhart," Willie stated.

Roger pulled up next to them, shut the truck engine off and hopped out of the cab. "Good afternoon gorgeous," Roger said, as he took Lilly in his arms.

"You're going to get a speeding ticket wild man," Lilly said, with a smile.

"Always the practical one," Roger teased. "I met the highway patrolman headed north as I turned south in E-town. I said to myself, 'self, this is your lucky day,' and I put the pedal to the metal."

"How did you get lost?" Lilly inquired, as Roger put his arm around her and the foursome headed to the lunchroom.

"Ah, I must've had a T.I.A. last night," Roger stated. "Things have been a little confusing all day. It should clear up in four or five days."

"You better not die on me," Lilly scolded. "Remember, you promised that I could go first. You know I don't want to be a widow again."

"I know," Roger chuckled. "I'm doing my best. I keep getting up every morning. That's always a good sign, I figure. However, I don't have complete control over that living and dieing business."

"Well, I've put up with a lot of years of being teased about robbing the cradle," Lilly retorted, with a smile. "I expect you to make it worth my while."

Willie and Janice were clearly amused by this mock argument.

"I'll do my best darling," Roger said, as he took off his cap and hung it on a peg in the lunchroom wall.

After Roger had said grace and they started eating lunch, Lilly told them about the telephone call from Marcy.

"Well it was bound to happen darling," Roger said. "When the chicks spread their wings and leave the nest, one occasionally catches an updraft and lands a long way from home. The Thompson's kids ended up living in France. Sam and Lori's only daughter, Sally Watkins, lives in San Francisco."

"That probably influenced Marcy's decision to work out there," Lilly agreed. "She did spent a lot of time with the Watkins family, while she was in school. Hopefully her work will keep her close to the Watkins."

"If Marcy gets a place big enough to put us up for a couple of weeks, I think we should pay her a visit next winter," Roger said.

"Oh Roger!" Lilly exclaimed. "You mean we can spend a couple of weeks in San Francisco during the winter months? That would be grand."

"Yep, I think we should," Roger replied. "We're not getting any younger. I'm going to move my office over to the American Legion club this fall. Those two woodcutters I contracted with last fall worked out real good. There are several more fellows who have hit me up for a contract. Most want to cut four or five cords. If I put ten men out there-that'll be forty to fifty cords. Sales are down to seventy cords. You and I easily make up the difference."

"That will be nice if you can slow down a little dear." Lilly said.

"Are you sure, darling?" Roger teased. "That will give me more time to chase you around the house."

Lilly felt the heat of a flush rise up her neck to her cheeks. *That randy old buck can still do this to me.* "Well----, what if I don't run?" she asked.

"Well---- then, I guess it will be put up or shut up for me, " Roger replied, with a chuckle.

"I think we're going to need a video camera set up at their place," Janice teased. "It'll help us prepare for our old age."

"If our kids are going to spy on us, we're going to have to do more traveling," Roger said. "Maybe we'll go back to Italy. Danny's in-laws wanted us to visit again."

"Remember we're suppose to go to France with Oscar and Jenny again next summer," Lilly said. "That's always a lot of fun. You've always enjoyed helping them on their dairy farm."

"Yes, France is pleasant, especially in the summer time," Roger agreed.

"Well Willie, Rainy, I believe this will be my last year with the business. From now on it'll be just monkey business," Roger said, with a smile while looking at Lilly. "After Christmas we go to San Francisco. We'll start thinking about seeing the rest of the world after that. I'm impressed with all the new fangled equipment you boys use," Roger continued. "However, I don't understand it. I feel obsolete. Heck, I can't even operate that new cash register you fellows installed last spring. I just can't learn new things anymore. The T.I.A.'s don't help. Most days my world is one of confusion. When that happens I don't want to be very far away from Lilly. She always makes sure I stay out of trouble."

"Thank you dear," Lilly said. "I think it will be nice to have you at home. I can boss you around more. That'll be good for you."

"Oh, oh, Dad, sounds like you'll be walking the line," Darcy said. "We can take turns dropping the grandchildren off. That will give you two a change of pace. Also a chance to change diapers."

"Yes that sounds like a terrific idea," Janice concurred.

"Just the ones that are potty trained," Roger said, with a chuckle. "We don't do diapers anymore. Arthritis makes it impossible." He held up a hand in a faked display of deformed fingers.

"Those are the ones we want to leave with you Dad," Darcy protested. "The other ones are easy to take care of."

Lilly found herself chuckling at the verbal exchanges. Their three daughters loved to gang up on Roger whenever they got a chance. They insisted that it kept him alert.

Chapter 31. Roger's Passing.
Autumn, 2010

L illy had awakened early on a Thursday morning. Looking out the window, she could tell it was going to be a sunny day. Roger was rolled up in the covers on the far side of their queen-sized bed. Lilly decided not to disturb him. It wasn't her intention to get up just yet. She would empty her bladder and crawl back into bed to sleep a couple more hours.

This was her habit of late. She required a lot of rest. Her doctors had told her that her heart was failing and she would probably live another six months. That was two months ago. Lilly knew her heart was failing faster than the doctors had estimated.

Since Roger had retired ten years earlier, they had spent almost all of their time together. He was devoted to her and was always quick to see to her needs. Roger was physically strong but experienced a lot of confusion because of all the transient ischemic attacks he was experiencing.

Their ailments had brought them closer together over the years. They had become more dependant upon each other. Roger had to get the cooking utensils out of the cupboards and load and unload the dishwasher. He had to help her with any lifting of heavy pots or pans. Lilly had to help Roger think. He couldn't remember where to put utensils away or where to retrieve them from, when she needed to use them again.

They spent a lot of their days sitting in the Japanese garden

Roger had constructed, after he had retired. Roger would push her, in her wheel chair, to the elevator. Then the two of them would ride down to the garage and Roger would push her out to the garden. She would have two books in her lap as well as two Afghans. They could sit in the sun and read. This had become their routine in what they both knew were their last days. At nearly seventy-eight years of age, and with her heart condition, she tired quickly. They both needed several naps throughout the day. She needed ten hours of sleep each night as well.

Lilly felt her time with Roger had slipped by to fast. Now, knowing they were nearing the end of their lives, she felt cheated. She had expressed this to Roger. She had suggested that they should've had more time together. Roger, the eternal optimist, had insisted they would spend eternity together. When Lilly had asked him how he could be so sure, he said, "God is fair. It won't be heaven unless I'm with you." And that was that.

After empting her bladder, Lilly crawled back into bed and was soon fast asleep. When she awoke again, about two hours later, the bedroom was brilliant with sunlight. Roger was still curled up in the blankets on the far side of their bed.

Lilly thought this strange because Roger was always up first. He would spend the early hours in the kitchen. Whenever he heard her stirring or the flushing of the toilet, he would bring her a cup of coffee and help her get dressed for the day. Lilly reached over to touch Roger's face with her hand. She quickly pulled her hand back when she realized his flesh was cool and clammy. Roger was dead! Lilly lay back on the mattress. What would she do now? She must collect her thoughts and be rational. How would Roger handle a situation like this? The first thing she must do is telephone nine, one, one.

After the phone call was made, Lilly emptied her bladder again. When she flushed the toilet, Marcy's voice came over the old intercom system, "About time you two sleepy heads got stirring," Marcy stated.

Marcy had moved back to Ashland Falls with the Lee family six months ago and was using the twin's old bedroom.

"Please come up and help me Marcy," Lilly said. "Your father's dead. He died in his sleep last night."

Lilly heard the elevator leave the basement and soon a tearful Marcy rushed into the bedroom. "Please Mom, say it isn't true," Marcy wailed, as she looked at the still form of Roger in the bed.

"It's true dear," Lilly said. "We knew it was coming. We always thought that I would die first. I've already phoned nine, one, one. With your help, I should be able to get dressed and down to the kitchen, with my wheelchair, before the ambulance arrives. Roger and I had talked about this day a lot," Lilly said. "I will be joining him soon. We will be together again without all the aches and pains of old age. I'm sorry we're going to miss your wedding. We knew neither of us was going to live long enough to see you married. Roger and I were very satisfied just knowing you would be marrying George Lee."

"But Rose and Chin never got a chance to meet Dad," Marcy tearfully protested. "They were going to meet him for the first time this coming Sunday."

"I know dear, but that's the way life is," Lilly said. "We never know what turn our road will take. We must have faith in God and trust that he will take care of us. However, George got to know your father well and they became good friends. Roger thought very highly of your George. You two will always have that."

"Oh Mom, why do people have to die?" a tearful Marcy asked, as she pushed the wheelchair with her mother in it to the elevator.

"It's God's plan dear," Lilly said. "As we grow older and the experience of living becomes more painful, we actually look forward to going home. I know I'm looking forward to being with Roger again. I hope I go as peacefully as he did. His days were rapidly getting harder for him to get through. His brain was slowly dieing because of all the T.I.A.'s. The attacks were coming so often his brain didn't have time to recuperate. He was actually far worse off than I was. He just wouldn't admit it. He seen it as his duty to take care of me."

When the two of them got down to the kitchen, the ambulance had arrived. Marcy took the elevator to the garage to escort the attendants in. After the ambulance left, Marcy joined Lilly in the kitchen.

"I've talked to the rest of the children and informed Oscar and Jenny Thompson," Lilly said, as she handed Marcy the telephone. "Maybe you should call George and let him know."

Friday morning brought Oscar and Jenny Thompson out to spend the day with Lilly. Oscar was also wheelchair bound. He and Lilly could get up and walk with the aid of handrails or walkers, but not for any great distance. After depositing Oscar on the garage slab, in his wheelchair, Jenny rushed to hug Lilly.

"You appear to be taking this quite well," Jenny said.

"Oh we knew it was coming," Lilly replied. "However, we always thought I would go first. Roger's going to owe me when we're together again," Lilly said, with a smile.

"The Lord has his reasons for doing things the way he does," Oscar stated. "If Roger hadn't died first, you wouldn't have gotten to know about his private war for survival. He never wanted you or the children to know. He didn't want you to be constantly living in fear of what could happen to him."

"I think Roger handled it the best way any of us knew how," Jenny agreed.

"I always thought there was something Roger wasn't telling me," Lilly said. "I suspected some dark secret when Irvin Callahan killed that Asian in prison. I didn't question it because so many of Roger's revelations were just to horrible to contemplate."

"You were wise to do that dear," Jenny soothed. "I believe it was the best way for you to handle that situation."

"Yes, you were better off not knowing," Oscar agreed. "You and Roger enjoyed all that time together cutting wood in your woodlot all those years. Could you have been at ease out there if you had known Roger had to kill a man in those woods? The man tried to murder Roger."

"Oh my God!" Lilly exclaimed. "And Kelly helped Irvin kill the Asian in prison because he was sent for Roger?" Lilly questioned. "Is that how it happened?"

"That's about it," Oscar confirmed. "Kelly made that decision on his own. Irvin was eager to do the job for Kelly. Irvin knew he would be executed if he survived the riot. He had argued with Kelly. Irvin seen it as his only chance for redemption. It would be his life for a deserving family man. Maybe it was truly God's will. Kelly said that was the only time Irvin called him Dad. Kelly thought it was Irvin's way of letting him and Colleen know that he appreciated their efforts. They were good parents. May God rest their souls."

"Lord how I miss them," Lilly said. "They were truly a wonderful couple. Oscar, how many people knew about Roger's private war?"

"All the war veterans on both forces," Oscar replied. "We knew they would be interested in protecting Roger, while providing the privacy he needed. The Vietnam vets were eager to help because in their minds successfully protecting Roger would mean victory. Victory was something they had been denied after ten years of war."

A very red-eyed Marcy with tear filled eyes brought out an insulated pot of coffee with mugs and cookies on a tray. Putting the tray down on a glass-topped table, she said, "If you folks wish to stay out here I'll bring three Afghans down. It's going to be a beautiful day."

"Thank you dear," Lilly answered. "That would be nice. We may even take our naps out here if it warms up enough."

"I'll be back in a minute," Marcy responded. "George is on his way out here right now. Rainy, Darcy, Janice and I will be meeting in Ashland Falls to make the memorial service arrangements this morning. Danny will be here with his family on Monday."

After George arrived, Marcy left to meet with her siblings for the service arrangements. George brought Lilly's cell phone to her. "I'll be up in the kitchen preparing lunch for everybody that shows up at noon," He said. "Call me if you need anything." Then George removed several shopping bags from his car and rode the elevator to the kitchen.

"Roger was to meet George's parents for the first time on Sunday," Lilly said. "He was looking forward to meeting them. Roger, George and Rainy all shared a love of history. I always thought they watched The Military Channel way too much. But, they always seemed to enjoy that time together."

Looking off to the northeast, Oscar said, "Looks like the Sheriff's cruiser coming in. Randy coming out to pay his respects, I suspect."

Sheriff Randy Slocum pulled up to the garage slab and exited the cruiser. He walked over to Lilly and taking both of her hands in his, he bent over and kissed her on the cheek.

"I'm sorry about your loss," Randy said. "Now Roger's war is over and he won. Trust me, Roger will be waiting for you with open arms. I'd hoped to spend more time with Roger after I retired, but we must accept God's plan. I know Roger was suffering in his human body."

"Yes he was," Lilly agreed. "After what Oscar and Jenny told me, I understand why God took Roger first. It's for the best and I'll be joining him soon, very soon."

Randy pulled a chair closer to the little group and sat down. "This is a business call also," He said. "Police Chief, Josh Smith investigated a break-in at Chin Lee's restaurant this morning. It wasn't actually a break-in. Somebody hid so they would be inside after closing. Josh and Chin were inside Chin's office and they had to close the door to get good pictures of the rifled safe. On the back of the door were two eight by ten photos. One was a picture of a communist Vietnamese officer in full dress uniform. The other was a picture of a much younger Roger in military fatigues. There was something written across the bottom of Roger's picture in Vietnamese. When Chief Smith recognized the photo of Roger, he called me."

"Oh Lord, now what?" Lilly asked. "Chin's son is engaged to my daughter."

"When Chin's family moved into this area they were checked out," Randy said. "Chin was in the Red Army of Occupation in South Vietnam. When he met Rose he converted to Catholic. Then they skipped from country to country until they were able to immigrate to the United States from Hong Kong. The Vietnamese officer in the photo is Chin's deceased father. Chin's father disappeared in this area back in the early seventies. The writing on the bottom of Roger's photo is Chin's father's hand. It simply states, 'A Brave Warrior.' Chin suspects his father was killed here. He would like to recover his father's bones. That's important to the Vietnamese. Chin insists he bears no ill feelings toward the man who killed his father. He didn't know the man in the photo was Roger. Chin only knew that the man in the photo was the man his father had been sent to kill. That's why he had the photo."

Lilly shook her head from side to side in disbelief. "Roger and Chin were going to meet for the first time this coming Sunday," Lilly said. "We were going to celebrate Marcy and George's engagement. Does George know about any of this?"

"He's probably hearing about it right now," Randy said. "Chin was going to call him. He wasn't sure of George's whereabouts. That's George's car next to mine, isn't it?"

"Yes, George came out here to make lunch while the children handle the arrangements for the memorial service," Lilly said. "I've made arrangements for Chin and Rose to ride with me at the service. I hope they're handling this latest revelation well. Roger felt the same way as Chin's father did. He never felt he was at war with a people as much as an ideology. He always expressed respect for the communist warriors. It was the politicians who angered him."

Just then Lilly's cell phone rang. Reading the message as she snapped the phone open, she said, "Hello Rainy. Okay. Oscar, Jenny and Randy are with me in front of the garage. George is in the kitchen preparing lunch. Sure, I can put it on speaker phone and we'll all listen."

"Mom, the memorial service will be next Thursday," Rainy said.

"Oh Lord, why so long a wait?" Lilly inquired.

"Many people are coming from long distances," Rainy explained. "Danny's in-laws from Italy will be the furthest. There will also be Oscar and Jenny's children from France. The memorial service will be at the armory."

"Why not my church?" Lilly inquired.

"Because of the number of people who want to attend," Rainy replied. "Over two thousand so far. The armory is the only building in the city with that capacity. It will hold four thousand people.

The Sheriff's Department and the Police Department are swamped with telephone calls. Pastor Johnson assured me your church group would coordinate lunch arrangements. He said just about every church in the county is involved. We must keep him updated on how many people to expect. The Sheriff's Department and the Police Department are taking care of the anticipated attendees count. We've started announcing the details on the local radio station. Dad's passing has been the news last night and all morning."

"Oh Lord! How did this all happen?" an exasperated Lilly inquired.

"Mom, Dad did business with a lot of people in the county," Rainy said. "He had most of the hillbilly trade before he met you. After you two were married he started getting the flatlander trade. We have been giving out five hundred calendars for the last five years. Remember, we give them out at our slowest time of the year."

"Well dear, what must be must be," Lilly stated. "When will you kids be home? It's near lunch time."

"In about a half hour," Rainy replied. "We have everything handled here."

"Rainy, this is Sheriff Slocum," Randy said. "I need to discuss something with you. It can wait until you get here."

"Good," Lilly said. "Randy, you must join us for lunch."

"Leaving right now," Rainy said. "Over and out." The telephone went to the dial tone.

Looking skyward, Lilly said, "Well Roger, you had to slam the door with another big surprise. Lord, you sure were chock full of surprises. Being married to you was like riding the wind, and I loved it."

"Yeah," Oscar chuckled. "It was like riding a whirlwind after Roger showed up in the county. Kind of like life began anew."

"It seems like just last week that Roger and I celebrated our wedding right here on this spot," Lilly concluded. "And what a family he gave me! I always felt like a magnet whenever we all got together. I can't help but wonder how God's going to handle this one. I loved my first husband and our two sons. But this family with Roger! Lord how they appreciated me."

"Well I'm sure God will come up with something special for you dear," Jenny said. "Do you realize that you took six people that the rest of society rejected and reared a good Christian family of wonderful citizens? That's quite an accomplishment my dear."

Chapter 32. Roger's War. Autumn, 2010

The fact that Roger was gone was finally settling in for Sheriff Randy Slocum. They had met often over the years. They always bought each other drinks. Randy's son, Willie, was married to Roger's daughter, Janice. Still, Randy some how felt cheated. They hadn't gotten together enough for fishing trips. They had always envisioned themselves doing just that often once Randy had retired. However, Randy had seen Roger's health failing much to rapidly over the last couple years for that to be a possibility.

Roger's children had come home after the arrangements for the memorial service were completed. George had put together a splendid lunch of oriental and western cuisine. After silently eating lunch, the group separated. Sheriff Slocum and Rainy got together for a private discussion. George and Marcy found a private place for George to tell Marcy about their families' past connections. Lilly, Oscar and Jenny with the rest of the children stayed at the dining room table.

"Roger wanted to be cremated," Lilly said. "He wanted me to spread his ashes over the hills around Mosquito Lake and on the lake. He said, 'I want to piss off the mosquitoes when they find they can't get anymore blood out of me.'"

This revelation got a chuckle out of the group.

"Actually I talked him into dumping his ashes over Mosquito Lake," Lilly confessed. "He wanted me to dump the ashes over St. Paul, for the same reason."

Oscar's laughter roared throughout the house. "Roger certainly knew how to get the best out of a bad situation," He said, as he slapped the table with his hands.

"Roger and I experienced a oneness that neither of us could have imagined," Lilly continued. "For that reason I'm going to save his ashes until mine can be added to them." Looking at her children, Lilly continued, "Then, we want you to take our ashes up in an airplane and spread them over Mosquito Lake and the hills surrounding it. We so loved that place."

Randy and Rainy had concluded their plans. Rainy knew where the grave, in the woods was. Roger had taken Rainy to the gravesite after his first stroke.

"Are you sure you can find it?" Randy had asked.

"Yesterday, after Dad died, I went out to the grave and said a prayer," Rainy said. "I thought that if they were going to meet up in eternity, a prayer would be appropriate. This was a distressful situation for both Dad and I. Dad said the soldier he had killed was a family man. He didn't want the location of the grave to be lost when he died. The grave is surrounded and protected by prickly ash. Dad said, 'God must be involved because there wasn't any prickly ash growing in this area when I killed him.' We'll need a chain saw to get close to the iron cross marking it."

Randy and Rainy made arrangements to meet at the lumberyard in Siding about five that afternoon. "I won't be able to get away from the office again until about then," Randy said. "I'll have Chin with me and we can load your equipment into the department's suburban. Then the three of us will go out there."

Marcy was devastated to learn her Father had killed George's Grandfather. George was doing all he could to console her.

"You must not come to work tonight," George said. "Mom and Dad will help me run the place."

"Ah, Rainy and I will be taking your Father out to you Grandfather's grave site this evening," Randy said.

"Oh George, I can't leave you and Momma Rose alone," Marcy wailed. "This is always our biggest night of the week."

"I think you should take Marcy to work with you, George," Lilly said. "Keeping busy will be good therapy for her. I also think she needs to be with you and Rose. It will be the easiest way for all of you to get through this."

Sheriff Randy Slocum snatched the keys for the department's suburban from the keyboard on the wall behind the Dispatcher's desk. "Headed for the woods," Randy said to the Dispatcher.

Randy drove over to Chin's restaurant and went inside to pick up Chin. Taking off a huge white apron, Chin said, "I'm ready to go." Chin kissed his wife and still dressed in a white dress shirt and tie, he left with the Sheriff.

The two men didn't say anything as Randy drove to the Siding lumberyard to pick up Rainy. When they got to the yard, Rainy was waiting out front with a chainsaw. Opening the back door of the suburban, Rainy set the saw in and closed the door. Then he took a seat behind Randy.

There wasn't any talking except for Rainy directing Randy down the different roads and trails to the secluded gravesite. When they left the county road they found the woods trails overgrown. There was very little evidence of Rainy's visit the day before.

"We haven't harvested any wood from this area for years," Rainy said. "Dad brought me back here to show me the grave site shortly after his first stroke. We were the only two to know the exact location. I'm so pleased to know this will be over with soon. Stop here," Rainy commanded, as Randy drove the suburban into a small grass filled glade. "We'll have to walk from here. It's only about fifty yards."

The sun was rapidly falling toward the treetops on its trajectory to the horizon. The three men were fast losing the direct lighting the sun had provided. As they approached a large thicket of prickly ash on a hillside, which sloped into the early dusk's shadows, the mosquitoes mounted a ferocious attack. Squatting down while slapping at the mosquitoes, Rainy peered into the thicket. Chin squatted down along side of Rainy. "There it is," Rainy said, as he placed his right hand on Chin's left shoulder. He pointed into the leafless thicket with his left hand. "You can barely see it in this light."

"I see it! I see it!" exclaimed an excited Chin. "Can we get closer?"

"First we have to cut some of this ash off and move it out of our way," Rainy said. "If we try to crawl through this thicket, we'll look like hamburger when we get back."

Rainy started the chain saw and began swinging the bar back and forth at the base of the brush. Most of it was twelve to fifteen feet in height. The growth was so dense that the bottom two-thirds of the stalks was leafless. The bottom branches, although leafless, were covered with flesh tearing spines. Chin grabbed the brush by the butts and dragged it away from the thicket. The mosquitoes departed when the sound of the chain saw and smell of exhaust gas permeated the work area.

"I'll go back to the suburban and get the portable spot light," Sheriff Randy Slocum said. "We'll need it before you get up to the cross."

When Randy returned with the light, he found both men working at a feverish pace. They were cutting and pulling the brush out of the thicket to produce a narrow path back to the cross. As Rainy cut further into the thicket, the narrow path became more difficult to drag the brush over.

The tops of the prickly ash were huge. The smaller bushes could be pitched on top of the twelve-foot high standing thicket. The bigger bushes had to be dragged to the outside of the thicket. Attempts were made to stack it. The tops were so huge that the ash reacted like giant tumbleweed once cut off it's stock.

"Ready for the flashlight," Chin announced.

Randy walked the narrow path back to the iron cross, which had been driven into the ground. The other two men had cleared a tight circle all the way around the cross. Randy shined the spotlight onto the cross arm of the iron cross. Written on the cross arm in Roger's hand, with an arc welder, were three words, "A Brave Warrior."

Randy noticed the two men had moved closer together and were facing each other. Momentarily shining the light on the two, he was struck by the strangeness of the scene. The men were face to face; their bleeding hands on each other's shoulders. Their bare arms were dripping sweat and blood. Their shirts were torn and Chin's tie resembled a scared cat's tail, ruined by the prickly ash. Blood, sweat and tears dripped from their faces, in spite of the chill of the autumn evening. The act of revealing the grave appeared to have brought closure for both men.

"I'll notify the Coroner tomorrow morning," Randy said. "We'll send out a crew with equipment to exhume the body. After identification, the remains will be turned over to Chin."

Saturday morning had dawned very dreary with a light drizzling rain and heavy fog hovering over the landscape. Lilly came down to the kitchen in bath robe and wheel chair to find Willie and Janice preparing breakfast and putting away dishes from yesterday's gathering. Marcy was still in bed after a late night at the restaurant.

Rainy had reported a successful night locating the grave in the woods. He had spent some time with Marcy and the Lee's at the restaurant after closing time. Chin and Rose Lee were very grateful for the care and consideration Roger had extended to their father, in spite of the horrible circumstances. They realized that these two warriors had shared a profound respect for each other.

Lilly wheeled to the table as Janice set a mug of black coffee in front of her. "Good morning," Lilly said. "Thank you, Janice. How's Randy doing? These have to be trying times for him."

"He was still sleeping when we went by the house," Willie answered. "We had a cup of coffee with Mom and then came out here. I hung a sign on the door of the lumberyard office saying we would be close until Monday morning. Most of the traffic we had yesterday was to inquire about the memorial service and to offer condolences. Dad said there are over two thousand people registered to attend the service already. American Legion clubs and The Veterans of Foreign Wars clubs from all over the state are sending Honor guards. Some are even coming from out of state."

"Lord, it sure will be noisy if they all fire their guns," Lilly stated.

"There will only be one twenty-one gun salute outside of the armory," Willie explained. "The rest of the Color Guards will line up along the route and present arms as your limo leaves the armory or passes by."

"Goodness, I'm glad I'm not involved in the planning of all that," Lilly said, with a sigh of relief.

"George will be out here as soon as he gets up," Janice said. "He's very concerned about Marcy. She was feeling much better by the end of the night. Working with George and Rose last night was the right medicine."

"Roger always said, 'Have faith in God when you're overwhelmed and everything will be okay,'" Lilly said. "He always said, 'We shouldn't fear going home to Jesus.' I guess maybe that's why we thought he was so brave. He always put his life in the Lord's hands, especially when he was in a tight situation. His faith in his Creator was unshakable. I often thought about that when I thought I was going to lose the twins to that Hargrove woman. Roger and I did a lot of praying when that happened. Roger knew the Attorney General had it in for him. We were sure there was going to be a huge court battle. Then all of a sudden Susan Hargrove took a job with the University and transferred down south. Janice, you remember how she threatened me, don't you?"

"Yes I remember Mother," Janice replied. "It was like you had a guardian angel watching over you."

When Lilly caught site of Janice winking at Willie, she asked, "And what do you two know about that incident that I don't know?"

"Mom was working at the courthouse at the time," Willie said. "All three of us were computer nerds. Dad was always buying new components and upgrading that computer Roger gave us. There weren't many people who understood computers like Mom and Dad did. Mom loved hacking. The state had just gone on line. Mom had gotten into the computer for the Attorney Generals office. Somebody had used that computer to type up the donation list for the Attorney General's previous campaign. That list didn't exactly match the list filed with the Elections Commission. Mom ordered the Attorney General to cease and desist in his case against you and Roger."

"Your mother did that!" Lilly exclaimed. "Well, if that doesn't beat all."

"Mom used her computer skills to level the playing field several times over the years," Willie continued. "She said it was so easy because almost everybody assumed she was the dingbat she always portrayed in the Summer Theatre productions. At the courthouse, she would slip out of her spike heels. Then she had the run of the place. She found the birth certificates for the twins in the Clerk of Court's office. They were abandoned in the dead letter box. Mom pilfered them and sent them to you. She always says, 'Possession is nine points of the law.' One time I asked what the tenth point of the law was. She said, 'Since our public officials display so much contempt for our constitutions, the tenth point will soon be a big club. Roger can handle that.'"

Lilly shook her head from side to side in disbelief. "No wonder Roger enjoyed the productions Jackie had parts in. We never missed one. Jackie must be as sneaky as Roger was."

"Yes, that she is," Willie assured her.

Chapter 33. Roger's Memorial. Autumn, 2010

The day of Roger's memorial service had arrived. It had been a week since he had passed away. Lilly had turned in early the night before and had been blessed with a very restful night. She was going to need it to get through this day.

Lilly was feeling very fortunate that she hadn't gotten her wish to die first. This past week had almost seemed like another lifetime. It seemed that every day brought some new revelation about Roger. It made her appreciate her time with him even more. The prospect of being without the pain and fatigue connected with her heart's failure, when she joins Roger, had given her a sense of anticipation.

The Lee's had helped Marcy put aside her feelings of guilt. Chin had insisted that his father and Roger had the same values, just different ideologies. "Why would they think of each other as brave warriors even though they were enemies?" Chin asked. "They clearly respected each other."

Lilly was concerned about the eulogy that Pastor Hennen was going to deliver. She had assumed Pastor Johnson, the leader of her church, would deliver the eulogy. Pastor Johnson had requested Pastor Hennen for the eulogy. Pastor Hennen was widely known for his excellent research.

Lilly had only met Pastor Hennen once before Roger's death. However, Pastor Hennen had spent a lot of time at their house the last week. The family had invited him to share several meals with them. They all agreed that he was a good man.

Pastor Johnson had read the eulogy and he had assured Lilly that it would be very befitting of her Roger. "There won't be a dry eye in the house," he had assured her.

"The limos are here Mother," Lilly heard Janice say. "Willie and Rainy will help get you and your chair into the elevator and down to the garage."

After Lilly was in the limousine, her children piled in. The grandchildren and other extended members of the family would ride in a second limousine. Both were stretch versions.

The driver confirmed with Lilly that he was to pick up Chin, Rose, Oscar, Jenny and Jackie Slocum at the church before going to the armory. After picking up the others at the church, even though two were in wheelchairs, there was still space in the limousine. Sheriff Randy Slocum should have been in the limousine with his wife, Jaclyn. However, Randy had begged the women to allow him to command his department.

"Well this is Roger's memorial service," Lilly had said to Randy. "I'm sure nobody would agree with you more than Roger. Duty has a strong hold on all you former military men."

Just then there was a commotion a short distance from the limousine. "Yes, we still have some minutes before we have to leave," Lilly heard the driver say. "We don't want these folks sitting to long in the armory before the service begins. Some folks here to see you, Mrs. Hartec."

Lilly peeked out to see a tall thin black man pushing through the crowd trailing a black woman, by the arm, behind him.

"Lenny Callahan," Lilly fairly shouted. "Oh it's so good to see you."

"I'm truly sorry about your loss, Miss Lilly," Lenny said. "My wife and I just arrived in town. We thought the service would be at your church."

"No, no," Lilly responded. "Lunch will be served here after the service. Actually, lunch will be served at three other churches also. Are you folks alone?"

"Yes we are," Lenny replied.

"Well crawl on in and ride with us to the armory," Lilly said. "We've plenty of room for two more."

"Yes by all means," the driver instructed. "There's plenty of room. We'll have to double back from the church to get to the end of the procession route," the driver informed Lilly. "The Honor Guards stretch away from the armory for at least a half mile."

Lilly quizzically looked at Rainy.

"All the military veterans consider Dad as one of their own," Rainy said. "There are a lot of veterans on both law enforcement departments. Veterans seem to run in families. Word of Dad's situation and passing spread like a wild fire in the veteran's community."

"There would have been an even larger crowd if all the politicians had gotten their way," Willie chimed in. The sheriff's department and the police department received numerous phone calls from politicians requesting escort service and protection. Dad and Chief Smith told them that they were on their own. Every Deputy, Officer, Fireman and EMT was assigned responsibilities. Dad told them, 'Everybody who knew Roger was aware of his distain for the political class.'"

"Chief Smith told them that because of all Roger's letters to the editor over the years, it's well know what he thinks of politicians," Rainy said. "The Chief said, 'Proselytizing at Roger's memorial service could be an insult beyond our control with all the veterans who will be in the area. Staying away from this crowd could be the only correct decision you've made in your life.'"

Lilly couldn't help herself as she began chuckling. Looking at Rose and Chin, she said, "Sheriff Slocum and Chief Smith knew my husband well. I believe their assessments are very accurate. I'm so pleased that Lenny and Camille are with us. Lenny's father and mother were very dear friends of our family. Both of them passed on a few years back. I'm sure Roger is with them right now."

After arriving at the armory, many volunteers under the direction of Pastor Johnson helped get the family seated in the reserved seats. Again Pastor Johnson assured Lilly that she would be pleased with Pastor Hennen's eulogy.

Then Pastor Hennen stepped to the podium and the service began.

The Eulogy

"It feels strange that I was selected, by my fellow men of the cloth to deliver the eulogy for Roger Hartec. As a matter of fact, this whole episode in my life will be fondly remembered as strange bordering on bizarre." Lilly saw a smile spread across Pastor Hennen's face. A low chuckle rumbled through the crowd.

"It all began when I received a telephone call, early last Friday morning, from a member of our congregation who wishes to remain anonymous. This lady asked if our congregation was getting involved in the memorial service for Roger Hartec.

"I said to her, 'not that I know of. I've never met Roger Hartec. As far as I know, he's not a member of any church. I'm not even sure if he was a Christian.'

"She said to me, 'Oh yes, he was a Christian. He didn't belong to any church. He was a seven-day-a-week Christian.'" Pastor Hennen's eyebrows shot up on his forehead.

"Soon after that telephone call, our office was flooded with telephone calls from our congregants wishing to help with Roger Hartec's memorial service. So we began to get involved.

"Then Pastor Johnson, the Shepherd of the church Lilly Hartec has belonged to for years, asked if I would produce and deliver the eulogy. He said to me, 'I've admired the research you do and the unique preparation that goes into your efforts. I thought it only fitting that I do this for this family.'

"Since our congregation is removed from the city, and since I'd never met Roger or Lilly Hartec, ah, actually I met Lilly once. It was for a very brief period of time years ago. We had both worked with the Cub Scouts. I realized that I knew very little about Roger Hartec.

"Here's what I did know. I knew that I had arrived in this area a few years before Roger had. After Roger arrived, I knew him to be a troubled ex-soldier who had killed a lot of men in the war. Some of his actions, as a citizen of this county, were of a violent nature.

"The definition of the word eulogizes means to praise. Now I realized I was very short of material." Many gray heads nodded in agreement, as a chuckle rolled throughout the assemblage.

"Then it hit me. Why did this woman describe Roger as a seven-day-a-week Christian? I would definitely have to follow up on that conversation. So I set out to learn more about Roger Hartec.

"From his customers, he was known as the man who's word was better than most written contracts. He was also known as the man who would lend a hand if he came upon them in distress. If they had a tractor stuck or an animal having a difficult time birthing, Roger knew how to right the situation. He gave freely of his time and expertise.

"From Roger's wife, Lilly, I learned he was a loving and protective husband. From his five children, I learned that Roger had instilled in them the value of being a seven-day-a-week Christian.

"Then, a strange thing happened. This is where my story gets bizarre. Roger's children had asked me to help them sort through Roger's personal papers. They knew that Roger Hartec wasn't really Roger Hartec. They wanted to know what his real name, the name he was given at birth, was.

"As a former military chaplain, I knew his military records would give us all that information. Roger had a four drawer steel filing cabinet packed full of personal papers.

"There were hundreds of letters to politicians and editors. Roger chastised them for supporting abortion. He chastised politicians for supporting or passing laws he felt were contrary to our constitutions. He railed about how the United States Constitution was a sacred document, inspired by God. He complained about how the laws they were supporting or passing were contrary to Life, Liberty and the Pursuit of Happiness. Very few politicians responded to Roger's criticisms in a positive manner. I calculated that number to be less than one per cent.

"In spite of negative responses, and in later years no responses at all, Roger continued his battle of writing and chastising. Only in the most recent years, because of failing health, he had to give it up.

"I must say that many a man who had received those letters had to be more than a little uncomfortable reading them. If they themselves believed they possessed an immortal soul, they had to have been shaken. I suspect that's why the number of returns from the politicians dwindled in later years.

"However, I was shocked to find that Roger had thoroughly purged his files of all records pertaining to his military service. His family knew he had spent over four years in the United States Air Force. They knew he had been recruited by the Central Intelligence Agency for clandestine operations as a sniper. They knew he had not served his country as Roger Hartec.

"I pursued my research with members of the law enforcement community. All of the men, who were veterans, weren't surprised that Roger Hartec wasn't Roger Hartec. They weren't surprised that Roger's records wouldn't reveal who he was. Each and every one said that the Roger they knew would do that. He would destroy his own military records to protect his family.

"I also learned from these men that the war didn't end for Roger when he left Vietnam. The nature of his duties, the duties assigned to him by our country in our defense, made him a life long target of our enemies.

"Many in our law enforcement community became involved in helping Roger win this war. Some extreme sacrifices were made. Of these sacrifices, I will tell you no more. What about a man could arouse this sense of duty in other men? I could only conclude that it had to be the way he lived his life. I could only conclude it could not be the life I had knowledge of.

"I returned to Roger's home to again visit with his family. I'd found his children had given up on learning his identity. I asked Roger's wife to express her feelings about Roger's true name. This was her response. 'I'm probably known as the nosiest person in the county. However, I fell in love with Roger Hartec. I married Roger Hartec and I want to spend eternity with Roger Hartec. I know that will be very soon because of my heart condition.'

"It was very clear to me that Lilly Hartec was very much at peace with what she was saying to me.

"Now, I began to understand. Roger didn't wear his Christian beliefs printed on his shirt cuff for all to see. Rather, he lived them and his example was his ministry. Roger Hartec didn't inflate his military service for political or financial gain, as we are seeing done so often today. Instead, Roger destroyed all evidence of his dedication and devotion to duty. All the records of his bravery, his medals, ribbons and certificates of accomplishment were destroyed. He had done this in the belief that it was required of him to protect his family.

"In conclusion, I have this to say: Holy Father, we commend to you the spirit of the man we knew as Roger Jerome Hartec. He was truly a warrior in our army as well as in your army. While he was never a member of any of our congregations, we know that he was a seven-day-a-week Christian. He was true follower of Jesus Christ. We can only hope that the same will be said of us."

There wasn't a dry eye in the armory. Lilly was very grateful for Pastor Hennen's eulogy. The fact that Roger's memorial service was held in a military facility was also befitting of Roger the warrior. Lilly was content. She would be joining her Roger soon.

Epilogue

Friday morning found Sheriff Randy Slocum in his office, contemplating the events of the past several days. The news of Roger Hartec's passing had been gut wrenching for him. They were of the same generation, and both had served their country in the same unpopular war.

Randy had been planning his own retirement this term. It wasn't his intention to run for reelection. Long ago, he and Roger had made plans for more time together. This was to be done when the duties of office were no longer a concern of Randy's.

Randy had offered to help Lilly with the memorial service. Then, suddenly his office had been swamped with telephone calls. Everybody wanted to know about Roger's memorial service. They all wanted to contribute in some fashion. Also, the robbery at Chin Lee's restaurant commanded a lot of his attention. Finally, he was able to beg off the limousine ride. He knew he would be better off working. It wouldn't give him as much time to dwell on his loss.

Lilly Hartec had proven to be a real trooper. She was truly worthy to be the wife of a warrior. She had understood well Randy's dilemma and insisted that he should command his department.

Nobody had realized how far reaching Roger's befriending of people had extended. While Randy had been chatting with Lilly, at her church, a young woman from California came to Lilly and introduced herself. She said, "We've never met. I'm married to one of your late husband's students of birthing. I married Glen Acton. He grew up on a farm northeast of Siding. That's him over there with our two sons and our daughter, Rogeina. When Rogeina was due, I experienced several false alarms. Glen was prepared for the worst. He took it right in stride when I informed him, at three a.m., that our baby was coming. My water broke while we were on the freeway. Glen pulled off to the side and proceeded helping me with the delivery. In short order, we had several members of the California Highway Patrol shining flashlights into the back of our station wagon. Glen had done a wonderful job of assisting me with the delivery. The troopers and Doctors were impressed with Glen's resourcefulness. He had an ice chest half full of warm water. There were lots of towels and pillows. He also had a quilt, scissors, alcohol and string packed in a small bag. Then Glen informed the staff that he had been taught all about deliveries by Roger Hartec. Lord, I was so happy that he didn't get time to tell them that it was calf deliveries he had done."

Randy smiled as he thought about how he and Lilly laughed until their ribs were sore. Lilly had told Randy that she had heard at least half a dozen more stories similar to that one before leaving for home.

The dispatcher interrupted Randy's thoughts: "Call for Sheriff Slocum, line one,"

"This is nurse Sonja Ortiz," said the voice on the telephone. "I've been General Maxwell Verney's nurse in the old soldier's home for many years. General Verney was one hundred and one years old. This morning he watched Fox News while eating his breakfast. There was some commentary about a Roger Hartec's memorial service. When General Verney was done eating, he wiped his face with his napkin and threw it down on his tray. Then he said, 'Roger Hartec is dead. He died in bed. We won.' Then he smiled, closed his eyes, and quit breathing. We were unable to resuscitate him. We are wondering, who is Roger Hartec?"

"That's a question for the ages," Randy replied. "Only Roger and General Verney knew. Now they've both passed on. It all had to do with Roger's service in Vietnam. He touched a lot of lives over there, unfortunately not in a good way." Randy silently snickered at what he had just said. "However, he touched a lot more lives, after the war, in a positive way. That explains the large turnout for his memorial service. Unfortunately, not even his family, which I'm an extended member of, knows his real name. His children have gone through four file cabinet drawers of Roger's papers. They've found absolutely nothing pertaining to Roger's military service. We feel he destroyed this part of his life to protect his family. He couldn't risk his true identity being discovered. The American Legion club has a copy of his DD214. It was obviously supplied by the Central Intelligence Agency. The name on it is Roger Jerome Hartec. His wife, Lilly, just doesn't care. She wishes to join him directly. She's expected to die of heart failure very soon."

"Well that certainly helps explain things on this end," Sonja said. "The General was always a troubled old man. When he stopped breathing, we saw him smile for the first time."